OUT OF THE MIST

"The story's robust momentum and lively characters make this a fun, energetic read."

—Publishers Weekly

"If you enjoyed the Callahan Brothers trilogy, you're in luck. *Out of the Mist* is Book One of JoAnn Ross's Stewart Sisters trilogy, and this one definitely sets the bar high. . . . Her characterizations are stellar and the setting of the beautiful Smoky Mountains comes alive with her evocative words."

—A Romance Review

"Ross weaves the search for the missing family treasure and the growing attraction between two creative spirits with aplomb in this charming romance."

—BookPage

"Fun, funny, sexy, and entirely enjoyable. Think *To Catch a Thief* with a twist—a Scottish twist."

—Susan Lantz,
Romance Fiction Team Captain, America Online

MAGNOLIA MOON

"Readers seduced by the first two books in JoAnn Ross's Callahan Brothers trilogy will be equally charmed by *Magnolia Moon.*"

—Publishers Weekly

"Perennial favorite JoAnn Ross wraps up the hugely engaging Callahan trilogy in great style. Filled with emotion, passion, and a touch of suspense, this is just plain fun reading."

—Romantic Times

RIVER ROAD

"Skillful and satisfying. . . . With its emotional depth, Ross's tale will appeal to Nora Roberts fans."

—Booklist

JoANN ROSS

Out of the Storm

POCKET STAR BOOKS

New York   London   Toronto   Sydney

Pocket Star Books
A Division of Simon & Schuster, Inc.
1230 Avenue of the Americas,
New York, NY 10020

This book is a work of fiction. Names, characters, places and incidents are products of the author's imagination or are used fictitiously. Any resemblance to actual events or locales or persons, living or dead, is entirely coincidental.

This Pocket Star Books paperback edition August 2008

POCKET STAR and colophon are registered trademarks of Simon & Schuster, Inc.

For information about special discounts for bulk purchases, please contact Simon & Schuster Special Sales at 1-800-456-6798 or business@simonandschuster.com.

Cover design by Lisa Litwack
Cover illustration by Melody Cassen

Manufactured in the United States of America

10 9 8 7 6 5 4 3 2 1

ISBN-13: 978-1-4165-8080-5
ISBN-10:   1-4165-8080-8

To Jay,
this time more than ever

Acknowledgments

Lauren McKenna, editor extraordinaire, for going way above and beyond the call of duty; Megan McKeever, who juggles myriad details with unfailing grace and good humor; my agents—the always amazing Robert Gottlieb and brilliant matchmaker Jenny Bent; and last, but certainly not least, my own personal Washington, DC, "inside source," award-winning investigative reporter, Patrick Ross.

Out of the Storm

prologue

The last day of Sissy Sotheby-Beale's life dawned another Low Country scorcher. It was dog days in the South, when any canine possessing the sense the good Lord gave a flea could be found sprawled on a veranda beneath a slow-moving, paddle-bladed fan.

Long after the blazing sun had disappeared behind the towering twin alabaster spires of St. Brendan's Cathedral—the boundary between city and marshland—the humidity-drenched air remained thick enough to drink. Sissy stepped through the French doors onto the balcony and felt as if she were walking into a sauna.

The sultry scent of night blooming jasmine wafted up from the formal courtyard garden ten stories below. Usually the sweet perfume bathed Sissy in a heady sensual pleasure.

Not tonight.

Fingers of white heat lightning danced on the horizon. Electricity from an approaching storm sizzled on her tongue, sparked beneath her glistening, damp skin.

A century earlier, Somersett's movers and shakers had decided to mark the bicentennial of the city's founding with a mock sea-battle which they'd hoped would bring much-needed tourist dollars to the town still suffering economic deprivation after losing the Civil War. Buccaneer Days quickly escalated into South Carolina's answer to Mardi Gras, allowing citizens to slip out of the reins of southern civility as they drunkenly reveled in Somersett's infamous pirate roots.

Bringing in more revenue than Savannah's St. Patrick's Day bash or Charleston's Spoleto Festival, Buccaneer Days was a week-long extravaganza of parties, masked balls, parades, street fairs, a beauty pageant, and nightly sea battles.

And, because the original colonists had the unfortunate timing to arrive from England in the middle of August, there was always the heavy, unrelenting heat.

Sissy's short silk slip—the deep hue of a late-summer rose, which complimented her magnolia pale skin—clung to a body firmed by diet and rigorous daily exercise. Tendrils of blond hair streaked that afternoon at Dixie Belle's House of Beauty trailed down her neck.

Cannon fire boomed from Somersett Harbor as wooden ships bearing either the tri-colored Union Jack or black-and-white skull and crossbones kicked off the week-long celebration.

As a fringed black carriage carrying tourists on a

Ghost and Graveyards tour passed on the street below the balcony, Sissy climbed atop the railing.

From the Victorian bandstand at the center of Market Square, the Somersett Pops Orchestra had just broken into a rousing rendition of "Dixie" when Sissy spread her tanned, toned arms and flew off the balcony railing.

1

Camp David, Catoctin Mountain, Maryland

"What are we doing here?" Laurel Stewart asked the man sitting next to her in the sanctuary of the presidential retreat's Evergreen Chapel.

"Praying for peace?" Max Kelly, a reporter from the *Boston Globe*, suggested.

"Granted, it's an admirable goal, but given that the Weather Service has declared this the hottest summer on record, what made the White House decide that August would be a good time to hold another round of Middle East Road to Peace meetings? Couldn't the State Department find a road map that leads to Maine?"

She slapped at yet another mosquito that had sneaked in through the window screen. "And how come they all invited us here to participate?"

She had to raise her voice to be heard over the huge pipe organ's rendition of "The Song of Peace." According to her program, Israeli prime minister Yitzhak Rabin had sung the song with over a hundred thousand people at a peace rally in Tel Aviv minutes before his assassination.

"This from the reporter who's always bitching that we don't get enough access when the president hides out at Camp David?"

"Like you think anyone's going to nail down a scoop here today," Laurel scoffed. Her dark auburn hair, styled in a sleek, no-nonsense cut that ended at her earlobes, hinted at a redhead's temper she usually kept tightly controlled. Her eyes were a cool, intelligent green in a pale complexion, her nose was straight, her mouth generous, and her chin as stubborn as she herself was. "We're being herded around the place like a bunch of senior citizens on an If-It's-Wednesday-This-Must-Be-Camp-David bus tour from hell."

"Hey, it's not every day you can watch two world leaders knocking down ten pins in the Nixon bowling alley."

"Bowling for Peace," she muttered. "Now, that's going to catch on. I'm still trying to find out if those were new shoes they gave the prime minister, but no one's talking."

"Go get 'em, Lois Lane. That story's bound to get you a banner headline."

"That's my point, Max. There *is* no story here. At least nothing new, other than their refusal to release the president's scorecard and the chef's diplomatic faux pas of serving sun-dried tomatoes with the beef tenderloin. I mean, really, no one's eaten sun-dried tomatoes since the Clinton Administration."

"I thought they ate Big Macs."

"Cute." Actually, a big, juicy cheeseburger with fries sounded a lot better than the uninspired deli spread of sliced cheese and cold meat that had been laid out for reporters in the mess hall. "It's an evil plot cooked up by the politicos to do away with us."

She felt the sting at the back of her neck and slapped again, an instant too late. "The gang in the White House is probably hoping all of us nuisances in the press corps will be attacked by a swarm of West Nile virus–carrying mosquitoes and drop dead before the election."

Unfortunately, the organ player wearing Marine dress blues chose that moment to pound out the last chord, which left Laurel's conspiracy theory hanging on the steamy air. The president and First Lady, displaying impeccable manners in the front row, did not turn around. Neither did the prime minister.

Her peers were not as polite.

Pretending vast interest in the flags on either side of the linen-draped altar at the front of the chapel, Laurel ignored their evil grins.

Two hours later, she was back in the Clinton Room at the Cozy Country Inn in nearby Thurmont, soaking in the Jacuzzi tub, when her cell phone started playing the theme from *Jaws*.

Buh dum. Buh dum.

"No one's home." She took a long swallow of the frozen margarita she'd brought up from the pub and savored the icy tartness.

Buh dum. Buh dum.

"Undoubtedly some jokers wanting to rag me about my big mouth." Journalism was a blood sport; she'd do the same thing if it'd been Max who'd jammed his Bruno Magli into his mouth.

Dum dum dum dum.

Some people might be able to ignore a ringing phone. Laurel was not one of them. Splashing water onto the floor, she lunged for the cell phone she'd left on the sink.

"Oh, hell." The caller screen identified her *Washington Post* editor. She punched Talk. "Yes, Barry, I'm afraid it's true," she admitted, not bothering to waste time with hellos. "I insulted the entire White House in front of a foreign dignitary. You can probably read all about it in tomorrow's *Washington Times.*"

"That's already old news," he said, brushing off her ill-timed remark. "Don't worry about it—I'm not calling to chew you out. I wanted to see if you've been keeping tabs on the AP wire."

"The Secret Service confiscated my computer and phone and held them hostage until we were finally released thirty minutes ago. Something about electronic bombs and homeland security."

Laurel noticed she was dripping on the floor. "What's up?" she asked as she pulled down a towel and wrapped it around her body, which was draped in fragrant white froth from the bubble bath she'd dumped into the tub.

"That's all they did?"

It was not unusual for Barry Yost to answer a question with a question. He was, after all, a newsman, more accustomed to delving for information than handing it out. "Yeah, which was too bad," she answered, "because there's this really cute, hot new agent I wouldn't mind being patted down by."

"Did they return your computer?"

"Of course." For a moment she thought her phone

had dropped the call. "Barry?" she said into the silence of dead air. "Are you still there?"

"There's been a leak."

"There are always leaks in Washington." She retrieved the margarita from the rim of the tub and took a sip. "Which is probably why those Watergate guys were called plumbers."

"This one concerns the vice president."

"Don't tell me someone else has my story." The printed note that had landed on her desk from the confidential, obviously high-level source had promised exclusivity. The first article of a five-part series had run this morning.

"Not exactly."

Silence descended again, thick and, this time, a little unnerving.

"Not exactly?" she coaxed, trying to ignore the little frisson of nerves that skimmed up her spine.

"The vice president's people are alleging that papers were stolen from their offices."

"That's certainly not unheard of." If the confidential report had been meant to be for public viewing, it wouldn't have had to be leaked.

"Yeah, but . . . shit."

Barry Yost was one of the most articulate men Laurel had ever met, which, in a city populated by glib-tongued politicians, attorneys, lobbyists, and fast-talking, charismatic television reporters, was really saying something. She couldn't recall ever hearing him at a loss for words. Until now.

"The story hasn't gone beyond rumor stage at this

point," he said. "But your name's being floated around town as a suspect."

"A suspect?" Laurel's fingers tightened on the stem of the glass. "As in, someone thinks I'm the person who stole the report?"

Her nerves began screeching like the civil defense siren Jamie Douglas continued to test once a year back in her hometown of Highland Falls on the Tennessee–North Carolina border.

He blew out a breath. "Like I said, it's just a rumor, but—"

"Hold that thought." An unmistakably authoritative knock had begun hammering on her door. Hopefully it was room service with the steak she'd ordered.

Oh, hell. It wasn't.

One look at the grim faces on the other side of the peephole and the idea of being patted down by the new Secret Service agent—whose thrust-out jaw was wide enough to land Air Force One on, and who appeared neither as cute nor as hot as he had this morning—suddenly lost its appeal.

"I'll have to call you back, Barry. I've got company."

The tart taste of lime and tequila turned coppery as Laurel tossed back the margarita, threw on a robe, sent a quick, abbreviated Hail Mary upward, then opened the door to face the inquisition.

2

"It could have happened that way," Derek Manning claimed, defending his jumper scenario as the four homicide detectives observed the broken female body sprawled on the hood of the black Suburban.

"No way." Caitlin Cavanaugh shook her head. "Even Wonder Woman wouldn't have been able to climb up onto that iron railing in four-inch Manolos. Some guy threw her over the balcony."

One of the high heels in question—flimsy bits of silver leather held on with a thin ribbon tie—was still on the dead woman's foot. Assigned to take the crime photographs, Cait lifted her 35 mm Olympus and snapped the other, which had landed in the "Frolicking Nymphs" fountain ten feet away.

Having never understood how women walked in ice-pick heels in the first place, Detective Joe Gannon decided Cait's murder scenario sounded more plausible than suicide.

"Vic probably weighs a hundred and five, tops," Manning estimated. About the weight of one of his muscular, tree-trunk-sized arms. Cait, who had a minor in psychology backing up her criminal justice degree, had long theorized that the bulked-up detective was overcompensating. "Could have been a woman doin' the tossing."

"Maybe a catfight," Lonnie Briggs suggested. His lips, beneath a mustache the color of a rusted-out skiff, twisted in a leer.

"Why am I not surprised you'd latch onto that idea?" Cait muttered.

On the days Briggs got to pick the lunch spot, he invariably opted for the harborfront Hooters. Little wonder his fifth marriage was breaking up.

Cait looked up at Joe, who'd remained typically silent since arriving on the scene that was beginning to draw a crowd. "Well? You're the hotshot Cop-of-the-Year medal winner. What do you think?"

He slapped at the back of his neck. The damn mosquitoes had been attacking like kamikaze bomber squadrons ever since he'd arrived on the scene. "I think I'll move to Maine."

Glacier-carved peninsulas, craggy seaside cliffs, icy waves, cool, crisp sea breezes, and the tart taste of an apple plucked right off the tree . . . If he left right now, then drove straight through up 95, he could be sitting down to a lobster dinner tomorrow night.

"Discounting the fact that you just happen to be a home-grown, deep-fried southern boy who'd freeze your very fine ass off by Labor Day, homicide's in your blood, Gannon. You'd be bored brainless investigating murder by moose before you were up in Yankeeland a week," Caitlin predicted. "So, getting back to the case at hand, do *you* think we've got a jumper?"

"Anything's possible."

Joe scanned the crime scene, his hands deep in the pockets of his humidity-rumpled jeans to keep himself from touching anything. One of the unwritten axioms of homicide investigation stated that the least competent cop would always be the first to arrive. Beat cop Dylan Thomas, son of an English professor at the nearby Admiral Somersett Military Institute, was the exception that proved the rule. Thomas had already cordoned off the crime scene and had begun taking the names of witnesses.

He'd also held firm when the owner of the SUV had demanded his vehicle back and the area cleared. No small feat, considering the Suburban was registered to the Secret Service.

Joe's gaze skimmed over the gathering crowd, looking for anyone who might appear a bit too interested, when he saw two guys in suits pacing impatiently on the other side of the yellow-and-black tape, talking back to whatever voices were coming through their earphones.

Since the vice president's advance team had been a royal pain in the ass since they'd hit town last week, Joe decided to let them cool their heels a while longer.

It had been twenty minutes since the first 911 call had come in. Not enough time for the victim's smooth, golden skin to turn blue-gray or lividity to begin to set in. Her nose had been broken, her cheekbones shattered like crystal slammed with a sledgehammer. Her still-clear hazel eyes, more green than blue, stared unseeingly up at the night sky, giving no clue as to the last moments of her life. They didn't look depressed, or surprised, or frightened. They just looked dead.

As a vision of another blonde, her face horribly broken, swirled through Joe's mind like smoke, sweat beaded on his forehead and above his lip; his heart felt as if it were pounding out of his chest.

"Joe?"

He blinked, clearing the memory from his mind. "What?"

"You okay?" Cait was looking at him as if she expected him to keel over at any moment.

"Sure." He hitched in a breath and swiped the sweat off his forehead. "This damn heat just got to me for a minute."

"You looked a million miles away."

"I was just thinking of how she might have ended up here." It was going to be okay. He no longer felt as if he were on the verge of a heart attack and his lungs were working again.

Caitlin was too good a detective not to spot the lie, but she was also a good enough friend not to push it.

A high-pitched whistle screeched from the old iron suspension bridge leading to Swann Island, a palm and pine tree studded barrier island three miles offshore; seconds later, a dazzling display of red, white, and blue exploded over the water. Buccaneer Days wasn't about to slow down just because some unidentified female had discovered the hard way that arms made lousy wings.

"I can't hang around here all night investigating a frigging murder," Manning complained with a whine that sounded ridiculous coming out of a guy with an eighteen-inch neck. "I've got a hot date with a hard body." He glared down at the corpse and shook his shaved head.

Cait, who'd had a one-night stand with the detective

after her divorce, had reported back that Manning also shaved his entire body. Which was a lot more personal information about the guy than Joe wanted to know.

"Vic could be a jumper who bounced off the side of the building after she was airborne," Joe surmised. "From the dent in the SUV's roof, she landed there first." Eventually coming to an abrupt stop on the hood.

He tilted his dark head back, looking a long way up at the balcony. According to the desk clerk, the twenty-something woman had checked into suite 1033 as Sissy Smith, from Charlotte. Her credit card was imprinted with the same name, but a computer check for a North Carolina driver's license had drawn a blank, which had Joe wondering about the slender gold band on her broken left hand. A woman meeting a man other than her husband at a hotel wasn't all that likely to check in under her own name.

"Jake and I tried counseling before the final breakup." Cait bent her knees to get a close-up shot of the wedding band. She'd always had a knack for sensing Joe's thoughts, which was only one of the things that made her such a good partner. "The counselor suggested hotel dates to spice up our marriage."

"Guess it didn't work," Manning said.

"No shit, Sherlock." She changed the angle of the camera to capture the angle of the broken neck.

Cait's marriage to a vice cop had ended in divorce. They were both good people who'd reluctantly decided that murder didn't make for scintillating pillow talk, something Joe had discovered for himself. Bad enough that murder cops were always on call. It was damn difficult to live in both worlds—to attend the autopsy of an innocent child in the morning, then show up at a family dinner a few hours later.

A raucous parade of wannabe-pirates sporting cutlasses and buxom would-be wenches in low-cut blouses passed by, the rowdy *yo ho hos* turning to complaints when they discovered their access to the waterfront restricted.

"Oh, oh," Cait murmured. "Things could get ugly."

The burly leader of the gang, who looked like a biker outlaw turned buccaneer, was wearing a lace-trimmed black silk frock coat over striped knee breeches. A bright-green parrot perched on his shoulder. The man's face was lobster red as he waved toward the yellow tape. Excited by his master's anger, the bird began squawking and flapping its wings.

The wannabe-pirate's cohorts, undoubtedly fueled by the lethal rum punches being served at walk-away concessions every few feet along the harbor, backed up their pirate leader with shouts and fists thrown in the air.

There was no way the tape could prevent them from surging into the crime scene. The other uniforms appeared to be taking their lead from the unflappable Thomas. Their mood was quietly authoritative without being overly aggressive.

The Secret Service guys, on the other hand, appeared to be going from pissed to edgy. Edgy and armed was never a good combination.

Joe watched one of the agent's hands ominously disappear beneath his jacket. Drunken pirates getting shot by government agents would undoubtedly land them all on the evening news on television sets all over the country. And wouldn't the mayor, who was already in a squeaker of a three-way race for reelection, love that?

"I'll be right back."

Joe walked the ten yards to where the confrontation looked more and more in danger of escalating.

"Cool threads," he said, moving between the pirate and the agent. "Not many guys can get away with wearing lace and red satin, but you sure pulled it off, son."

One eye was hidden behind a black patch. The other, as red-veined as a South Carolina road map, narrowed suspiciously. "Would ye be insulting the dreaded Bastard Jack?"

"No way would I do that, sir." Joe smiled reassuringly, managing not to flinch as a burst of rum-scented breath hit him in the face. "See those guys over there?" He nodded toward the agents. "They're Secret Service agents, who, between you and me, are genetically unable to have a good time. They'd just as soon haul people in as look at them, and I'd sure hate for your holiday to include an up-close-and-personal tour of the brig."

"Would that be a threat, ye cursed bilge rat?"

"No, sir." Since the pirate had a good two inches on his own six-two, Joe took half a step back as the giant swayed. "I'm just trying to help y'all avoid any unnecessary trouble that'd cut short your fun."

"If you backtrack half a block and make a right at Lanterns and Lanyards, Harbor View Drive will take you straight to where the *Queen Anne's Revenge* is docked," Patrolman Thomas offered helpfully.

The *Queen Anne's Revenge* was a replica of the French slave ship Blackbeard had captured and converted into a forty-gun warship; it had been one of several ships the pirate had used to blockade nearby Charleston's harbor back in 1718. This twenty-first century replica, which had sailed from New Zealand, was one of the special attractions of the festival.

The pirate looked tempted. But it was obvious that he didn't want his band of merry men to see him backing down to authority.

"Aargh! Bloody flaming hell!" He looked over his shoulder to where his pirate gang was waiting to see if he'd run up the white flag. "Come about, stripeys," he said finally, "we be goin' to the *Revenge.*"

A hearty cheer rose up. In decidedly less than drill-team precision, the ragged band turned around and staggered back the way they'd come.

Having feared that if Bastard Jack had told his ragged band to hang Joe by the yardarm, they'd have started trying to drag him to the ship, Joe was glad to see them go. "Now that we've solved that little problem," he said to the agents, "why don't we agree to keep our weapons in our holsters?"

The taller of the two agents jutted out his jaw. "Who the hell are you?"

Like the guy couldn't read the badge he'd clipped to his shirt pocket? "Joe Gannon. Lieutenant, Somersett PD." There'd been a time, when Joe had been young, green, and eager, that he might have welcomed a pissing contest. Right now he just wanted to work his crime scene with the least amount of interference. "Homicide. And you are?"

"Gerald MacNab." The guy's accent was County Cork by way of Boston. "Secret Service." He flashed his own credentials like a gunfighter pulling his Colt revolver at high noon. The five-sided star reminded Joe of the badge he'd gotten with Cheerios box-tops when he was seven. "And we want our vehicle back. Now."

"Sorry." *Not.* "Your vehicle just happens to be evidence. You'll get it back after the crime lab finishes with it." If he hadn't already decided to impound the Suburban, this Yankee's hostile attitude would have ensured that the agents weren't getting it back anytime soon.

"That vehicle happens to be the property of the US government. You don't have the authority to commandeer it."

Unintimidated, Joe flashed a grin that was pure pirate. "Watch me, matey."

He turned to the uniformed cop whose eyes had widened as he'd watched the exchange. "Everything copacetic, Thomas?"

"Aye, aye. I mean, yessir!" Dylan Thomas, who reminded Joe a lot of himself when he'd been young and eager and actually believed he could save the world, stopped just short of saluting.

"Then I'll leave things on this side of the tape in your capable hands and get back to work."

Ignoring the steamed Secret Service guys, he strolled back to his crime scene.

"How do you think Feds walk with those sticks jammed so far up their tight asses?" Caitlin wondered out loud.

Joe had been pondering the same thing since Noble Aiken had been elected to the vice presidency seven years ago, which had resulted in the plague of government guys riding like gunslingers into Somersett whenever the former governor returned to his home town to shake out donors' pockets.

"Everyone has his talents."

Joe shifted his gaze from the now more-subdued crowd back to the body. The vic's skirt had twisted up, revealing a skimpy scrap of pink silk.

After the dark day their only son had died, the day that had changed their lives and doomed their marriage, his now ex-wife had started going to bed in sweats or one of his raggedy old SPD T-shirts. Not that he would have noticed if she had suddenly taken to wearing some frothy, come-screw-me-big-boy nightgowns, since most nights, when he finally did come home, he'd fall asleep on the sofa in the den in front of the TV to avoid risking any intimacy. Unfortunately, the same ability to disengage emotionally that was a necessity in the cop business had proven very unhelpful in a relationship.

Three years after Austin's death, memories of his son still hurt. Joe, a cradle Catholic who'd been brought up to believe in the concept of penance, figured it should. His brother Mike, a Jesuit priest, had told him God didn't work that way and suggested counseling. Joe had passed on the idea. It was his fault his dinosaur-loving child was dead. Therefore, retribution was due. You could take the former altar boy out of the Church, but as he'd already discovered, it was a helluva lot more difficult to take the Church out of the man.

"A chick doesn't put on butt floss and hooker heels to attend a garden party," Briggs said, drawing Joe's mind back from that rainy afternoon when he'd stood beside his Valium-numbed wife and watched their brown-eyed boy's body being lowered into the ground.

"If she was trying to spice up a marriage, she definitely picked the right wardrobe," Manning agreed.

"How come the woman's always the one who has to make the extra effort?" Caitlin complained around the plastic pen stuck in her mouth.

She snapped a longer shot of the SUV, capturing the crowd of lookie-loos—every once in a while you got lucky and caught a photograph of the perp who'd stuck around for the fun—then scribbled the photo sequence in her notebook.

"Because they outnumber men. It's a competition thing," Briggs claimed. "Chicks need to attract males so they can get laid to keep the species going."

Cait made a low sound of disgust.

Joe, who'd also gotten fairly good at reading *her* thoughts, suspected Cait was thinking the species would have been a great deal better off if Briggs's mother hadn't attracted Briggs's father.

"Unless she's a Victoria's Secret model, that's sure as hell not everyday underwear," Manning pointed out. "Which fits the pattern of women prettying themselves up before they check out." He was still pushing for suicide, which wasn't surprising, given all the unsolved murders they were trying to juggle.

All summers in the South Carolina Low Country were hot, but this one was breaking records every day and crime had escalated right along with the temperature. The hotter it got, the more tempers flared. Minor fender-benders exploded into road rage, bar arguments became brawls, date rape rose in direct proportion to increased alcohol consumption, patrol cops couldn't keep up with the increased number of domestic disturbance calls, which were leading to murder, and just last night, unhappiness about an umpire's "safe at home" call at a kids' play-off baseball game had started bullets flying.

"Jumping off a ten-story balcony is not exactly the way to leave behind a good-looking corpse," Joe countered.

One more half-twist in the air and Sissy Smith, or whoever she was, would have left a face print in the windshield. The investigative unit hadn't arrived to set up the klieg lights yet, but the flashing red, white, and blue bubble lights from the cruisers illuminated a bit of pink on the dusty brick hotel roadway. Joe crouched down, picked up the lacquered tip of a fingernail, and slipped it into a glassine bag.

"Make sure you get some close-up shots of her hands," Joe advised Cait as the medical examiner's van arrived at the scene and a man dressed in a suit even Joe could tell was Italian climbed out of the driver's seat. Despite the sweltering, breath-stealing heat, the nubby silk jacket didn't appear to have a single wrinkle and the crease in the slacks could have cut glass. It was not your usual medical-examiner attire.

Then again, Drew Sloan was not your usual medical examiner. Son and grandson of plastic surgeons to generations of the Deep South's society belles, rather than use his talents with a scalpel to pretty people up, he'd chosen an occupation that had him cutting them up.

His good looks, near genius IQ, and ability to make

the complexities of forensic medicine understandable to the layman, had created a demand for his expert testimony among both prosecutors and defense attorneys. A frequent guest on *Court TV*, he'd written a book profiling a few of his more gruesome cases, which had landed on the best-seller lists and paid for his designer duds and the batmobile-black Porsche he drove when not on duty.

For Dr. Drew Sloan, crime not only paid, it paid handsomely.

"So, boys and girls, what's the flavor of the day?" he greeted the detectives.

"Suicide," Manning prompted hopefully.

"Sounds like someone's got a hot date." Sloan tugged a pair of blue paper shoe-covers over his handmade Italian loafers; white talc puffed as he snapped on a pair of latex gloves.

"Better put your hot body on hold, Sherlock," Cait advised the detective. Aware of the Eyewitness TV 3 news van that had pulled up right behind the ME, and the video camera now focused on them, she refrained from smiling. But Joe could hear the grin in her voice. "Because I've got ten bucks that says murder."

"This sucks," Manning complained.

As the sky overhead exploded in a grand finale that drew *oohs* and *ahhs* and appreciative applause from the crowd, and gave the broken, near-naked body atop the shiny black SUV a surrealistic look, Joe silently agreed with him.

Maybe he'd become a lobsterman, piloting his boat through the cool morning fog, setting his traps, returning when they were full to harbor in some small, unpretentious, picturesque little town of gray clapboard buildings.

Unfortunately, if there was one thing he'd learned in twenty years in the cop business, it was that appearances could be deceiving. A lobsterman's life undoubtedly wasn't as uncomplicated as his fantasy. But as he swatted away another attack of vampire mosquitoes, Joe couldn't help wondering if those Downeasters had any idea how fortunate they were to spend their days breathing in the crisp scent of salty sea air instead of death and despair.

3

Laurel opened the door to the men, one clad in a stiff, off-the-rack blue suit which immediately gave him away as FBI, the other two wearing the Secret Service's cockamamie idea of an invisible cloak. She had no idea what former bureaucrat had decreed that polo shirts and khakis would be the uniform of the day whenever Secret Service agents wanted to fit into the scene with casually dressed civilians, but she could have saved them a lot of the bucks they'd spent at Brooks Brothers and the Gap by pointing out that most civilians, when relaxing, didn't stand at attention while talking into their collars.

The agents themselves would have been bad enough news. But the fact that they hadn't come alone made matters even worse.

Lois Merryman had been appointed managing editor of the *Post* last month, having been hired away from Seattle's *Post-Intelligencer*. To say her name was an oxymoron would be a vast understatement and although it made no sense, she and Laurel had disliked each other at first sight—so much so that if Laurel actually bought into all the hocus-pocus, New-Age pagan stuff her aunt Zelda,

Highland Falls's self-proclaimed witch, believed in, she'd have thought she and Lois had been mortal enemies in a previous life.

"Are y'all lost?" she asked helpfully after acknowledging the editor. "Camp David's a bit down the road."

Not one of them so much as cracked a smile. No surprise there. They went through the identification ritual, flashing their badges with military precision while Lois Merryman's face wore its usual stony expression. The new Secret Service guy, Laurel discovered, was named Jack Wagner.

"Okay, I get it." Laurel sighed. "You're pissed off at what I said during the peace prayer. But last time I read the Constitution, irreverence toward elected officials wasn't a federal crime."

"We're not here regarding your ill-chosen or poorly timed remarks, Ms. Stewart," FBI Special Agent James Doherty said with a west-Texas twang.

His mouth was set in a grim line, but his jug-handle ears took a bit away from what Laurel supposed was meant to be an intimidating tone. Having worked for six months on a now-defunct afternoon weekly in the Permian Basin, she could recognize a guy who'd grown up wearing Stetsons at too young an age. The weight pressed down on a child's growing cartilage, and by the time a cowboy reached manhood, his ears could appear capable of manned flight.

"We're here about that story you ran in the *Post* this morning," Dumbo Ears revealed.

"Ah, yes. The one about petroleum company executives who—wow, what a surprise!—bought special favors."

Since such behavior went on all the time in Washington—the back-room wheeling and dealing wouldn't by itself be a political bombshell—the difference was that this time the fat-cat contributors were hiding behind the Terrorism Act.

"Where did you get your information?" he asked.

Laurel had worked in national politics long enough to know that not all FBI agents were so blatantly obnoxious. This one, however, was totally deficient in people skills. Obviously, Efrem Zimbalist Jr. had not been Special Agent Doherty's role model.

"My information?" She lifted a tawny brow as she glanced over at Lois Merryman, whose grim expression gave nothing away. Not a good sign. "Are you, by chance, referring to my facts? Which include the fact that, if elected president, Vice President Aiken plans to fight terrorism by drilling for oil and gas in fragile coastal wetlands?"

"Facts can be debatable," the agent pressed on, in a way that told Laurel he was one of those holdouts who refused to buy into the idea of global warming.

"We're not here to debate the merits of the case, Ms. Stewart," the second Secret Service agent, who'd remained silent until now, intervened smoothly.

Unlike the Texan's twang, his smooth tone conjured up images of Virginia's rolling green Shenandoah mountains. Laurel and J. T. Malloy had gone out a few times last year, but their demanding schedules had made it impossible to carve out enough personal time to see if drinks and two dinners interrupted by work-related calls could evolve into a relationship. She'd told herself that even if they had kept dating, the inevitable career conflict would have eventually gotten in the way. "We're investigating the leak of important government documents."

"Leaks happen," Laurel said, repeating what she'd told Barry when he'd called. "This is Washington, aka Sieve City. If any alleged leaked documents did somehow happen to end up on my desk, and I happened to turn them over to my editor, who, in turn, published them, that's not against the law."

This time her smile, directed at the Texan FBI agent, edged on feral. "Perhaps you missed class the day your American Government teacher taught the Pentagon Papers case, where the people's right to know trumped a corrupt administration's right to keep secrets from its citizens."

"Thank you, Ms. Stewart, for the civics lesson." The Fibbie's sarcasm was even sharper than hers. "Being such a student of history, have you happened upon another incident from the Nixon administration, called Watergate?"

"Of course." Other teenage girls had crushes on rock stars; Laurel's idols had been Woodward and Bernstein.

"We're investigating the possibility of another break-in and theft. This time at the vice president's office."

Her heart was clattering so hard against her ribs she was surprised the men couldn't hear it. "Someone stole something from Vice President Aiken's office?"

"Are you saying that comes as a surprise, Ms. Stewart?" Doherty demanded. She had the feeling he was wishing for the bad old days of law enforcement when he could drag out the bright lights and rubber hoses.

"I'm stunned." Laurel suspected her breezy bravado wasn't fooling any of them. But it wasn't exactly a lie. She had, indeed, been stunned when Barry had informed her that her name was being tossed around inside the Beltway as the source of the leak. "If someone can break into the vice president's office, when he's surrounded by Secret Service protection, what hope is there for the rest of us?"

The flush that rose up from the collar of Secret Service Agent Wagner's navy blue polo shirt suggested he was not amused. Dumbo Ears glowered while J. T. merely slanted her a veiled warning look.

"Would you happen to recall the last time you were in the vice president's office?" J. T. asked.

Okay. You've obviously landed in some serious shit. And having made that stupid remark during the prayer for peace, your chances of a presidential pardon are probably slim to none.

"Last week. But I never made it past the dragon guarding the door to his inner office."

She'd been stuck in the reception area for hours, proving, at least to her mind, that the stories of secret passages leading out of the White House were true, since she'd sat long past dark on that couch and Aiken had never walked past her.

"Would you swear to that?" Doherty looked as though he'd love to pull out his cuffs, haul her in, and ship her off to a cell in Guantanamo.

"Absolutely." Despite the blistering heat wave, Laurel was now very, very cold.

She wasn't guilty of breaking into anyone's office. Nor would she have ever hired anyone else to do her dirty work for her. She was admittedly dogged when she was working on a story, but she wasn't guilty of anything other than aggressive reporting.

"I told the agents you didn't steal any report." Lois Merryman finally entered the conversation.

"Thank you." Laurel was surprised by the vote of support. Lois questioned everything Laurel wrote. Not in Barry's hard-driving, dig deeper way. She held up stories beyond deadline by flagging so many minuscule details that two fact checkers had actually quit and rumors were that four others were threatening a walkout. Worse yet, although Lois's job was administrative, she edited Laurel's copy to death, even going so far, on occasion, as to change her prose style until her unique voice was nearly unrecognizable.

Just as Xena, Warrior Princess, had Callisto, and Buffy the Vampire Slayer had the evil god Glory, Laurel had Lois Merryman. Frustrated, she'd been just about ready to turn in her resignation, when the leaked memo arrived in the mail.

"You couldn't have stolen that report because it's patently false," the editor revealed, her expression matching her grimly dark, off-the-rack charcoal suit. Her hair had been pulled back into a French twist so tightly Laurel suspected her head must hurt.

Laurel's own head went light. "That can't be." She tried to focus as a bubble of panic rose in her throat. "I checked it out. I have the required three sources."

"Well, either they're lying or you've turned to writing fiction."

That sarcastic accusation cleared the fog from her

head. Laurel shot her a look. "I uncover stories. I don't need to make them up."

Laurel's nemesis had tried to confine the story of smoke-filled room deals and illegal drilling to limbo, but after she'd spiked it, Barry had bucked the chain of command, taking it directly to the publisher, who'd warned Laurel that her sources be damn better than golden; this story demanded platinum credibility.

Credibility she'd assured him she had.

Unfortunately, her sources had insisted on speaking only on deep background, which meant that nothing she wrote could identify the person in any way or even allude to the organization he worked for.

"We have a responsibility to our readers," Lois said. "They trust us to be unbiased and accurate, and I'm not going to allow our credibility to be questioned under my tenure."

"I may not have revealed my sources in my article," Laurel argued. "But they're in my notes." It was standard practice to always record names, even those promised anonymity. "Which you're welcome to see."

"I've assured legal that they'll have all your notes by the end of the day." The editor extended her hand. Laurel took her notebook from the hobo bag she used for a briefcase. The fear that she'd never see it again caused a jolt of loss. "I also informed them you're no longer on staff. As we speak, your desk is being cleared out; I'll have your belongings and your final check sent to your home."

A week ago she'd been on the verge of quitting. But resigning was one thing; getting fired was an entirely different kettle of koi.

"My story may turn out to be false," Laurel allowed reluctantly. "But I did *not* make it up."

"That remains to be seen." Assassination completed to her satisfaction, Cruella nailed Laurel with a satisfied look and left the hotel room. Probably off to roam the streets of the District searching for dalmation puppies to skin.

"We'd like you to come downtown with us," Doherty said, breaking the silence that lingered momentarily after the editor's departure.

"Downtown?" Just when she'd thought things couldn't get any worse. "As in, the Washington field office?"

"Questioning in an office with proper recording facilities is in your own best interest," J. T. supplied. "And if you're telling the truth—"

"I am," Laurel interjected.

"—then you shouldn't have any objection to answering a few questions," Secret Service Agent Wagner said.

"It'll help us eliminate you as a potential suspect, so we can concentrate on catching the bad guys," Doherty said.

Maybe he *had* watched all those FBI television shows after all. Because she'd bet that line had been said in most of them. Usually right before the blue-suited agents arrested the perp they were falsely claiming to want to eliminate from the suspect list.

"If dragging in reporters who dare write anything negative about the administration is standard operating procedure in post-9/11 America, our system is in even worse trouble than I've been telling readers."

"You have the right to remain silent," Doherty reminded her.

Laurel's hot temper warred with iced fear. She folded her arms and dug her fingers deep into the sleeves of her robe to prevent the agents from seeing her hands were shaking. "Are you reading me my Miranda rights, Special Agent?"

"Just pointing out a fundamental rule of American justice," he said with strained politeness.

"I assume you'll allow me to get dressed."

"Of course."

She went over to the closet and pulled out the overnight bag she'd learned to keep packed after a trip to Paris for a European Summit. After a hotel fire alarm had blasted her awake in the dark, she'd ended up outside the Hilton on the Place de la Defense at three in the morning with only a three-hundred-count Egyptian cotton sheet wrapped around the black bra and panties she'd stripped down to after finally falling into bed an hour earlier. The photograph of her standing on the sidewalk, looking like a refugee from a college toga party while puffing on a Gauloises, had landed her on the front page of both *Le Monde* and the *International Herald Tribune*.

She returned to the bathroom, dressed quickly, then, although it was one of the most difficult things she'd ever done, second only to that time when, at five years old, she had forced down her blazing anger as she watched her dead mother being lowered into the snowy ground, Laurel walked out of the inn, accompanied by the three agents, with her head held high.

She had just reached her lipstick-red Audi when a man wearing a casual blue golf shirt and sporting a dark televangelist's pompadour, came up to her.

"That was quite a performance in the chapel, Lois Lane," Warren Wyatt greeted her. A smirk played at the corners of his thin lips.

Grateful that the agents had continued on toward their black Suburban, Laurel pulled her keys from her bag. "I'm so pleased you enjoyed it."

Politicians and other government functionaries tended to view the press as annoying speedbumps in their otherwise smooth road to being seen as flawless human beings. Laurel didn't take their animosity personally, since most of the time she didn't like politicians, either. Hell, if the White House liked her, she wasn't doing her job.

But this man was different. Known inside the Beltway as "Aiken's brain," Warren Wyatt was a slick operator who'd crawled his way up the top rung of the Washington political and social ladder on the backs of countless victims who'd made the mistake of underestimating his grifter's grin. Since he was also Noble Aiken's college roommate, close friend, and chief political consultant, there were many who believed the vice president owed his successful career to Wyatt's maneuvering.

"Hey, you were the hit of the conference." He treated her to another of his trademark smirks, then strolled off toward his metallic-blue Jaguar, his hands in the pockets of his khaki Dockers. He was jauntily whistling "Hail to the Chief."

"You wish," she muttered.

Alone in the privacy of her car, she finally gave in to frustration and hit the steering wheel with her palm. "Damn, damn, damn!"

She'd spent the past fourteen years since graduating

from Northwestern's Medill School of Journalism honing her craft and building a reputation for tough, honest reporting. How could anyone ever think she'd ever stoop to even shading a story, let alone making one out of whole cloth?

It was unbelievable. It was infuriating.

And worst of all, it was so impossibly, excruciatingly painful.

Laurel took a deep breath and struggled for focus. Her hand was shaking so hard it took three times to insert the key into the ignition.

The thing to do, she decided as she reluctantly followed the black FBI Suburban out of the lot, was to concentrate on getting through the next few hours.

It was dark when she finally escaped the FBI Washington field office. She drove home in a fog, double-parking in front of a small market a few blocks from her house to dash inside and grab a pint of Ben and Jerry's Chocolate Fudge Brownie ice cream, a bottle of Pouilly-Fuissé, and on impulse—though she hadn't smoked for nine months, ten days, and eighteen hours—a pack of cigarettes.

Giving herself a mental pep talk the rest of the way home, Laurel remembered something her aunt Zelda had told her when she was sixteen and had discovered her date, Bobby Finn, making out with Holly McLean—a girl she'd thought was her best friend—in the parking lot during the Robbie Burns Birthday Bash Ball.

"You'll get over this," Zelda had reassured her. "But if you want to be a writer, you must remember what you're feeling right now."

She'd been feeling a hot and hungry need for retribution. The idea of reenacting the prom scene from *Carrie* had been hugely appealing.

"Everything's copy to a writer," Zelda had said. "You'll be able to use this later."

As usual, her aunt had known best. Bobby had gotten a comeuppance when Holly told her girlfriends—who quickly spread it all over school—that Bobby Finn didn't know how to French kiss worth a damn. Better yet, six months later Laurel earned twenty-five dollars from a science fiction magazine for a short story about a pimply faced boy who'd broken up with a sweet, pretty, small-town girl on Valentine's Day, only to turn into a rat by midnight.

Someday you'll probably write about this as well.

As she pulled up in front of a pretty yellow-and-white Victorian town house, Laurel hoped she wouldn't be writing from a federal prison cell.

4

A full, white moon was floating across a midnight sky studded with stars. You couldn't see so many stars in the city, Joe thought. There were too many lights. But out here, seven miles off the South Carolina coast, they glittered overhead like diamonds.

When a shriek of drunken female laughter split the salt-tinged summer air, Joe sighed and pressed the button to light up the dial of his watch. Shit. There were still two hours until the rendezvous. He'd never been known for his patience, and having worked this case for eighteen months, he was damn ready to close it and move on.

His mind drifted back to the argument he'd had before leaving for the yacht. He rubbed his cheek and imagined he could still feel the imprint of Gwen's hand. He hadn't been the least bit tempted to return his wife's slap. But dammit, why couldn't she understand that his work was his life? He couldn't separate the two even if he wanted to. Which, he privately admitted, he didn't.

Don't let yourself be distracted. Take your mind off the job and you can end up shark bait.

He heard the high heels tapping on the mahogany

deck as a woman approached in a cloud of gardenia perfume.

"You're not joining the party," she complained prettily. She held out to him one of the two glasses she was carrying.

"I was just looking at the stars." He took a sip of the martini.

"All by yourself?" She leaned her bare back against the railing and looked up at him. "That's not very sociable."

"Sorry." Since her feline smile suggested Joe look at her instead, he took a slow, masculine perusal, from the top of her brunette head down to her feet, clad in platform sandals that added at least five inches to her height. She'd poured herself into a low-cut, figure-hugging minidress that looked as though a man would have to peel it off her.

"I don't know what I was thinking." He allowed his gaze to drift lazily back to her breasts. He'd never been able to get all that excited about breasts that had been pumped up with silicone; he much preferred the natural B-cup ones waiting for him at home. Still, sometimes, for the job, you just had to fake it.

The moonlight shone in her eyes as she looped an arm around his neck. "That's better," she purred as his body responded to her lush female one as she rubbed it up against him. Some things a guy just couldn't fake. "I was beginning to worry that you didn't like me."

"Now, who wouldn't like you?" Her skin was warm and soft and fragrant. There'd been a time, back in his wilder and crazier days, when he might have taken her up on what she was offering. But no longer. He and

Gwen might not be getting along all that well, but narcs had to set their own limits as to what they were willing to do for the job, and adultery was over Joe's personal line.

Two hours, he thought as she lifted her lips to his, her tongue action as sensual and as practiced as he'd expect from a woman who, rumor went, had once commanded three thousand bucks a night before getting into the even more profitable drug trade. What the hell was he going to do for the next 120 minutes?

He was about to suggest that he refresh her drink when there was another cry from behind Joe. And this time the woman wasn't laughing.

He looked around just in time to see a girl, no older than eighteen, get hit in the face hard enough to turn her bleached head around.

"It's just Ramon," the brunette told Joe. "He likes things physical."

The girl didn't seem enamored by the idea of rough sex. The drug dealer was also flying high on meth, which could result in a trainwreck tonight and ruin months of investigation. Blood began streaming from the girl's nose.

"Hey." Scarlet-tipped fingers splayed against Joe's cheek, turning his face back to hers. "Don't worry. Jasmine's a big girl. She can handle one Miami homeboy."

Grabbing Jasmine by the hair, Ramon dragged her down onto a mahogany deck that had been waxed to a glassy sheen. He threw his body on top of her, clamped his mouth onto her breast, and thrust his hand between her kicking legs.

"She doesn't look like she's handling him very well."

The woman laughed. "They didn't tell me that you were a Boy Scout, Joey." She trailed her hand down his neck, caressing his chest, then lowered it further to the erection that had deflated the minute Ramon had torn open Jasmine's short, too-tight red dress. "Believe it or not, I was a Girl Scout in a former life." She played with the top button of his jeans. "How about we go below deck and I show you my cookies?"

Damn. Jasmine was now screaming her head off. Joe wasn't particularly surprised when not a single person, including his effing partner whom he'd last seen disappearing into the VIP suite with two of the girls hired for tonight's party, paid any attention to the pair. In the drug business, teenage whores tended to be disposable.

You've spent eighteen months working on this. You're on the verge of bringing down a major kingpin. Don't screw it up now.

Jasmine might be down, but she wasn't out. Her knee connected. Ramon rolled off her, roaring as he clutched his balls in his hands. He staggered to his feet.

"Hey, son." Joe tried the good-old-boy routine that oftentimes could diffuse a dicey situation. "Let's not get carried away."

Ramon paused, spinning around on still unsteady legs to stare at Joe. His dark eyes filled with fury. "This isn't any of your fucking business, *cacorro*." He pulled back a booted foot and—*aw shit!*—kicked the girl, hard, in the ribs.

Jasmine was now curled up in a fetal position on the

moon-spangled mahogany deck, sobbing for mercy from a hopped-up drug dealer who didn't know the meaning of the word.

Joe might have been in deep cover, but, dammit, he was still a cop. He pulled the concealed Glock 26 from his ankle holster just as Ramon put the barrel of a TEC-9 against the girl's head.

The muzzle of Joe's Glock flashed. The smell of cordite overpowered the fragrance of gardenia perfume. Ramon stared in disbelief, then crumbled onto Jasmine, who was now screeching loud enough to make ears bleed.

Then all hell broke loose.

Stuttering bursts from automatic rifles shattered the peaceful summer night as bad guys began running toward him. Joe rolled behind the deck house.

"Kill the damn lights," he shouted to his partner, who'd finally emerged from below on the port side of the yacht. Glass shattered as Joe shot out a pair of lights himself. His partner hit a third. The night went black.

People were shouting and cursing in Spanish, but Joe couldn't hear what they were saying over the earsplitting sound of all the guns—his included—firing. He dove behind the locker where the life jackets were stored. Bullets spattered across the mahogany deck, whistled overhead, creating little sparks of flame as they tore through the sheet metal.

Joe slammed his spare magazine into the Glock and fired to cover his partner's zigzag sprint to the locker.

"Are we having fun yet?" Trace Harding, a former running back from Texas A&M, asked.

"I suppose that depends on what your definition of fun is." There was a loud crack from overhead. Hell, now the scumbags were firing from the flybridge!

"Feels a lot like Crockett and Bowie at the Alamo." Trace sounded as if he were actually enjoying himself as he blasted away in the direction of the shots.

Left out in the field for too long with too little supervision, narcotic cops tended to get crazy, on a good day. Trace was the most insane narc Joe had ever worked with, and this was turning out to be a far cry from a good day.

Joe felt the hot sting on his neck as fragments ricocheted off the metal locker; the moon drifted behind a deep purple cloud. He held the Glock high, blindly firing upward into darkness that was now lit only by stars, while Trace yanked a pair of orange life jackets out of the locker and threw one toward Joe.

Someone screamed from the flybridge. There was a momentary silence.

"Hey, bro, I think you got him."

The words had no sooner left Trace's mouth when there was another deafening *rat-a-tat-tat* from above, the bullets wiping away Joe's partner's grin, along with the rest of his face. More dead than alive, he staggered backward, falling into the water with a loud splash.

Struggling to fasten the bulky life jacket with his left hand, Joe kept firing with his right.

He heard someone come up behind him, and spun around to see the woman who'd propositioned him earlier pointing a pistol at his chest.

Time slowed.

The pistol's *pop* wasn't nearly as loud as the earlier automatic fire.

Joe saw the flame headed toward him, felt the impact of the slug slamming into his chest, tearing through tissue, shattering bone. He doubled over as the breath left his scorched lung in a painful *whoosh*.

"I'm very disappointed in you, darling," the brunette said.

Pop!

Joe's arm was on fire. The Glock dropped from his numb fingers.

Cool as a cucumber, she kicked it with her dainty sandaled foot, sending it sliding across the deck.

Deciding not to wait around to see what part of his anatomy she was going to shoot next, Joe dove off the yacht, into the wine dark sea . . .

The shock of the water jerked him from the nightmare. Gasping for breath, he was bathed in sweat, shaking like a damn crackhead in serious withdrawal at the memory of that gun battle three years ago.

When you lived above a pub, you got used to the sound of night music. Tangled in the wet sheets, all Joe could hear was the light patter of summer rain on the roof and the lonesome sound of a buoy tolling somewhere out in the harbor, suggesting that it was late. The glowing blue dial of his bedside clock confirmed that it was four a.m.

He dragged himself out of bed, stumbled on rubbery legs over to the loft kitchen, and ran a glass of water from the tap, gulping it down to put out fires he could still feel burning inside him. As bad as the memory of the gun battle was, what had come next was far, far worse.

When he'd gained consciousness two days later, he was lying in a hospital room. Apparently the Coast Guard had pulled him out of the water. The first bullet had broken a rib, collapsed a lung, then lodged in his heart. Although he'd been declared dead on the table at one point, the surgeon had managed to dig the slug out of him. The other bullet had merely grazed Joe's upper arm, taking some flesh and muscle with it.

His partner was dead. Joe had felt bad about that, but all cops knew the risks going in, especially those adrenaline junkies—like himself—who'd chosen narcotics. He was also humiliated that he'd blown the case that had taken the joint task force so many months to set up.

That embarrassment had been short-lived, swept away by the unthinkable news a sad-eyed nurse had reluctantly broken to him. While he'd been on that sleek white yacht, drinking martinis and swapping spit with a drug dealer, his son was being rushed to this very hospital with an antibiotic-resistant strain of streptococcal pneumonia.

While he'd been floating in the water, Austin had fallen into a coma.

And while he'd been lying on the operating room table, five-year-old Austin, who'd been disappointed by Joe's erratic working schedule far too many times during his too brief life, had been waiting yet again for his father to show up—this time to be in attendance when the life-support was disconnected.

Since Joe had been in a damn wheelchair, weak as a baby, Austin's doctor had been the one into whose arms

Joe's sobbing wife had collapsed after they'd turned off the respirator.

Joe still heard the mechanical whisper slowly and inexorably ceasing, in his sleep.

He figured he was cursed to hear it the rest of his life.

5

No Retreat. No Surrender. Springsteen's gravelly voice boomed from the speaker of Laurel's bedside CD player/alarm clock the following morning, yanking her out of a hot dream where she'd been having impossibly steamy sex with a photographer for Stockholm's *Dagens Nyheter* newspaper, after she'd modestly accepted a Nobel Prize from the King of Sweden.

Never mind that the Nobel committee didn't hand out prizes for journalism. Laurel had never done the hokey-pokey with a blond Viking in a sauna, either, but that hadn't stopped her from waking up tingling in all the right places. Unfortunately, the Boss had interrupted just as Sven was going in for a close-up.

The maniac living inside the CD player was pounding the song into her brain with a sledgehammer. Blindly reaching for the switch, she cut it off just as the singer's walls began closing in.

"I know how you feel," she groaned into the silence that was shattered when a bird warbled outside the window, its relentlessly cheerful morning song grating like fingernails on a chalkboard.

She gingerly opened her eyes, flinching as a laser-like sun blinded her. Hungover and dehydrated, she dragged herself out of bed; when her stomach turned over, she sank back down onto the edge of the mattress.

"That's what you get for breaking your one-drink rule."

Once upon a time ago, DC reporters had kept whiskey bottles in their desk drawers and passed the days and nights getting plowed in the Senate cloakroom with the very same politicians they covered. Although these days the watering holes may have mostly moved out of the Capitol, more than a few journalists believed in keeping up the tradition. Not wanting to miss breaking an important story because her head was fuzzed with alcohol, Laurel had always limited herself to a single glass of white wine.

Until last night.

The FBI questioning had been civil, but Laurel had sensed an undercurrent that told her that this mess wasn't necessarily going to go away just because no one shined bright lights in her face or brought out rubber hoses. Exhausted both mentally and physically, and not yet prepared to talk about what had happened to her, she'd been relieved to discover a note from her housemate, White House staffer Chloe Hollister, saying she was working late.

Laurel had gone upstairs to her bedroom, where she'd sat alone in the dark, her thoughts spinning around and around as she tried to figure out who would have gone to all the trouble of setting her up. And why. Unfortunately, answers hadn't been forthcoming. Which was how she'd somehow managed to work her way through that entire bottle of wine.

She turned on the television—already tuned to CNN—atop the dresser and, despite her pounding head, turned the volume up loud enough to hear it in the adjoining bathroom.

The row house was conveniently located three blocks from Union Station. It was one room deep, the downstairs taken up by a living room, dining room, and kitchen while two bedrooms and a connecting bath made up the second story. In contrast to her housemate, who'd seemingly tried to corner the world market in chintz, Laurel's only concession to decorating were the floor-to-ceiling shelves groaning with books.

A guy wearing epaulets on a shirt that looked as if he'd bought it at a West Bank Banana Republic was reporting on violence in the Middle East. Cringing at the deafening *rat-a-tat-tat* of automatic-weapon fire, Laurel stumbled into the bathroom, splashed cold water on her burning eyes, and brushed her fuzzy teeth. She swallowed two aspirin with a glass of water from the tap, then, after reconsideration, tossed down two more.

She twisted the shower to cold, partly because the ancient air conditioner in the house wasn't up to DC's staggering August heat, but mostly because if she was going to get any work done today, she needed to blast Sven and his wickedly clever fingers out of her imagination so she wouldn't be fixating on sex all day.

Which would, she admitted as she gingerly massaged shampoo into her hair, be an improvement over worrying about what would happen when the news of her firing, and the reason for it, became public.

It had been—what, three months—since she'd had sex? *Damn, longer than that.* Her last lover had been a documentary cameraman she'd met at her father's wedding last summer. They'd gotten together twice since then, once when they'd both been in New York on assignments, once when she'd been covering a meeting of the G8 in Stockholm and he'd flown over from Oslo, where he was filming a project.

Six months. Worse yet, you didn't even notice.

"That's just too purely pitiful for words."

It also explained why her sex-starved brain had created Sven and his long lens.

Shampoo streamed into her eyes, stinging like nettles.

"Dammit," she yelled, then wished she hadn't as a lightning bolt flashed through her wine-sodden brain.

She flung open the glass shower door and groped blindly for a towel.

You might as well have flipped an off-switch on your body.

It was only because it was an election year, she decided as she braved the seeming jet-roar of the hair dryer to blow her short auburn hair dry.

"Once the campaign season's over, you're going to prioritize your life."

She dusted some makeup across the bridge of her nose to cover up some freckles, then returned to the bedroom where the scene on the screen had shifted from the Middle East to Cincinnati's River Downs Racetrack.

"The annual Weiner Dog races are the most popular summer event in the city," the local anchorwoman breathlessly informed viewers as a frenzied pack of more than a hundred dachshunds madly raced for the finish line. If she'd seen the frenzied dash last night, Laurel would've feared she'd been suffering an alcohol induced hallucination.

She switched to C-Span, where a Kentucky legislator was giving a speech to an empty chamber, his words obviously directed toward his home audience, since he'd managed to praise a coal-mining company three times in as many minutes.

After dressing for the heat in a taupe, sleeveless silk shell and a pair of white shorts, Laurel followed the scent of fresh-brewed coffee downstairs, nearly stumbling over the pile of Louis Vuitton luggage in the foyer as she went to retrieve the paper.

When the *Post* wasn't sitting on the front stoop where it was supposed to be, she belatedly remembered it was Wednesday, food section day, the one day a week Chloe— who was a champion recipe clipper—would beat her to it.

Her housemate was seated at the kitchen table, her expression that of a woman who'd just lost her only friend. The cheerfulness of the tulips blooming on her short silk robe contrasted with her downcast expression.

"What's wrong?" The kitchen TV was tuned to *Good Morning America*. With every cell in her body screaming for caffeine, Laurel poured a cup of coffee, then cut off Diane Sawyer's preview of a fall fashion show in Paris to switch to C-Span2, which was airing a month-old tape showing dueling senators arguing about health care. So far, no news was good news. "Is there a goat cheese shortage?"

Or, perhaps, Laurel thought, noticing that the paper hadn't been opened, another breakup.

Chloe Hollister was bright, beautiful, and blond, which, along with her magnolia southern accent, usually had her opponents on the front lines of legislative battles underestimating her intelligence. She was also disgustingly, unrelentingly cheerful, even in the mornings. Except when a romance went south, which they did with predictable regularity, due to her penchant for getting involved with unavailable men.

Her last relationship had been with a married tobacco lobbyist who'd assured her that he and his local wife had an "understanding." Apparently there was some difference of opinion on the meaning of the word *understanding;* two weeks into the brief affair, the wife bought a can of fire engine–red paint from the Fairfax Home Depot and sprayed *whore* and *slut* all over Chloe's titanium-silver BMW convertible.

Laurel didn't need reporter skills to recognize the clues. The pattern was always the same. Chloe would begin humming love songs by Barry Manilow and the Carpenters, until Laurel would threaten to give the stereo to Goodwill if she had to hear "We've Only Just Begun" one more time.

She'd change her perfume, disappear at odd hours, return home at the end of the day laden down with pink Victoria's Secret shopping bags. She'd even begun buying *Bride* magazine, which might have been an okay thing— though Laurel would rather be covered in honey and staked out on a fire ant–hill than sentence herself to a life of domestic "bliss"—had she not also been uncharacteristically close-mouthed about the man who'd apparently stimulated this latest bit of romantic behavior.

"Nothing's wrong," Chloe alleged. She'd always been a terrible liar. Her speculative gaze swept over Laurel. "Perhaps I should be asking how *you* are. And why aren't you dressed for work?"

"I'm hung over," Laurel admitted. Feeling a bit as if she were on the rolling deck of a ship, she sank down onto one of the Windsor chairs Chloe had sponge painted a cheery sunshine yellow.

"You never drink more than a single glass of wine."

"Unfortunately, I forgot that last night after I was hauled into the FBI."

"What?" Cornflower blue eyes widened.

"Apparently someone broke into the vice president's office. One theory making the rounds is that I'm the one who did it."

"You didn't!"

"Of course not. You can't possibly believe I'd have the guts—or the practical knowledge—to break into the office of the vice president of the United States?"

"You're the gutsiest woman I know," Chloe said loyally.

"Thank you." Laurel took the compliment in the spirit which she knew it'd been offered. "But I'm not suicidal. Even if I did know how to avoid security, then pick a lock, which I don't, the odds of getting caught would be astronomical."

"A bit like the odds of nailing that award-winning interview you got with the DOD whistle-blower who ended up testifying before the Senate committee about military contracting kickbacks."

"There was no breaking and entering involved in that story." Just a clandestine trip to Colorado and a lot of whistle-blower hand-holding. "Nor was there in this one. Christ, if I got caught taking papers from a government office, at best my career would be toast. At worst I'd end up in a federal prison."

"You know *I* believe you. But I'll bet people never believe they're going to get caught. So, what did you tell the FBI?"

"The truth. That I didn't do it."

"Do you think *they* believed you?"

"I can only hope, since the idea of writing a jailhouse column is less than appealing. Besides, even Houdini couldn't break into the West Wing undetected, especially these days, and I'd have to be insane to try to sneak into a building that has all those sharpshooters and missile launchers on the roof. It gets worse," Laurel admitted. "That story I wrote? The one I got from an over-the-transom tip that ran yesterday? There's a chance it may be false."

"You're kidding!"

"Getting fired is not exactly a joking matter."

"You were fired?"

"I was. And I do believe it made Cruella's day." Month. Year. "She showed up at Camp David with the FBI in tow. And *that's* why I'm not dressed."

Chloe's expression turned speculative. "I'll bet those agents were just trying to back you into a corner and scare you into naming your source."

"A journalist never burns a source." It was a cardinal law; sources were, after all, the lifeblood of journalism. "I wouldn't tell even if I did know, which I don't, because the leak was anonymous."

Lines furrowed Chloe's brow. "I wonder if it was Cody Wunder."

"Why would you think that?" Laurel wasn't prepared to admit the same thought had flashed through her mind when she'd been told the story was fake.

Cody "Shadow Hawk" Wunder was the self-proclaimed leader of CHAOS, a radical environmental group which, ironically like the very industries they protested, believed that their ends justified any means. They'd gotten their start spiking trees in northwestern forests a decade ago and more recently had been accused of attacking oil companies by throwing down the sort of spike strips used by police in high-speed chases in front of fuel trucks on the highway.

"It'd be just like Wunder to spread lies. He's been following the campaign all over the country, trying to paint the vice president as anti-environment." Chloe's lips, painted the same petal pink as the silk tulips on her robe, pulled into a tight line.

"The vice-president *is* anti-environment," Laurel argued. "Look at his Senate voting record; Aiken and environmentalism are oxymorons."

"You're just too jaded to ever allow a politician the benefit of the doubt."

"That's not true." Not exactly.

Laurel supposed there were some good ones—okay, she'd met a handful over the years who came to Washington to do good, but even the most idealistic soon discovered that the nation's capital was a political version of

Let's Make a Deal. Factor in the old saying about money being the mother's milk of politics proving, indeed, true, and politicians tended to lose their virginity real fast.

Damn. She never mixed metaphors. How many brain cells had she killed last night?

"The media misunderstand the vice president's policies," Chloe argued. "The campaign's been working on a forum to take environmental issues directly to the voters."

Meaning Wyatt had pulled out the green paint and brushes to add some much-needed chlorophyll to the vice president's image.

Chloe contributed to both the Sierra Club and Greenpeace, which was only one reason why Laurel couldn't understand her steadfast support of Noble Aiken, who, if given the opportunity, would probably plunder every last resource from the planet, then pave it over and turn it into one gigantic parking lot.

The stepdaughter of a former ambassador to the Court of St. James, Chloe had arrived in DC seven years ago with a collection of sparkly beauty pageant tiaras, a silver Olympic medal for dressage, a calligraphied, gilt-framed diploma from charm school, dual bachelor's degrees in political science and French from Somersett University, and a steamer trunk of designer clothing that nearly had Laurel salivating.

After leaving a job at the State Department, she'd been working as protocol officer to the vice president for the past—*shit*—six months. The missing piece of the puzzle that was Chloe's romantic life fell into place with a resounding thud.

"Oh, Lord." Laurel pressed her fingertips against her temples, which were now throbbing like a bass drum. "Please don't tell me you're having an affair with the vice president."

"Don't be silly." Chloe stood up and pretended a vast interest in sweeping crumbs from her cinnamon raisin bagel off the counter. "What an idea."

"Chloe." This could be a nightmare. "Does the name *Monica* mean anything to you?"

"Of course. But what on earth does she have to do with me?"

"You might find out if you land in the middle of a national scandal."

"Are you saying that if—hypothetically speaking—you knew something about me and some high level married politician, you wouldn't write about it?"

"Of course I wouldn't. Even if you weren't my best friend, if the paper reported on every case of adultery in this town, there wouldn't be space for anything else. But if—hypothetically speaking—Aiken is reckless, not to mention hypocritical enough, to run for leader of the Western world on a platform stressing a family values plank while having an affair with a staffer, that story will eventually leak out. And all the vice president's men won't be able to put the campaign together again."

"Noble Aiken's not a hypocrite," Chloe said loyally. "And he's going to be elected."

"If that dark day actually arrives, Mrs. Aiken will be First Lady." She felt the need to bring some reality into this conversation.

"Well, of course she is." Suddenly paling, Chloe put

a hand over her mouth and raced from the room.

The walls of the town house hadn't been built for privacy; Laurel listened to the gagging coming from the downstairs powder room, heard the toilet flush, and then the water in the sink run. She put her elbows on the table, lowered her aching head into her hands, and hoped like hell she wasn't the only one in the house suffering a crushing hangover.

"Please tell me you're not pregnant," she said, looking up when Chloe returned on legs that looked as unsteady as Laurel's felt.

"Why on earth would you think that?" Chloe's blue eyes fluttered around the room like butterflies, never landing anywhere. "It's just a case of flu."

"It's not flu season."

"A stomach virus, then. Or food poisoning." She filled the tea kettle and put it onto the range top. "I shouldn't have had those raw oysters at last night's fund-raiser."

Chloe was a vegetarian; as far as Laurel knew, she'd never eaten an oyster in her life. "We've been best friends for seven years. I hate the idea of you being in trouble."

Chloe sucked in a deep breath, and let it out on a long sigh. "You're like the sister I always wished for, and it's not that I don't want to tell you, but I just need a little time to work things out first." The doorbell rang. "That's the car I booked to take me to the airport."

Remembering that Chloe was accompanying her employer on a working vacation/fund-raising trip to South Carolina, and knowing how stubborn she could be beneath that blond magnolia belle exterior, Laurel reluctantly decided to shelve the discussion for now. "Where are you staying in Somersett?"

"The usual place the staff stays whenever the vice president goes home. The Wingate Palace."

"I'll call you this evening. Meanwhile, promise me you won't make any rash decisions until we can hash this over."

"Everything's going to be fine."

Laurel recalled the captain of the *Titanic* saying much the same thing. "Promise," she repeated.

"Heavens, you can be pushy."

"When you were wishing for a sister, you should have been more careful to specify that you didn't want the big, bossy one."

Chloe managed a laugh. "Next time I'll watch that fine print," she said as they hugged. "I'll bet both our problems will be all straightened out by the time I'm back home Monday morning."

Laurel stood in the doorway as the uniformed driver loaded the mountain of suitcases into the trunk. As the black limo glided away from the curb, Laurel wished she could believe that all their problems would disappear in the next five days. Unfortunately, while Chloe might be an optimist, Laurel was not.

6

Laurel's belongings arrived from the office by messenger shortly after Chloe's departure. Even in her numbed state, she was surprised by how few personal effects she possessed. Inside the box there was an autographed copy of *All the President's Men*, a slim *The Elements of Style*, a framed photo of her family taken at her sister Lark's wedding, another one of Laurel with quarterback Steve McNair taken during a very brief stint working the sports beat at the *Tennessean*, a small clay pot that held the shriveled, dried remains of an African violet, and a white coffee mug with the suggestion *If you don't like the news, go out and make your own*, printed on the side in bold black type.

As she tossed the plant out and took the other things upstairs to her room, Laurel couldn't get her brief conversation with Warren Wyatt the day before out of her mind.

He'd never pretended to like her. Could he have set her up? But why go to the trouble of creating a phony leak? A leak which had led her straight into a web of lies and seemed to have been designed solely to get her fired.

"It's not as if you're a household name." She was, in fact, only one political reporter on the paper. Of course it *was* the same paper that had brought down a sitting president.

Wyatt was an accomplished political duelist who wasn't above using anything or anyone as a weapon. Having been described as the most powerful unelected politician in America, he was the go-to guy whenever there was dirty work to be done on which the vice president didn't want his fingerprints.

But surely the vice president of the United States—the man a heartbeat away from the Oval Office—wouldn't stoop to engaging in a conspiracy to get rid of a reporter.

Oh yeah, her more cynical self responded. *Like Woodward and Bernstein and Lord knows how many other people weren't threatened with a lot more than the loss of their jobs during Watergate.* Hadn't Katherine Graham herself been warned that if the paper continued working on Nixon's ties to the break-in, she'd find her "tit in a wringer?"

But while she'd amassed an admirable collection of tear sheets over the years and some affirming awards from her peers, Laurel wasn't anywhere near the lofty level of either Woodward or Bernstein.

"Of course neither were they when they were running around chasing wild geese, trying to follow Deep Throat's instructions."

The trick was to distance herself and treat this debacle like a story she was tracking down. It was classic, connect-the-dots journalism. Someone had leaked her that file; three sources had lied. "But why?"

If she were a paranoid person, she might have thought this was all some scheme of Lois Merryman's to get rid of her.

"She wouldn't have to go to so much trouble," Laurel muttered while she paced a path on the living room plank floor. "As managing editor she could just fire you."

Like a leaf caught in a whirlpool, her mind circled around and around, finally returning to Wyatt, which, because two of her three sources had come from the West Wing, in turn pointed toward the vice president.

She'd never trusted the charismatic southern politician who'd been on the track to the White House since being elected the youngest governor of the state of South Carolina twenty years ago. After a single term he'd been elected to the Senate, where his voting record, from campaign finance to the environment to the economy, was to the right of Attila the Hun.

He was also the king of pork, even though he traveled around the country—on the taxpayer's dime—making speeches about his "tax and spend" opponents. In a town of self-serving individuals, Noble Aiken wore the hypocrite's crown.

Still, Wyatt and Aiken weren't the only suspects. After all, it still strained credulity that the vice president of the United States would stoop to such dirty tricks. There was still Cody Wunder to consider. She could easily picture him doing just about anything to grab some free publicity for CHAOS. But if he knew the environmental story wasn't true, he'd also know that it could easily be proven false.

But retractions weren't printed on the front page,

which meant a lot more people would remember the headlines, never knowing the truth.

Preferring fact to hypotheses, Laurel wasn't a big believer in conspiracies. She'd never bought into the argument that rogue elements in the British Secret Service had killed Princess Di, thought the people who kept insisting that the moon landing was a hoax perpetuated by NASA were flat-out nuts, and was firmly convinced that the words *grassy* and *knoll* should be expunged from the English language.

But it was looking more and more as if, for some reason, she'd landed on someone's enemy's list. But if whoever had done this to her expected her to just give up without a fight, they were hugely mistaken.

No retreat. No surrender.

Chloe reminded herself, all during the flight to South Carolina, that southern women were not the shrinking violets so many people—especially those living in the capital where people would probably run over their own dog if they thought it'd get them a vote or a headline—believed them to be.

She might have a bit of a problem—all right, a huge problem—but she'd been brought up to tackle adversity, and her mama, a multimarried southern beauty, would be beside herself if she knew her only daughter had ever stooped to sinking into a defeatist attitude.

After those two little colored lines had shown up on the pregnancy test kit, she'd been indulging in a pity party when her mama's voice suddenly echoed in her head.

"Better to have a broken heart than broken china, Chloe, darling." It was what Margot Rose Hollister had said after her third husband, Bradford Hollister, a sinfully handsome scion of a cotton fortune who had an unfortunate gambling habit had committed suicide at the tragically young age of thirty-three.

"There's a reason we're called steel magnolias," Margot declared bravely as she and her seven-year-old daughter watched the auctioneer taking all their furniture out of their home, Dogwood Hall, when it was discovered that Chloe's father had gambled away the family's future by losing a game of high stakes poker to Buckley Stuart Montgomery, a real estate developer who'd made millions building homes with such names as Tara, Twelve Oaks, Magnolia Point, and Graceland on fallow farms all over the South. Dogwood Hall, built in 1845, was destined to become the clubhouse for Montgomery's latest upscale subdivision.

Buck was to Bradford Hollister what Rhett Butler had been to Ashley Wilkes, a wheeler-dealer who had more money than God. But, having pulled himself up by his bootstraps, all Buck's money was "new" and he'd been looking for a way to break into old Somersett society. Margot might not have so much as a Confederate dollar left to her name, but her blood was as blue as the field on the Palmetto State's flag. As she explained to her daughter on her wedding day, a scant three months after having buried husband number three, Bradford wouldn't have wanted her to waste away her life mourning.

It had been a match made, if not in heaven, of convenience. Eighteen months after the wedding held in Dogwood Hall's English garden, Margot caught Buck having a sleepover with his secretary at the Savannah Marriott Riverfront Hotel. Taking responsibility for his wandering ways, Buck had dutifully written out a healthy divorce settlement check that kept Chloe in ballet lessons and Margot in Zandra Rhodes dinner gowns.

Two more marriages, to a Charleston cardiologist and a Somersett attorney and political fund-raiser who'd been appointed ambassador to Great Britain, followed. Margot had divorced the physician for the cardinal sin of being boring and was widowed for a second time when the ambassador skied off the side of mountain in the French Alps.

Twice divorced, twice widowed, Margot Rose Sotheby Channing Hollister Montgomery Bremer Talmadge, had not let life defeat her. She kept her hair a bright and sunny blond, her refrigerator stocked with Dom Perignon, and this past winter had cruised the Greek Islands with a blues musician from Memphis half her age.

"A positive attitude is like kudzu," she'd said once, when Chloe had called in tears after a college romance had crashed and burned. "It spreads like crazy and can't be stopped."

Reminding herself of another one of her mother's favorite sayings, that a magnolia didn't fall far from the tree, Chloe vowed that whatever happened in Somersett, she would not wring her hands or fall on her knees and grovel. She also wished she could borrow Laurel's brassy balls.

7

Laurel wasn't feeling all that brassy at the moment. Even having been on the other side of the press blitzkrieg more times than she could count, she hadn't been prepared to land in the spotlight. Being lumped in with all the other recent high-profile journalists who'd plagiarized or simply made up stories was not only humiliating, it was downright infuriating.

Unsurprisingly, the Washington media went into a full feeding frenzy as she became the topic du jour on the radio and political talk shows.

Journalism could, admittedly, be a competitive, cutthroat business, where getting the story first was, unfortunately, often more important than getting it right. Especially here in duplicitous Washington where enemies shook your hand with a smile while patting your back, looking for the soft spot into which to plunge the knife.

"Vultures." Conveniently ignoring the fact that there were many who might consider her to have been one of those carrion feeders, she used the answering machine to monitor the phone, which had begun ringing off the hook.

Knowing that anything she said could end up a headline or soundbite at eleven, she'd called her family from her cell phone to tell her side of the story and assure them that things were going to turn out just fine. Her aunts and sisters had been understandably concerned, but remained stalwartly supportive. For a while she'd been afraid her father was going to come down from his mountain and tear the *Post*'s editorial offices apart, but she managed to distract him by asking about his work. John Angus Stewart was an artist, and like many creative people she'd met, he tended to be self-absorbed.

"Hey, Laurel," Barry's familiar voice growled from the machine. "Pick up."

She did. "I don't suppose you're calling to tell me this has all been a mistake and you want me back at my desk."

His slight pause spoke volumes. "It'll all work out," he assured her.

"Of course it will." She could not allow herself to think otherwise. "But meanwhile my reputation goes down the toilet."

"You'll probably be the hot topic for a while," he allowed. "But you know how it is in this town; by this time tomorrow, copies of the front page will be covered in parakeet shit." His voice turned unnaturally soft. Almost gentle. Laurel hated the idea of anyone feeling sorry for her. "People will move on."

The fact that he was right didn't make her feel a damn bit better.

She'd no sooner hung up when the phone rang again. "*Beep* . . . Hello, Ms. Stewart?" The female voice sounded a bit hesitant, but friendly. "My name is Sandra Squires, editor of the *Falls Church Bee*. You may have seen our weekly shopper in your local Safeway? We're the paper who's been pushing for the District to adopt a national courtesy week, like they do in Culpepper?"

"Boy, do you have the wrong person," Laurel muttered as she lit a cigarette. Chloe didn't like her smoking in the house. Fortunately, Chloe wasn't here. Laurel vaguely remembered Sandra Squires's paper to be a free shopper, seemingly addicted to cutesy clip art, with a heavy emphasis on hearts and flowers.

"Well, I've always been a huge fan of your work, and I was thinking, now that you seem to be, uh, between jobs?" Another pause. "Well, I know we'd be a step down for you—"

"How about a giant leap?"

"But I was thinking perhaps, while you weigh other offers, you'd consider the idea of coming to work here at the *Bee*. The stories aren't as hard edge as you're used to covering—"

"Talk about your understatements."

"—but our readers enjoy them and they're often very informative. Of course our claim to fame is our 'amazing but true fact' which we run right below the banner on the front page. Last week's revealed that the life span of a taste bud was ten days. Can you imagine that? Who knew? But now our readers do, and we're proud of our contribution to the District's body of knowledge. Please call 703-555-1212. We'd love to chat with you."

Talk about hitting rock bottom. "It sure as hell can't get any worse than that." Laurel stabbed the cigarette out in the kitchen sink, then yanked the phone out of the wall.

Buh dum. Buh dum, her cell phone rang.

Buh dum. Buh dum.

Laurel squeezed her eyes shut and tried to ignore it.

Dum dum dum dum.

Oh, hell. Unable to resist at least looking to see who was calling, she flipped it open when she saw it was Chloe.

"Are you all right?"

"That's what I was calling to ask you."

"I'll be fine." Someday. Maybe when she was a little old lady in a nursing home for disgraced journalists and people had hopefully forgotten her name.

"Of course you will," Chloe responded on cue. "I've been thinking a lot about what you said, and have decided you may be right."

"Of course I am," Laurel answered automatically. "About what?"

"I can't talk now." Chloe's voice dropped to little more than a whisper. "But I think I might have a line on who set you up. And why . . .

"I'll be right there," she called out to someone. "I should know more by this evening." She was back to whispering again. "I'll call again when we break for dinner."

She immediately hung up.

"Well." Laurel blew out a breath as she stared down at the phone. She'd never been known for her patience. So, what was she supposed to do for the next six hours and thirty-five minutes?

8

Laurel was disappointed, but not particularly surprised when six o'clock came and went and Chloe didn't call. After all, six was still early for dinner and she knew how difficult it was to schedule regular meals during a campaign.

By eight o'clock, she was growing impatient.

By ten she was annoyed.

By eleven, when Chloe didn't answer her cell phone, Laurel was worried.

By the time the sun was rising in a pink and purple haze over Capitol Hill the next morning, when all she'd received all night long was a recorded voice telling her that Chloe was unavailable to take her call, Laurel began packing. She'd already decided to go to South Carolina to investigate Warren Wyatt's role in her problems; now she was also getting concerned for Chloe.

"What do you mean, she's left town?" Laurel asked Wyatt after she'd arrived at the Wingate Palace hotel.

"We'd barely arrived in the city when she decided to take a vacation."

"A vacation?"

"Yeah, an eight-letter word meaning 'ditch your responsibilities.' You, being a wordsmith, ought to know that one," he sneered. "Apparently, while the rest of us are working our tails off, the Dixie belle is off working on her tan."

"But that doesn't make any sense."

A self-professed workaholic, and proud of it, Laurel hadn't taken a vacation since the first Clinton Administration. Oh, she had, reluctantly, attended her father's wedding last year and raced home from Camp David after her sister's plane had crashed in the Smokies, but even on those brief trips she'd continued to work, conducting phone interviews and posting stories from Highland Falls. She'd never understood the need people seemed to have to lie like beached whales on the sand, or sway in a hammock on a screened-in porch in some cozy mountain cabin, and do nothing.

But Chloe was not one to leave a job undone. She'd also spent weeks shopping for the perfect dress for the black tie fund-raiser at Aiken's Somersett home. If she *were* having an affair with Aiken, wouldn't she be curious to see inside the antebellum mansion the vice president shared with his wife?

Laurel certainly would be. Then again, that was a moot point since she'd never allow herself to fall in love with another woman's husband. Actually, she didn't plan to ever fall in love with any man. Granted, her sisters seemed to be floating around on cloud nine these days, but they were merely the exceptions that proved the rule.

Although she'd throw herself off the top of the Key Bridge before admitting it, Laurel had always feared falling in love. Feared being consumed by it. Because, then, when it was gone, what were you supposed to do? Shake yourself off like a dog shaking off rain, then move blithely on, as if you hadn't lost a big chunk of your heart? Better—and a helluva lot simpler—not to get emotionally involved in the first place.

"What, exactly, did Chloe say?" she asked Warren, dragging her mind back to the problem at hand.

"Not much. She left a message saying she was taking some personal time and not to bother to try to call her back, because she doubted there'd be that many cell towers where she was, so there probably wouldn't be any signal."

"Message?" Her tawny brows dove toward her nose. "You didn't speak with her directly?"

"I'm not Chloe Hollister's secretary," he reminded her stiffly. "But no, I must've been on the phone when she called because she landed in voice mail."

"Where did she go?"

"Who knows?" He glanced out the hotel window at the huge, white wedding-cake-tiered ship docked across the street. "I suppose she could have taken a cruise."

"Chloe gets seasick on a waterbed."

Something was terribly wrong. Laurel would bet the award she'd received last year from Investigative Reporters and Editors on it. Not that she'd gotten any money from the IRE, but the recognition was what counted.

Laurel had never played well with others. Although she could certainly contribute to a team investigation, she'd always preferred working on her own, digging around in secret closets, shining light in dark corners.

Now, dammit, it was looking as if she was going to have to do something totally alien to her nature. She was going to have to ask for help.

The police station was located in the courthouse, a stately Greek Revival building which, from the outside, reminded Laurel of *Gone with the Wind*. Inside, it was bedlam. Desks were crammed close enough to give a fire marshal apoplexy, phones were jangling off the hook, one cop was pounding on the top of his computer monitor while cursing a blue streak, people were shouting back and forth, and were it not for the two drunken pirates in handcuffs and a transvestite wearing a huge black wig and silver beaded dress that was all wrong for his/her coloring, she could have been back in the *Post*'s editorial office.

The sergeant sitting at the front desk had hair like a rusty Brillo pad and a mustache to match. His cheeks were ruddy, his nose bulbous, and his expression less than welcoming as she approached his desk. Having worked a police beat in Reno, Laurel wasn't intimidated by his scowl. Squaring her shoulders and dragging her wheeled carry-on behind her, she walked into the lion's den.

9

There'd been a time when just walking in the cop shop door had given Joe a boost, a buzz, as if he'd been free-basing coffee beans. Now coming to work just made him tired.

Burnout, the little voice inside him whispered as he walked up the cop shop steps, which the heat and humidity were turning green.

No. It wasn't burnout. He'd know burnout, Joe assured himself. He was just tired. And bored.

Find a body, solve a murder, and there'd be more tomorrow.

Murder was Joe's business. And business was good.

Especially in this damn, unrelenting heat.

The temperature outside the building had been inching up into the nineties since dawn, with the humidity just as high. Inside, which smelled of mold, sweat, cheap perfume, and scorched coffee, it wasn't any more comfortable and the ancient ceiling fans creakily circling overhead weren't helping.

Despite directives from the commissioner for every-one to look snappy while the VP was visiting their fair city, Joe had refused to dig out the suit and tie he was forced to wear on those occasions when he had to go to court to testify in a case.

Still, even in short sleeves, he was hot. Hot, and frustrated, and bored.

But not burned out.

A voice managed to make itself heard through the babble and din of computer keys clacking, phones ringing, and file drawers slamming shut.

"I realize she's a grown woman," the woman seated in front of the shift sergeant's desk was saying. "Which is exactly the point I've been trying to make. Chloe Hollister is responsible. And reliable. She wouldn't decide to take off on some spur of the moment vacation."

"It's Buccaneer Days," Sergeant Frank Hogan, a former street cop who'd been assigned to the desk after his third donut-induced heart attack, pointed out. His tone was dry and blatantly disinterested, but his gaze, as it skimmed her over from the top of her head to the pointy toes of those high heels, was anything but.

Joe didn't need any detecting skills to know that Frank had pissed the woman off. Her eyes narrowed as she folded her arms across a silk blouse which amazingly didn't have a single wrinkle.

She leaned toward Hogan across the desk.

"I don't give a damn about whatever provincial little festival your chamber of commerce has come up with to snag tourist bucks. I don't care if Blackbeard himself is going to show up tonight to sing *Louie Louie* on that rock stage you've set up on the waterfront. My friend, who just happens to be a very important aide to the vice president of these United States," she stressed, "has gone missing.

"Now, unless South Carolina seceded again while I was flying down here this morning, the state's still in the Union, which suggests that the Somersett police department just might have a passing interest in the disappearance of Noble Aiken's protocol advisor."

"She's an adult," Hogan said doggedly. "If she's still not back in twenty-four hours, you can file a missing person report."

She leaped up from the chair, eyes blazing like green flames.

"Newsflash, Kojak," she shot back, unerringly zeroing in on the detective's weak point with the accuracy of a heat-seeking missile. Hogan was sensitive about his male-pattern baldness, which he hadn't exactly solved by wearing a rug that looked as if he'd stuck a road kill raccoon atop his head. "This happens to be a free country. Which means that I'm free to file a damn report whenever the hell I want."

"Fine." The Kojak remark had obviously pricked Hogan's cop ego. His face flamed as bright as her auburn hair. "And I'm free to wait another twenty-four hours before I read it. I'm also free to book you for disturbing the peace."

She actually growled. Joe was finding the little standoff interesting, when he noticed that her hands had curled into fists.

"You call this peace?" She flung an arm toward two prostitutes, one clad in a barely there sequined halter and sprayed-on hot pants, the other sporting a visible five o'clock shadow, screeching obscenities at each other from opposite sides of the room. From what Joe could tell they'd been hauled in on a dispute over turf; unfortunately for them—and the police who had to deal with the additional disturbances—some of the prime corners had been shut down because they were along the vice president's motorcade route. In a few days Aiken would be back in DC, the prostitutes would be back in business, and life would pretty much go on as normal.

There were times, and this was one of them, when Joe felt like the guy with the wheelbarrow and shovel following the elephants in the parade.

However, since the redhead was providing the first entertainment he'd experienced in a very long time, he'd hate to see her end up getting arrested for assaulting a police officer. Even one who sat around eating Krispy Kremes and impersonating a cop while he waited for retirement.

"May I help?" he asked mildly.

She spun around. Age, early- to mid-30s; 5'6", 115 pounds nicely arranged on a long, leggy frame. No visible distinguishing scars, tattoos, or other marks that he could see. Hair dark red, eyes the velvet green of summer grass, face fantastic.

"Who the hell are you?" Her gaze was as piercing as shards of glass.

"Detective Joe Gannon, Ma'am." His voice dipped deep into a South Coast drawl; if he'd been wearing the straw planter's hat he kept on the backseat of his unmarked police car, he would have tipped it. "Do you have a problem?"

The back-and-forth motion of a jaw that was a bit too strong for conventional beauty suggested she was grinding white teeth that were either the result of having sprung from a great gene pool or several years of orthodontia. "No, I just dropped by for afternoon tea because there's nothing I'd rather do than sip Earl Grey in a damn sauna with cops."

She had a quick and sharp tongue, but she'd have to do a helluva lot better than that little dig to score a hit. Using a technique he'd learned his first year on the beat on Somersett's iffy Northside, Joe moved a step closer, forcing her to look up at him. Then, having achieved the necessary dominance, he rocked back on his heels.

"The only tea we've got is from the vending machine," he said. "I doubt it's Earl Grey, but it's probably a sight more drinkable than the coffee, which is just a step above toxic waste. Want me to get you a cup? Then you can tell me your problem."

Suspicion shadowed eyes that gave him a sweeping, openly skeptical glance. So, was it him, or cops in general that she didn't trust? "You said you were a detective." She didn't appear to believe him. Hell, there were days he hardly believed it himself.

"Lieutenant." He tapped the shield fastened to the pocket of his shirt. "First grade."

Unlike most civilians, who accepted a police badge with barely a passing glance, she leaned closer and took the time to study his ID.

"Why don't you come on back and we'll talk," he said in the same voice he'd once used to convince inebriated drivers to walk the line.

She angled her head as she considered the suggestion, and put her hands on her hips, which momentarily drew his gaze downward. Her slim-cut purple slacks, paired with heels, made her legs look a mile long.

"Fine," she said. "And when we're done, I'm filing a report."

"That's what we're here for," he said agreeably, not rising to the challenge in her tone. There was a brief tug-of-war as he tried to help her with her black canvas suitcase. When she refused to relinquish control, he shrugged, took her elbow, and guided her through the chaos toward the relative quietness of the homicide bullpen. Her stilettos clicked with purpose on the tile floor. "To protect and to serve."

"Yeah, I saw the motto on Barney Fife's mug." She shot a fulminating glance back toward a dour-faced Hogan, who glared back. "Someone ought to remind him to read it once in a while."

Joe kept his agreement to himself.

"And he sets a terrible first impression. What ever happened to southern hospitality, anyway?"

"This is a police station. If you're looking for southern hospitality, you might be better off at the Welcome Wagon offices. They're down the street, in the green-and-blue Victorian house facing Heron Square."

"Just what I need," she muttered. "A cop with an attitude."

Hey, kettle, he thought as they walked down the hallway to the bullpen. *This is the pot, calling you black.*

10

She paused when she spotted the metal plate on the wall beside the open doorway. "Exactly what kind of detective are you?"

"A good one."

"I mean what department? This sign says Homicide."

"Things get a little crazy during Buccaneer Days so everyone tends to pitch in wherever they can."

She gave him a longer look, then apparently decided to buy his explanation. Or, he considered, more likely she'd decided arguing would lessen her chances of achieving her goal.

"I would've guessed vice," she said. "Or narcotics."

Three years ago she would have been right. Joe led her to the back corner of the cramped, hot room that was at least a helluva lot quieter than the madhouse they'd just passed through. He grabbed a stack of murder books piled on the battered wooden desktop and placed them on the floor.

"Don't narcs tend to be the worst dressed in most departments? So they'll fit in with drug dealers?"

The disparaging remark toward the vintage Hawaiian

shirt he'd picked up at the Salvation Army had Cait, who was seated at a nearby desk, openly listening to the conversation as she dialed the phone, spewing her Diet Pepsi onto her computer monitor.

"Drug dealers only look like dealers on TV." Joe didn't like to talk about his days in narcotics. Didn't like to think about them. "Most of the time they look like everyone else." He gestured toward a chair beside the desk.

"Thanks, but I'd just as soon stand." From the barely suppressed energy radiating from every fragrant pore, Joe suspected she'd rather pace.

"It's sturdier than it looks. And if it does break, hey, you can always sue the city." He paused a beat, waiting for an answering smile, then shrugged when it didn't come. Just what *he* needed—a civilian with a fantastic face, a chip on her shoulder the size of Jupiter, and no visible sense of humor.

"It's going to take me a while to fill out your complaint, so you might as well have a seat," he repeated.

He wasn't sure whether her frown was directed at the wobbly looking wooden chair or his suggestion that this could take a while. She perched on the edge, crossing her legs with an impatient, uptown-girl swish.

"I'll get that tea. Sugar?"

Her eyes narrowed dangerously.

"Would you like sugar in your tea?" he clarified.

"I'd prefer water." She lifted her hand to wipe the back of her neck. The gesture did interesting things to the breasts beneath the spotless blouse. "I'm on the verge of melting."

"You hide it well." She looked cool and collected. But

not, Joe thought, calm. He doubted this woman even knew the meaning of the word.

"It's one of the first things you learn in my business." When she caught him looking at her chest, she frowned and lowered her arm. "Never let them see you sweat."

"And your business would be?" Her face was fine-boned and classy. Except for those full, lush lips, which looked more suited to a high-priced call girl.

She crossed her legs again. The irritation in her gaze turned to a challenge. "I'm a journalist."

Damn. He should have known she'd have a fatal flaw. Though she could have been created for television; the electronic "if it bleeds, it leads" universe was populated by pretty women and buffed up men who'd breathlessly report on stories chosen more for their ratings potential than any honest desire to inform the public.

"I'll get that water," he said.

He could feel her appraising gaze as he walked across the room to the water cooler and mentally cursed himself when he realized he'd squared his shoulders which, when he'd first arrived at the station, had been slumped from the weight of responsibility.

Christ, he could have been a twelve-year-old kid popping wheelies on his dirt bike to impress the neighbor girl. Not that they'd had any girls who looked like her out in the working-class neighborhood of cops and firefighters where he'd grown up.

Weaving his way back to his desk with water for her and a cup of coffee for himself, Joe noticed that it wasn't just him she'd been watching. Her intelligent eyes scanned the office, taking everything in, filing everything away. He could practically see her writing notes in a mental notebook, much the same as he would have been doing under the circumstances, which was surprising since he doubted there was much he and Miss Don't-Ever-Let-Them-See-You-Sweat had in common.

"Here you go."

"Thanks." Their fingertips brushed as she took the foam cup from his hand. Joe assured himself that the odd little tingle that shot from that inadvertent touch down to more vital regions was merely static electricity.

Her long, thirsty swallows reminded Joe of a guy tossing back a beer in a dark pub after a hot round of hoops. "Is it always this damn hot down here?"

"You're in the Deep South," he pointed out. He perched on the edge of the desk and took a drink of black sludge. "Summer's never a picnic. But it's worse than usual because we're in the middle of a tropical heat wave."

"I thought it was sweltering up in DC, but you win the prize."

"So you're from Washington?"

He sat down behind the desk, leaned back in the wheeled chair, and linked his fingers behind his head. Too late, he remembered the wet circles beneath his arms. So what? He was a guy. Guys sweat.

"I'm originally from Highland Falls, a little town in the mountains on the North Carolina–Tennessee border.

He nodded. "I've heard of it." He doubted there were many—especially cops—in America who hadn't; the story of singer Lark Stewart's stalker escaping from prison and tracking the singer to the mountain town had dominated the headlines for days.

"I've lived in the District for the past few years. I'm a political reporter for the *Post*."

Joe found the idea of this woman working in the bare-knuckles arena of American politics a bit of a stretch. Then he took in the stubborn tilt of her chin, thought how she'd gone after Hogan, and reconsidered. "I'm impressed."

"It beats slapping together Happy Meals." She plucked one of his business cards from the plastic holder on the desk. "Joe Gannon," she mused. "Wasn't that the TV cop—"

"From *Dragnet*. But Gannon's first name was Bill. The other guy was Joe Friday."

"That's it." She nodded. "You probably get that a lot."

"Every so often. I was baptized Joseph Xavier, but since that sounds more like a priest than a cop, I settled for Joe."

"Sounding like a priest might encourage people to confess."

"I'll keep that in mind."

She crossed her legs again with another impatient swish, putting an end to the little getting-to-know-you part of the conversation. "Well, I'm sure you have better things to do than fetch drinks for reporters, who, I suspect, aren't your favorite people."

He lifted a brow, ignoring her less than subtle suggestion that they get down to work. "Did I say that?" It was true, but since he might need to work with her, he wasn't prepared to admit it.

"You didn't have to. I worked a police beat for a few months." When she leaned forward to place the empty cup on his desk, he caught a glimpse of cream lace and an even more intriguing curve of breast beneath her blouse.

"Look, Lieutenant," she continued, "we're both busy people with things to do, people to see, places to go. We also know that your occupation and mine have probably been natural enemies since the first reporter scratched the story of Cain murdering Abel onto a stone tablet."

He was thinking that technically there wouldn't have been any reporters around to report on the first human murder, when that sneaky serpent in the garden of Eden came to mind. She was right; as a rule he didn't like the press. But since it'd been a very long time since he'd felt any sexual tugs, he decided he might be willing to make an exception in her case.

Besides, the chances that the woman she was looking for would turn out to be his still unidentified Sissy Smith were slim to none, but one of the things he liked best about the cop business was the unpredictability. You just never knew when you'd uncover the final piece of the puzzle; sometimes it even fell into your lap, like the Son of Sam getting a parking ticket.

11

"So," she was saying, when Joe brought his wandering mind back from wondering if that pale skin he'd glimpsed beneath her blouse was as soft as it looked, "why don't we get to filling out that report on Chloe Hollister, then I'll get out of your hair."

"Chloe Hollister being your friend you believe has gone missing."

"I don't believe. I know."

"Okay." He hit Enter on his keyboard, bringing the form onto the screen.

"And your name would be?"

She paused. He glanced up in time to view the flash of surprise in her eyes; her wide mouth turned down in chagrin. "I didn't tell you?" The fact that she was obviously unhappy at the oversight suggested perfectionist tendencies.

"No, Ma'am," he drawled, chalking up a point on a mental scoreboard. "You didn't."

"I'm Laurel Stewart."

The name rang a loud and instantaneous bell. He remembered reading her coverage on a serial killer the

FBI had apprehended in Fairfax, Virginia a few years ago.

"I've read your work." It occasionally got picked up by the *Somersett Beacon-Sentinel*. "You're good."

"Thank you." He liked the way she took the compliment in stride, neither using it as an opportunity to boast, or claiming false modesty.

She'd also obviously picked up a lot of polish since leaving that small town tucked away in a hollow in the Smoky Mountains. Everything about the woman—the spiffy clothes, sleek hair, and edgy energy—said City Girl with a capital C. Her scent, while decidedly female, was as crisp and no-nonsense as the rest of her. But, he decided, that lace he'd glimpsed showed promise.

"Laurel Stewart," he murmured. "That would make you Lark Stewart's sister, wouldn't it?"

"That's right." Temper flashed in her eyes; Joe watched her fight her emotions for control and win.

"Helluva thing that happened to her." He couldn't recall her reporting on that particular story, but she was probably the only journalist in the country—perhaps the world—who hadn't.

"There are those who believe stalkers go with the celebrity territory."

"But you don't agree."

"That if someone has the talent to become rich and famous she has to automatically give up every vestige of privacy and become a target for a psycho with guns? No." She met his questioning gaze straight on. "And I realize the privacy issue sounds hypocritical, given what I do for a living."

"It's only natural you'd want to protect a family member." He'd testified in enough trials to know how to dodge a verbal trap.

"Yes." She looked surprised he could understand that, giving him the impression that she didn't trust his occupation any more than he did hers.

He returned to the form. "Your friend's full name?"

"Chloe Anne Hollister."

He glanced up from his two-fingered typing. "The former Miss Buccaneer Days." Whose late stepdaddy, the ambassador, had been the only person in the state whose political clout had come close to equaling Noble Aiken's.

"She may have mentioned that once. Chloe probably has more tiaras than Queen Elizabeth."

"Pageants tend to be a big deal down here in the Lowlands."

"So she tells me. But Chloe's never skated on her looks. She's smart as a whip and works her ass off."

"Good for her." Joe wasn't sure he liked the thorny Laurel Stewart all that much, but he couldn't fault her loyalty. "Height? Weight?"

"Five-seven, probably one-thirty, give or take a couple pounds. Hair blond, eyes blue."

Naturally. The South was partial to its blondes; even his mother, who could never be considered the least bit vain, went to Dottie's Curl Up and Dye every month for a touch-up to keep her hair a soft honey color.

"Address?"

She rattled off an address. "It's on Capitol Hill."

"And the reason you didn't contact the Washington police is?"

"I would have, if that's where she'd gone missing

from." Her voice shimmered with icy uptown-girl impatience again. "Chloe's a protocol officer for the vice president. She left DC yesterday after breakfast."

"Are you sure she actually left the city?"

"Absolutely. She called me yesterday from here."

"On a cell?"

"Yes." Impatience was shimmering around her like a force field.

"Then you don't have any way of knowing that she actually called from here, do you? Since your Caller ID would've shown her Washington number."

"Good point," she allowed. "But not only was she on the Air Force Two passenger manifest, she checked into the Wingate with the rest of the vice president's staff—"

His fingers paused on the keys. "The Wingate Palace?" The long-shot odds of Laurel Stewart knowing his jumper just got shorter.

"That's the one." Her eyes narrowed, her body grew taut. She reminded him of Orbison, his old German shorthair, on the scent of a covey of quail. "Why?"

"I need to put it on the form," he said, dodging the question, wanting to finish filling out the complaint before mentioning the woman who'd learned the hard way last night that arms made lousy wings. Not that he figured Laurel Stewart to be one of those hysterical people who'd fall apart at the seams, but you never knew. "So you last saw her yesterday?"

"At 7:18 a.m.," she confirmed.

"You're that sure about the time?" Most people weren't.

"I was watching C-Span; they flash the time on the screen periodically."

"Okay. And you believe—*know*," he corrected at her sharp look, "that this is a matter for the police because . . ."

"Because Chloe takes her work very seriously. This trip is vastly important to Aiken, which, as protocol officer, makes it important to her, and she spent weeks shopping for a dress."

"What color?" They'd found a purple silk dress on the floor of the hotel suite.

"Orchid. From Bill Blass's spring line."

Joe wouldn't recognize a Bill Blass if Hedi Klum sashayed into the station wearing one. But even he'd been able to tell the dress puddled on the plush hotel carpeting had been expensive. "Orchid. Is that purple?"

"Sort of. It's lighter than purple, between violet and plum."

"Like your blouse?"

"My blouse is lilac." Impatience flared like red flags on the slash of her Kate Hepburn cheekbones. "Is any of this relevant or are you cramming for a final at the Fashion Institute?"

Christ, the woman had a mouth on her! Which, perversely, had Joe wanting to take a deep gulp of it. Just to shut her up.

"You never know what's relevant. The more info I have to add to the report—the report you asked for—" he reminded her "the better."

As he dutifully noted the color as purple, the cell phone he'd placed on his desk chimed. Joe glanced down at the Caller ID, then let it ring. And ring.

"Besides," he said, "I think we've already determined I'm not a candidate for any fashion institute."

"That crack was probably unwarranted." She skimmed a hand through her short-cropped swing of hair. "Look, I'm not usually this rude." Her huff of breath kept it from being much of an apology.

The phone continued to ring.

"Okay, that's not true," she conceded. "I can be rude and I'm admittedly impatient, but Chloe's a close friend and I'm positive she would never walk away from her job. Besides—

"It sounds as if someone really wants to talk to you," she said as the damn phone continued to ring.

"That's okay. It'll go into voice messaging." Though he knew this particular caller wouldn't leave a message. He returned to the report. "And besides, what?"

"As I said, she called me yesterday. Around one." The chiming of the cell phone had finally stopped. "We didn't talk long because she had to get back to work. But she promised to call around dinner time, which she didn't do. I kept trying to get hold of her all night, but she never answered my messages."

"Do you always keep such close tabs on your friends?"

She gave him a hard look.

Joe kept his fingers on the keys and waited. The ability to wait a person out had given him one of the best confession rates in the precinct.

"She was having some personal problems," she said finally, on another frustrated breath. "I was worried about her."

"Worried enough to come down here?"

"Yes. She's not at the hotel and she left a message with the vice president's political advisor that she was taking a few days' personal time." Her fingers swiped through her shiny cap of hair again. "But he didn't talk to her personally; the message was left on Warren Wyatt's—the advisor's—voice mail. But I don't believe it for a minute."

"Did Wyatt recognize it as Chloe Hollister's voice?"

"He's sure it was her, but I wouldn't believe a thing that man told me."

"The entire city's in party mode," Joe said. "Maybe she got down here and decided to take some time off to work on her tan."

"No way." That diamond sharp jaw shot up like a rocket. "Chloe doesn't go out in the sun. She always says she doesn't want to look like a raisin when she hits forty. Besides . . ."

She slammed her mouth shut, but it was too late. He looked up at her over the wire rims of the half glasses he wore for computer work. "Besides?"

"Look, this is just conjecture, okay?"

"Sure." He didn't point out that so far, everything she'd said past her friend's name and address, was pure conjecture.

"I think she's having an affair." Her deep breath lifted her breasts, momentarily drawing his mind off the missing persons report again and making him wonder if she'd look as good out of that purple outfit as she did in it. *Dangerous thought, Gannon.*

"Maybe she's off with her boyfriend."

"I don't think so."

"Why not?"

"I don't know for sure," she admitted reluctantly. "But I think he may be married."

"All the more reason to maybe want to get away and think things through." He decided against pointing out that perhaps Chloe Hollister wanted to work out her problems on her own. "You want to share this maybe married guy's name with me?"

She opened her mouth. Closed it. Frowned as she studied short, unlacquered fingernails, which had been buffed to a glossy sheen. "Is this absolutely germane to the case at this point?"

"We don't have a case, yet. But if it turns out your friend really is missing, you never know what might turn out to be important during the investigation."

"Okay. I can't swear to it, but my best guess would be Noble Aiken."

"The vice president?" The lady was turning out to be one surprise after another. At least Joe wasn't bored anymore.

12

Dammit, they were wasting time. There were those over the years who'd accused her of bumping heads with authority. Laurel wouldn't deny it. Others called her impatient, hardheaded, and stubborn. She wouldn't deny those descriptions either; on the contrary, she wore the labels with pride. She'd also always trusted her instincts, which had begun to blare like a fire alarm.

"The vice president," she confirmed. "Who probably would have a bit of a problem running on his family values platform if he's sleeping with his protocol advisor. And now that I've leveled with you, why don't you come straight with me and tell me what you know about Chloe's disappearance that I don't?"

"This is the first I've heard her name."

"But?"

He studied her with a silent intensity. His eyes were bloodshot. Probably one of those alcoholic cops who drowned their dissatisfaction with a life spent chasing lowlifes in the bottle, Laurel thought. Not that she hadn't polished off that entire bottle of wine the other night, but that'd been out of character.

He glanced up at a map hung on the wall behind him, the cross grid of streets studded with pins topped in red, yellow, and blue, then looked back at her and began tapping the tip of a ballpoint pen on the manila folder. She counted fifteen damn taps until he finally spoke.

"Does the name Sissy Smith mean anything to you?"

"No." She'd grilled enough politicians to know when someone was holding back. "Why?"

"I've got an unidentified body that physically matches the description you've just given me for your friend. She died last evening, but no one's come forward to identify her yet."

Laurel's blood chilled. She reached for the water again, belatedly realizing that the cup was empty.

He stood up. "Let me get you a refill."

"I'll take the coffee this time. Black, two sugars." Her head was spinning; she needed the sugar burst to clear it.

Fears and possible grim scenarios swirled in her mind. As she fought to keep from putting her head down on the metal desk piled high with folders and three-ring binders, Laurel watched Detective Joseph Gannon walking back toward her across the room. He didn't look like any homicide detective she'd ever seen. Nor did his appearance give her a great deal of confidence.

"Here you go." His smooth as silk drawl, at odds with his rough-around-the-edges looks, was obviously meant to calm rattled nerves. Laurel suspected in his line of work he dealt with a lot of nerves.

She took a sip and burned her tongue. The thick, dark sludge tasted like overly sweetened motor oil and was even worse than he'd threatened. He was looking at her closely, carefully, as if concerned she was going to pass out on him.

Needing more time to gather up her scattered thoughts, she dragged her gaze away, only to have it land on the large dry-erase board on the wall across the room. There were far more red names than black; the bottom name was Sissy Smith.

"What happened?" she asked. "To the woman who died?"

"She appears to have fallen off a balcony at the Wingate."

"Was she pushed?"

"That hasn't been determined."

"If she jumped, it wasn't Chloe."

"You said your friend might be having an affair with a married man—"

"Newsflash, Lieutenant, we've entered the twenty-first century." Laurel was grateful for the temper that rose to burn off the lingering cobwebs in her mind. "Women are allowed to vote, have careers, and even down here in Moonlight and Magnolia–land, I suspect they have affairs without feeling the need to commit suicide."

He leaned back in his chair, took a drink of his own industrial waste, and grimaced at the taste.

"Would you be willing to look at some photographs?"

"Absolutely." She wouldn't just be willing, she'd insist on it.

He picked up the binder on the desk and flipped through the pages while Laurel downed the sweetened coffee in long swallows.

He held the stack of eight-by-tens toward her. "They're not pretty."

"I told you, I was a police reporter; I've seen bodies before."

Too many. She saw no point in mentioning that after six months on the police beat, she'd asked for an assignment change because after spending all day watching that disregard for human life, she'd go home every night needing a bath. Politics might be a blood sport, but at least most of the time it wasn't fatal.

She steeled herself before looking at the photos. Back when she'd covered the cop shop, the photos had been black and white. These were in color, which made them even worse than the gory ones cops got a kick out of showing to rookie reporters. The woman's cheekbones, jaw, and nose were shattered, her right pupil blown.

God, she couldn't tell. It couldn't be Chloe. Laurel refused to let herself think it was. "How high was the balcony?"

"Ten stories."

Laurel cringed. Briefly closed her eyes. Then reluctantly opened them again. Although it was painful, she continued looking through the photographs. Why the hell couldn't she tell?

She frowned when she got to the first long shot, taking in the crowd on the other side of the tape. "Those are Secret Service agents."

"You've got a good eye."

"I live in Washington," she reminded him. "You get used to seeing them all over the place." Laurel saw no reason to bring up her recent problems with the Secret Service. "That black SUV is theirs?"

"Yeah."

"Did you impound it?"

"For the moment."

"I'll bet they loved that."

"The agents understood the need to protect a crime scene."

Laurel caught a fleeting flash of shared humor in those tired blue eyes. "I don't suppose the vice president was at the scene?"

"He was speaking at that hotel." He glanced down at his notebook. "On domestic terrorism at a meeting of the Rotary Club."

"He can call it anything he wants, but everyone knows it was a fund-raiser paid for by the taxpayers."

His only response was a shrug. The garish shirt would suggest he wasn't a right-wing Noble Aiken fan, but appearances could be deceiving.

"I want to see her," Laurel decided. "In person." She tapped a nail on the top photograph. "I refuse to believe this is Chloe, but I need to prove it isn't, so you'll start looking for her."

He eyed her mildly over the rim of the mug. He was, she understood, summing her up.

Just as she was him.

"Okay," he said finally.

13

"I know it's unexpected," Chloe said, smoothing nonexistent wrinkles out of the short, pleated plaid skirt she was wearing with Mary Janes polished to a mirror sheen, ruffle-top white socks, and crisp white blouse. It was her sexy Catholic-schoolgirl look, one she enhanced by pulling her blond hair back with a shiny black ribbon. Her only makeup was a bit of pale pink lip gloss.

"But I've been thinking about it, and I believe it could be a positive thing." Childhood elocution lessons could not keep her voice from trembling. "A blessing, even."

The man she loved to distraction looked at her with patient indulgence. "Are you suggesting this child is heaven-sent?"

Unsure of whether or not she was being teased, Chloe tossed up her chin. She was not accustomed to being laughed at. "Aren't all children?" She'd certainly heard that often enough during twelve years of parochial school.

When he chuckled softly, the chains that had had her stomach tied up in knots loosened ever so slightly. "I should know better than to argue theology with a woman who considered becoming a nun."

She never would have confessed to that if she'd known he was going to bring it up every time they were together. Her short-lived Bride of Christ vocation had been born during a weekend-long marathon of Audrey Hepburn movies on television during a bout of flu. Two weeks later, Jimmy Bower kissed her in the dark of the Paramount theater, giving her a firsthand look at sexual temptation.

Six months ago, her life had been in flux; she'd just moved from the familiarity of the State Department to her new job as protocol officer, her romance with that lying weasel of a tobacco lobbyist had come to an inglorious end, and she'd felt adrift on a wide and lonely sea.

Depression had slammed down on her during a casual conversation, and she'd burst into tears.

"There, there. What brought all this on?" the man she'd been speaking with asked in a deep, soothing voice.

"My life is a mess," she'd wailed. "Everything is so, so hopeless."

She'd been humiliated when the waterworks started in again.

"Nothing's hopeless." Rather than appear appalled by her behavior, he'd taken out a crisp white handkerchief and calmly patted the hot tears away.

That was when she'd fallen in love with him.

"You'll see," she assured him now, forcing her bright, beauty queen smile. "Everything will work out."

"Of course it will," he said benevolently. "Why don't I make you a cup of that ginger tea you like so well, sweetheart? Then we'll talk about what we're going to do about your problem."

A subliminal feminine intuition stirred. "It's not a problem. It's a baby. *Our* baby."

Chloe might have been on the verge of hormonal meltdown but the blood of steel magnolias ran in her veins. Admittedly all the other times she'd gotten herself in romantic troubles, she'd crumbled like a store-bought shortbread tea cookie.

Not this time, she vowed. This time there was more at stake than just her heart—this time she was fighting for her child.

"Of course it is," he agreed quickly. He smoothed a hand down her hair.

"I love you," she said.

His benevolent smile had gilt-edged fantasies of happily-ever-afters shimmering in her mind.

"I know," he said.

14

It was a great deal darker when Laurel and Joe walked out of the station than when she'd gone in. Deep pewter clouds were clustering overhead.

"It'll rain tonight," Joe offered.

"That'll be a relief."

"Actually, probably not." As they walked across the parking lot, Laurel's heels sank into the melting black asphalt. "It'll just get steamier."

"If this air gets any wetter, fish are going to start swimming by," she said, then felt petty for complaining about something so trivial when some woman—but not Chloe!—was lying on a slab in the Somersett morgue. She rubbed the back of her neck, which was moist and knotted with stress. "How do you stand it?" It'd be like living in a terrarium.

"Can't have fall without going through summer."

Displaying old-fashioned southern manners a DC cop would never demonstrate, he opened the passenger door of a black Ford Crown Victoria that had definitely seen better days. Heat exploded outward, hitting her like a fist. Fastening her seat belt as he walked around the front of the vehicle, Laurel decided that whoever had chosen a black car here in the Deep South ought to have their head examined.

"Autumn here is terrific," he continued conversationally as he muscled the car into traffic. The interior smelled of French fries and Big Macs, along with a vague odor of mold riding the hot air blasting from the vents in the dashboard. Cop talk crackled on the radio. "Though spring's probably our best time of year. The tourism bureau always has something goin' on, but our biggest crowds are college kids on Spring Break in April and the May Garden Festival."

He darted in and out of traffic as if he were driving a Mini Cooper in a Hollywood chase movie, rather than a battleship-size Ford. Apparently driving was the one thing he did fast. Who'd have thought she'd have anything in common with a cop?

The streets were wide and lined with magnificent old moss-draped oaks whose leaves filtered the light. The buildings were decidedly eclectic, revealing three hundred years of architecture: gray brick and stucco town houses with high front stoops stood next to gingerbread-trimmed Victorian flights of fantasy, while across the street a grand, pillared antebellum mansion with double colonnades stood as a reminder of when cotton was king.

Boisterous, colorfully dressed people crowded the sidewalks and sat beneath striped umbrellas downing pitchers of rum-spiked fruit punches and beer. Dueling electric guitars blared through outdoor speakers in a battle of rock bands from bars on opposite sides of the street.

"I'll bet the gardening fans aren't nearly as rowdy as the pirate-wannabes," she said.

"You'd think so, wouldn't you?" Brakes squealed as he swung around a lemon-yellow Volkswagen Beetle. Seemingly oblivious to the blaring horns, he gave the drivers a casual wave. "This year things were fixin' to get ugly when Miz Lulu Bell got in a tussle with Miz Theodora Odem over a window box of geraniums at the Green Thumb charity raffle. They're half sisters; their daddy had two families, each kept in houses on opposite sides of the Somersett River. To hear my grandmother tell it, everyone knew about Spencer Bell's two wives, but it would've been bad manners to bring it up in polite society, so things mostly stayed on an even keel with Spencer splitting his weeks between the two houses.

"Then came the Cotillion, which is a big deal down here. I guess Spencer wasn't all that farsighted, or perhaps he never thought both marriages would last, but his house of cards pretty much came tumbling down when both Lulu's and Theo's mothers insisted their daughter be presented to society. According to how I always heard it, Miz Lulu's mother—who was the second wife—got herself a swamp witch to put a fatal voodoo curse on Spencer."

"Surely you don't believe that?"

He rubbed his sexy cleft chin. "Well, I'm not saying I do, and I'm not saying I don't, but the story goes that Spencer dropped dead of a heart attack right there on the ballroom floor while he was dancin' the waltz with Theo. Theo's always blamed Lulu for ruining the Cotillion, but since no society mother would let her son marry into such a scandalous family, Theo also ended up a spinster."

"Which isn't exactly the end of the world."

"Not to some women, perhaps. But Miz Theo took it real personal. She's been carrying a grudge for seventy-some years, and when Lulu—who's buried three husbands—won the window box of geraniums her half-sister had her heart set on, Theo took that box and dumped the potting soil over Lulu's head. According to witnesses, that's when the hair pulling started."

"This has been going on for seventy years?"

"Give or take a few years either way. Neither one will admit to being over sixty, but the tombstone in the Bell family plot has Spencer dying in 1934."

Laurel did the math. "Which would make them in their late eighties?"

"That'd be about right. But they're pretty damn feisty for senior citizens."

Laurel started to laugh, then remembered where they were going. And why.

It couldn't be Chloe, she assured herself.

So, that argumentative voice in her mind challenged, as she stared ahead out the windshield at the road that curved around the bend of the harbor, where tall green palmetto trees were silhouetted against the darkening sky, *where the hell is she?*

Laurel had no idea. Not yet. But she wasn't going to stop looking until she found her. It wasn't just that she cared about her friend. But there was also the little matter of Chloe's call. Laurel needed to know what she'd found out about those false leaks that had gotten her fired and sabotaged her reputation.

Not that her reputation was anywhere near as important as Chloe's life.

If the worst case scenario proved to be true, and the body in the morgue did turn out to be Chloe, Laurel was going to find out who was responsible for her best friend's death.

Then make him pay.

Unlike the 1800s courthouse, St. Camillus Hospital was a sleek, modern building located on the verdant green banks of the Somersett River.

"Used to be the morgue was in the courthouse," Joe said as he pulled the Crown Vic up in front of the entrance. "The rotunda was used as a field hospital during the War Between the States. Between the fires set by Sherman's troops and the battles raging in the streets, it was too dangerous to have funerals, so bodies were kept in the basement."

"Which was cooler," Laurel guessed.

"So they say." He reached into the back seat, retrieved an On Duty sign, and tossed it onto the cracked vinyl dashboard. "Tradition being what it is down in this part of the country, the morgue remained in the basement until a few years ago when this hospital was being designed and it finally dawned on someone that it'd be more convenient just to move it here."

The sliding glass doors gave way to a lobby that was both open and inviting. Natural light from towering windows and the glass canopy of the atrium flooded the

space; a fountain at the center of the room burbled soothingly and leafy green ficus trees and tall palms in clay pots
contributed to the peaceful setting.

They passed a gift shop, its windows filled with balloons—gaily colored ones wishing Get Well, pink proclaiming It's a Girl, blue for boys. Sunny displays of fresh
flowers jockeyed for space with plush stuffed Nemos and
pyramids of best-selling paperback novels featuring
pirates, cowboys, or bloody daggers on the glossy covers.
Laurel experienced a spark of family pride when she
viewed several of her aunt's novels.

The cobalt-blue elevator doors opened with a discreet
ding. A young man clad in a powder blue "New Dad"
T-shirt got out.

"We just had a baby," he announced.

Despite her concern for Chloe, Laurel smiled. "So I
see." Paternal pride shone in his face like a thousand
suns.

"His name is Thadeus Jackson Lee, IV." His grin
could have lit up the entire Eastern Seaboard for a
month.

"Congratulations." Laurel had no choice but to accept
one of the blue-banded cigars he thrust at her as she
entered the elevator.

The doors closed. "He's going to fly home," she murmured.

"I sure as hell hope he's not driving," Joe said. "From
that luggage he's carrying beneath his eyes, he looks as if
he was up all night."

"Give the guy a break, Gannon." You'd think a guy
wearing parrots and surfboards on his shirt would be

more easygoing. "He's a new dad. Going without sleep is part of the deal. Or so I hear."

"Spoken by someone who isn't going to have to tell his widow that he's wrapped his car around a lamp post on the way home."

"Gotta love a positive outlook." And people called *her* cynical.

"I'm a cop," he said, as if that explained everything. Which, Laurel decided, it probably did.

"Do you have any kids?" Since he looked somewhere between thirty-five and forty, it was likely he'd been married. Which, in turn, suggested he could be a father.

Unless, of course, he was gay.

Right. And the Confederates had won the Civil War. Detective Lieutenant Joe Gannon was, hands down, the least gay man she'd ever met.

"No."

His curt, monosyllabic response seemed a bit out of character, but Laurel didn't dwell on it. "Me neither."

That topic exhausted, they were silent for the rest of the ride to the basement.

15

Somersett, South Carolina, was large enough to support the arts—the symphony orchestra predated the Civil War—and sports, represented by a Triple A baseball team, a minor league ice hockey team (which, Joe would admit, seemed out of place in a city where the last snow had fallen in 1957), and a NASCAR track thirty minutes out of town. The city was also small enough for nearly everyone to be connected in some way. The rest of the world might believe in six degrees of separation, but here in the Deep South, you'd be hard-pressed to find four.

Including the residents scattered over the various barrier islands, the city boasted a population of a quarter of a million, which, given the annual statistical death rate of 1 percent of any given population, meant that 2,500 citizens could be expected to die in any given year. Since autopsies were only conducted on "suspicious" deaths, one-quarter of those deceased—approximately 620—would likely end up on a metal table in the hospital basement.

John Lennon's "Imagine" was playing from hidden

speakers when Joe and Laurel arrived at the morgue.

"We have to stop meeting like this," the ME greeted Joe.

Icy air blasted through the wall vents. The morgue was probably the only place in town that was cold. Cold as death, Joe considered as he introduced Laurel to Drew Sloan.

"Ms. Stewart's here to see if she can identify that jumper who came in last night."

"That'd sure be a help." He flashed a warm but sympathetic smile at Laurel. "She's in the annex. Drawer 313." He handed Joe a pair of latex gloves. "I'd get the lady for you, but I've got customers stacking up like planes in a thunderstorm."

There'd been a time when, under the old regime, the morgue had been a gathering place for cops to hang out; the morning equivalent of the cop bar where uniforms and detectives alike stood around, drinking coffee out of 7-Eleven cups, smoking cigarettes, and munching down Krispy Kremes.

All that had stopped when Drew had come on board with what several regarded as a quaint notion: that people should be accorded the same respect in death as they deserved in life. He banned the cigarettes, coffee, soft drinks, and donuts and limited witnesses to his assistant, the detectives who'd caught the case, occasionally some of the street cops who'd worked the scene, and the prosecutor, if he deigned to show up, which he usually didn't.

"You're not going to throw up or anything, are you?" Joe asked Laurel as he located the drawer.

"I told you that I've seen bodies before."

"Yeah, but you didn't tell me whether you tossed your cookies, and I just want to know whether to be ready to get out of the way."

"You're such a white knight."

"I'm a realist. With new shoes."

She shot a skeptical glance down at the snazzy black, blue, and silver Nike trainers. "Are you sure you're a cop?"

"You're not the first person to question that." Including himself, more and more, lately.

He opened the drawer, tugged on the latex gloves, then unzipped the thick white bag just low enough to reveal the victim's face. Even with the refrigeration slowing physical deterioration, it wasn't any surprise that Sissy Smith, if that really was her name, looked worse than she had last night.

He felt Laurel flinch and cast a sideways glance toward her, watching as she bit her lip. But at least she didn't hurl on his new Air Zooms.

The face she was studying with intensity was not a pretty sight. The blond hair was matted with dried blood and lividity had turned her fractured face the deep color of Merlot.

"It's not her."

"You sure about that?"

She tilted her head, looked a bit longer. "Yes." Joe belatedly wished he'd thought to ask Sloan for some Vicks to help her with the smell that she'd be taking out of here with her on those spiffy clothes and in her glossy hair. He watched the lump rise and fall in the smooth white line of her throat as she swallowed. "At least I don't think so." She rubbed her forehead with her fingertips. "It's harder than I thought."

Misidentification wasn't that unusual. He'd seen it happen before, partly because people couldn't bear to look at the remains of what had once been a living, breathing friend or family member. He'd seen people literally cover their eyes, peek through spread fingers, and not realize it wasn't their loved one until the day of the viewing at the funeral home, when they'd finally dare look at the face that the mortician's cosmetologists had restored as close as possible to its original state and start screaming that the body laid out on white satin wasn't Uncle Jack or Grandma Ruby one after all.

He waited patiently. Laurel squeezed her eyes, tight, as if trying to merge the image in her mind with the damaged one from the drawer.

"No," she said, more firmly this time. "It's absolutely not her."

"Okay." He zipped the bag again, rolled the drawer back in, shut the door, pulled off the gloves, and tossed them into a medical waste bin near the door.

"So now that we've determined your body isn't Chloe Hollister, will you start looking for her?"

"I'll call my partner from the car and have her file a BOLO. That's a—"

"Be on the lookout for," she translated the police acronym. "But that's not going to jumpstart any search, is it?"

He hesitated, then decided there was no point in beating around the bush. "Having worked the cop-shop beat, you should be familiar with the system."

"I know enough to realize that all that'll happen is that Chloe will, at the very best, become a subject of what you law enforcement types refer to as a "passive" search. Meaning that she won't be found unless she somehow comes in contact with a cop."

"If you had every police officer in South Carolina, hell, even here in Somersett copying down the info on every BOLO that comes across the wire, they wouldn't get anything else done," he said evenly. "Besides, on average, 98 percent of missing people are found, or return home on their own within 24 hours."

"There's nothing *average* about Chloe Hollister. And even given your statistics, that still leaves 2 percent who aren't found within that 24-hour window." She tucked her hair behind her ears. "Which is why cops should take those alerts more seriously."

They were nearly to the door when a brunette woman about Laurel's age called out to him.

Laurel felt Joe stiffen and glanced up just in time to see him briefly close his eyes. Then he let out a measured sigh between his teeth and turned around.

16

"Hey, Gwen," he said.

A brunette about Laurel's age wore blue scrubs over a body a Playmate would have killed for. Her name tag read simply Gwen, with a bunch of letters Laurel took to be nursing degrees. Her attitude said she and Joe were far from strangers.

His attitude, as he introduced Laurel to Gwen Hemming, suggested he'd rather be somewhere—anywhere—else.

"You're a hard man to pin down," the nurse said. Her smile didn't meet her brown eyes.

"You know how busy things get during Buccaneer Days."

He was obviously uneasy. A romantic dodge, Laurel decided, suspecting this was the person who'd been trying to get in touch with him earlier when he'd ignored that ringing phone.

"It's always bad when the festival falls during a full moon," Gwen agreed. "Last night we had three aliens who supposedly escaped from some mother ship that had landed out on one of the barrier islands and were conducting medical experiments."

"Gotta love the mother ship wackos," Joe said.

"They do keep things from getting dull," she agreed dryly. "Unfortunately, one of the wackos showed up missing a penis he insists was taken in the name of interstellar research."

"Ouch." Joe grimaced.

"In addition to the Bobbitized guy, we had two vampires, a werewolf, and one guy who took the story of Bluebeard seriously and strangled his eighteenth wife."

"Who, was, in reality, not his wife at all, but a twenty-year-old cocktail waitress who made the mistake of letting him pick her up in the bar," Joe said.

"Called it," the nurse agreed. "When I heard you caught that case, I expected you to show up in the ER."

He shrugged, obviously uncomfortable. Laurel wouldn't have been surprised if he had started rubbing the toe of one of those snazzy new sneaks into the highly waxed floor. "I got tied up with a possible jumper, so I handed Bluebeard off to Harkin."

"Yeah, Detective Harkin mentioned something about you having a full plate." The woman didn't look as if she believed him for a minute. Neither did Laurel.

She was vaguely disappointed to discover he was a rat. For some reason, although he might not dress like a responsible grown-up, she would have expected better from Joe Gannon.

"Well," Gwen said briskly, getting down to brass tacks, "now that I've finally caught up with you, we need to talk."

"I'm working a case." He cut a glance to Laurel, as if expecting her to help him out.

No way, buster. Laurel folded her arms. *You're on your own.*

"I don't mind waiting outside if there's something the two of you need to discuss," she said, getting a perverse enjoyment from leaving him out on that limb. "I'm dying for a cigarette."

"Smoking's bad for your health," the nurse said, on cue.

"I'll keep that in mind," Laurel responded sweetly.

"She's attractive," Gwen murmured as she and Joe watched Laurel walk away toward a glass door leading to a small patio that had been carved out of the grassy slope of lawn leading up to the ground floor. There were a pair of metal tables and chairs for the morgue employees' coffee breaks.

"I suppose so. For a reporter."

"One of your favorite people."

After seven years of marriage, she knew him too well. He skimmed a slow look over her. "You're looking great."

"Thank you." She smiled. "While you, on the other hand, look exhausted." She brushed a finger beneath an eye that felt as if it was filled with sand. "You're also in need of a visit from the Fab Five."

"You don't like Hawaii?"

"I'm wild about the state; it's your tacky tourist look I take issue with."

"There was a shooting at the Salvation Army thrift store a couple weeks ago. A grab-and-run gone wrong. A crackhead got hold of a gun and blew away the clerk behind the register." A former alkie who, after more than a decade on the streets, had finally managed to crawl out of the bottle. And what had he gotten for the trouble? A slug between the eyes. Yet more proof, not that Joe needed it, that life wasn't fair.

She arched a brow. "And you just happened to do a little shopping while waiting for the victim to be bagged?"

"Shows how much you know. He was already in the ME's van."

He'd bought the shirt on an impulse, because the shrink he'd gone to when the cold sweats had returned with a vengeance had said that keeping all his emotions locked in, along with the usual stresses of police work and the upcoming anniversary of the shooting and all that came after it, was causing the renewed attacks of PTSD that were stealing his sleep. Tens of thousands of dollars had probably been invested in those fancy diplomas hanging on the wall, and that was the best insight the guy could come up with?

The shrink had suggested a leave of absence—which is what he got for going to a non-departmental therapist who didn't understand that taking off during a heat wave or Buccaneer Days wasn't an option—then had written out a script for Wellbutrin, which Joe still hadn't gotten filled, since he preferred to keep his private life exactly that, which wouldn't happen if he got tapped for one of the department's random drug tests.

Since he couldn't sail off into the sunset to Kauai, or Key West, the shirt had seemed like the next best thing to a vacation. The funny thing was, while it hadn't completely banished the problems, when Joe realized he actually felt a little better while wearing it—or, more accurately, not as bad—he'd gone back and bought six more for a buck fifty each.

He idly wondered what folks wore up in Maine when they weren't fishing for lobster. Probably L.L. Bean khakis, plaid shirts, and penny loafers. None of which sounded all that appealing.

Gwen swept another, more judicial glance over him. "Strangely, on second thought, the look sort of works for you." She glanced out the glass door, where Laurel was smoking and pacing like Maggie the Cat on the postage-stamp-size patio. "Your reporter friend's a little tightly wired."

"She's not my friend. And tightly wired is putting it mildly. She's a textbook type A, which is short for pain in the ass." Though, he admitted, her ass, in those snug pants, was easy on the eyes.

"What's she doing here?"

"She's got a friend who turned up missing after arriving here yesterday from DC. I've got a jumper I can't identify. I was hoping they might be the same person." He shook his head. "They weren't."

"Too bad." She drew in a breath. Let it out slowly. "The reason I've been trying to reach you is to tell you that I'm getting married again."

He'd figured as much. Other than when he'd end up in her ER to question a witness, Gwen hadn't initiated any conversation with him since the marital Ice Age had descended on their lives three years ago. The fact that she'd been leaving messages all over town for him to call her had been out of character.

He was glad she was moving on with her life, but wished he could ask her what trick she'd discovered that allowed her to put the past behind her.

"Good for you. So, who's the lucky guy?"

"Gene Newsome."

The name hit like a sledgehammer to his solar plexus. "Christ Almighty, Gwen . . . How can you . . ." He raked a hand through his hair. "Doesn't it bother you that . . ." He couldn't think it, much less say it.

"That Gene was Austin's doctor?" She finished the question he couldn't ask. "He did everything he could to save Austin."

"Well, obviously everything he did wasn't good enough," Joe snapped.

Her eyes narrowed. "I wouldn't think you'd want to go there."

"And you wonder why I've been dodging your calls." Joe didn't need to be reminded of that time. Didn't need her piling more guilt on top of the shitload that was coming close to suffocating him.

"I'm sorry. Accusing you was a knee-jerk response." She took his fisted hand in both of hers. "It wasn't your fault. Terrible things happen, Joe. Even to good and innocent people like Austin."

Hell, Joe knew that. Didn't he see it every day?

"Even if Austin hadn't died, I don't think our marriage would've worked, Joe. Between the two of us, we've seen enough grief for several lifetimes," she said, as if reading his mind. "Death doesn't make for very good pillow talk."

They may have fallen out of love, but Joe still cared for her. Would always care. They had, after all, had a child together. Once upon a time ago, he'd been that goofy, giddy guy handing out the blue-banded It's a Boy cigars.

He skimmed his knuckles up her cheek. "Are you happy?"

He knew she'd truly moved on when she didn't push his hand away. "Yes. Very."

"Good." He nodded. "You deserve to be happy."

"So do you." Her gaze softened; little horizontal lines of concern furrowed her forehead. "What are you going to be doing Friday night?"

He knew she wasn't asking him out for pizza and a beer. "Probably work."

"That's probably a good idea. Rather than be alone."

"I'll be okay." Actually, he'd planned to get drunk, like he had the past two years on the anniversary of the night that had changed both their lives, but Gwen was a born nurturer and the last thing he wanted was to have her inviting him to spend the evening with her and her doctor fiancé so he wouldn't have to suffer alone. "I talked to a shrink. Worked some things out."

"I'm glad you got help." Relief flowed into her warm Bambi eyes. Her gaze returned toward Laurel, who was still pacing and puffing. Joe wondered if the woman ever relaxed. "Maybe that reporter irritates you because she's gotten under your skin."

"She irritates me because she's about as prickly as a damn cactus."

"I imagine she's concerned for her friend. Maybe under other circumstances—"

"She'd still be a pain." He felt the need to set her straight before she got the wrong idea. "I'm happy for you, darlin'." He'd never said a truer thing. "But just because you're getting hitched doesn't mean you have to play matchmaker for your ex."

"You need a woman in your life." She smiled up at him in a fond way he hadn't seen in years. Joe figured he had Clean Gene Newsome to thank for that. "If for no other reason than to have someone take charge and burn that shirt."

They shared a laugh.

"I have to go," she said as a page advising of the impending arrival of an EMS copter was announced in a calm tone from the speaker above their heads. "We're getting married next Saturday at St. Brendan's. At two. I don't suppose—"

"I don't think that'd be such a good idea." He might be okay with the woman he'd once sworn to love until death they did part pledging her troth to some other guy, but Joe didn't want to witness the event.

"I suppose not."

The page repeated. The copter ETA was two minutes, and all emergency staff were directed to return to the ER STAT.

"That's me." She blew out a frustrated breath. "I hate Buccanner Days."

Yet another thing they could agree on.

17

Hoping that Chloe might have called home, Laurel called the house again while Hawaii Five-O dealt with his romantic problems, to check for messages.

"Beep . . . Hey, Laurel. Kevin Hawkins, here, from the *Weekly Worldwide View*, the must-read tabloid that's taking a million readers a day away from *Star Magazine* and the *Enquirer*. We here at the *View* are highly impressed with your creativity and your willingness to write outside the box, sweetheart.

"We understand you're currently between jobs and would like to offer you the position of our very first Washington correspondent. We were thinking along the lines of 'First martian ambassador caught in love nest with Capitol Hill intern.' Or, hey, how about 'Senator with two personalities—one Democrat, one Republican—runs against himself'?

"But, hey," he continued in a rapid, machine-gun-fire, New York delivery, "who am I to suggest story ideas to a writer with your imagination? Call me, sweetheart." He rattled off a 212 area code phone number. "I think we're a match made in journalistic heaven."

"More like hell," she muttered, punching End. Just what she needed, she thought, as the electronic doors swept open and Joe Gannon came out of the hospital, to be embraced by the Loch Ness crowd.

"Sorry about that," he said.

"Hey, everyone's entitled to a personal life. Even a cop." In truth, had it not been for Kevin Hawkins, she'd been grateful for the time alone; it had given her jittery stomach time to settle.

"I love the way you throw that verbal acid on my job." He plucked the cigarette from her fingers and took a long drag. "Like I took to police work after giving up grave robbing," he said on a stream of smoke.

"It's nothing personal. More than a few people have suggested that I'm not particularly fond of authority figures."

"I suspect those people would be right."

"Like journalists are your favorite people," she scoffed when he handed the cigarette back to her.

"If I fell into the trap of responding to that sweeping statement, you'd accuse me of profiling."

Laurel hated that he was right. "I'm a reporter, which means that I'm naturally curious. So shoot me." She remembered the gun he was wearing beneath that blinding shirt. "I was speaking figuratively."

"I figured that out," he said. "Bein' a detective and all."

"Did you and your lady friend get things worked out?"

"She's not my lady friend. And what makes you think there was anything to work out?"

She shot him a look.

He shrugged and dipped his hands into his pockets. "She's my ex-wife."

"Ah." Her tone invited elaboration.

"She's getting married."

"Ah." Laurel took another hit on the cigarette, the slight spinning in her head reminding her that until two days ago, she'd no longer smoked. She wasn't surprised he was divorced. From the statistics she'd read, divorce went with the territory when you were in law enforcement. Not that journalists were a group renowned for matrimonial bliss. "And we're not happy about that?"

"I don't know about you, but since Gwen's a good person who deserves to be happy, yeah, I am." He took the cigarette away and stabbed it into the sand-filled container beside the door. "She's also right about these things being bad for you."

Although she found his behavior obnoxiously bossy, Laurel couldn't argue that point. She also decided that the detective must be doing his Snoopy happy-dance on the inside, since he sure hadn't looked all that thrilled during the intense conversation with his former wife.

"So, was it a nasty divorce?"

A look of pained irritation moved across his face. "Anyone ever tell you that curiosity killed the cat?"

"Sure. Lucky I'm not a cat." It was all Laurel could do to keep from fluttering her lashes just to annoy him.

"It was painful," he said through set teeth. "And messy, as all breakups probably are. But it wasn't nasty." He paused and plowed his hand through his sun-tipped hair. "And I've no damn idea why I'm even telling you this."

"Because I'm a crackerjack reporter." Laurel suspected that not many people could throw Detective First Class, Lieutenant Joe Gannon off balance. She liked the idea of being one of them. "People tell me stuff. I think it's because I've got one of those faces people trust."

"Or it could be because they realize that you're going to just keep after them until they give in, so it saves time and energy all the way around just to tell you what you want to hear."

"There is that," she agreed. "So, if you had such a friendly divorce—"

"I didn't say that."

"I stand corrected. If the divorce wasn't nasty, why have you been dodging her calls?"

"You don't miss much, do you?"

"Nope. Since it appears the blushing bride-to-be's happy and you're happy that she's happy, what's the problem?"

"The problem is that I've got an unidentified dead woman lying on a slab in the morgue and I'm wasting time I could be using to find out who she is—or was—being grilled on my personal life by a nosy reporter."

"If you're trying to insult me, you're going to have to do better than that."

He rolled his eyes. His gorgeous, knee-weakening gold eyes. "I wasn't trying to insult you; I'm trying to get back to work. Where are you staying?"

"The Wingate," she decided. It would stretch her budget, but in case everyone was right about Chloe having taken off for a few days vacation, which she still didn't believe, Laurel wanted to be there when she returned. It would also keep her close to Aiken so, once this problem was solved, she could get back to tracking down who, exactly, had pulled the strings to ruin her reputation and get her fired.

"Fine." When he put his hand on her back in a casual, natural gesture, Laurel assured herself that the burst of heat racing up her spine had everything to do with the steamy August temperature and nothing to do with him. "I'll drop you off on the way back to the station."

"Good idea," she said as they walked toward the ugly Crown Vic with its Unmarked Police Car sticker she suspected he'd put on the bumper. "You can tell me what we're going to do to find Chloe on the way."

18

"Have you ever killed anyone?" she asked as he peeled out of the parking lot.

"Why? You asking for my cop credentials or for a personal reason?"

"As a reporter, I'm naturally curious about things. People. And I like knowing who I'm working with."

"I hadn't realized we were working together."

"Of course we will. I'll wear you down, Gannon."

Joe decided her confidence fit her as well as those snug purple trousers.

"I always do," she continued.

He shifted gears, uncomfortable talking about killing with a civilian, even one who'd worked a cop beat. Unless you'd found yourself in a situation in which the only way to end things was to pull a trigger and cut a life short, there was no way to understand how shootings in real life were a lot different than the way they were depicted in the movies.

"Yeah. Once." He kept his eyes on the traffic, but Joe could feel her looking at him. "When I was working narcotics."

"You didn't like it," she said quietly.

"Hell, no." All in all, it had been the worst night of his life.

She didn't say anything more, but he could feel her thinking about it.

A crowd had gathered a block away from the hotel, the mood as loud and boisterous as among those celebrating Buccaneer Days. But this group had an entirely different agenda. Apparently a contingent of various environmental groups, they waved placards proclaiming such slogans as Back the people, not the polluters, and No drill, no spill.

They were being held back with rope and yellow police tape which, if they decided to surge forward to the hotel, certainly wouldn't have stopped them. The armed cops on the other side of that tape, though, might have.

"Interesting how the police moved the protestors around the corner so Aiken won't have to see them," Laurel murmured over the clang of cowbells.

"Don't blame us," Joe said. "The department's just following the Secret Service's dictates by keeping any protestors in a First Amendment zone."

"Now there's a nifty governmental euphemism. It's almost up there with collateral damage."

Joe couldn't argue.

Laurel watched as Cody Wunder, clad in his usual black, led the group in a not all that original, "Ho Ho, Hey Hey, how many trees have you killed today?" chant.

"So," she murmured, "if protestors speak from a First Amendment zone, and no elected official hears them, is it really free speech?"

He shrugged. "You've got me."

"I see." She flashed him a false smile. "You're just following orders. Someone also might want to inform the police department that it might not be a bad idea for the vice president of the United States to see what democracy looked like."

"It's not my call. Personally, I'm a big fan of trees. It's anarchy—and the people who encourage it—I'm not real wild about."

Remembering a tractor-trailer rig that rolled and exploded in Louisiana, killing the occupants of two SUVs and a Ford Escort that had had the misfortune to be on that particular stretch of highway at the same time, Laurel couldn't argue.

She'd met the forty-something environmentalist once, at a Georgetown party hosted by a political society maven who, if you were to believe the whispers, was having an affair with him. He'd been striking, with his silky black hair pulled into a ponytail, blue eyes vivid in a copper complexion that revealed his Native American roots, and an intriguing crescent-shaped scar at the corner of his mouth. He'd worn a fringed, black leather jacket over a black silk T-shirt, lean black stacked jeans, and black lizard cowboy boots.

The rebel outfit alone would have caused him to stand out like a blizzard in July amidst the old time pols, party fat cats, and social movers and shakers arriving for the fund-raising dinner in black ties and beaded designer gowns. Considering that he'd ridden to fame on the hard luck story of having grown up impoverished on a reservation in Oklahoma, if the three diamond studs blazing at his earlobe were any indication, radical environmentalism paid very well. Or perhaps, she'd thought while watching the same women who were accustomed to dining with the president flutter around him as if he were a rock star, rumors about the generosity of his female "patrons" were true.

He'd been incredibly striking, even in a town where charisma was the coin of the realm. But while he was speaking forcefully on the need to save the planet, his eyes had never caught fire; even when he'd had the five-hundred-dollar-a-plate crowd cheering along like fans at a Redskins game, those hooded, slightly slanted eyes had glittered like blue ice. She'd caught a glimpse of him in one of those rare instances he was alone, observing his donors with the same cold-blooded detachment with which a python might watch a group of unwary mice.

"Chloe invited me to that party."

She hadn't realized she'd spoken out loud until Gannon asked, "What party?"

"It's not important." At least she didn't think so.

"If she really is in trouble, anything could be important," he reminded her.

"It was a fund-raiser. Something about saving baby sea turtles." She told him about the party, but couldn't recall whether or not she'd seen Chloe and the environmentalist together.

"Kind of a coincidence, both of them coming here to Somersett at the same time."

"Not really. Chloe's job is to travel with the vice president whenever an important social event's on the calendar. Another reason she wouldn't have just taken off, by the way. While Wunder's self-proclaimed mission, along with cleaning up the planet, is to make certain Aiken doesn't get elected, so the CHAOS crowd has been following him around. Maybe you should question him," she suggested.

"Maybe we should get you checked in. Your friend's probably already back in her room waiting for you."

Okay, so Detective Joe Gannon still wasn't exactly chomping at the bit to start investigating Chloe's disappearance. At least she'd gotten him thinking about it. That, Laurel decided, as she climbed out of the car, was something.

19

They'd no sooner entered the gilt and marble splendor of the lobby when she was confronted by Warren Wyatt's all too familiar face.

"Fancy meeting you here," he said. "Doing a little breaking and entering?"

Knowing full well that the dig was meant to rile her up, Laurel refused to respond to the bait. "That story is an off-the-wall rumor that's not even going to be a blip on the news cycle before it's proven false." Somehow. She hoped. "I'm currently working on a story about financial corruption and the misuse of power in the executive branch."

"Really?" He didn't appear to be trembling in his tasseled Gucci loafers. "And here I thought I'd also heard a rumor about you being fired."

"I'm on a temporary leave of absence." Having Chloe go missing might have sidetracked her temporarily, but Laurel had every intention of salvaging her reputation. "I was hoping to speak to the vice president."

"If you want to apologize for that bogus story about the offshore drilling, you needn't bother. The matter was settled when your paper ran a retraction on page A2 this morning," he said smoothly.

"Now how did I know you were going to say that?" Laurel had literally seen red when she'd read that retraction on the Corrections page. She wasn't angry that the *Post* had run it; she was furious that they'd *had* to.

Remembering a bit of the manners her aunt Melanie had tried to drill into her, she turned to acknowledge Wyatt's companion, who, despite the stifling heat, was clad in a tropical-weight black wool suit and stiffly starched Roman collar. Gold-and-onyx cufflinks gleamed from the French cuffs of his shirt.

Bishop Damian Cary had had the propitious timing to inherit a rice farm from a great-uncle the same week the diocese's elderly bishop resigned after being diagnosed with Alzheimer's. The then-monsignor lost no time in donating his inheritance to the diocese, which had been seeking land for a new Catholic high school. The pope, appreciating Cary's generosity, appointed him bishop and moved him into the vacancy.

"Hello, Bishop Cary."

"Ms. Stewart." His smile was brief, then his gaze turned sympathetic. "I was sorry to hear about your recent troubles. But you seem to be holding up quite well."

"I am, thank you." He was a good-looking man, tall and athletic, with just enough gray at the temples of his thick, swept-back black hair to give him a bit of gravitas. Since he was a frequent visitor to Washington, Laurel had run into him on several occasions and not once had she seen him looking anything but Cary Grant elegant.

"And, as I told Warren, my recent problems are merely a misunderstanding I intend to clear up."

"I have not a single doubt you'll be successful," he said enthusiastically. Laurel had always thought that if the bishop hadn't gone into the God business he would have made a dandy politician.

"Well, while I'd love to stay here and chat, I really have to get checked in." She turned to Wyatt. "It was nice running into you, Warren." *Not.* "By the way, have you heard from Chloe?"

A frown darkened his brow. "No, but if she happens to call you before she checks back in with the campaign, tell her to call me and explain why I shouldn't fire her lazy ass." He glanced over at the priest. "Sorry, Your Excellency."

Bishop Cary's frown did not appear to be due to Wyatt's language. "I can't imagine anyone could ever considering Chloe Hollister lazy. And it's very unlike her to ignore her responsibilities." Seeds of concern darkened his slate-gray eyes. He was the first person, other than Laurel herself, who seemed at all concerned with such uncharacteristic behavior and she was grateful for his support. "I do hope she hasn't gotten herself in romantic hot water again."

His comment came as a surprise. Then again, the bishop was Aiken's unofficial "spiritual advisor." It was possible Chloe might, at one time, have unburdened her heart to the bishop. Perhaps he knew who she'd been having the affair with?

"I hope that as well, Your Excellency." Unfortunately, she couldn't very well ask him if Chloe had been sleeping around with the vice president, with Wyatt looming over them.

Laurel took a business card from her bag. "I have to admit I'm worried about her. If she happens to contact you, will you let me know? You can reach me on my cell." It was a long shot, but at this point long shots were all she had. "And perhaps you could tell her to call me?"

"Of course." His bishop's ring, a large, gold-set amethyst with an intaglio design of the cross on its surface, flashed as he tucked the card into his pocket.

"Thank you." She glanced back at Wyatt. "Well, I guess I'd better be checking in so I can get to work on my story."

The politician's smile, as false as hers, didn't reach his eyes. If a cobra could smile, it would look just like Warren Wyatt, she decided. "Don't let me stop you," he said in that slow, deep syrupy South Carolina Low Country drawl that had caused so many people to underestimate his treacherous nature.

Dammit, he had to be the one who'd set her up. Now all she had to do was prove it. After she found Chloe.

"Neither one of them seemed real worried about your friend," Gannon pointed out as they continued across the red-and-gold carpet.

"They don't know her as well as I do."

"The bishop knows her well enough to know about her boyfriend problems."

"Bishops might be more into the politics of the Church than any spiritual aspect, but he *was* a priest before getting bumped up the career ladder. He's probably used to listening to people's problems, which is undoubtedly why Chloe felt she could open up to him."

It was not often Laurel felt guilty about anything; she did at the thought that Chloe might have found her too judgmental to share her problem with. Laurel sighed at the memory of how she'd lectured her friend yesterday morning instead of providing a shoulder to cry on.

She was going to try harder. Be more empathetic. Maybe her family was right when they accused her of being too cynical. Pollyanna would've lasted five minutes in the dog-eat-dog world of Washington politics, but surely there was a middle ground . . .

Unfortunately, Laurel's intention of trying to soften up a bit was about to be tested. "What do you mean you don't have any rooms?" she asked the clerk standing behind the oak front counter.

"It's Buccaneer Days," the young woman—were all the females down here in Magnolialand blond?—replied, voicing what Laurel had decided must be the city's motto. She gestured toward a large, calligraphied events board on an easel. "As you can see, we're also hosting two wedding receptions, and, of course, the vice president's staff has booked the entire top floor."

"Just any old room will do," Laurel assured the clerk, whose badge declared her to be Tiffany Madison, assistant day manager. "In fact, I'll even take one of those cramped pie-shaped rooms no one ever wants between the elevator and the ice machine."

Tiffany squared her shoulders clad in a burgundy twill blazer with cheap gold piping that Laurel wouldn't have been caught dead in, but she gave the assistant day manager reluctant points for having had it tailored. "We have no cramped rooms," she sniffed.

"My mistake. I'm sorry, I guess this southern heat's frying my brain. I'd forgotten what a class operation you're running here." She opened her billfold, pulling out the spare press pass she'd had printed up after having hers stolen from a Moscow hotel room. "I'm from the *Post*. The *Washington Post*," she clarified with a smile designed to help Tiffany see the resemblance to her photo.

"We're always happy to host the press. But at the moment there aren't any rooms available. Unfortunately, I suspect you'll find the same story all over town. It is, after all—"

"Buccaneer Days," Laurel said flatly.

Tiffany bobbed her teased blond head. "That's right."

Damn. The clerk was probably right about the other hotels being filled up. In any case, even if Gannon were willing to taxi her all over the city in search of a room, she wasn't eager to drag her suitcase around in this heat. Especially with the threatening thunder that was beginning to sound a great deal louder than it had while they'd been driving here from the hospital.

"Look." Laurel leaned conspiratorially toward the intransigent assistant manager, trying a new tact. "I do a lot of traveling in my work. I know hotels always hold back a few rooms for celebrities; I'm sure your establishment does, as well."

Tiffany eyed her suspiciously. "We do."

"Well, then." Laurel discreetly pulled a twenty dollar bill out of her wallet. "What would it take to get one of those rooms?"

"Perhaps be a celebrity?" Her catty response had Laurel thinking perhaps Tiffany shouldn't have chosen a career in the hospitality industry. "Though it wouldn't matter even if you were Nicole Kidman," she tacked on. "We still wouldn't have accommodations."

"How about suite 1033?" Joe, who'd been standing silently by during the exchange entered the conversation.

"1033?" The clerk's perfectly arched blond brow winged upward. "But that's a crime scene."

"*Was* a crime scene," Joe corrected. "I'm Detective Gannon, primary on the case." He showed her his shield. "I don't believe we've met."

"I was off yesterday." She hadn't even bothered to check out his badge. For all Tiffany knew, he could have been a serial killer. Laurel thought perhaps someone should let the hotel's home office know about the lax security. "But I certainly heard all about the incident." Tiffany shuddered dramatically. Her eyes, which Laurel was surprised she could even open, given how many coats of navy blue mascara were coating her lashes, widened. "We've never had anything like that happen here."

"Well, since we're all finished up there, there's no reason for you not to open it up. Unless," he said, glancing over at Laurel, "Ms. Stewart is disturbed at the idea of sleeping in a former crime scene."

"Doesn't bother me at all," Laurel said, responding to the faint challenge she thought she detected in his voice. A moment later she was rethinking her fast decision. She didn't, after all, know how nasty a crime scene it was. If they were talking blood or any other bodily fluids, she'd rather take her chances sleeping on a bench in that pretty little park she'd seen across the street from the court-house.

"Except for some fingerprint dust, the room's clean," Gannon said, seeming to sense her thoughts—which, for some reason she'd think about later, piqued Laurel's irritation.

"I'll take it." Beggars, after all, could not be choosers. Laurel pulled out her American Express card.

"That's not necessary," Joe said.

The assistant manager's hand, tipped by acrylic nails just a scant shorter than Freddy Krueger's and polished the deep burgundy shade of her blazer, paused over the top of the counter. "It's customary to run a card at check-in."

"Usually," he agreed. "But this isn't exactly business as usual, is it?" He rubbed his chin, bringing both Laurel's and Tiffany's eyes to that deep cleft. Damn, the man may have had his faults, but if *People* magazine ever wandered down south for Buccaneer Days, Joe Gannon could definitely be in the running for Sexiest Man on the Planet, provided he ditched that god-awful shirt.

"Ms. Stewart's had a long day," he said. "She may look as cool as a cucumber"—he slanted her an appraising look and a smile not nearly as warm as the one he'd bestowed upon Tiffany—"but as much as I hate to challenge the chamber of commerce's Sultry Somersett tourism slogan, the fact is that it's hot enough to poach eggs in the harbor today. I imagine she was lookin' forward to going up to her suite, havin' herself an icy drink from the mini bar, and a long cool shower.

"Not that you need a shower, of course," he assured

Laurel in that smooth as warm honey drawl that seemed to deepen when he was talking to women. All women except, Laurel had noted, his former wife. "You smell as fresh as sun-dried sheets."

"Why, aren't you just the sweetest thing," Laurel said in what she considered a damn good replication of her aunt Melanie's North Carolina–belle drawl. Her smile was sweet enough to rot teeth.

"It's the truth." He held up a hand as if swearing an oath. "The thing is," he continued, turning his attention back to Tiffany, "it'll be a little hard for Ms. Stewart to get any work done with housekeeping bustling around the room, cleaning up the mess."

"A mess that wasn't our doing. *Or* our responsibility," Tiffany pointed out, proving that she wasn't quite as malleable as her spun-candy looks might suggest.

"Well now, I'm not one to duck responsibility," Joe said. "We're sure enough the ones who spread that nasty old dust around, but only because we were trying to wrap up a mysterious death before the media started writing stories falsely suggesting that your fine establishment isn't all that different from those hot-sheet motels across the county line." He paused for effect. "Bein' as how the lady whose unfortunate death set the investigation in motion appears to have checked in without any luggage."

"It's not our business to prescreen our guests by asking what they intend to do in their rooms." Tiffany was sounding a little bit testy. "The last time I looked, no one had elected me—or any other employee of the Wingate Palace hotel—morality czaress."

"Czarina," Laurel murmured.

"Excuse me?" Definitely testy.

"*Czar*'s a masculine word that tended to be used inter-changeably with *emperor.* The feminine version is czarina, or, *tsaritsa*, which means either the wife of the czar or an empress."

Tiffany just stared at her.

"The thing is," Joe pressed on, trying to make his point, "it doesn't seem right that Ms. Stewart should be put out because of an unfortunate incident that had nothing to do with her."

"Ms. Stewart is free to attempt to locate lodging in some other hotel." The smile Tiffany flashed at Laurel was as false as her platinum hair color.

"And write about the experience," Laurel said. "The Washington Wingate Palace hosts a great many political and social events; I've no doubt readers would appreciate reading about my personal experience with your hotel chain."

It was a threat, pure and simple, and subtle as a sledge-hammer. Laurel might not be as smooth at verbal maneu-vering as Joe Gannon, but she damn well knew how to get a point across.

"I'm sure the manager would want me to comp your room," Tiffany replied stiffly, switching gears on a dime, "to make up for your inconvenience."

Laurel put her card back in her billfold and filled out the registration form the assistant manager somewhat petulantly shoved across the polished desk.

20

"Thank you," Laurel said to Joe as they walked to the elevators, "Not only for getting me the room, but for pushing for the comp."

"This place isn't cheap and I figured the paper probably isn't springing for your tab, since you seem to be down here on a personal matter."

"With Aiken in town, I could have turned in an expense sheet." *Once I get my job back.*

"But you wouldn't. Because you're not down here to cover the vice president."

He was right. She wouldn't have tried to get her expenses reimbursed even if she hadn't been fired. She'd long ago come to the conclusion that she was the only reporter alive who didn't fudge on her expense sheets. One reason was her admittedly black-and-white view of things and the fact that it seemed hypocritical to expect others to live up to ethical standards she didn't demand from herself. Staying rigidly honest also helped her sleep at night. Or at least she *had* slept well, until her integrity had been challenged.

"That's very good profiling.

"I told you, I'm—"

"A detective."

"Got it." He pressed the Up button.

"You don't look much like a detective." She skimmed a look over him. "Magnum, PI, maybe. But he was a private eye. And worked in Hawaii."

"Maybe you never heard of *Hawaii Five-0.*"

"Got me," she allowed. When she was ten, she'd had such a major crush on James MacArthor, the hunky actor who'd played Detective Danny Williams, she'd actually fantasized about moving to Hawaii and becoming a policewoman. That was, thinking back on it, the only time she'd wanted to be anything other than a writer.

"My partner went to Maui on her honeymoon," Joe said conversationally when the elevator reached the lobby. "She stayed at this resort with an indoor waterfall. Said the island was a real pretty place."

"It is. I went there for an economic convention."

"You're lucky your work lets you travel." The elevator doors closed behind them. "Ever been to Key West?"

"I worked there for a few weeks." Six, to be exact.

"What's it like?"

She glanced over at him, surprised at what appeared to be idle conversation. "Sunny. Laid back."

Too laid back for her, where people actually gathered every evening to celebrate the sun setting over the Gulf of Mexico.

He nodded thoughtfully. "That's what I always figured."

They fell silent as they watched the numbers light up above the door.

"How about Maine. Ever work there?"

"I spent six months writing obits and covering school board meetings." The latter of which had taught her exactly how messy pure democracy could be. "It's got magnificent scenery."

"And is a lot cooler than here," he guessed.

"Hell would be cooler than here. But yeah, they seem to have two seasons—winter and August." It was during the long Maine winter that she'd begun her still unfinished novel, writing on her laptop in bed hunkered beneath a stack of down comforters.

Another not uncomfortable silence settled over them.

"Is it true what that guy downstairs said? About you losing your job?" Joe asked.

"That guy is Aiken's chief political advisor. And my temporary unemployment is due to a misunderstanding." She sighed at his pointed, patient sideways glance, knowing he was willing to wait until doomsday for her to elaborate. "I received an anonymous leak about Aiken getting a no-bid contract for one of his cronies' companies to drill off the South Carolina coast inserted into a terrorism funding bill."

The door opened and they exited onto a floor lit by wall sconces and scented by a vase of fresh flowers. "So, I got my usual three sources, two of which came from the vice president's office, the third from the Department of Energy. All three would only talk on deep background."

"Which allowed you to use the information, but without attributing the source, right?"

"Right. So, once all three had confirmed it, on the

record, I filed my story, which landed on the front page. When the story turned out false, I was out of a job."

"Just like that?"

"Just like that." She snapped her fingers as they walked side by side down the hall, her high heels sinking into the plush burgundy carpet.

"I hadn't realized journalism was a 'one strike and you're out' business."

"It's not, which is why papers run corrections as a matter of course. But except for a few supermarket tabloids, publishers tend to frown on writers making stuff up."

"Gotta wonder why someone would go to so much trouble to get you off the paper."

She was surprised he so quickly, without any further questions, not only accepted her side of the story, but echoed her own view about a conspiracy. Then again, cops were probably a lot like reporters when it came to distrusting most of the population.

"My thoughts exactly. Which was why I came down here. To get to the truth."

"But then your friend went missing and you got sidetracked."

An unpalatable thought suddenly occurred to Laurel. "You don't think the two could be related?"

"Hey, you haven't even convinced me Chloe Hollister *is* missing," he pointed out. "But when you work in the cop business, things eventually stop surprising you," he said.

They stopped in front of 1033. He pulled a Swiss Army knife from his pocket—who knew they made them in purple?—and sliced open the yellow crime tape sealing the door.

"You going to be okay?" he asked as he took the card key from her hand and stuck it into the slot.

"Of course. If I can handle viewing a body, I'm not going to be bothered by a little fingerprint dust."

The gritty fingerprint dust didn't get to her.

But something else, much, much worse, did.

21

The scent—a heady cloud of jasmine, orange blossoms, wisteria, and sandalwood—hit her the instant he opened the door.

"Extravagance," she murmured.

"It's not exactly Motel 6," Joe agreed, taking in the very good reproduction furniture, the satin upholstery, the lace bordering the French doors, the art on the walls which could have washed off a misty Impressionist landscape.

"*Extravagance* is a perfume. By Givenchy. Chloe wears it."

"Are you suggesting she's been here?"

"No. But someone who wore the same fragrance. A man gave it to her." Laurel could feel the light spray at her wrists. At the hollow in her throat where her pulse picked up a beat. "He told her it suited her—it was sophisticated and modern and bright." Laurel smiled at the memory. "Just like her."

"Who are we talking about?" Joe asked.

"I'm not sure." Laurel's head was going a little light. Damn. That's what she got for not eating lunch. "They had champagne."

A scene shimmered in front of her eyes, more shadow than substance, as if she were watching it from the other side of a silk curtain.

"It was French." The bottle was deep green, the label gold. The man opened it with expertise; the cork came out with a discreet, sexy whisper. "She normally doesn't drink alcohol, especially during the day, but champagne isn't really like drinking."

Laurel was being drawn from behind that veil into the scene. She could taste the bubbles dancing on her tongue like sparkling liquid sunshine.

"She's turned up the air-conditioning, but it's still so very hot in the suite." She stroked her fingers down her throat. Lifted her hair off the nape of her neck. "Or perhaps it's their lovemaking that's left her feeling so warm." A moist sheen glistened on Laurel's arms.

"A shower sounds like heaven. She scoops up her underwear, leaves her dress on the carpet, and goes into the bathroom."

Joe followed her through the bedroom. The bathroom shower was tiled in blue and white, echoing the harbor outside; the whirlpool tub had been built on a pedestal and was large enough to swim laps in.

"She turns on the shower."

Laurel's eyes fluttered shut as if she were in some sort of trance. Since it was the first lead he'd had on the Sissy Smith case, Joe hesitated doing anything to bring her out of it. "She calls out to him. 'Aren't you going to join me?'

"There's no answer. She hears voices. Has he turned on the television? God, she knows it's an election year but there are still months to go and she's sick, sick, sick of politics!

" 'I'm going to start without you,' she threatens playfully.

"The voices on the television get louder.

" 'You said we don't have much time,' she complains."

Laurel's use of present tense, as if she was actually in this room right before Sissy Smith's death, caused the hair to stand up on Joe's arms.

"She's a bit irritated, but she's learned the hard way that getting angry and having a confrontation can be dangerous. Painful. She decides to charm him. Seduce him.

"She's smiling as she plans her seduction while she takes a cool shower. She dries off with a white fluffy towel and puts on the thong panties and silk slip she bought at the Victoria's Secret at Harbor View. The first time they'd been in such a hurry he hadn't even gotten a good look at the pretty new lingerie. This time she's going to make sure he notices."

The docks where the merchant marine ships had once arrived with foreign cargo from around the world had recently been regentrified into an upscale shopping and tourist mecca called Harbor View. Joe wondered if Laurel had known about that. He also made a mental note to check and see if there was a Victoria's Secret in the center, which resembled a New England fishing village.

"Her strappy sandals with the pretty ribbons and silk flowers are Manolo Blahniks. They were ridiculously expensive, but since nobody makes fuck-me shoes like Manolo, they're worth every penny."

That's what Cait had called them. Manolos. There was *no* way this woman could have known that.

"She spins around, takes a long look at herself in the mirrored wall, and likes what she sees." Laurel did a short spin herself, like a little girl showing off a new party dress. "It's been a long time since she'd thought of herself as pretty. A long time since she'd allowed herself to be happy.

"But she's met someone. A man who appreciates her for who she is. A man she can talk to about all sorts of things that she cares about. A man who listens to her, who values her opinions, a man who actually likes the insecure woman lurking beneath her smooth and perfumed skin. A man who—amazingly!—loves her."

Joe watched Laurel fluff her hair, then pick up an imaginary bottle and go through the motions of spritzing perfume behind her ears and between her breasts. Watched her pantomime tossing back the champagne.

"The sky is darkening and thunder rumbles from somewhere out on the horizon as she glides out of the sumptuous bathroom, enticement on her mind. She senses the difference the instant she enters the living room suite. A vile, dark force of evil. She starts to hyperventilate, then assures herself that her near panic attack is only due to the building storm outside.

"A man's standing by the window; she draws in a sharp, painful breath when he turns toward her. Her heart begins hammering against her ribs. He's found her out!"

There was no mistaking the fear that suddenly filled Laurel's eyes. Joe could have sworn his own heart stopped.

" 'Your lover's gone,' the man says in that calm, reasonable voice that she knows from experience means he's on the verge of exploding. 'It seems he remembered a pressing emergency.'

"It hadn't been the television after all. The voices she'd heard had been the two men. Had they been arguing about her? What threats had he made? And why had her lover left her to face this alone?

"His smile is cold, so cold. She drops the glass onto the carpet and braces for his attack. But he surprises her."

Joe watched the terror on Laurel's face change to puzzlement, tinged with suspicion.

"He says he's hurt. She should have told him she was unhappy. She's afraid to remind him that she'd tried to share her feelings in the beginning. When he'd first begun to hit her. But not lately. Lately she's been afraid to say anything.

"Then he surprises her again. He says that he doesn't want to be with anyone who doesn't want to be with him. Oh, he still loves her, he assures her in that mild tone that sends shivers through her. But, as he told her lover, he cares for her enough to let her go."

Laurel glanced over to the coffee table where Joe knew the empty champagne bottle had been found. "He wants her to drink one last glass of champagne with him. To toast the good times. She thinks that they haven't had that many good times, but she's also afraid of setting him off. The last time she'd made him angry, she'd been so bruised and battered, she hadn't been able to leave the house for two weeks . . .

"He hands her a glass he's already poured. At the first

sip, the bitter and nasty taste slaps her tongue. Does he really think she's so stupid she won't realize he'd drugged it?

"His fingers curl around hers on the stem of the glass. 'Drink it all,' he says.

" 'I don't want to,' she argues weakly, sensing that if she doesn't, he'll force it down her throat.

" 'You liked it before,' he reminds her in a coaxing tone, like a parent bent on convincing a child to eat the vegetables on the dinner plate.

"She liked the floating soft feeling, the pretty colors, and the way it could make her feel so sexy, but she didn't like when the trip went bad. And she hated waking up the next morning with bruises and deep red scratches, not being able to walk without terrible pain, not remembering what she'd done the night before.

"She'd never done drugs before meeting him. In the beginning, she'd only taken the pills to make him happy. Later, she'd been more willing to resort to them to escape from the horror of her situation, if only for a little while.

" 'It's a smaller dose than last time,' he assures her. 'One last trip, darling. For old times' sake.'

"His hand tightens like a vice around hers, so tight she's afraid the matchstick stem of the glass will break. She knows she has two choices. To go ahead and swallow, or be beaten senseless. Surely he wouldn't give her enough drugs to kill her. She is not so deluded as to believe he loves her, but murdering her would destroy the career he's worked so hard for.

"His fingers tangle in her long hair; he jerks her head

back, then, with his other hand still tight over hers, tips the glass against her lips. She realizes that her newly found courage that had allowed her to fall in love, and that warm sense of wonder and security she'd felt while primping in the bathroom, were as ephemeral as sea foam. And the man she'd believed to be her knight in shining armor hadn't stayed to rescue her, which just proves, she supposes sadly, that she has terrible choice in men.

"Resigned to her fate, she closes her eyes and swallows.

" 'Good girl.' He actually pats her on top of the head, as he might a pet dog, then puts his hand on her back and leads her over to the couch."

With her gaze still focused inward, Laurel sat down on the sofa covered in blue-and-white-striped satin. Another change seemed to come over her. No longer tense, she was turning practically boneless in front of his eyes. As if, Joe thought, she'd been drugged.

"It doesn't take long for the floaty, dreamy feeling to begin to wash over her.

" 'You know you don't want to leave, baby.' His deep voice is warm and soothing. 'You belong to me.' At first the hands moving over her feel like a caress. 'You always have.'

"She's restless. Confused. She can't remember where she is. Or who she's with. All she knows is that she needs . . . something.

"She feels a cool breeze on her legs as he lifts her slip. His fingers slip beneath her panties. Soft, pretty pink-and-gold clouds are floating across her mind," Laurel said tonelessly. "Her arms and legs are getting numb. Her muscles are so lax her thighs fall open.

" 'Slut,' he growls. 'You'll open your legs to any man who comes along, won't you, whore?' "

Joe's gut clenched when the voice coming out of Laurel's lips suddenly changed to something that sounded a helluva lot like the devil in *The Exorcist*.

"Her eyes fly open. She recognizes the rage growing inside him. His face is twisted. Ugly. Like an evil mask. Fear burns off enough of the drug haze that she can remember exactly where she is. He tells her all the time that she's stupid. For a while she actually believed that, until these past months, when the man she mistakenly thought would be her savior showed her it wasn't true. But she still can't understand why he'd give her drugs to loosen her up, then become furious when they do their job and make her more sexually uninhibited."

Joe was torn between calling a halt to whatever was happening right now, before she had to suffer any more, and needing to discover something, anything, that would help him solve the mystery of Sissy Smith's death.

What he hadn't fully realized, until this week, was that after twenty years on the force, he was getting to hate mysteries.

Give me a name, goddammit. Then we can get the hell out of here.

"He's so angry." Laurel was squeezing her hands together so tightly her knuckles had turned white. "He hits her so hard her vision blurs.

"She cries out. She's never seen such murderous fury on his face, in his eyes. Perhaps this is the night that he will kill her, after all. 'Please don't,' she begs."

Joe's sense of dread intensified as tears—Sissy Smith's

tears—seeped from beneath Laurel's lashes, trailing down her cheeks.

"His signet ring slashes her cheek when he backhands her." Laurel's own hand lifted to her smooth, unwounded face, slowly, jerkily, as if it were being pulled upward by a puppeteer's strings. "She tries to fight him, but he's so strong and the drugs have made her so weak . . .

"She falls off the couch onto the floor. He kicks her in the side, then puts his foot on her back and pushes her facedown onto the carpet.

"He loves her like this. When he can make her cringe like a whipped dog. The thrill of absolute power surges through him like electricity. Watching her so helpless, so humiliated, makes him feel invincible. He can do any-thing—absolutely anything!—to her.

"He rolls her onto her back so he can enjoy the terror in her eyes. 'I could kill you,' he says with a cold, devil's smile. She's weeping now, silently, resigned to her fate. His blood's running high and hot as he forces her thighs even further apart.

"He knows what she's expecting, but he isn't ready to give it to her yet.

"He takes a knife out of his pocket; light from the overhead chandelier glints off the thin, stainless-steel blade. 'I could cut you into little pieces.' He skims the tip of the blade down the inside of her thigh, not deep enough to draw blood, but to raise a thin red line. 'And then I could throw the pieces to the sharks.'

"She's trembling so hard her teeth begin to chatter. He covers her mouth with his hand. His penis swells as her eyes widen, huge and white with terror. He presses his palm hard against her lips, swallowing her scream as he slams the gleaming steel blade into the floor between her legs. Then he yanks down his zipper."

Hell. It was bad enough that Sissy Smith could have been raped and murdered. There was no way Joe's conscience would let him stand by and allow Laurel to suffer the same horror in her mind.

"Okay, that's it," he muttered. This had gone far enough.

He crouched beside Laurel, took hold of her trembling shoulders and shook her. Once. Twice. "It's okay." A third time. His voice was harsh and strained in the stillness of the room. "Look at me." He caught her chin in his fingers and forced her unseeing gaze to his. "It's me, dammit. Gannon."

Laurel stared up at him, her eyes a deep and fathomless green.

Finally, just when he was considering calling for a doctor, she said, "Gannon?"

"Yeah." He blew out a relieved breath. "Where the fuck did you go?"

"Nowhere." She glanced around, blinking as she struggled to get her bearings. "I was here, but not in this time."

"I'm trying to go along with the program here, sugar. But time travel's stretching my belief system."

"Mine, too." She blinked again. "But I was here," she insisted. "It must have been when she was here."

"Who? Not your friend? Chloe Hollister?"

"No. Not Chloe, thank God." She dragged both hands down her pale-as-glass face. "That woman at the morgue. Sissy whoever."

She was trembling like a willow in a hurricane. The woman who'd confronted a uniformed police officer back at the station had vanished. In her place was a frail, shaky wraith.

"I'm okay," she insisted, sounding just the opposite.

"Yeah, and I'm Johnny Depp."

Since the only thing he and that megabucks movie star had in common was a Y chromosome, Joe knew she still hadn't come entirely back to the land of the living when she neither smiled or challenged that statement. No longer boneless, she was now sitting stiffly on the edge of the couch. Joe had the feeling that if he so much as said *boo*, she'd take off flying out of the room.

"Why don't I get you some water."

She didn't answer. Just sat there, spooking the hell out of him, staring out the French doors. He got a glass from the bar and went into the bathroom.

He was only gone a second, but, dammit, when he came out, she was gone!

22

Annoyance changed to icy fear when Joe viewed Laurel standing out on the balcony. That very same balcony Sissy Smith might or might not have been thrown from.

He put the glass down on the marble coffee table, crossed the room, and gingerly, carefully, walked out onto the balcony.

"Hey," he said in the same calm, low voice he'd once used in his patrol days to talk a would-be jumper off the bridge, "why don't you come on back in?"

The sky had opened up, the downpour driving all the merrymakers indoors. The only sound was the hiss of wet pavement beneath the tires of the cars on the road below, and the drumming of the rain on the blue canvas awning above the balcony.

"She was trying to get away from him," Laurel said in a flat, emotionless voice. "When he drove that knife into the floor between her legs, the adrenaline rush from the fear gave her the strength to grab the champagne bottle and hit him on the head.

"She tried to run for the door, but even with the blood

streaming over his eye, he blocked her way. So she spun around and ran out here. Which was, of course, her final fatal mistake. But her mind was all fuzzy from whatever drug he'd given her. And possibly from having been hit so hard herself."

Laurel lifted a trembling hand to her own forehead. Sighed. Went silent.

One of the first things a good cop learned in the police academy was not to jump in at the first pause in conversation when questioning a suspect or witness. Joe was a good cop; he'd never run across anyone he couldn't wait out.

So he let the silence linger between them, even as he inched forward, prepared to lunge in case she decided to surprise him by reenacting the rest of what he'd suspected from the beginning was a murder scene, right up to its gory conclusion.

"She thought she could fly away." Laurel shook her bright head. She closed her eyes and although she seemed to be coming out of whatever trance she'd been in, she began to tremble again. "She'd fought so many times before and he'd always won, because he was stronger. Crueler. She knew she couldn't win, so this time she chose flight over fight. So she could finally be free of him."

She opened her eyes again; her fingers curled around the lacy wrought-iron railing as she stared down into the cobblestone courtyard. "I guess she finally is. Free."

Joe thought death was one helluva way to gain freedom. Had the woman come to the cops before? Had anyone taken the time to really listen? The idea that she might not have had anyone she'd felt she could tell her ugly truth to was damn depressing.

"She didn't scream. If she had, perhaps someone would have noticed. Perhaps he wouldn't have been able to get away without being seen. But she was silent, which gave him just enough time to wipe his glass clean, put the champagne bottle back on the table, and escape."

"Let's get you back inside." Joe slowly uncurled her hands from the railing, one cold, slender finger at a time. "There's nothing you can do for her now."

"He didn't throw her over the railing. But he's responsible for her death." She'd wrapped her arms around herself. "No one has the right to treat another person so horribly."

"I'll get him." Joe made the oath not just to Laurel Stewart, but to himself. And to Sissy Smith, or whoever was lying dead on that slab in the morgue. "He won't get away with it."

"Good," she said simply.

She exhaled a deep, weary sigh as her gaze drifted out over the foggy harbor.

"How long has it been since you had anything to eat?" he asked.

"I don't know." Neither did she seem to care. "I had a carton of yogurt for breakfast, why?"

"Because I need some dinner and I figured you could keep me company."

"You're just trying to get me out of here."

"Would you rather stay?"

Dazed, she looked around. Then shivered. "No."

"Okay, then. That's settled." Not that she'd had any

real choice. She couldn't have looked any paler if Dracula had drained all the blood out of her body and if she hadn't agreed to leave, Joe would just have flung her over his shoulder and carried her out of the room. "I'm hungry enough to eat a moose and you're looking as if a strong gust of wind would blow you away."

She considered his words. "I suppose I could eat something."

"Good." He ushered her back across the room to the door.

"I don't usually take my suitcase to dinner," she said when he picked it up.

"I'll bet you don't usually stay in hotel rooms that creep you out, either."

"No." She glanced around, shivered. "Can't you feel it? The evil he left behind?"

"No." Joe was vastly glad to be spared that little insight.

He closed the door behind them, unable to ignore the feeling that he was locking some malevolent force inside. "It's obvious you can't stay here. Not if you want to get any sleep."

"I'll be fine." She didn't sound all that sure. "It wasn't real."

"Maybe it was, maybe it wasn't," he said. "But the way I figure it, you've got two choices—either I stay here with you, just in case you go into some sort of woo-woo trance and wander out onto that balcony again—"

"I think this is where I point out that *woo-woo* is not exactly complimentary." She might look as fragile as glass, but that stubbornness that he'd already seen went deep into her bones was beginning to kick in again.

"Excuse me. My point was that you shouldn't be left alone in case you suddenly fall into some sort of psychic trance." He lifted a brow. "Is that better?"

"A bit."

"Good. My second suggestion—and the one I intend to push for—is that we find you another place to spend the night."

"That manager—Tiffany—said all the hotels are full."

"We'll think of something." He figured he'd have better luck pitching his idea once he'd gotten some comfort food into her. "After we eat."

Afraid to leave her alone, Joe tipped the doorman ten bucks to retrieve his car from the parking lot.

He decided she must really be out of it when she didn't complain about his driving as he peeled out of the parking lot. Rather, she leaned her head against the back of the passenger seat and closed her eyes.

"It must be hard," he said.

Her eyes blinked open and she slanted him a brief, sideways glance. "What?"

"Being psychic."

"I wouldn't know. Because I'm not."

"If that was an act, sugar, you ought to give up the journalism business and set up one of those 1-900-Madame-Laurel-Knows-All hotlines."

"It wasn't an act." She turned, pretending interest in the spotlighted sails of the *Queen Anne's Revenge*. "Since I've never experienced anything like that before, I don't know what, exactly, it was."

"You saw what happened."

"No." She shook her head, still a little sluggish, but thoughtful. "It was more sensing. Experiencing what she was feeling."

She paused again.

Three sweeps of the windshield wipers later, Joe was still waiting.

"My aunt Zelda's psychic," she eventually said. "There've been lots of times in my life that she's known what's about to happen. Not the details, necessarily, but she gets these feelings. And signs. But this wasn't like that. I only knew what was happening as your victim saw it. I only sensed her thoughts."

"Did you see her assailant?"

He felt a little guilty turning the cop on after the emotional hit she'd taken, but just in case she was on the level, he wasn't about to turn down an opportunity to close a case.

"No. Yes." She shook her head. "Not really. I just had a sense of him. Of what he was thinking." She shuddered. "And feeling." She reached into her purse and pulled out the cigarettes, then, on second thought, paused. "I suppose it's against the law to smoke in a cop car."

"Probably is." He leaned forward and punched in the dashboard cigarette lighter. "But if there isn't a law against murder cops having to drive around in rattletraps with cracked vinyl seats, there should be, so don't let that stop you."

"Thanks." The lighter popped out. The red tip glowed as she lit the cigarette with hands that weren't nearly as steady as they should have been, then cracked the passenger window. The air smelled of rain, oil from the ships docked in the harbor, salt, and faraway places.

She blew out a stream of smoke, then turned in her seat and studied him. Both her eyes and her expression were grave. "I'll bet you don't believe in precognition, or psychics."

"Better not wager the family farm on that one, sweetheart. Because you'd be wrong. Whenever we have a high-profile case, a lot of charlatan spoon-benders come crawling out of the woodwork. But I had a case a few years ago, right after I transferred to Homicide, where I knew damn well that this scion of a cotton fortune had killed his wife, but we couldn't find her body. Then, out of the blue, this woman called us from Savannah saying she'd sensed things a lot like you just did."

The logical part of him had considered her just another wacko headline-grabber, but following a cop's hunch that had served him well and kept him alive during all those years working vice, he'd driven to Georgia.

"She didn't look much like a psychic—"

"Meaning she wasn't wearing flowing robes, a turban, and Gypsy hoop earrings," Laurel murmured. She was definitely getting her spunk back. "You realize that you are, once again, skimming that profiling line, Detective."

"Okay, so I was expecting the fortune-teller lady from the carnival." He pulled around a beer truck. "Stephanie Long, that was her name, looked like a soccer mom. Actually, she *was* a soccer mom. She was also right on the money."

"You found the body?"

"In the swamp about fifty miles from here. The victim's husband's currently doing life plus ten."

"Maybe you should call your soccer mom about Sissy Smith."

"Why should I do that," he asked mildly, "when I've got you?"

23

The rain that had begun while they were in the hotel room was letting up. The wipers slowed. And still she didn't answer right away.

"That was an anomaly." Laurel frowned, scooped the toll bridge change from the ashtray, and jabbed out the cigarette. "I haven't had much sleep the last few days. It was undoubtedly an overly active imagination talking."

"Could be," he allowed as he pulled into the cobble-stone parking lot of the gray-stone building flying the orange, white, and green flag of Ireland next to the Stars and Stripes. "But if that's the case, your imagination hit on one thing no one but a handful of investigating cops know."

"What's that?" She didn't sound real happy to hear that little bulletin.

"There was an open champagne bottle on the coffee table. But only one glass. With her fingerprints." Which he'd sent in to IAFIS, but the FBI was occupied with terrorism these days and hadn't yet gotten back to him on whether Sissy Smith's prints were in the national data-bank.

"There, see? I was wrong." She sounded relieved about that. "A single glass suggests she was drinking alone."

"Champagne is for celebrating." He cut the engine. "Seems odd to break out the bubbly when you're depressed."

"Alcohol's still alcohol, whatever you call it. I went through a bottle of French Chardonnay the day I lost my job." She frowned at the memory. "If there was a man drinking in the room with her, why wouldn't he wipe off both glasses?"

"He might have wanted to wash out any drug particles left in the bottom of the glass. Plus, leaving one glass out tends to point more toward solitary drinking, which in turn could make cops more likely to call the death a suicide."

"I suppose so." She unfastened her seat belt. "Do you intend to close it out as a suicide?"

"That depends partly on tomorrow's autopsy report. But no, I don't feel comfortable with it."

He didn't think that gleam in her eyes was solely a reflection from the dome light when he opened the driver's door.

"It seems to me we've got ourselves a quid pro quo situation here, Gannon."

"Oh?" He could see it coming, like a runaway oil tanker headed straight toward him.

"I gave you a clue—"

"A *possible* clue," he pointed out. "Like you said, neither of us knows if you've suddenly turned psychic."

"You have more of a case than you did two hours ago. You know your body isn't Chloe Hollister, and you have reason to believe that a man, if he didn't actually cause her death, was in that hotel room with her right before she took a header off that balcony. Seems only fair that you do some detecting for me in return for my good citizen's assistance."

"I took your missing person's report," he reminded her.

"Yeah, a BOLO." She opened the passenger door, forestalling him from going around the Crown Vic's massive hood and opening it for her. "Which, with a five dollar bill, will get you a cup of designer coffee."

They dashed through the rain and though he'd shortened his stride, just a little, Joe was still surprised how fast she ran on those needle heels.

"Did you happen to see that case board on the wall in the precinct office?" he asked as he pulled open the heavy oak door with a sign stating, Open when we're here, closed when we're gone.

"The big dry-erase board with all those names written in magic marker?"

"That's the one." The place, decorated with smaller Irish flags than the one flying out front and framed photographs of green hills, sparkling lakes, and castle ruins, was packed with pirates and wenches. Joe returned the wave of the dark-haired Irishman building pints behind the horseshoe-shaped bar and with a hand on her back, began lightly guiding her to a table that was just emptying up in the far corner of the room. "Those red names represent open cases."

"Even if I hadn't been a cop reporter, I'd know that. Along with everyone who ever watched *Homicide*."

"Well, then, it might occur to you that I already have my hands full."

"One more case isn't going to make that much of a difference in the whole scheme of things," she pointed out as she climbed up on the stool. He decided she really did know something about cops when she left the stool against the wall for Joe, letting him see the entire bar. "Besides, you've got a partner."

"I know. She was the strawberry-blond detective one desk over back at the station. The one talking on the phone. Her name is Cait Cavanaugh."

"Oh." She frowned at that. "I'd forgotten detectives travel in pairs, like nuns."

"Touché. You're obviously feeling better than you were back in that hotel room."

"You ever been to a county fair, Gannon?"

"Sure. Mama used to sweep the blue ribbons in cakes and pies 'most every year and there were more than a few times her huckleberry pie won best overall in the baking category."

The brash, city girl edge that had returned to her eyes eased up a bit. "That's nice," she said, sounding as if she meant it. Then, as if afraid of being thought soft, she shook it off like a dog shaking off water after a bath. "The point is that I'm like one of those blow-up clown balloons with the big feet you could score throwing rings around milk bottles."

"I stayed away from those. They tended to be rigged. I did better shooting mechanical ducks with the air rifles."

She rolled her eyes. "Are you always so literal?"

"I don't know." He considered the idea.

"Never mind." Her impatience was back, shimmering around her like a force field. As she crossed her legs with a frustrated swish, he wondered if she spent her entire life at warp speed, which in turn made him wonder if she'd be just as quick and efficient in bed. "My point was that I may get knocked down from time to time, but I always pop back up."

"Sorta like Glenn Close in *Fatal Attraction*."

Joe had to give Laurel credit for coming back from whatever had happened in the hotel room. She was a good actress, but he'd gotten damn good at reading people over the years—his job, and often his life depended on it—and he sensed Laurel Stewart was trying to backpedal away from whatever had happened up there in suite 1033.

She huffed out a breath, but he thought he saw a reluctant smile tug at the corners of those full lips. "Okay, so now we're even for the nun crack. And, for the record, unlike that movie bunny-assassin, I don't date married men, which brings me back to my main reason for being here in your charming little city in the first place."

"Chloe Hollister."

Light from the heavy wood and wrought-iron chandelier overhead flashed like sparks in her hair when she nodded. "Chloe has a great many good points. Her choice in men is not one of them."

"Sounds like something she might share with Sissy Smith," he said.

"I don't want to talk about that. Not now." She had herself under control again.

"I can understand that. We'll have ourselves some dinner, a little conversation. Get you some sleep, since you look like you've been, as my uncle Stew, who worked at a Florida racetrack used to say, rode hard and put away wet. But we *are* going to have to discuss it. Even if he didn't physically throw Sissy Smith off that balcony, that second guy in the room with her was responsible for her death. You wouldn't want that to happen to any other women."

"Damn it, Gannon, of course I wouldn't. But if you're counting on me to pull a bit of eye of newt and toe of frog out of my witch's bag and spin some bubble, bubble, toil and trouble voodoo hooey to solve your hotel murder, you've definitely got the wrong woman."

The conversation briefly came to a stop when Brendan O'Neill, owner of The Black Swan, came over to their table to take their order. A Guinness for Joe, who decided what the hell, he wasn't technically on duty, a glass of wine for Laurel, and a double order of fish and chips. Joe, who'd dated too many women who refused to let anything more substantial than lettuce past their glossy lips, found her willingness to eat pub grub one more thing they had in common.

Not that he was keeping score.

The hell he wasn't.

24

Two little girls wearing green dresses and ribbons in their hair were step dancing to the tune of a penny whistle on a postage-stamp-size dance floor. The TV over the bar was tuned to a rugby game; the Kilkenny Cats were giving the Limerick Shannonsiders a shellacking.

She followed his glance up at the screen where a fistfight had broken out. "Rugby's got to be the toughest team sport going."

Surprised such a classy, feminine woman could recognize a scrum, he wondered how much else about sports she knew. "I don't suppose you like football," he said.

"I just happen to have an autographed McNair photo." She leaned her elbow on the table and rested her chin in her palm. "The *Post* has season tickets to the Redskins, but in my heart, I'll always be a Titans fan. Why?"

"Just wondering. You root for the wrong team, but we can deal with that," he stated. He'd gotten hooked on the Chargers back when he was a kid and Dan Fouts, Kellen Winslow, and Charlie Joiner were revolutionizing the passing game with their "Air Coryell" offense.

"How about baseball?"

"Yankees all the way."

He grimaced. "Diamondbacks."

She surprised him again by considering that. "They took a hit in their rotation when they lost Shilling to Boston, so Webb's got some large shoes to fill. But he did have the best ERA in the National League last season. And sixth best in the Majors." She smiled. "But of course, we have A-Rod."

"And the best team money can buy."

"You get what you pay for."

"You must've covered sports for a while."

"In Nashville. Next to politics, it was my favorite beat."

"Okay, that does it. You like greasy food and sports, and since I'm a magnanimous guy, I'm willing to overlook the fact that you've gone over to the dark side by rooting for baseball's Evil Empire."

"Thank you," she said sweetly.

"You're welcome. So, how about marrying me?"

"Sorry. I'm allergic to matrimony." She smiled up at Brendan, who'd arrived with their drinks. The bartender returned the smile with one that, though the Irishman wasn't one to spread tales, Joe suspected had charmed more than his share of Somersett females. He placed the wine and beer on the table with a bowl of cocktail nuts, then, with a knowing look at Joe, left them alone again.

"My career takes a lot of time and energy," she picked up her answer again. "I suppose it's selfish, but I like being able to come and go as I please, do what I please, without having to feel guilty about screwing up a relationship."

"There's more to life than work." And hadn't he learned that the hard way?

"You're telling that to a person who's just joined the ranks of the unemployed," she reminded him. "But this is only a temporary setback, and one I intend to straighten out once we find Chloe. Besides, while I'm a damn good reporter, I know my limitations. I'm not the type of woman who falls in love."

"And what kind is that?"

"Women like my sisters, who are willing to give their hearts away for all time." Her eyes softened again when she mentioned her sisters, and while she might not be the type of woman who fell in love, it was more than a little apparent that she loved Lily and Lark Stewart. "There's a reason they call it holy wed*lock*. Even thinking about getting shackled to another person for the rest of my life makes me break out in hives." Laurel took a sip of the ruby Merlot, then eyed him over the top of her glass. "All over."

Heat spread, like slow-flowing lava through his veins. Joe took a swallow of the foam-topped Guinness to cool it. "You did that on purpose."

"Did what?" she asked with the same faked innocence Joe had heard at least a thousand times before.

Was I speeding, Officer? . . . But, Officer, someone hypnotized me into stealing those cashmere sweaters from Nordstrom . . . I have no idea what that human head is doing in my freezer, Detective.

"Tossed in that feminine sweetener to your quid pro quo offer."

"Are you suggesting I'd trade sex for your cooperation?"

He shrugged. "It's been known to happen."

She took a deep breath, then leaned back and gave him a long, pointed look as she swirled her wine in her glass. "But you've never worked that way."

"No."

"I didn't think so. Let's lay our cards on the table, Gannon. It can't have escaped your attention that other than an appalling lack of fashion sense, you're an attractive man."

"Thanks," he said dryly.

"Despite recent attempts to make it seem otherwise, I deal in facts. Also in your favor is the fact that some women might find that Good Old Boy southern drawl appealing."

"But not you?"

Her shoulders lifted beneath that silk blouse that clung in all the right places. "If I were down here to cut loose for Buccaneer Days and play pirate-wench, sure, I might consider a bit of no-strings slap and tickle. But that's not what I'm here for, so if you've got any ideas along those lines, you might as well forget them."

"Here's a suggestion, sugar. If you don't want a guy to get ideas, you shouldn't invite him to imagine your naked body. All over," he reminded her.

"That was a mistake," she allowed. She picked up her wine, studied it thoughtfully, then put it back down again without drinking. "I've had a stressful couple days, which sure as hell wasn't made any better by our little visit to suite 1033, and I know enough not to drink wine on an empty stomach."

On cue, Brendan O'Neill delivered two oversize platters of fish and chips.

She ignored the little bottle of vinegar and poured a liberal amount of catsup onto the heavy white plate and dipped one of the golden French fries into it.

"The only idea I want you to get is to help me make Noble Aiken tell us what he's done with Chloe. There's not going to be any sex stuff going on."

"How about this? I'll pretend I'm not attracted to you. And you do the same."

She stabbed a piece of heavily battered fish. "What makes you think I'm pretending?"

"Bull's-eye, Annie Oakley." He rubbed a hand over his heart. "You do realize that it's going to be a little hard for me to solve your so-called missing-person case while I'm bleeding to death here."

"It's not so-called. And you'll survive. Now, getting back to Aiken—"

"It also strains credulity to believe the vice president of the United States would have anything to do with a missing-person case."

She pointed her fork at him. "Harder to believe he could get elected with a mistress young enough to be his daughter."

"I sure hope you don't make these huge leaps of logic when you're reporting." He held up a hand and ticked off the flaws in her reasoning on his fingers. "Number one, unless you're holding back evidence, you've no proof that your friend is having an affair with anyone. Let alone the vice president."

Laurel decided that keeping her suspicions about Chloe's pregnancy to herself were not exactly holding back evidence. After all, she didn't really know Lieutenant Joe Gannon yet; didn't know whether or not she could trust him.

"I've lived with her for seven years. I know her pattern. Hell, so does anyone who knows her. Even Bishop Cary knows her personal life swings from messy to disastrous," she reminded him. "Besides, women sense these things."

Even without that spooky episode in the hotel room, Joe had been married, and partnered with Cait long enough not to discount female intuition.

"Number two," he ticked off his second problem with her accusation, "even if we assume, for argument's sake—though there's still a reasonable doubt—that you're right about the affair, there's no way of knowing Aiken's the guy."

"If he isn't, why did she leap to defend him?"

"Maybe because she respects him and you can come on a little strong at times?" Like a damn pit bull, Joe thought, but had the sense not to say it.

"Hmmph." She bit into another chip and chewed that one over. "Once you question him, we'll have a better handle on their involvement."

"What's this *we, kemosabe?*"

She waved off his objection. "Oh, don't play hard to get. We both know that you're going to take my case."

He didn't have a problem with her brassy confidence, having plenty of his own. He pulled a pen out of his pocket and held it out to her along with the cocktail napkin that had been beneath his beer.

"Write this down," he instructed. "I'm still not sure I believe you *have* a case. And what makes you think I'd take it even if you did?"

"Because if she isn't involved with Noble Aiken, the undeniable fact is that Chloe Hollister, who grew up teething on Amy Vanderbilt and whose behavior could make Miss Manners look like a punk rocker at a rave concert, has blown off her responsibility and disappeared from the face of the planet. Now that, Detective, is a puzzle. And if you didn't get off on solving puzzles, you wouldn't be a murder cop."

"Good try. Except there's one little piece of information you don't know that might screw up your pithy analysis."

Her fork paused on its way to her mouth. "And that is?"

"What if you've hooked up with a burned-out cop who just wants to slide through the next couple weeks until he gets his twenty years and leaves with his pension?"

Her grass-green eyes nailed his. "Are you burned out?"

"Maybe." He said aloud what he hadn't even admitted to himself.

"Then deal with it." That said, she dug back into the mountain of fried food.

Like she was dealing with the loss of her job, what she believed to be the disappearance of her friend, and that weird channeling she'd been doing earlier, he considered as they ate for a while in oddly companionable silence.

"Do you eat like this all the time?" The woman had the body of a ballerina and the appetite of a linebacker.

She glanced down at her empty plate. "On the days I'm not out Washington power-lunching trying to worm secrets out of people, I tend to grab a candy bar or fast food on the run."

"I'm amazed you don't weigh a ton."

"I've got the metabolism of the Energizer bunny. Nothing ever seems to stick. Which, while a good thing in my thirties, drove me to tears in my teens, since high school boys tend to ignore brains for tits and ass."

"*Some* high school boys." He imagined the coltish girl she must have been at seventeen, all penny-bright hair, huge green eyes, and those mile-long wraparound legs. "Sounds like you've got some idiots up in those mountains."

"I was too tall, too skinny, and had a mouthful of railroad-track braces. I also had one sister who was, and still is, one of the most beautiful females on earth, and another who was pretty, unrelentingly chirpy, and queen of the Highland Falls Highlander's yell squad."

Joe knew he was getting to the slippery edge of a dangerous cliff when just the idea of this woman wearing one of those short, flirty little pleated cheerleader skirts and waving pom-poms made him hard.

"You could have been a cheerleader if you wanted to be."

She stared at him, then burst into a rich, throaty laugh that drew definitely interested looks from a trio of pirates playing darts, which in turn caused an uncharacteristic jealousy to twist inside him.

"Are you up for dessert?"

She shook her head. "I think I'd just like to find someplace to crash."

"We can do that." He stood up. "Let's go."

"You're forgetting the check."

"I run a tab and settle up with O'Neill once a month."

"Oh." He knew exhaustion was finally setting in when she didn't question that statement. "Where are we going?"

"See that door?" He gestured toward the heavy wooden door he knew to be original to the building. "There are two lofts upstairs. One belongs to O'Neill—"

"Let me guess. The other belongs to you."

"Got it on the first try." He put his hand on her back, but she didn't budge.

"I'm not sleeping with you, Detective."

"If rolling around on some hot sheets is what I had in mind, I doubt we'd spend much time sleeping. But you don't have to worry, sweetheart. Because you look dead on your feet and the prospect of having a woman start snoring while I'm making love to her is definitely less than appealing."

"I don't snore," she grumbled. "And I don't sleep with men I've just met."

"Newsflash, buttercup. Not every man you meet wants to get into your lace panties."

"My name is Laurel. Not *sugar*, not *sweetheart*, and definitely not *buttercup*. *Laurel*. I'd appreciate you remembering that. And what makes you think they're lace?"

"We detectives get paid for deductive reasoning. You're wearing lace beneath that silk blouse—"

Her hand flew to her breast. "You copped a look at my bra?"

"Hey, you practically flashed me back at the station."

The way she was looking at him, like he was some Peeping Tom pervert, had him almost forgetting how pale and needy she'd been back in that hotel room.

"I did not," she muttered.

"That's okay." He shrugged. "I'm a twenty-first-century man. Sexually aggressive females don't wound my masculine ego."

"It'd take a Bradley tank to make a damn dent," she muttered.

"My place has two bedrooms," he said, steering the conversation back on track as he pulled his keys from the front pocket of his jeans. "Well, I guess what you'd call the master bedroom is part of one big room, but there's a smaller one I slept in while I was doing renovations. I'll crash on the couch in there and you can take my bed."

"Are all the cops in Somersett this accommodating?" she asked as she stepped into the cargo elevator.

"No." He grinned. "You just got lucky."

Lucky. There were a lot of words Laurel could use to describe her last few days, but that certainly wasn't one of them.

25

Laurel knew that a lot of women would consider spending the night with a man they'd just met to be risky. Even dangerous. But a lot of women hadn't camped out with Doctors Without Borders in Afghanistan. Or been embedded on an aircraft carrier during the Shock and Awe campaign of the Iraqi war.

The elevator cranked its way up to the second floor, opening to reveal two doors. Joe opened the left. The loft-like floor plan reminded her of her own space on Capitol Hill. The ceiling towered over them, at least twenty, maybe thirty feet high, exposing dark beams. The furniture was sturdy and leather, the kind a man would feel free to put his feet up on.

She paused in front of a huge empty tank filled with water and some sad-looking plants. "What happened to the fish?"

"I got busy and they died. It's—"

"Buccaneer Days." Laurel assumed the same neglect had caused the pitifully bare ficus tree by the huge window to have dropped all its leaves. Remembering her poor dead African violet, she could identify with a career that killed plants.

During the day she imagined the loft would be flooded with sunlight, but right now all she could see were the lights of the bridge, looking like blurred stars through the rain-streaked wall of glass.

Ever since her mother had died the winter of her fifth year, Laurel had learned to compartmentalize, locking negative experiences away into little boxes in the back of her mind where she could deal with them later, when she was ready. Occasionally, if an event was too painful, she'd force herself to ignore it entirely. Which was what she'd been attempting to do with that frightening time in the hotel room when it had felt as if she'd been inside Sissy's skin and mind, looking at events through the other woman's eyes.

Then, even more terrifying, for that fleeting moment, slipping into Sissy's murderer's thoughts, as well.

The hocus-pocus stuff was what her aunt did. Laurel was the practical, down-to-earth person in her family. She was a sensible woman. A reporter who dealt in facts, who believed in *five* senses, not six. If she couldn't see it, smell it, touch it, taste it, or hear it, it didn't exist. At least not in her world.

Sarcasm had always been one of her most powerful weapons, something she'd pull out when she was feeling her most vulnerable. She'd developed the brassy, wise-cracking style of a 1940s movie heroine, like Katharine Hepburn, or Rosalind Russell, whose ace-reporter character, Hildy Johnson, from *His Girl Friday*, was Laurel's personal role model.

She'd always been proud of her independence, secure in her ability to survive whatever storms came her way. But something had happened tonight. Something that had left her feeling stripped naked, then turned inside out.

Having had plenty of practice over the years, she'd managed, with considerable effort, during the drive to the pub, to slip back into character. Admittedly she'd gone too far when she'd made the mistake of coming on too strong to Gannon, but her emotions had been jumping all over the place, like steel balls in the pinball machine she'd seen in the corner of the pub, and given the choice, behaving a little sexually over-the-top was a helluva lot better than falling apart in public. Now that facade was threatening to crack.

"You sure you're okay?"

He was standing close behind her. Too close.

"Of course." Intent on moving away, she spun around fast enough to risk whiplash.

He took hold of her shoulders. "You don't look okay."

The building pressure in her chest was painful. She wanted to lock those mumbo-jumbo moments back at the hotel in a mental box and bury the key somewhere no one could ever find them. "You know what they say about appearances being deceiving."

"And sometimes they're not." His gaze roamed over her face. "You were starting to get some of your color back in the pub." His knuckles skimmed down her cheek. Around her jaw. "But now you're looking like a ghost again."

"She just wanted someone to love," she murmured. "Wanted to be loved in return." It might not be Laurel's fantasy, but it had been Sissy's. "She shouldn't have died for it."

"No." His grave expression turned reflective.

"What now?"

"Just a minute," he said absently.

He cupped her chin in his fingers. Moved a little closer.

He lowered his head until his lips were a whisper from hers.

You remember how to breathe, she told herself as she watched the gleam rise in his eyes. *So, why aren't you doing it?*

His mouth was softer than it looked as it brushed against hers, retreated, then returned to brush again. He took his time, tempting, tasting—then, as he took the kiss deeper, savoring.

Laurel's blood was humming when he lifted his head again. "Much better," he decided.

Shaken that one kiss—and he hadn't even used his hands!—could nearly cause her bones to melt, she took a step back. "What was that for?"

"You were looking a bit lost." His benevolent smile was warm with sympathy. "I thought maybe it'd make you feel better."

"Lost? You thought I was looking lost?" Overlooking the fact he was right, she shoved her hand against his broad chest. "That was a pity kiss?"

He didn't budge. She might as well have been trying to move Mount Rushmore. Ignoring her rising temper, he skimmed a finger along the top bow of her still tingling lips. "Well, pity's a bit strong—"

"Don't deny it!" Could she feel any more stupid? "You were feeling sorry for me."

"Hell, yes." He moved his shoulders. "You've had a rough couple days and a miserable experience in that hotel room. I figured it was the least I could do."

"The least you could do?"

"Hey, it seemed like a good idea at the time. And you seemed to enjoy it well enough."

There was no point in trying to deny that. "You said you didn't have any ulterior motives in inviting me to stay here tonight."

"I don't have a single ulterior motive," he said. "So why don't I apologize for misreading the situation, restate my promise to keep my hands off you, and we'll move on."

"All right." It was, after all, the reasonable thing to do. "And I may have overreacted." It was not often Laurel apologized. But she wasn't about to let him claim the high road all to himself.

"You've had a long day," he said mildly. "The bathroom's over there." He pointed across the loft. "There's a new toothbrush in the cabinet."

"Handy." Talk about being prepared. "I'll bet you were a Boy Scout."

"You'd lose," she heard him say just before she shut the bathroom door behind her.

Leaning against the pedestal sink, she washed her face and brushed her teeth. When she came out, her suitcase was sitting on a bed covered in midnight blue sheets and Gannon was nowhere to be seen.

Apparently he was going to keep his word and leave her alone.

As she carefully folded her blouse and slacks and pulled a sea-green satin nightshirt over her head, Laurel almost managed to convince herself that she was glad about that.

"So," Cait said when Joe showed up at the precinct house the next morning, "did you get an identity on our Jane Doe?"

"Not yet."

"Then that redhead you left with yesterday—the one who looked as if she stepped out of *Vogue*—didn't know anything?"

"Nope."

"Too bad."

"Yeah." Joe pried the lid off the brown cardboard cup of coffee he'd overpaid for across the street. "Maybe the autopsy'll give a clue."

"Clues are good," Cait said with a nod.

The mass of hair she'd tied back with a clip at the nape of her neck was red, but more of a strawberry, shades lighter than that of the woman he'd left sprawled on her stomach in his bed, dead to the world. Laurel's sheet had slid down a bit, revealing a nightshirt the color of sea foam, trimmed in lace. Wondering if her skin would taste as smooth as that pale-green satin, he took a swallow of too hot coffee and reined in his galloping hormones.

"We caught a new case right before you came in," Cait informed him. "Looks fairly open and shut. According to the uniform who called it in, a couple of neighbors were arguing over a Great Pyrenees that had barked all night.

Things got heated, the dog kept woofing, and according to witnesses at the scene, the guy who apparently hadn't had a decent night's sleep in two years, retrieved a .44 Magnum out of his truck and decided to play Dirty Harry. It was not the dog owner's lucky day. Since you're due at the morgue, I figured I'd take Donahue."

"The new guy?" Joe glanced over at the detective who'd transferred from robbery/arson last week. He was busily sorting through files, trying to pretend he wasn't watching them and failing so badly Joe figured it was a good thing the kid hadn't gotten transferred to vice or narcotics, since he seemed to have zero undercover talent.

"He's no rookie," Cait said, a little too defensively, Joe thought. "He's been a cop for five years, and made detective two years ago. Plus, he happens to have set a squad record for closing cases."

"Of course the fact that he looks like one of those guys on the cover of those paperbacks you read on lunch breaks didn't come into play when you were choosing between him and Manning."

"Been there, done that." She winced a bit at the memory of that one-night stand. "And you're a fine one to talk."

Joe lifted a brow.

"Like you were searching for clues when you were looking down that redhead's blouse?"

"Can't fool you."

"Hell, no. I'm a detective. A regular Christine Cagney." She pulled her Glock out of the desk drawer and dropped it into her purse. Across the bull pen the new guy leaped up like someone had set fire to his chair. "Let me know if you get a line on our jumper."

The kid might have been a hotshot in his old squad, but if he'd had a tail, he'd be happily wagging it as he and Cait left the squad room. Joe dragged a hand down his face and felt a million years old.

Unfortunately, since the bad guys didn't often stroll into the police department to turn themselves in, crimes didn't get solved drinking coffee, so he was going to have to head over to the hospital.

The truth was that cops seldom solved cases with clues and brilliant detective work. More often than not, the perpetrator was turned in by family members, friends, or a rival. What clues and a strong, documented investigation did was get the perp convicted.

Which was something, Joe considered as he was forced to creep down Harbor View with the rest of the rush hour traffic.

Drew's eyes narrowed as he took in Joe's haggard appearance. "You look even worse than you did yesterday. When was the last time you got a night's sleep?"

"Sleep," Joe said as the medical examiner's assistant—a huge African American who'd played offensive linebacker for the University of South Carolina, only to have his pro career taken away with a brutal knee injury in the Orange Bowl—transferred Sissy from the cooler onto the metal autopsy table. The perforations in the top tier of the table allowed fluids to drain; the scale, which resembled the ones in the vegetable section of the Somersett Piggly Wiggly, was to weigh organs. "I vaguely remember that. Isn't it what you do in a bed that feels real good?"

"That's sex."

Joe remembered that, too. Of course during Buccaneer Days, even if he did get lucky, he probably wouldn't have enough energy to do anything about it.

"Speaking of which, that was one fine-looking female you brought by yesterday. Since she didn't identify our Jane Doe, I take it she's looking for someone else?"

"Yeah." Although he'd been primary on the scene when the body had been taken away, Joe did one more check for evidence in the thick white bag that he might have missed. "Her roommate."

"And here I thought homicide detectives only showed up after the bodies were found," the ME said mildly. "Or did you get transferred to missing persons in the past two days?"

"Logan was being his usual *helpful* self when I showed up at the station yesterday. As much as I would have enjoyed watching her deck him, I decided to save the court the time, trouble, and expense of processing an assault case."

"Speaking as a taxpayer, I'm grateful." Drew's eyes danced knowingly as they met Joe's over the woman's body. "I'll bet that leggy redhead was, as well. 'Man, you ain't lived' "—his baritone broke into the Springsteen lyric—" 'Till you've had your tires rotated by a red-headed woman.' "

"It's not like that." Joe frowned, unreasonably irritated by his longtime friend's lusty tone. They had, after all, grown up sharing locker room talk together, first in high school gym class, then later, after Drew had come back to town from Yankeeland, eating pizza, and downing suds while watching ESPN.

"It's just as well. Given the money thing."

"What money thing?"

"She's obviously got dough. You're a civil servant with a killer mortgage. Some guys might be intimidated by a woman with more money than them."

"I'm not some guys." O'Neill's pub was drawing a standing room only crowd every night. And not just tourists, but locals. Joe had sold the Irishman a share of the building six months ago, cutting his monthly payments nearly in half. "Besides, how do you know she's got bucks?"

He thought about the photographs he'd seen of the huge stone castle the Stewart sisters had grown up in. "Her father's some big shot artist and her aunt writes mystery novels, but Laurel Stewart's a reporter, and I don't think journalism pays that well."

"Those were Jimmy Choo shoes, son. The belt was Chanel, and I'll bet you a month of Krispy Kremes the blouse was a Dolce & Gabbanna."

As much as the money thing didn't bother him, it did point out the vast differences between them, which was another reason why he shouldn't even think about getting involved with Laurel Stewart.

"I've got cases up the wazoo. Can we just get on with it?"

"Sure thing." Drew looked a little surprised at the sharp tone, then got down to business. He ran his fingers over the rose-hued slip. "Nice. You don't find silk this smooth in your average mall-store lingerie department."

Never having wandered into a lingerie department in his life, Joe took his word for that. An image of porcelain-pale arms extending from pale-green satin popped into his mind. He ruthlessly forced it down.

"The fact that she was in the Wingate already suggested the victim had bucks. Or she could have been a call girl with a client who had reasons for preferring the room be booked under her name."

If Laurel's vision, or whatever the hell it was, was true, Sissy wasn't a call girl. But she *had* been having an affair. Something a political candidate, especially one from a conservative state, would want to keep quiet.

"She'd been drinking," Drew said as they both breathed in the familiar sweet scent of ethanol.

"That jibes with the empty champagne bottle at the scene."

That single glass found in the hotel room had been niggling at Joe even before Laurel had suffered that weird trance, or whatever it was, last night. How could a woman down an entire bottle of bubbly, then climb up on a waist-high railing in spindly high heels? Joe's first inclination had been that she was pushed. If Laurel was right, adrenaline, fear, and despair had propelled her right over it.

Either way, he needed to find the guy she'd been running from. He might not be able to prove Murder One, but he damn well would make certain he got locked away where he belonged.

"Great Miss America teeth," Sloan murmured. "Lady had good oral hygiene."

"There'll be dental records somewhere." The Miss

America comment had Joe taking out his notebook to make a note to check out former beauty queens in the area. Which, in the South, was akin to searching out a single grain of sand on one of Somersett's beaches.

"Undoubtedly so."

Sloan removed the brown paper bags from her hands, then ran a file beneath the white moons of her fingernails. The only sound in the hushed chill of the room was the running water washing blood from the lower tier table into the floor drain.

"Manicure looks new," he said. "I'd say that morning, or the day before, at the latest. It looks professionally done."

Joe made another note and wondered how many nail salons there were in the city. However many, they'd all need to be checked. Perhaps, since the new kid hadn't been assigned a partner, he and Cait could make the rounds after they finished up the paperwork on their dog-barking homicide. Although it could get tedious, footwork was a detective's best tool.

"No defensive wounds. No blood, skin, or fibers beneath the nails."

"Of course there aren't. That'd be too easy, if there was a damn piece of DNA evidence."

"Win some, lose some. We've still got a lot to go; you could still get lucky."

Hopefully luckier than Sissy Smith.

"You'll want a tox screen."

"Absolutely." Even if Laurel was off the mark about the guy giving her dope, the champagne could have been drugged. Or Sissy Smith and her boyfriend could have been partying with recreational drugs, things had gone south, and the guy might have panicked and tossed her body off the balcony to stage a suicide.

After taking the weights and measurements, and photographing her clothed, Drew bagged the slip and thong. Then began his study of the naked body. "Don't see many natural blondes."

The pubic curls between the broken pelvis bones were as pale as those on her head. Enough time had passed since her swan dive that her skin had turned pale and waxy. "She could have dyed it."

"Could have, but didn't. This is virgin hair. We're definitely talking Scandinavian descent."

The machine whirred as Sloan's assistant took X-rays of the dead woman's broken bones. It was more a case of which bones weren't broken than which ones were. It would have been worse if she'd landed on the cobblestones instead of the Suburban, but in the end that didn't make any difference. Dead was dead.

The order of the autopsy was from top to bottom. After making a note of C-cup breast implants into the overhead microphone, Sloan held up the jet black hair he'd combed out of the pale white curls. "I do believe you have yourself a piece of evidence, Detective."

"Intercourse doesn't necessarily lead to murder."

"Lucky us." He plucked out a second hair. "Or the world's population would've gone the way of the Shakers." Sloan turned off the lights, then used an ultraviolet light to scan the body, but after finding none of the purplish-white patterns of fluoresced semen, he instructed his assistant to turn the overheads back on.

"I've always wondered if the founders realized the flaw in creating a celibate religion."

Sloan took out his swab kit.

"I guess they figured they'd get recruits."

"Who'd want to join a group that didn't allow sex?"

Since it was a rhetorical question, Joe didn't respond. Neither did he admit that if his current sex life was anything to go by, he could easily fit right in with the Shakers.

Which brought his mind back to Laurel Stewart. If he'd met the reporter any other way, he might have asked her out. Nothing fancy that would set off her anticommitment alarms. Maybe a pizza, then a movie.

Did people still do that on dates? Did people even date at all? Or did they just have a couple drinks and move straight to sex?

Which wouldn't be so bad, especially since his job didn't make for very appetizing dinner conversation.

Joe didn't need a secret decoder ring to know he wasn't the only one who'd felt the sparks last night. Maybe the thing to do was to track down this Chloe Hollister, then he and the reporter could fan the flames a bit before she went back to DC.

The problem with that idea was that there'd always be more cases to solve, more murder books piling up on his desk, more neighbors shooting neighbors, more Sissy Smiths. Laurel Stewart didn't seem like a woman willing to hang around and wait for him to free up some quality time to spend on her. A lot of women liked the idea of being with a cop, but eventually they'd discover they liked the fantasy better than the reality.

Which was one of the advantages of dating someone who worked in the department, someone who knew the pressures and wouldn't give him the silent treatment for a week if he forgot to call and cancel a dinner date. A woman whose world didn't revolve around him.

But Joe didn't like to sleep with cops because it inevitably complicated the job.

Then again, life tended to get complicated when you slept with a woman who wasn't a cop.

Hell. Maine was looking better and better.

26

Laurel awoke to the sound of silence. She lay there for a moment, her head buried in the pillow, listening for any signs of Joe Gannon in the loft.

Nothing.

She glanced over at the alarm clock/radio. "Christ, nine o'clock." She couldn't remember the last time she'd slept so long. Or so deeply.

Feeling a bit logy, but still a lot better than she had when she'd woken with the mother of all hangovers, she was pushing back the sheets when the view outside the window caused her to draw in a sharp breath.

The rain had stopped sometime during the night. The loft overlooked an impossibly blue harbor bustling with boats—fishing boats, tugboats, sleek sailboats—their sails fluttering in the breeze. A gleaming white ferry steamed away from the dock toward a palm studded island in the distance.

She left the bed and made her way around a half wall to the kitchen, where she found a pair of Post-It notes stuck to the Mr. Coffee.

Coffee's in the carafe. Help yourself to anything in the

fridge. Don't go anywhere, I'll be back before noon. Then we'll talk about what to do next. It was signed simply with a bold, scrawled *Gannon.*

Laura snorted at the *PS,* unable to decide whether to be annoyed or amused. *And don't get into any trouble.*

She poured a cup of coffee from the black, insulated carafe, checked the refrigerator, which had the typical, but unappealing bachelor contents of leftover Krystal burgers, two pizza boxes containing something that looked like the penicillin experiment she'd made for the sixth-grade science fair, a brick of cheddar cheese, a half-empty jar of blackberry jelly, two six-packs of Sam Adams and a bottle of Jose Cuervo margarita mix. The cupboards weren't any better, yielding peanut butter, Cheetos, a box of Coco Puffs, a PowerBar, and a bottle of tequila to go with the mix.

Deciding to walk to the small market/café in the quaint little dockside shopping village she'd seen a couple of blocks away, she was in and out of the shower, dressed, and on her way out of the loft in record time.

Brendan O'Neill caught her as the steel-cage elevator door opened onto the ground floor. "Good morning." His smile was drop-dead gorgeous and Laurel felt a twinge of concern when it didn't move her nearly as much as one of those faint, reluctant twinges of Joe Gannon's lips.

"Morning." She returned his smile.

"What would you be liking for breakfast?"

The question surprised her. "I haven't decided. Why?"

"Because I promised Joe I'd cook it for you."

"You don't have to go to all that trouble." And Gannon shouldn't have gotten it into his head to arrange for it.

"It's no trouble at all. I'm here doing some odds and ends, paying bills, that sort of thing, so you needn't worry about making conversation."

"You're very perceptive." She didn't reach human until at least her second cup of coffee.

"Years running a pub back home has given me a bit of insight into people."

"Back in Ireland."

"Castlelough," he confirmed. "That's a little village in the back of beyond near—"

"Clare."

He looked a bit surprised. "Would you have been there, then?"

"Last year. The press caravan drove through it on the way from Shannon to Galway on some cultural exchange thing the president was using for a photo op." He'd also stayed three more days for what had been billed as a working vacation. An oxymoron if she ever heard one. Which was why Laurel didn't take vacations. "It's a pretty little town."

"I wouldn't be arguing that description."

"What brought you to America?"

"Well, now, that's a bit of a story." He flashed another one of those warm smiles. "Why don't I tell it to you over a short stack and bacon?"

He was, in his own way, as bossy as Gannon. But the lilt of Ireland singing in his voice kept her from being irritated.

"If you're sure it's no trouble."

"Cooking for a beautiful woman is no hardship," he assured her.

Five minutes later, she was settled at the bar, drinking the best coffee she'd ever tasted from a thick, white mug, skimming through the *Somersett Beacon-Sentinel* while Brendan O'Neill banged pans around in the kitchen.

The front page of the paper featured a police artist's sketch of the woman known as Sissy Smith. The caption beneath the photo asked readers who knew anything about the woman to notify Detective Joseph Gannon of the Somersett Police Department.

There was trouble in the Middle East, speculation here at home on the outcome of a Supreme Court case concerning free speech on the internet, and the latest tracking polls had Aiken winning his home state by a comfortable margin.

Usually reading the morning paper, seeking an angle on a story a reporter may have missed, jump-started Laurel's day. Now, with all she had on her mind—the loss of her job, Chloe's disappearance, and, although she hated to admit it, the way Gannon had gotten under her skin—she couldn't concentrate.

She was just tired, she assured herself as she folded the paper and put it aside to dig into the stack of pancakes Brendan O'Neill had put in front of her. He refilled her coffee, then, as promised, left her alone.

The pancakes were even better than the coffee. Drenched in melted butter and maple syrup that tasted as if it had been drawn from some tree in Maine just this morning, they almost made her moan.

The syrup, along with Gannon's comment yesterday

about Maine, had her thinking back on the six months she'd worked for the *Brunswick Times Record*, writing obituaries and reporting on raucous school board meetings which lasted long into the night. Anyone who truly wanted to learn how government worked should spend six months attending local school board meetings—the World Wrestling Federation of community politics.

After a freezing winter which taught her at least forty new words for *cold*, she moved to Florida for a job with the *Key West Citizen*. Determined to write her way to a bigger market where crime was a little more exciting than kids getting drunk at spring break, she hadn't fully appreciated the island while she was living there.

Now, as scenes of palm trees, blue water, and dazzling sunsets came to mind, she fantasized about lounging in a hammock, drinking lemonade, and reading a book. And not her usual thick, dry political nonfiction, but a book written solely with the purpose of entertainment, like the novel she'd been working on since that winter in Maine.

It suddenly dawned on Laurel that Joe Gannon was a lot like her fictional hero.

Gannon? Oh, please.

She polished off the pancakes and pushed the plate aside, resisting the urge to lick it. Oh, the Somersett detective was pretty enough, and his slow sultry drawl could undoubtedly melt stone. But she had to wonder what O'Neill had put in her coffee to have her thinking the affable, southern-fried, Good Old Boy in the obnoxious shirt was anything like her Armani-wearing relentlessly dogged fictional detective who toed the line just enough to keep from getting kicked off the force, but was willing to cross that line, if that's what it took to solve the crime and put the bad guys behind bars. And looked damn good while doing it.

Maybe her family was right. Maybe she *had* been working too hard.

Perhaps she ought to think about taking some time to recharge her batteries. After she got her job back. After she ripped away Aiken's mask and revealed the venal, dangerous politician to the voters. And most of all, after she found Chloe.

"Could I be getting you anything else?" Brendan asked, interrupting her thoughts.

"No, thank you. The pancakes were delicious. The lightest I've ever tasted."

"Well, I couldn't be taking total credit for them, since it's me mam's recipe," he divulged. "It's the buttermilk that adds the air." Eyes as blue as a County Clare lake deepened with concern. "Joseph told me about your friend who's gone missing."

"Did he also tell you he doesn't believe I have a case?"

"Now, he didn't say he didn't believe. Nor did he say he did," he admitted. "But I can tell you that you couldn't have a better man looking for her. He's like those Mounties up in Canada. He always gets his man. Or woman."

"He sure doesn't look much like a cop."

"Ah, now, aren't appearances often deceiving? I remember, when I first began building pints at The Irish Rose back home, there were those who didn't think I looked like a publican. Which probably wasn't surprising, since I didn't much think of myself as one, either."

"Then why did you take the job?"

"It was more a case of inheriting it. My father developed a bit of a heart problem, so I moved back from Dublin to help him out with the pub that'd been in the O'Neill family for three generations."

"And what did you do in the city?"

"I practiced law."

"You were an attorney?"

Laurel usually didn't like lawyers any more than she liked politicians, but pouring Jameson's in a pub, no matter how cozy, and flipping pancakes seemed a career stepdown.

"A barrister," he confirmed. "I chose family law because it allowed me to avoid those frightful formal wigs and black robes worn by those arguing in criminal or commercial law." He reached over, took the carafe from the burner, warmed up her coffee again, and poured a mug for himself.

"I'll bet the wardrobe wasn't the only reason."

"Aye, you'd be betting right." She liked the way his eyes smiled. "Standing up for the underdog had its appeal."

"And you didn't mind? Giving it up?"

"Ah, didn't Joseph say you had a quick and curious mind?"

"I'm a reporter. Curiosity comes with the territory." Laurel hated that she wondered what else Gannon had said about her.

"Aye, so he said. And building pints of Guinness isn't that different from practicing the law, really. Don't both involve listening to people's concerns, offering a sympathetic ear and a bit of advice?"

"I suppose so." She tried to recall the last time she'd met a bartender in DC who'd take the time to listen to a customer's concerns, and came up blank.

"The difference—and to my mind, it's a good one—is that working at The Irish Rose—and now, here at The Black Swan—gives me a sense of freedom I'd lost living in the hustle and bustle of Dublin."

"Here when we're open; gone when we're closed," she quoted the sign on the pub's door.

"Aye." Little lines crinkled outward from the corners of his eyes, adding not age but character. She liked Brendan O'Neill. The fact that he and the detective were friends was a point in Gannon's favor.

"Is this pub like the one you ran back home?"

"A bit." He glanced around. "There are some differences, of course, but the buildings are both about the same age. Did Joseph happen to mention that the stones used to build this entire waterfront block came from the holds of coffin ships?"

They'd been called coffin ships because so many Irish immigrants had died while crammed like sardines in the stench of below decks, she recalled. "It didn't come up."

"They were used as ballast." He skimmed a broad hand over the wall. "Since Southerners and Irish share a tendency toward making over, making do, or doing without, they were turned into construction material. You'll be seeing them all around town turned into our roads, walls, and buildings, as well as shoring up the walls of the tunnels."

"Tunnels?"

"Oh, the city's laced with them. They lead from several of the old homes to the water's edge. Stories go that pirates, smugglers, and blockade runners used them to bring their booty into the city. They were also supposedly part of the Underground Railroad, and from a few bottles of moonshine I've uncovered beneath this pub, I suspect bootleggers made use of them as well during Prohibition."

"We had a bootlegger in our family," Laurel revealed. "My great-aunt Edna used the recipe my family brought over from Scotland to make moonshine. She was the black sheep of the family." She'd also supposedly been the fastest driver in the hills, which had prevented government agents from ever catching up with her. Laurel had often been accused of inheriting her love of speed.

"You'd be Laurel Stewart of Stewart's Highlander's Pride," he said as he connected her name with the mention of the whiskey. "It's excellent. We serve it here."

"I'll tell my family you said so. Well, thanks for the breakfast." She pulled out her billfold.

"It's on the house," he said.

The flint of Irish stubbornness that sparked in his eyes told her there was no point in arguing. "Thank you."

"As I said, cooking for a bright, beautiful woman is no hardship."

Laurel decided to let that little bit of Irish chauvinism pass; besides, he had called her bright.

A frown dove between his black brows as she slid off the stool and headed toward the door. "Would you be going out?"

She could tell from O'Neill's tone that he knew Gannon wanted her to stay put. Tough. The one thing in the paper that had captured her attention was the news that Vice President Aiken would be meeting with staff at the Wingate, then hosting a coffee for some of his supporters. Laurel didn't need to be psychic to know that if she shared her plans to confront the vice president, the hospitable pub owner would be on the phone to his cop friend before she got two feet from the door.

"You've piqued my interest in the city," she said. "I thought I'd do a little sightseeing."

It was a lie and they both knew it.

They also knew that short of tying her up, there was no way he could stop her.

27

Gannon had been right about the rain; while the clock thermometer on the village tower revealed the temperature had dropped by a few stingy degrees, the humidity had skyrocketed. The sky had already begun lowering while she'd been inside the pub eating breakfast, turning from blinding blue to tarnished silver.

Not wanting to get caught in a rain shower and show up at the hotel dripping wet after a mere two blocks, she dropped her plans to walk along the harbor to the hotel and flagged down a passing cab. A cartoon Blackbeard leered at her from the side of the door; the driver was wearing a hoop earring the size of the wrist bangle she'd bought on sale at the Chevy Chase Tiffany's.

"Ahoy, me beauty," the driver said with a flash of gold front tooth. "Where ye be headed, darlin'?"

"The Wingate."

As she climbed into the back seat to Gilbert and Sullivan's *Pirates of Penzance* blasting from the cab's speakers, Laurel wondered how long Buccaneer Days lasted.

While in the car, she checked the DC phone for messages again.

"Hello, Ms. Stewart," the now familiar voice said. "This is Sandra Squires again. Editor of the *Falls Church Bee?* I just came from a meeting with Lois Nettleman, the head of our advertising department, who assures me that having your byline appear in our little shopper will bring in enough extra revenue that we'll be able to pay a bit more. Not that we could equal what you were making at the *Post*, of course, but we like to think of the *Bee* as a big happy family. I believe you'd fit right in."

She repeated the number she had given the first time she'd called, and although Laurel had no intention of calling, she couldn't fault Sandra Squires's enthusiasm.

After getting out of the cab in front of the hotel, Laurel couldn't stop herself from looking up at the balcony where Sissy had spent her last few moments. Ice skimmed up her spine and she considered returning to the loft to wait for Gannon.

But she'd always fought her own battles. She wasn't going to turn tail and run just because things had gotten a little—okay, a lot—uncomfortable.

A doorman in gold braid and epaulets held the door open for her. The blast of refrigerated air hit like a dart to her temple as Laurel entered the hotel lobby.

Unsurprisingly, while they hadn't been banished to that ill-named First Amendment zone, reporters were being held behind a rope line guarded by a burly pair of local cops. Embarrassed to have landed in a scandal, and secretly afraid that those who didn't believe her capable of fabricating a story might be enjoying some schadenfreude at her misfortune, Laurel paused.

Retreat was tempting. Reminding herself that she had

nothing to be ashamed of, she waded into the breach.

Her former colleagues reacted like a pack of hounds who'd just had a fox wander into their midst. "Hey, Stewart," an all-too-familiar voice bayed out, "a little birdie tells me you've been offered a new job working on the *Drudge Report.*"

She'd rather have her fingernails ripped out and her charge cards taken away than work on what she considered more gossip column than news website. The cretin who'd called out to her was a former low-level House staffer turned CNBC political pundit who'd held a grudge ever since she'd kneed him after he'd cornered her on the way to the lavatory restroom on Air Force One, grabbed her breasts, and drunkenly suggested they join the Mile-High Club.

"And your wife tells me that your dick's three inches long." His face flushed an angry scarlet as the others laughed at her put-down.

Playing on a seniority she'd had until three days ago, she edged her way through the crowd, earning shouted questions she answered with the standard "no comment" she'd always hated to get thrown at her, low grumbles from some, a couple of cold, hard stares from people who either believed she was guilty or wanted to believe that, and, thank heavens, more than a few supportive or sympathetic remarks.

"I've been wondering when you were going to show up," Max Kelly greeted her when she finally managed to make it up to the rope.

"I got sidetracked." She paused, wondering what he thought of her current troubles. She and the *Boston Globe* reporter had been friendly rivals, respecting each other's work while trying to grab the same scoop. "I didn't make that story up."

"Never thought you did. The prevailing wisdom among those who don't automatically hate you because you're a bright, gorgeous, competitive journalist who's managed to collect a list of go-to unnamed sources longer than reporters who've been here twice as long as you, is that the West Wing set you up."

So, either she was right, or prevailing wisdom was as paranoid as she'd become. Which, in the capital, could be either one. "But why would they do that?"

"Probably because they can," he said mildly. "You'd be a thorn in any politician's ass. Mixing metaphors here, you're also like a damn terrier who won't stop digging for the rat. The rat, in this case, being Aiken. They probably would have loved to have you gone when you first hit town, but the powers that be at your paper wouldn't have caved into political pressure."

"Until Cruella de Merryman hit town."

"Word is that she's up for a cabinet spot when Aiken gets elected. She happens to have been a big fund bundler for the ticket when he ran for vice president."

"I knew she was after me, but I figured we'd just been mortal enemies in a previous life."

He looked at her a little curiously. "Didn't know you believed in that sort of stuff."

"I don't. Not really." When last night's unsettling episode reared its ugly head, she slammed the door on the memory.

She spotted the Secret Service officer who'd just come

out of the banquet room where the brunch was taking place. Sometimes you just got lucky.

"Wish me luck," she said as she ducked under the rope.

"If you're not careful, what you're going to need is a bail bondsman."

"I'll be on my very best behavior." Ignoring Max's snort, she greeted the agent with the dazzling smile that had earned her offers from all the major networks and several twenty-four-hour cable news shows. "Hey, J. T."

J. T. Malloy didn't look the least bit happy to see her. "Reporters are supposed to stay on the other side of the rope line."

"You know I'm not dangerous."

He smothered a laugh by coughing into his fist. "That's a matter of opinion."

Laurel's aunt had always told her that determination and grit could move mountains. Laurel had both those attributes in spades.

"Come on, J. T.," she wheedled prettily. She did not often stoop to using her femininity, but since Aiken's gang had declared war on her, she decided she was entitled to use every weapon in her arsenal. "I just want to slip in the back door of the banquet room and listen to the speech."

She could tell he wasn't buying it. He folded his arms. Held firm. "No press allowed."

"But I'm not press anymore."

"Yeah, I heard you got fired. Sorry about that."

She believed him. Unfortunately sympathy didn't solve her problem.

"How about I just stand outside and maybe I can hear something through the door." She glanced over at the little notice stating Private Party right below the Admiral Somersett room sign.

"How about you just give it up?" he suggested mildly. "I have instructions to arrest you if you get within a hundred feet of VPOTUS."

"What?" Goosebumps rose on her flesh at the idea of being lumped in with all those crazies who wrote threatening letters in crayon to elected officials. "Who determined that?"

"The order came from higher up."

"Oh, I believe that. And I'll bet the buck stops right on Warren Wyatt's desk."

She knew she'd hit the bull's-eye when he wouldn't meet her frustrated gaze. "You shouldn't even be here, Laurel."

Her mind was scrambling to come up with a new tact when a hand coming from behind clamped onto her shoulder.

Laurel's response was pure instinct. She swung around, her left hand shooting out before she could pull it back.

The resounding *crack!* of bone on bone reverberated around the lobby like a gunshot and a flare of camera flashes lit up the area as Laurel's fist connected with Secret Service Agent Jack Wagner's face.

Joe was pissed. After the autopsy, which hadn't given him a whole lot of clues, other than the fact that Sissy Smith had had sex shortly before she'd died, he'd gone straight from the hospital to the courthouse, where he'd spent an hour on the witness stand getting hammered by a lawyer who, having no other defense for his douche bag of a client who'd murdered two teenagers parked in a lover's lane, had decided to try to blame the cops.

The attorney attacked the chain of evidence, falsely claimed that Joe had failed to Mirandize his client, and came right out and accused the entire Somersett PD of being prejudiced against the rich and powerful. To which Joe had snapped back that, last he checked the Constitution, there weren't two different sets of laws in America—one for the regular guy and one for the rich and powerful. The defendant killed two innocent kids and if he wasn't prepared to do the time, he shouldn't have committed the crime.

Not all that sure he'd made his point—despite what he'd testified, defendants with big bucks walked more often than those left to overworked public defenders—he left the courthouse in an ugly mood and was halfway to the Wingate Palace to interview a few of the vice president's staff about what they knew about their protocol advisor's so-called disappearance, when his cell phone, which he'd turned down for court, vibrated.

"What the hell do you mean, she left?" he shouted when Brendan O'Neill told him the reporter was no longer in the building. He plowed a hand through his hair, which he suspected had begun to go gray over the past two days. "No, of course I wouldn't have wanted you to sit on her." Though hog-tying the woman sounded appealing right now. Or better yet, cuffing her to the bed before he left.

Joe was even more ticked off when the idea of the leggy redhead handcuffed to the metal frame of his bed caused a stir of heat in his gut. "She's probably headed to the hotel," he muttered. "I'll try to cut her off at the pass before she gets into any more trouble."

He suspected *trouble* was Laurel Stewart's middle name—a suspicion that was confirmed when his cell phone rang again.

"Hey, Joe," Cait said. "Thought you might be interested in knowing that dispatch just took a 10-87 call from the Wingate Palace."

There were only three reasons why Cait would phone him for a "situation" call at the hotel. "I don't suppose this has to do with our possible murder vic."

"Nope."

"The CHAOS protestors?"

"Last I heard, they were still safely tucked away in their tidy little Free Amendment zone."

He'd worked with Cait long enough to know that she was enjoying this. "Could you be more specific about what kind of situation we're discussing?" he asked through gritted teeth.

"All I know is that it involves a 10-15." A significant pause. "Concerning your new friend."

What a shock. Hotshot reporter Laurel Stewart involved in a disturbance. The surprise would be if she'd actually stayed in his apartment like he'd told her to do. More heat stirred, this time in Joe's chest. He reached for the bottle of Tums he kept in the jockey box.

"I'm headed to the scene now," he said around the handful of chalky antacids he'd dumped into his mouth.

He hit the blue-and-red dashboard strobe light plugged into the cigarette lighter.

"Have fun." Cait didn't bother to keep the laughter from her voice. "Oh, and needless to say, the order from the captain, which in turn came from the Feds, is to keep this signal 11."

The Feds and the brass were living in the State of Denial if they thought not talking on the police band about whatever the hell was happening at the hotel would keep it out of the press.

From what he'd been able to tell over the years, reporters were like sharks—the faintest scent of blood and they'd show up, hoping for a big meal. Having one of their own involved would undoubtedly send them into a feeding frenzy.

"This is turning out to be one fucked up day," he muttered as he pulled up beneath the porte cochere.

A patrolman—Thomas, again—was waiting for him in front of the door. They waded through the throng of reporters who'd been corralled in the lobby, and rode down the escalator to a small office in the conference room area. Sure enough, there she was, looking unbelievably hot in a silky cream dress that clung to her sleek body in all the right places and another pair of those ice pick heels.

When he viewed the handcuffs around her wrists, Joe decided his lousy day was going to get even worse.

28

"Well, well." She did not seem particularly distressed by her situation. Her eyes swept over his suit in a quick, judicial study. "I had no idea you'd clean up so well."

"I was in court."

"Ah." She tilted her head. "Geoffrey Beene's a good look for you. It's not as well draped as an Armani Black Label, or as cutting edge as a Gucci or Etro, but I suppose the traditional look plays better to a jury. And the navy goes well with your coloring."

She may as well have been speaking Aramaic and the only *Black Label* he'd ever heard of came in either a whiskey or beer bottle. "You've no idea how relieved I am you approve." He'd gotten the suit at the Men's Wearhouse ten years ago and had never bothered to check out the label.

"Though you could do a lot better than that safe Republican-red tie," she tacked on.

"And you could do a lot better than those silver bracelets you're wearing." He turned to the Secret Service agents who'd been watching the exchange like spectators at Wimbledon. Joe was good at spotting clues; the fact that one of the agents was nursing a shiner was not a positive one.

"Joe Gannon, Somersett PD." He flashed his shield. "Want to tell me what's going on here?"

"Ms. Stewart was asked to leave." An agent whose ID revealed his name to be J. T. Malloy shot Laurel a look that appeared nearly as frustrated as Joe himself was feeling. "She chose not to."

"Then she assaulted a federal officer." Agent Wagner's left eye was nearly swollen shut. What was visible was turning an ugly bluish-purple.

Joe drilled her with the stare he usually reserved to earn a confession from gangbangers in the box. "You slugged a Secret Service agent?"

"It was an accident, Detective. I'd certainly never strike a law enforcement officer intentionally."

"Let me guess. The altitude from those high heels made you dizzy, so you reached out for balance and your hand just accidentally *bumped* against his eye?"

His sarcasm caused a line to furrow between her russet brows. "Agent Wagner came at me from behind. He startled me when he grabbed my shoulder, my instincts kicked in, and, well . . ." Lips painted the soft hue of the inside of a seashell, those same lips which, dammit, he'd dreamed about taking last night, pulled into a regretful line.

"I was only responding the way any woman would respond when she's suddenly, unexpectedly assaulted from behind. It was even more startling because I've been mugged before," she tacked on with a smaller than usual lift of that stubborn chin that gave him the impression that she might be a bit more upset by events than she was letting on. "Certainly, as a law enforcement officer, you're a proponent of women taking self-defense training?"

Hell, he'd taught some of those classes himself. But that wasn't the damn point.

"Look," he heard himself saying to the agents, "it doesn't look as if any real harm has been done."

"It's a federal crime to assault, resist, or impede a Secret Service agent," the polo-shirt-wearing hunk quoted the criminal statute.

"It was an accident," Laurel insisted.

Joe and Malloy exchanged a look. The agent's slight, resigned shrug suggested this might not turn out as badly as Joe had at first feared.

"How tall are you?" Joe asked Laurel.

"Five-six. Why?"

"And you weigh, what? One-fifteen?"

"One-twelve. And six ounces. Why?"

He didn't respond, just turned to Wagner. "And you?" Six-three, Joe guessed. One-ninety pounds with about a 2 to 3 percent body fat ratio. That was seventy-five vertical inches of nearly pure muscle mass against sixty-six inches of whip-slender female.

The guy got it right away. "That's not the point. If she'd had a weapon—"

"But she didn't." Joe was grateful when Laurel surprised him by actually seeming willing to keep her mouth shut and let him handle this. "The picture of you being decked by a woman is already going to land on the front pages of newspapers all across the country.

"Despite having already screwed up by letting a civilian get the drop on you, if you back away from this now, you could end up with a lot of embarrassment, a slap on the wrist, and a transfer out of this detail for a while until things blow over. Play hardball and keep the story alive and who knows, you could find yourself checking out counterfeit twenty-dollar bills in Boise."

The guy might not have been fast enough to duck Laurel Stewart's fist, but like all Secret Service agents who'd risen to the lofty ranks of the White House detail, he was no dummy. He'd admittedly made a major mistake that, if things had been different, could have resulted in an assassination. He'd have to pay for that, probably lose a pay grade or two, and find himself back behind a desk.

But it could be worse. He could become a staple of late-night comics—the Secret Service agent who couldn't take a punch from a girl.

Watching the wheels turn in the agent's head, Joe suspected he was probably also imagining Dr. Phil and Oprah discussing post-traumatic stress syndrome in female crime victims.

"She's already stolen classified papers." Wagner was still hanging in there, but there wasn't any real force in his tone. Joe understood the need to save face.

"I did not steal any papers from the West Wing," Laurel shot back on a flare of heat that caused Malloy to drag a hand down his face. Joe knew just how the agent felt. "Or anywhere else, for that matter. I was set up."

"Whatever, you can't deny that you're stalking the vice president," Wagner accused.

"Stalking?" Her voice rose like a soprano practicing her scales.

"That's a pretty strong word," Joe broke in mildly, even as he shot Laurel a *back-off* warning look.

"VPOTUS's scheduled to leave to meet with Bishop Hagen in five minutes," Malloy, who appeared to be leaning toward her side in the debate, reminded his partner. He cut a significant glance at his watch. "You know what a stickler he is for punctuality. We've got four minutes and counting to settle this."

Wagner was self-deflating, like a helium balloon with a slow leak. "The damn woman needs a keeper."

"Good idea," Joe said. "Since I know you've got more important things to do than hang around here, I'll just take her off your hands."

"We can release her to your custody." Malloy's relief of being given a way out of this potential tar pit was obvious.

"I'll take full responsibility for Ms. Stewart," Joe promised. Green heat flashed in Laurel's eyes, but Joe had to give her credit for not flying off the handle.

"I suppose that'll work." With obvious reluctance, Wagner pulled the handcuff keys from his pocket, and unlocked them.

"Thank you," Laurel said politely. She did not, Joe noticed, rub the faint red marks on her wrists. "You might want to try a compress of cool water spiked with essential oils," she told the agent helpfully. "My aunt has a garden, so I know a bit about herbs. Yarrow, hyssop, or lavender, followed with ice wrapped in a towel, will help keep the bruising down."

From the glare he gave her with his good eye, Joe got the impression that the agent wasn't all that grateful for her advice.

"You come within a hundred feet of the vice president, and we'll have to take you in," agent Malloy warned.

"Don't worry." Joe put his hand on Laurel's back, hoping to get her out of the hotel before someone said something to set her off. Or worse yet, Nobel Aiken left that meeting room. "She'll behave." Her back stiffened beneath his hand but she walked out of the office with her head held high.

"She'll behave?" Laurel ground out, her heels tapping sharply on the steps as he led her out the back way to where he'd parked the car. "That's incredibly bossy, even for a chauvinistic cop."

"Excuse me. Next time I'll keep my bossy, chauvinist cop mouth shut and let your ass land in federal prison." Knowing it'd piss her off, he reached past her and pushed open the heavy steel door, forcing her to duck under his arm.

"For your information, Detective, I've been taking care of myself for a very long time." The rain that had been threatening earlier had begun to fall, somewhere between a mist and a drizzle.

"You'd better be careful getting up on that high horse, sugarplum. Because it could be a very long fall."

"I'm simply saying that I could have handled the situation just fine without your charging in like the Lone Ranger."

"Goddammit!" The frustration that had been rising to the boiling point all day burst out. When she started to walk away, he snagged her arm, spun her around, dug his fingers into her shoulders, and pinned her against the red brick of the building.

Dark clouds, purple-and-black edged with a sheen of silver, were boiling in from the water, thunder rumbling dangerously behind them.

"You just don't get it, do you?" Her total lack of contrition, let alone any appreciation for having been bailed out of a potentially bad situation, hit a nerve already rubbed raw from a day that had started out bad and gone downhill from there.

"Get what?" Rain sparkled in her hair as she tossed her head. Her eyes flashed with a redhead's quick temper, but she didn't push him away.

"That if you're right about having been set up by the VP, charging in like Custer at Little Big Horn is definitely only going to make things worse. You're supposed to be such a hotshot reporter, I'm surprised you've never heard of finessing a situation to get a damn source to cooperate."

"Well, of course I have—"

"Could have fooled me. In case you were too dense to tell, sugar, you were skating on very thin ice down there."

"I'm not too dense to recognize when someone's mixing metaphors. I don't recall hearing anything about ice at the battle of Little Big Horn."

Her show of bravado only pissed him off more.

Joe had wanted to taste her from the instant he'd laid eyes on her. After that sample the night before, he'd spent a long frustrating night, with the ancient air-conditioning he still needed to replace doing little to cool either the air or his too hot body.

Just one more taste, he'd told himself again and again. One taste to prove to himself that the reporter with the smart mouth and wraparound legs was no different from any other woman. One final taste, he told himself now, to get Laurel Stewart the hell out of his system.

He splayed his fingers against her throat.

"Let go of me."

Lightning crackled across the darkening sky; when the sizzling green-white flash of light illuminated the bold dare in her eyes, Joe could no longer come up with a reason not to take that taste.

"Too late." His gaze took on a predatory gleam that had Laurel's breath backing up in her throat even as she knew the hand there posed no real danger. The peril was in the edgy, needy way he made her feel.

His head swooped down just as the sky opened up.

Unlike last night's tender kiss, the first contact of his lips brought on a full scale explosion; when blinding lights and colors flashed behind her eyes, Laurel's first thought was that someone had made a mistake and set off the nightly fireworks early.

She lifted her hands to push him away, but instead her rebellious fingers grabbed his dress shirt, crumpling the white cotton.

The kiss was carnal, but not cruel. Thrilling, but not threatening.

Rain was falling, streaking over her upturned face, cool against her cheeks.

His afternoon beard was rough against her skin; she sighed with the pleasure of it.

He savaged her mouth, deepening the kiss; she moaned as raw need shot through her.

The wind keened and rattled the fronds of the palmetto trees lining the curved driveway to the hotel. Laurel heard a low rumble of thunder and had no idea whether it was coming from the sky or from inside herself. The rising tide slapped against the stone seawall; the crash of the distant waves out beyond the harbor echoed the roar in her blood.

Feeling as if she'd been hurled headfirst into those waves, afraid of being swept beyond some point of no return, she lifted her arms around his neck, arched against him, and clung.

He murmured something against her mouth—it could have been a curse or a prayer, she couldn't tell which—then pulled her even closer, so tight against his body that a drop of rain couldn't have gotten between them, so close that Laurel was amazed the heat of their skin combined with their wet clothes didn't create steam.

His heart battered against hers. His teeth nipped at her lower lip. His wonderfully wicked hands were everywhere, stroking, kneading, claiming.

And then, as quickly as it had begun, he dropped his hands and pulled back.

"Christ." He was winded, his chest heaving like a man who'd just run a marathon. "I apologize for that." He dragged a hand down his wet face. "I lost control."

Laurel took a deep gulp of air, licked her bottom lip, and tasted a hint of blood. "You weren't the only one."

The way the soaked cotton clung to the muscles of his chest had her wanting to touch him, all over. Taste him, everywhere.

Lord, she had gone *way* too long without sex.

"You don't get it. I *never* lose control." His fingers curled into a tight fist which, for a fleeting moment, Laurel feared he was going to slam against the bricks. "Not ever." He spat out the word between clenched teeth.

"Join the club." She understood, even as she struggled to regain her equilibrium, that he'd meant to shock her, to press the point home that she couldn't break into private meetings and assault Secret Service agents.

Unfortunately, as much as she was not prepared to admit it, he had a point.

He gave her one of those long, hard cop stares that were really starting to annoy her, then turned and walked away.

29

"Where do you think you're going?" She hurried after him. No way was he going to turn things upside down then leave without discussing what could end up being a very big problem between them.

"Unlike some big-city people, I have enough sense to get out of this damn rain." He jerked the loosened tie from around his neck, balled it up, and jammed it into the pocket of his suit jacket. "Then I'm going to go home and change clothes. Since your clothes are at my place, you can come along if you want. Or, you can go back into that hotel and get arrested. It's your call. Then I'm going to continue with my murder investigation which was so rudely interrupted when I had to come pull your fat out of the fire."

She scooped some wet hair out of her face. "Well that's a flattering way to put it."

"I didn't intend for it to be flattering."

Wet and angry, he made the mistake of indulging himself with a long look down at her.

The wet silk was the color of buttermilk, fit like skin, and had been rendered nearly transparent by the rain. She was wearing another of those lacy bras and a pair of barely there panties low on her hips that had him fantasizing about pulling them down her legs.

"Okay, I take back what I said about your fat. It was just an expression. And that's one helluva killer dress."

She glanced down. A bit of color rose in her cheeks, but he was grateful when she didn't move to cover herself. "It's meant to be worn dry. Wet it looks like I'm auditioning for a triple-X-rated movie."

"Wet it looks terrific." Knowing that if he gave into temptation to touch, he'd never be able to stop, Joe pulled the remote from his pocket; the door chirped as it unlocked. "And it's obvious you don't watch a lot of porn movies or you'd realize that none of the actresses are as classy as you."

Her lips quirked. "Watch a lot of porn, do you, Gannon?"

"Only during my vice days. As part of the job."

"Yeah, right." Laurel stopped and stared at the torch-red Mustang Cobra convertible. "This is *your* car?"

"What, did you think I look like a Crown Vic guy?" He frowned at that idea.

"No." The smile that had been teasing at the corners of her mouth a moment earlier broke free. "The old-man boatmobile definitely isn't you."

"I only drive that piece of junk because the city makes me. Now this"—he smoothed his hand over the shiny fender, the way some men might caress a woman—"is a car."

A driver's car, for someone who liked speed and power. Laurel had always liked both herself. She reached for the door handle, only to get beaten to the draw again. Feeling uncharacteristically gracious after he'd admittedly saved her hide back at the hotel with the Secret Service, she didn't complain. The leather bucket-seat was smooth against the back of her thighs. And speaking of being gracious . . .

She waited until he was in the car, then said, "Thanks." He slanted her a sideways glance as he twisted the key in the ignition. "For what you did back in there. I owe you." There. The words were out, and amazingly, she hadn't choked on them.

"No problem." Actually, she was turning out to be one problem after another, but after what had happened a minute ago, Joe wasn't going to risk triggering another argument. He also suspected she was not a woman who enjoyed being rescued. "That Secret Service agent's never going to be able to live down a black eye by a one-hundred-and-twelve-pound female."

"You're forgetting the six ounces. And he surprised me, coming up behind me that way. He's just fortunate I recognized him when I did. Another second and I'd have kicked his balls into his throat."

Joe felt his own pull up in response to that mental image. "You've taken kickboxing?" It seemed her mouth would be weapon enough on its own.

"It's good exercise and a lot more interesting than the treadmill at the gym. Besides, I was telling the truth about having been mugged at the ATM. The guy got two hundred bucks and, for a while, my self-confidence. It was right after I arrived in DC and it scared me so much I almost turned tail and left the city."

"But you didn't."

"No. I started taking self-defense courses instead."

"Any of those courses teach you to choose your battles?" Even being able to kickbox a guy's nuts up against his tonsils wouldn't do her a damn bit of good against a knife or gun.

"Of course." She sighed. "Look, I know I'm not exactly your favorite person right now, but I really do appreciate your coming to my rescue," she admitted as he pulled out of the parking lot. "I was afraid Wagner was going to arrest me."

"You did a pretty good job of hiding it." Three-hundred-and-ninety horses growled a complaint as they got stuck behind a linen-delivery truck. He'd seen stone cold killers edgier than she'd looked when she'd made that crack about his Republican tie. "I guess that's part of the never-let-them-see-you-sweat thing, huh?"

"Yeah." And she'd worked damn hard to develop that skill. He shifted down, stepped on the gas, and swung around the truck. Seconds later, it was disappearing into their rearview mirror. "Do you have to do that?"

"Do what?" He leaned forward and hit the CD player, transporting them from rain-drenched Somersett to sunny Margaritaville, where Jimmy Buffett was growing up but not old.

"Drive like you're on the track of the Indianapolis 500." Laurel thought the car should be covered with advertisements for detergent and auto parts.

"Don't worry. I aced my high-performance driving class. You should see my slalom."

"I'd pay good money not to." She stomped on an imaginary brake as the light turned red.

The Mustang stopped on a dime. He glanced over at her again. "I'd think anyone who drives around in DC wouldn't be bothered by our small-city traffic."

"The difference is that in DC, I'm the one doing the driving." She'd also gotten more than her share of complaints from passengers about her total disregard of speed limits when she was behind the wheel of her Audi TT, which might not be a muscle car like this one, but she still loved its sporty lines.

"I should have figured you for a woman who likes to be in the driver's seat."

"I'm a woman who'd like to live to see thirty-five." She dug in her bag for her cigarettes. "And there's nothing wrong with wanting to maintain some control in life."

"You're not going to get any argument there. The problem is, life gets messy. Sometimes you've just got to loosen up and go with the flow."

She cracked open the window. "I'd expect nothing less from a man who owns a parrot shirt."

"That shirt happens to put suspects off guard. It's a lot easier for them to relax and spill the beans to a guy wearing a Hawaiian shirt than someone in a starched white shirt and tie."

That made a bit of sense. "Like Columbo's raincoat."

"Exactly. So, did they give you a badge?"

She blinked at the non sequitur. "A badge?"

"When you joined the Fashion Police."

"Cute, Gannon," she said on a stream of smoke. Dammit, she was beginning to like him. Which could be even more dangerous than wanting to jump his sexy male bones every time she looked at him. "So, did you learn anything at the autopsy?"

"Only that you were right about the victim having had sex before she died. We got some hair samples, so we'll be able to test for DNA when we track down who may have been in that room with her. I'm still waiting for the tox screen. She also had a tattoo of a butterfly on her butt."

A butterfly wasn't such an unusual tattoo for a woman. Still . . .

"CHAOS uses a butterfly as part of their logo," Laurel said.

The radical environmental group had taken their name from the chaos theory that the flapping of a single butterfly's wing can produce a tiny change in the state of the atmosphere; over time, the atmosphere diverges from what it would have done, and a tidal wave that might have devastated Maui might not happen. Or a volcano in Ecuador might erupt. Or a drought might devastate the Sub-Sahara.

"Yeah. I know."

"I just remembered something else," she said.

He gave her a sideways glance. "You going to tell me, or just sit there with those damn canary feathers sticking out of your mouth."

"That party I told you I went to? The one Chloe invited me to where I met Cody Wunder? It was held to raise funds for CHAOS's work protecting baby logger-head sea turtles down here in South Carolina. Guess who cohosted it?"

"I'm beat, wet to the skin, and in no mood to play

Twenty Questions. So, how about just cutting to the chase?"

"Happy Aiken."

Ha! She could tell from the way his eyes narrowed that she'd surprised him with that one.

"Noble Aiken's wife." He rubbed his chin as he mulled over the possibilities. "It could just be one of those small-world things."

"Or there could be a link. Which means Wunder needs to be questioned."

"As a matter of fact, I'd already thought of doing that tomorrow. Which is why the city pays me the big bucks for detecting," he said dryly.

"I'm coming with you."

When he didn't immediately respond, Laurel thought he might not have heard her over Buffett ranting about wanting his Junior Mints. "I said—"

"You want to come with me. Now there's a big surprise." Joe flexed his fingers on the steering wheel and blew out a frustrated, but, Laurel thought hopefully, resigned breath. "Okay, just to make sure we're on the same page here—you allege you have a missing friend—"

"I don't just allege it—"

"You *allege*," he repeated, cutting off her planned argument, "that your friend and housemate is missing. That friend may, or may not, have had a connection to Cody Wunder, who may in turn be linked to one of my current cases."

"You have to admit it's a coincidence."

"Juries don't tend to convict that often on coincidence, which is why I concentrate on gathering cold, hard facts. But yeah, the fact that Wunder and Aiken's wife are both in Somersett when one of the women who may have ties with the guy turns up dead and another may have gone missing, is interesting."

"It's more than interesting, it's—"

"So, here's what we're going to do," he said, overriding her again. "If you promise to keep your mouth shut, I'll take you along when I talk to Wunder. However"—he held up a hand like a traffic cop—"you need to get it through that stubborn, reckless red head of yours that this isn't DC."

"I know that."

"Then you should also know that the rapid-fire, take-no-prisoners attitude of yours that may work in the nation's capital just doesn't cut it down here. This is *my* town."

He actually jammed his thumb against his chest! Me Tarazan. You Jane.

Not in this lifetime! Laurel thought.

"I know these people," he was saying when she dragged her mind back from the enticing mental image of Joe Gannon stripped down to a loincloth, swinging on a vine through some dense green tropical jungle. "I know the way they think, know their prejudice against fast-talking Yankees."

"Excuse me?" She lifted a brow. "DC just happens to be below the Mason-Dixon line."

"It also happens to have been the headquarters of the Union army. And my point, if you'll let me finish, is that like it or not, when it comes to any investigation I may decide to undertake regarding Chloe Hollister's alleged disappearance, from now on you answer to me. Because I'm the boss."

"No one's the boss of me."

"That's right." He snapped his fingers as if remembering. "You don't have a boss because you got your ass fired."

Now that, Laurel thought darkly, was a low blow. "I didn't get my ass fired. Aiken, or his people, framed me. And in case you haven't noticed, Detective, we're not in Kansas, Somersett isn't Dodge City, and you're not Marshal Dillon."

"Damn. Remind me to leave the shiny tin sheriff's star I got from all those cereal box-tops at home when I pay a visit to our environmental friend."

"*We* pay a visit to him."

"There's only a *we* if you keep your mouth shut and let me do the talking."

"Perhaps you ought to stop at a bookstore on the way back to the loft. To buy a stack of bibles for me to swear on," she elaborated sweetly when he cut her a questioning look.

Joe managed, just barely, to restrain a smile. "Why don't we just skip the bibles and I'll take you at your word."

Damned if he wasn't starting to enjoy her. Which just showed that between the job and the heat, he was definitely being driven around the friggin' bend.

30

It was dark when Chloe awoke. Her head was pounding like a tympani and her arms were numb. Logy and confused, she tried to move them, afraid at first she'd somehow become paralyzed. Then she realized she was lying on a mattress. Impossibly, she was chained by the wrists to a stone wall.

Wherever she was, it was probably the only cool place in Somersett. She blinked, squeezed her eyes shut, then opened them again, trying to adjust her sight to near-enveloping blackness. The only light came from a tall container candle set on a wrought-iron table; the flickering light caused shadows to dance eerily on the damp gray stones.

The last thing she could remember was having a cup of ginger tea to ease a bout of morning sickness made even worse by an attack of nerves. Chloe had no idea why they called it morning sickness when she suffered from it all day, but she'd found that the spiced tea helped and she'd taken the sign that a man who was not accustomed to doing menial chores would go to the trouble to brew it for her as proof he loved her.

The wheels in her head turned sluggishly, creakily, as she struggled to sort things out.

Could he have put something in the tea?

Thinking back on it, she'd thought it had tasted more bitter, but artificial sweetener always left a bad taste in her mouth.

Oh, God! What if he had drugged it? And what if the drug had hurt her baby?

She struggled to think through the clouds fogging her brain.

Perhaps this was a new game. It wouldn't be the first time he'd tied her up. He liked to act out his fantasies, and although in the beginning she'd been embarrassed by the things he'd wanted to do to her, wanted her to do to him, she'd wanted to make him happy.

But now there was someone else to consider—an innocent life totally dependent upon her for its existence. That idea was even more terrifying than whatever situation she'd awoken to find herself in.

If this is a game, it isn't fun!

If this is a nightmare, I want to wake up!

It was the last thought she had before drifting back into the darkened void.

After changing into dry clothes, Laurel stood in front of the glass wall of Joe's loft and watched lightning streak across the storm-dark sky. Music was drifting up the stairs from the pub as Joe handed her a drink.

"You really seem to take this Margaritaville theme seriously."

"And here I thought the point of Margaritaville was not to take anything seriously."

She took a sip, enjoying the contrast between the smooth gold tequila and tart lime. "Easier to say than to do."

"Unfortunately, that's true."

They both fell silent, sipping their drinks while watching the storm.

"That thing earlier," she said.

"Thing?"

"You know." She waved a hand. "In the parking lot."

"Ah." She sensed his nod. "That thing where I kissed you." He paused another of those beats he used so well. "And you kissed me back."

"It was the adrenaline. People do things they wouldn't normally do when they get all wired." She glanced over at him. "As a homicide cop, you've probably seen it happen a million times."

"Not quite a million." The hint of a smile quirked at his lips. "But yeah," he agreed in a drawl as sensuous as black silk, "stuff happens in stress situations, though I can't remember the last time I locked lips because I got juiced up."

He'd changed into another of those shirts—this one featured white hibiscuses growing on a scarlet background—and white cotton pants with a drawstring waist. He'd left the shirt unbuttoned and Laurel decided it should be against the law to cover such a magnificent body with such ugly, boxy clothes.

She'd put him in snug silk T-shirts, though she imagined he'd also look gorgeous in black tie. Better yet, she thought as her fingers itched with the desire to follow that arrowing of burnished gold hair down to the drawstring waistband riding low on his hips, would be for him to wear nothing at all.

Laurel realized she was getting in deep, deep trouble when she found even the man's bare feet sexy. "It didn't mean anything," she said.

He cocked a brow.

"Dammit, it was the adrenaline," she insisted, wanting, *needing* to believe that herself. "That and the fact that it's been a long time since I've been with a man. It was only repressed sexual desire."

She slammed her mouth shut an instant too late. Oh, God. What on earth had her telling him that?

"That hiss of air you hear is my male ego deflating." He didn't look wounded. In fact, from the laughter in his eyes, he looked as if he was enjoying himself.

Laurel snorted. "It'd take a whale harpoon to even make a dent."

"Shows how much you know." Ice cubes clinked as he put his glass on a nearby table. "Maybe you ought to give me another try." Joe put his hand beneath her chin. "See if we can do something about all that repressed sexual desire." His thumb brushed over her lower lip. "It can't be healthy for you to keep it all bottled up."

"Why don't I worry about my health?" It was difficult to think when his light, seductive touch was sending quicksilver tremors through her. "While you worry about landing on your back across the room if you don't knock it off. I just happen to have been the best student in my jujitsu class." She'd only earned a yellow belt, but he didn't know that.

"Now that's an appealing scenario." Rather than take a defensive step back, he moved nearer. "Me on my back." He took her glass from her hand, placed it beside his, then slid the fingers of his free hand into her hair, cupping the back of her head. "Your sexy-as-sin legs straddling mine."

Somehow, he'd shifted their positions so her back was literally against the glass wall. "I've been accused—recently as a matter of fact—of being just another chauvinist, Good Old Boy southern cop, but I'm real open-minded when it comes to sex." There was a predatory gleam in his lion-gold eyes. "I'm more than willing to let the woman be on top."

"Dammit, Joe." His name came out in a soft, shimmering whisper barely heard over the rumbling of thunder outside and the thrumming of a bass from downstairs.

"Do you know, that's the first time you've called me by my first name. I like the way it sounds." He moved even closer, splaying his fingers against the small of her back, holding her against him, allowing her to feel the hot, thick ridge of his erection through the thin cotton of those low slung pants. "Maybe you can say it again when I'm inside you." He bent his head and touched his lips to hers. "And I sure wouldn't object if you scream it real loud the first time I make you come."

"The first time?" She hated how he could be so damn arrogant. Hated even worse that the way his words had her already wet suggested he might just be right.

He smiled against her mouth. "You're the one who brought up having a lot of repressed sexual need," he reminded her. His hand slid between them. One blouse button gave way. "It'll probably take a few times to get it all out." Another button. "I figure, three, maybe four orgasms, at the very least."

"You're pretty damn sure of yourself," she complained, tilting her head back to give his roving lips access to her throat.

"No point in doin' something if you can't do it right." His words vibrated against a pulse that was beating hotter. Faster.

He pushed the blouse off her shoulders, then slowly, with what seemed to be infinite patience, tugged down the elastic straps of her bra.

"You may have noticed that things don't exactly move at warp speed down here in this part of the country." He peeled the lacy cups down, then watched her face as he closed his hands over her breasts. "We southern boys like to romance our women with slow hands. Even if it takes all night."

"I didn't come here for romance."

"Too bad, sugarplum, because you're going to get it."

Her body bowed back and she shuddered as he replaced his hands with his mouth. Her breath caught, her heart pounded, her head swam. The deep rumble of thunder, the pelting of the rain against the window, the pulse of the music from the pub all receded into some hazy, distant place as Joe pleasured Laurel with wickedly slow lips and tongue.

A distant voice reminded her that her behavior was

rash, even for her. What did she know about Joe Gannon, really?

Other than the fact that he could make her melt with a single touch.

Which, she considered as his tongue made a wet swathe across her sizzling flesh, wasn't necessarily a bad thing.

He brought his lips back to hers, letting them linger in an impossibly slow, sexy kiss that had her floating back into the mists, when the strident demand of the desk phone brought reality crashing back.

"Ignore it." Without taking his mouth from hers, he began walking her backward toward his huge lake of a bed. "Whoever it is will go away." He caressed her from shoulder to thigh. "Now where were we?"

Laurel was desperately trying to shut the intrusion out. "I believe you were going to try to make me scream."

"No try about it." He lifted her hand to his lips and pressed a kiss against her palm that shot directly to that hot, tingling place between her legs. "That, sugar, is a given."

The back of Laurel's knees were against the mattress.

"You know what to do," Joe's deep drawl rumbled from the answering machine. "I'll get back to you soon as I can."

"Joe, it's Mike," a disembodied voice said. "If you're there, pick up."

The zipper at the side of her skirt whispered in the darkened room as he lowered it.

"The woman on the front page of the paper?" A voice that sounded a great deal like Joe's intruded yet again.

Dammit. Laurel and Joe both tensed. Looked at each other.

"The one in the sketch? I think I know who she is. I think she's a parishioner. Call me." There was a click. Then a dial tone.

"Shit." Joe lowered his forehead to Laurel's and sighed deeply as he ran a palm up her bare leg and brushed his lips against hers. "Keep that thought."

The real world had just intruded. As she buttoned her blouse, Laurel reluctantly decided it was for the best.

"When he says a parishioner—"

"Mike's my brother. Who just happens to be a priest at St. Brendan's."

"The Cathedral?" You could see the twin spires from all over the city.

"Yeah. Damn. While it definitely isn't my first choice of ways to spend a rainy evening, I'd better take those morgue shots over to him."

Despite the seriousness of the call, Joe was suddenly grinning down at her. "I like that look."

"What look?" She smoothed her palms down the wrinkled blouse, frowning when she saw that she'd rebuttoned it crooked.

"That slightly rumpled look. A little tousled. Makes me wonder what you're going to look like after a night of hot, steamy sex. After you've let your hair down."

She batted at the hand playing with her hair. "My hair's short. There's no letting down to do. And I don't think there should be any more tousling or rumpling. So you might as well not waste time thinking about it."

"Actually, I enjoy thinking about it. Who was it who said

that time spent in pleasurable pursuit is never wasted?"

"I've no idea." She folded her arms. "Neither do I care."

"God, I must be getting perverse in my old age," he murmured. "Because that snotty attitude of yours is actually turning me on."

"Turn it off."

"You know you don't mean that." He was too close to her. His eyes too warm. Too wicked. "I could take you. Right here. Right now."

She tossed her head. "And I could have had you on your knees," she shot back. "Begging."

"Christ, you're competitive. I love that about you." He skimmed a hand down her hair again, smoothing the strands he'd tousled. "Like the song goes, I ain't too proud to beg, sweet darlin'. If Mike hadn't called, you'd be naked in my bed right now." He lifted her hand; nipped at her fingers. "And I'd be inside you."

"In all my years in Washington, land of oversize egos, yours may just be the most Herculean I've ever come across."

She belatedly realized the Freudian slip and was madly trying to think up a comeback to the obvious response when he grinned.

"Too easy," he decided.

Laurel was distracted by the way he seemed to know just which buttons to push. Dammit, *she'd* always been the one who pushed the buttons; until this latest debacle with the Aiken story, *she'd* always been the one who controlled the situation.

Buh dum. Buh dum.

"Nice ring," he said when the instantly recognizable opening notes of *Jaws* sounded from her purse.

"It seemed like a good idea at the time." Okay, so maybe it wasn't the friendliest tone available in the cell phone databank.

Dum dum dum dum.

Her heart skipped a beat when she saw the number on the Caller ID. "Barry, please say you're calling to tell me that a tornado spun through the District and dropped a Kanine Krunchies factory on Cruella."

"One can only hope," her former editor said. "But I've got some other news that should end up good."

If he was calling to say she'd gotten her job back, surely he'd sound more upbeat?

"Okay." As her nerves jangled, Laurel wondered if dramatic pauses were a guy thing she'd never noticed before.

"There's going to be a board looking at all your stories."

"A board?" She sank down onto the edge of the bed as the blood drained out of her head. "As in an investigatory board?"

"Made up of a mix of print and television reporters."

The warnings of a headache stirred. "And this is good news, why?"

"Because once they start digging into your work, they'll confirm every quote and source."

At least the named ones. Fortunately, she tried not to rely on confidential sources as much as so many other DC-based journalists did. Which was why it was so ironic she'd get caught in that fake story snare.

"But it'll take months to investigate them all."

"More like a few weeks," he allowed. "But hopefully by then the other papers you've worked for—"

"Other papers?" When she started digging around one-handed in her bag again, Joe took it, retrieved her cigarettes, lit one, and handed it to her.

"Thanks," she murmured as she drew in a deep drag. "Are you saying that every paper I've worked for in the past fourteen years has started investigating my credibility?"

"Not all of them. That I know of anyway," he amended. "But I've gotten some calls." He blew out a long breath. Cursed. "Okay, so maybe this isn't the best news I could have called with. But you'll see, kiddo, this time next year all this will be forgotten."

By this time next year she'd be living on the street holding up a "Will Write for Food" sign. She glanced over at the shoes lying on their sides, just inside the door. Perhaps she should have put the $450 she'd spent on those in treasury funds, or some such conservative investment. Then again, frugality hadn't been encouraged while she'd been growing up in a massive stone castle that boasted battlements, Norman towers, arrow slits, and an entry hall with twin fireplaces high enough for a man to stand up in.

The fantasy Stewart home set in the hills of South Appalachia had been built after the Revolution by an ancestor with money he'd acquired by selling some silver pieces Paul Revere had gifted him with. Andrew Stewart had gone on to make his fortune selling whiskey made from a recipe he'd brought with him to America from the Scottish Highlands. The Stewarts had always been given to grand gestures and Laurel would be the first to admit she liked nice things. Oh, not crystal, or silver, or art—things that would slow you down as you moved from place to place—but if you had to wear clothes, why not look nice?

"Every time a reporter's accused of plagiarism or filing a false story, my name's going to come up," she complained. "And after a while, no one will remember—or care—that I've been found innocent."

Barry couldn't argue that point and Laurel wasn't naive enough to believe that she'd ever be able to prove the vice president had used Warren Wyatt to set her up. It had, after all, taken Sam Ervin's committee nearly nine months to wrap up the Watergate hearings, and there were still questions that'd never be answered.

Hell. This could very easily follow her, becoming her own personal albatross, for the rest of her life.

"Well," she said, dredging up some false enthusiasm from somewhere deep inside her, "thanks for the update, Barry. No, she hasn't shown up." She'd called him yesterday, just in case Chloe might call the paper looking for her for some reason. "Of course I'm going to keep looking."

After promising to keep him updated, she said goodbye and closed the phone with a decided snap.

"That was Barry Yost. My editor," she told Joe. "Correction. *Former* editor. Looks as if I'll be out of work a little longer."

She let out a long, stuttering breath and stabbed the cigarette out in the mug he'd brought her to use as an ashtray while she'd been on the phone with Barry.

"Damn, damn, damn." She pressed the heels of her hands against her eyes where the headache had exploded full blown. "Having total strangers, who've never met me, who don't know what kind of person I am, going through my work, scouring through phone logs and travel vouchers, calling up sources for verification of quotes, all that other crap, is just going to keep the story going." Her breath hitched. "And it's going to make it look as if I really did invent that story just to get my name on the front page."

"This is America. Where people are innocent until proven guilty," he said, unknowingly repeating what she'd said when those federal agents had first shown up at the inn.

Laurel shot him a look. "And wouldn't it be pretty to think so." She plowed her hands through her hair. "Jesus, listen to me. My best friend's gone missing, another woman's dead, and here I am, fretting about my reputation."

He went over to the sink and returned with a glass of water and two Tylenol. "You're trying to find your friend, Sissy Smith isn't your responsibility, and sometimes a reputation is all a person has."

"I have more." She swallowed the pills and even before they'd had a chance to work she began to feel a little better. "I have my family. Friends." There was Chloe. And Max. And Barry. And, as strange as it might have seemed only yesterday, Joe Gannon seemed to be fitting into that category.

Laurel managed a weak laugh. "My health. People always say if you've got your health you've got everything, right?"

"That's what they say." The sympathy in his eyes was

laced with a genuine kindness that she found harder to fight than the sexual attraction.

"Dammit, Gannon." She sniffled back the tears, refusing to let the bastards make her cry. "I'm starting to like you."

"Well now, that's convenient." He pulled a handkerchief out of his pocket. "Because I'm finding you real likable, sugar."

She blew her nose. "The timing sucks."

"Since I figure you'd be on about your third climax right about now if Mike hadn't so rudely interrupted, I'm sure as hell not going to argue with that."

Her laugh burst free, taking with it most of the frustration and worry brought on by Barry's phone call. "You really ought to do something about that deplorable lack of confidence," she murmured.

"I'd rather do something about you." His lips touched hers in a slow, delicious kiss that untied the last of the nerves that had knotted in her stomach. "I want you in my bed, Laurel. I want to be in you. All night long."

"We have to stop this," she complained, even as her lips plucked at his.

"Why?"

She drew her head back. "I don't know. Dammit, Joseph Xavier Gannon, you make it hard to think straight."

It was, for her, Joe knew, a huge admission. He flashed a satisfied grin. "I know the feeling, buttercup."

He kissed her again, hard, fast, and was hugely proud of himself when he resisted the urge to grab her by that shiny red hair and ravage her silly.

"I'll order a pizza from downstairs for when I get back," he said. "What do you want on it?"

"Anything but anchovies."

"Loaded," he agreed. He'd grabbed one of the six-packs of Sam Adams from the refrigerator and was almost to the door when Laurel called to him. "Joe?"

He glanced back over his shoulder. "Yeah?"

"She didn't commit suicide. Sissy Smith," Laurel clarified. "No matter what that letter says."

Joe froze, his hand still on the doorknob. "What letter?" He hadn't told Laurel anything about a letter. Even more to the point, he didn't know about one himself.

She blinked. Slowly, like a sleepy owl. "I'm not sure." She rubbed her temple with her fingers. "But it's out there somewhere. And while she may have written it, she didn't kill herself."

"Well." It was his turn to blink. "Got any more insights?"

"No." She hadn't even known she had that one, until the words had come out of her mouth. "I don't need this." She looked small, pale, and vulnerable, and Joe felt something turn over in his heart.

"Want me to stay?" It wasn't as if he was the only murder cop in Somersett. He could find someone else to send over to the church to take Mike's statement.

"No." She shook her head and managed a faint smile. "I'll be fine. Really. I've got a couple calls to make."

Never let them see you sweat. As he left the apartment, Joe couldn't help wondering if the sexy reporter had the motto embroidered on that lacy underwear.

31

Joe called Cait on the way, to fill her in on Mike's message, but she and the new kid had been called to a shooting at Admiral's Park. A family, in a hurry to get out of the rain, had been taking a shortcut across the park to their car when their nine-year-old daughter had suddenly fallen down.

At first her parents had thought she'd merely stumbled. Until she didn't get up; she'd been shot in the head and from the angle of the trajectory, Cait suspected the injury was the result of some liquored-up yahoo discharging his gun into the air.

The girl was in surgery at St. Camillus; Cait and Donahue, along with two teams of uniformed cops pulled off patrol, were canvassing the neighborhoods within a mile radius trying to find the shooter.

Two more days to go. Christ, he was going to be glad when Buccaneer Days were over!

Laurel had been trying to write off the strange feelings that had begun bombarding her ever since she'd walked into that Wingate Palace hotel suite.

She'd attempted to tell herself that it was only over-work, and stress, which had her imagination working overtime. She didn't want to think about the alternative. That they were all too real.

What if they were the damn legacy of the blood Laurel had spent her entire life trying to escape? A legacy she feared she could no longer ignore.

She'd just picked up the phone to call her aunt when it *dum-dummed*.

It figured.

"Darling!" Her aunt Zelda chirped cheerily. "How are you?"

"Just fine." Not.

"I've been worried. I've been getting some very strong vibes that something isn't right. This morning I read your cards and the Eight of Wands came up."

Laurel sighed. "Which means?"

"A swift release of raw power, cutting through your confusion and indecision, which at first I had to assume was a result of you losing your job."

"I'm going to get that straightened out."

"Of course you are, darling. We're all pulling for you. I've been burning so many candles Stewart's Folly is in danger of burning down, and after Soledad O'Brien mentioned it this morning on CNN, Melanie even flashed off an e-mail to the network this morning informing them that in her opinion, if Ted Turner were still running the show, he'd be the first to offer you an apology for even passing along such lies."

"That's very nice of Aunt Melanie." And out of character, since her aunt had always insisted correspondence should only be written by fountain pen on hand engraved Crane & Company stationery from Tiffany's.

"It gets better. She also pointed out that it's obvious from their willingness to put mean-spirited gossip on the air that they don't have a decent reporter on their entire network."

Laurel didn't need to be psychic to know what was coming next.

"So, naturally she suggested that they'd be doing themselves, not to mention their sponsors, a huge favor by hiring you," Zelda reported proudly.

Although she knew many would consider her short-sighted in the days when daily newspapers were disappearing like dinosaurs, Laurel had never been attracted to television news. How could you explain the fall of Communism, or a war, or even the complex politics of an election in two- or three-minute soundbites?

"I appreciate everyone's support." She tried not to groan at the idea of her aunt's remarks showing up as a CNN crawl.

But this was not what she needed to talk about. She skimmed a hand through her hair, feeling foolish for even bringing the subject up. "You're right about me having been confused. But not about my job. I know I didn't lie, and I know that'll be proven and I'll get my job back." And wouldn't she enjoy watching Cruella de Merryman grovel?

"Of course you will, darling."

"But I've been getting these strange feelings."

She went on to explain about Chloe's disappearance, and the episode at the hotel, and finally that letter she knew about that didn't even seem to exist. Yet.

"If you believe Chloe's still alive, she is," her aunt said.

"Believing doesn't always make it so." Laurel could *believe* she'd won a Pulitzer prize until doomsday, but that didn't mean the Pulitzer jury was going to award her one any day soon.

"Of the three of you girls, your intuition has always been the strongest. But you've always fought against accepting your gift. In order to find Chloe, you're going to have to open your chakra centers."

"Right," Laurel said flatly.

"I know you're skeptical, darling, but you can't deny that your first impression of someone is usually accurate."

"You learn to read people in the journalism business." She'd certainly known Aiken was a lying weasel the first time she'd met him. And while she might have been a little off the mark thinking Joe's tired eyes had been due to nursing a hangover, she'd definitely been right about him being too sexy for his own good.

"Or, perhaps you've gone into the business of journalism because you're good at reading people."

"Ah, the age old question of which came first, the chicken or the egg."

"You can scoff all you want, but we all choose lives most suited to our talents. Now, if you want to find your friend—"

"Of course I do."

"Then you're going to have to plug yourself into the switchboard of the collective unconscious."

Laurel loved her aunt Zelda. Really she did. But at times, and this was one of them, she could be more than a little frustrating. You wanted answers, she reminded herself. No fair blaming the messenger if you don't like them.

"It's always been more than a little obvious to me that you're an empath, Laurel, dear." Zelda continued to press her point. "It's not enough to write stories that connect on an intellectual level; even a journalist must tap into readers' emotions. Thoughts and emotions are, after all, merely psychic energy. You're one of those special people who can pick up on that energy."

"I'm not a mind reader," Laurel insisted. "I was exhausted the other night, my brain was on the verge of a meltdown; it was probably just suggestion and imagination. I can't believe it was real."

"Reality is where you find it, darling,"

Her aunt had always insisted that Laurel was a natural-born storyteller. But if it was merely a case of her having woven a story around Joe's Sissy Smith, if what had happened in the hotel room was only her imagination, how could she have known about the champagne?

The Sight. That gift of the blood—or the curse, depending on the viewpoint—that had been passed down over the ages through the women in her aunt's family.

Laurel had never envied Zelda that power. On the contrary, she'd always been relieved to be spared the legacy that had allowed her aunt to know, even before her sister-in-law became pregnant with Lily, even before that snow started flying on the night Laurel's mother had died, that the birth of the third Stewart sister would end in tragedy.

"Why me? And why now?"

"Why not you? As for why now, you've spent all your life, at least the thirty years since your mother's death, with your emotional shields up. With all that's happened to you the past forty-eight hours, it isn't surprising that they'd start developing cracks."

Laurel hated that about this, at least, her aunt might be right. She hadn't done as good a job at protecting her feelings as she usually did. How else to explain her reaction to Gannon?

She wasn't going to worry about that first kiss, which had, at least on his part, been solely an act of pity. And that hot, wild, wet kiss had been due to the storm. After all, their tempers had flared while the thunder had rumbled and the lightning flashed through a sky the color of ripe plums. Any woman would find the devil himself seductive under those circumstances.

But what about earlier? If Joe's brother hadn't called, she would have ended up going to bed with a man she'd known only two days.

"There's something else."

"You've met a man."

"How . . . Never mind."

"The stars are in perfect alignment for you to fall in love."

"It can't be love." It was only chemistry. Attraction. Lust.

"Why not?"

"In the first place, it's too soon." She had, after all,

been a very long time without a round of hot, steamy jungle sex. Her body was just reminding her of that.

"When something's right, it's right. Harlan and I were friends for a very long time—"

"That's my point," Laurel said.

"If you'll let me finish," her aunt said in an uncharacteristically testy tone.

"Yes, Ma'am."

"We'd been friends for a very long time; I was very close to his wife. Yet there was one night, after he'd had to move her to a nursing home because he couldn't take care of her Parkinson's any longer, that something sparked between us. We fell in love that night, Laurel. Some might call it lust, but it was the real thing. Of course we couldn't be together, because Harlan wasn't about to leave Abby. Only true love could have lasted all these years."

"You know I'm happy for you and Harlan." The widower and Zelda had gotten back together during Lark's stalker troubles. "But I really don't believe this is the same thing at all. Joe Gannon and I don't have anything in common; even our careers are like cats and dogs. I'm a writer, he's a cop—"

"So is Harlan." And, of course, Zelda was a writer.

"It's not the same thing," Laurel insisted again.

"Whatever you say, dear," her aunt replied serenely.

It was only lust, Laurel told herself yet again.

That was all she'd allow it to be.

After promising her aunt that she'd keep in touch and work on centering those chakras, she began pacing the hickory floor of the loft.

Patience had never been Laurel's strong suit. Forty-five minutes after her call to Zelda, she was still pacing the floor when her cell phone rang again.

Snatching it from the table where she'd left it, she immediately flipped it open. "Joe?"

"Ms. Stewart?" the male voice inquired.

"This is Laurel Stewart."

"I'm pleased to have reached you. This is Cody Wunder. Of CHAOS."

"I know who you are Mr. Wunder."

"I was wondering if you and I could meet."

She paused to look at her watch. What was taking him so damn long? She understood the need for Joe to take care of his own cases, but meanwhile, they weren't making any progress finding Chloe.

"I believe you'll find it well worth your while," Wunder said. "It's about our mutual friend, Noble Aiken."

Every instinct in her body went on red alert. "He's not my friend, Mr. Wunder."

"Then we have that in common. Which is why I want to give you a story that will blow the man's campaign right out of the water. And, if we're lucky, bring about the impeachment of the vice president."

Her mind was scrambling, trying to figure out what, precisely, he could be talking about. Did he know about Chloe? Did he know where she was? Was, as she'd feared, Aiken involved?

"I don't suppose you'd care to tell me what your story concerns?"

"I'm not foolhardy enough to discuss it over the phone. You never know who may be listening."

"There's never been a vice-presidential impeachment," she pointed out, trying to stall to allow Joe time to return. Vice presidents had always left office one of three ways—they became president, resigned, or died.

"Article 2, Section 4 of the Constitution states that the president, vice president, and all civil officers of the United States shall be removed from office on impeachment for, and conviction of, treason, bribery, or other high crimes and misdemeanors," he quoted the ruling.

"I realize that. But there's no precedent."

"Then we'll set one." His tone was cool and confident.

"Noble Aiken's leading by twenty-eight to thirty-five points in all the tracking polls." Damn. Where was Joe?

"That's because voters don't have the information I do. Which is where you come in."

She found his proposal intriguing, but decided that she couldn't very well complain about her reputation being ruined if she didn't stick to her scruples. "Perhaps you haven't heard the rumors, but I'm not working for the *Post* at the moment."

"I heard you'd been let go. It's an unfortunate incident, but I've read your work long enough to know that you'll find another position in no time. Perhaps, after the campaign is over, you'd consider coming to work here at CHAOS. Meanwhile, it's precisely the fact that you're currently without press ties that makes you the perfect person to entrust with this story. I'm giving you a head start, Ms. Stewart. An exclusive. So long as you can be at my hotel—the Palm Harbor Villa, two blocks south of the Wingate Palace—within the next fifteen minutes. I'm in the penthouse. I'll leave instructions at the desk to give you an access key to the tenth floor. Sixteen minutes after I hang up, I'll offer my information to the highest bidder."

"I'll be there." Joe was going to be furious, but there was no help for it. "Oh, and Mr. Wunder?"

"Yes?"

"I'd also like to ask you a few questions. About a friend of mine, Chloe Hollister." Laurel thought for a moment he'd hung up. Finally, he said, "Of course."

Then she heard the click, followed by dead air.

The rain hadn't let up; not wanting to risk getting drenched trying to find a cab on the street, Laurel called the taxi company and, with her nerves feeling as if they were being stabbed by red hot needles, impatiently watched out the window as a mental stopwatch clicked off the time.

Fifteen minutes.

Fourteen.

Thirteen.

Dammit! Did everything move with the speed of molasses down here?

Twelve.

The cab finally arrived, giving her eleven minutes to get to Wunder's hotel. Not wanting Brendan O'Neill to hear the elevator, Laurel ran down the back stairs, escaping the pub without being spotted by the bartender who was busy drawing beers and frying chips for the boisterous crowd.

She climbed into the same cab with the leering Blackbeard on the door, and pulled a twenty out of her wallet. "I need to be at the Palm Harbor in ten minutes."

"Aaar, me buxom beauty! We be haulin' out." The driver slammed a booted foot down on the gas and the cab tore away from the curb before she had a chance to buckle her seat belt.

32

"These photos were taken at the annual Fourth of July Summer Daze Festival," Mike told Joe. "The sketch in the paper looked so much like Sissy, I decided you should check it out."

"Sissy?" Joe looked at the pretty blond woman wearing shorts and a strappy white tank top with a little red embroidered heart between Clemson and University.

"Sissy Sotheby-Beale," Mike elaborated as he popped the top on one of the bottles of beer Joe had brought with him.

She was holding a stuffed tiger, the kind you'd win at a carnival, smiling at the camera as if she didn't have a care in the world. A man was standing beside her, his arm around her shoulders.

"Yep," Joe confirmed. "That's my Sissy Smith."

"Damn." Mike shook his dark head with regret. "I was hoping I was wrong. She's a very special person. Sissy and her husband joined St. Brendan's when they first arrived in the city last year, and she's been active in the community from day one. She teaches first grade catechism, has done some work with the bishop's council on cleaning up the harbor, helps out with the literacy program, and is assistant director of the children's choir . . . At least she was."

He briefly closed his eyes. Joe wondered if he was saying a prayer, and if so, envied his brother his belief.

"The article said she fell off a balcony at the Wingate?" Mike asked. He was turning the bottle around and around between his hands.

"Either fell or was pushed."

"That's impossible." Mike looked up again, surprised. "I can't imagine anyone wanting to kill her."

"Can you imagine her committing suicide?"

"Not on a bet," Mike answered without hesitation.

"Who's the guy standing with her?" The photographer had cut off her companion's head.

"It's hard to tell, but it's probably her husband. Doctor Robert Beale."

"Medical doctor? Or professor type?"

"Medical. He's on staff at ASMA."

The Admiral Somersett Military Academy, at the far edge of the city, had been established in the 1800s, prior to the War Between the States, and was often mentioned in the same breath with the Citadel and VMI.

"I called him earlier," Mike divulged.

Joe's brows dove toward his nose. "You called him?"

"Before I called you," Mike said mildly, proof that family dynamics never changed. Joe hadn't been able to intimidate his little brother when they were kids, either. "I figured there was no point in stirring things up if the sketch wasn't of her—if she was safely home with her husband watching television."

"Damn. You could have tipped him off."

"Excellent point. And, I suppose, one I should have thought of. Which is why it's a good thing you grew up to be the cop in the family, and I joined the priesthood."

Mike wouldn't have lasted a day as a cop. He'd always been an optimist. Joe figured it took a bushel of optimism to tackle the never-ending work of saving souls.

"Was Beale home when you called?"

"If he was, he didn't pick up. I suppose he could have been busy with something else."

Joe knew he was in trouble when the memory of what he and Laurel had been doing when Mike's call came in stirred those now familiar feelings of lust and need.

"I left a message for him to call me back," Mike revealed. "I said I had some questions about the Labor Day picnic."

"I didn't think priests were allowed to lie."

"It wasn't a lie. More of a hedge. We need a head count so we can order the burgers."

"You'd think a secretary would usually handle details like that. Or at the very least, a picnic committee person."

Mike flashed a guileless smile. "I guess I'm just a hands-on guy."

Joe wasn't going to dignify the lie with a comment. "Did you try to reach Beale at the Academy?"

"No. I figured that if the sketch *was* of Sissy, tracking him down at work might be crossing the line into an investigation, so I decided to leave it to my hotshot homicide detective brother."

"Any signs of trouble in the marriage?"

"None that I could tell."

"You've never witnessed any jealousy from Beale?"

Mike's brow furrowed. "No. But people tend to be on their best behavior at church, and unless they bring you their problems, you can never be sure what goes on behind closed doors."

Having gotten all he figured he could get from his brother, until he talked to the doc, Joe decided to do a little digging for Laurel.

"So," he said casually, "I guess the bishop's going to be spending a lot more time up in Washington."

"I suppose so. If Aiken's elected, that is."

"What's the book around here?"

"Gambling's illegal."

"This from a man who runs the weekly Bingo games."

"There's always been a dispensation when it comes to gambling for God. As for the upcoming election, you never know what skeletons might come tumbling out of a candidate's closets."

"Aiken got any in particular you know about?"

Mike shrugged. "Probably no more than any other politician."

"Ever hear anything about him womanizing?"

His brother's intelligent blue eyes narrowed. "This isn't a casual conversation, is it?"

"Not really." Joe might lie to a suspect, but he'd never lied to family. Except during that time when his life had collapsed around him and he kept assuring them he was doing just fine and dandy while spending long, lonely nights contemplating eating his Glock.

"Does it have anything to do with the Beales?"

"No." Another true statement. Joe figured he was on a

roll. "It's a missing-person case, not that I'm convinced the woman's actually missing. I don't suppose you've ever heard Aiken's confession?"

Black brows shot up. "Are you asking me to breach the confidentiality of the confessional?"

"Of course not. Unless you want to."

"Not today."

Joe shrugged. "Can't blame a guy for trying."

"I suppose not." Mike tilted back in his chair and took another pull on the beer bottle. "There have been rumors from time to time."

"Oh?"

"About questionable campaign contributions."

"Well, hell, I already knew that."

"Did you also know that a leading campaign contributor switched parties a few years ago?"

"Is that so unusual?"

"Not that I know anything about politics, but I suppose not. The family was one of the original founders of the parish, back in the 1800s. They're still active—the father's in Knights of Columbus, the mother's in the Altar Guild and one of a group of ladies who coordinate funeral supper groups. Their daughter—a Merit Scholar—was an intern in Aiken's DC office the summer between her freshman and sophomore years of college. The way the story goes, she quit out of the blue and came home. Two days later she and her mother took off on a two month trip down to St. Lucia."

"Must be nice." Sun, surf, catching sailfish. Margaritaville in spades.

"Must be," Mike agreed. "But it was odd timing

because it caused Madison—that's their daughter—to miss the first term of her sophomore year. They also didn't return to Somersett alone." He paused. "The wife adopted a baby while they were down there."

"That happens."

"True. But they asked for a private baptism, rather than the more public one, which was certainly their right, but unusual for a couple as active in the community as they are, and besides, all three of their other children had been baptized at Mass. And what do you think the odds are of finding a blue-eyed blond baby girl available for adoption in the Caribbean?"

"Not great." Joe drank his beer thoughtfully as he considered the idea. "So there was gossip?"

"There's always gossip and my secretary takes vast delight in filling me in on the juicier parts. There are times I think she's trying to make me blush."

Knowing that Mike hadn't exactly been a choirboy, Joe didn't figure he blushed all that easily.

"But part of this story seemed to carry a bit more validity than others," Mike allowed.

"Okay, let's say, for argument's sake, that the Merit Scholar got pregnant, gave birth to a baby, but the family decided, for the sake of appearances—since the father wasn't proposing to make an honest woman of her—to pass it off as the mother's," Joe said. "That doesn't necessarily implicate the vice president in her pregnancy."

"An honest woman," Mike mused. "What a quaint term. And people accuse the Church of being behind the times."

"You know what I mean."

"Yes. And actually, my guess would be that the girl's father, who's both politically and morally conservative, would feel much the same way. And you're right, of course, there's nothing to implicate the vice president." He polished off the Sam Adams. "You do have to wonder at the timing, though. An intern suddenly quits, disappears for two months, comes back home with a newborn baby sister, and the next thing you know a major campaign fund-raiser is not only switching candidates, but actively working for the opposition."

"If it walks like a duck, quacks like a duck—"

"So the saying goes. I don't have to be a Hardy Boy to suspect something went wrong up there in DC that summer."

They both fell silent.

"So," Mike asked, "does this line of questioning have anything to do with that *Post* reporter who's staying at your place?"

"How did you know about her?"

"I called the station looking for you earlier and spoke to Cait, who told me you were out playing detective with some redheaded reporter."

"She's got this theory about her missing friend." Joe shrugged. "I figured it wouldn't hurt to ask around."

"Probably not. I hadn't realized you'd gotten moved from homicide to missing persons."

"It's Buccaneer Days." Joe repeated what he'd told Laurel. "Everyone sort of pitches in."

"I see." Blue eyes honed in on him like a laser. "Cait says she's attractive."

"She's drop-dead gorgeous." There was no point denying it. "She can also be a pain in the ass."

"Which is why you moved her into your place."

"Every hotel room in town is booked up. Can't encourage folks to break the law by sleeping on the street."

"I've always enjoyed the parable of the Good Samaritan. So, how is the rest of life treating you?"

Joe knew what his brother was asking. And dodged the question. "Just jim-dandy. I've been thinking about going to Key West."

"That explains the shirt. A vacation's a good idea."

"Not for a vacation. I was thinking about moving there, opening up a bait shop and spending my days fishing. Or maybe taking up lobster trapping in Maine."

Mike threw back his head and laughed. "You'd last a week, tops, in Maine."

"That's what Cait said," Joe grumbled.

"Cait's a good-looking woman. Smart, too. You should listen to her."

"I didn't realize priests looked at women."

"Celibacy doesn't preclude looking. Our maker created a stunning world—we should all take the time to appreciate a dazzling sunset, a rainbow after a storm, a beautiful woman."

"Perhaps. But isn't lusting in your heart supposed to be a sin?"

His brother laughed again, sounding like the sixteen-year-old kid he'd once been. "What do you think reconciliation is for?"

"Spoken like a true Jesuit. So," Joe said with a feigned

casualness he suspected didn't fool his brother for a moment, "I guess Aiken calls on the bishop when he wants his sins expunged."

"What makes you think he commits any? From the commercials his campaign team has been putting out, you'd think the candidate walks on water."

"Last time someone claimed that, he ended up on a cross."

"Good point. And you're right. If Aiken does receive the sacrament of reconciliation, it's from the bishop. They go back a long time and they're pretty tight."

"And no wonder, since Cary's been on the list of campaign contributors since Aiken's first run for the senate." The courthouse was a Wi-Fi hotspot; Joe had used the wireless internet access to look that up on OpenSecrets.org while waiting to testify.

"The bishop's got family money and priests don't take a vow of poverty. Plus, it's no secret Rome bumped him up to bishop after he donated all that land he inherited to the Church. Money talks."

"In politics and religions," Mike agreed.

"Which seems to get a little untidily mixed when an important local figure in the Church spends so much time bundling money for political campaigns."

"The bishop has a great many influential friends. But if you're about to ask me—"

"Don't worry." Joe waved away his brother's concern. "I'm not going to ask you for names of his rich and famous parishioners. Although—"

"I knew the beer would come with a catch."

Joe no longer bothered to deny it. "What I'm interested in is someone else the bishop might have been spending time with lately. Someone less of a mover and shaker. Less reputable. Have any of the men from the shelter been hanging around here?"

"Sure. A lot of the men do manual labor around the rectory—gardening, painting, basic handyman stuff. It makes them feel as if they're contributing to their keep, which, in turn lifts their pride and helps them gain the confidence to stay out of trouble.

"Then there's the literacy classes I started last year. As I said, Sissy often helped out with those; she had a Masters degree in education and was a natural born teacher, but her husband's former career in the military made it difficult for her to work, since she never knew when Robert would be transferred. She was relieved to have finally settled down."

"So she didn't appear depressed?"

Mike thought about that for a moment. "No, if anything, she seemed even happier the past month or so."

"Perhaps like a woman who'd fallen in love," Joe suggested.

"Not that I have any personal experience, but it seems adultery would tend to make a person more conflicted. And unhappy."

"I suppose that depends on the spouse." Joe definitely wanted to talk with Doctor Beale. "Let's get back to the shelter group."

"The literacy classes meet weekly on Mondays in the library. Then there's AA on Tuesdays, NA on Wednesdays. We used to combine both of those on Tuesday nights until the drug abusers decided they didn't want to hang out with 'common everyday drunks.' SAA meets on Thursdays—"

"SAA?"

"Sex Addicts Anonymous."

"They meet here, at the church?"

"The world is filled with more and more temptation, as the Church's own sex scandals have shown. People accuse us of a lot of things, including being a fourteenth century institution, but here at St. Brendan's we try to keep up with the times."

"Ever think the times suck?"

"Occasionally. Then I think about slavery, polio, and the Cold War that had kids ducking beneath desks, and today starts looking a lot better."

"You might have a slightly different view if you were in the murder business."

"Granted. Which is why, given the choice, I'll take the miracle business any day. But what does this have to do with our shelter residents?"

"Any of those residents you think might be capable of murder?"

Mike didn't immediately dismiss the idea. "There may be some who've killed," he said thoughtfully. "Hopefully not recently. Why?"

"This woman with the missing friend, she doesn't seem like a wacko. She's also accusing Aiken of having an affair with the woman, which, needless to say, if true, wouldn't be all that good for his campaign."

"It wouldn't be helpful. But even if it's true, where does the bishop come in?" Mike stared at Joe as comprehension sunk in. "Surely you don't think . . ." Joe could see the wheels turning around inside his brother's head. "You're not suggesting the bishop—a man chosen to represent the Church's Good Shepherd—might, at the vice president's behest, have used the homeless shelter to find himself a hit man to get rid of a troublesome mistress?"

"A shelter'd probably be easier than recruiting an assassin at a Knights of Columbus meeting. And it's not as if Cary doesn't have a vested interest in the campaign. After all, if Aiken doesn't make it to the White House, the bishop's chances of becoming spiritual advisor to the president go down the drain."

"My God." Mike's lake-blue eyes deepened with sadness. "You don't trust anyone, do you?"

Joe shrugged. "I'm a cop. I can't afford to."

"That's damn depressing."

"Not as depressing as the idea of one woman jumping off a tenth story balcony to escape her attacker and another who, if she doesn't turn up pretty soon, might just end up with her name on the murder board, as well."

Mike couldn't dispute that.

33

As the cab rumbled over the cobblestone streets Laurel called the house yet again. The fact that there was only one message on the machine suggested that the news cycle had moved on without her. That was the good news. The bad news was that the message wasn't from Chloe.

Beep. "Hey Laurel, it's Joel Sienfield, from the *Star*, America's number one celebrity weekly news magazine. A little birdie told us you've been talking with *Worldwide View*. You don't want to work there, sweetheart. The people have no class and we offer a much better benefits package.

"As it happens, we were working on a story about Elvis sightings when this blockbuster idea that's right up your alley hit like a lightning bolt outta the blue sky. So, Elvis has been working undercover for the FBI for all these years, and his cover's blown when he singlehandedly foils a terrorist plot by Bat Boy to blow up the White House. Whattya think? Dynamite, huh?" He rattled off a number. "Call me, sweetheart."

"Sure thing, Joel. As soon as Elvis sprouts wings and

he and Bat Boy start dive-bombing the Capitol building," she muttered as the driver ran a red light, ignoring the angry blare of horns, and came to a screeching, rubber-burning stop in front of the entrance to the hotel, with two minutes to spare.

Fortunately she didn't have to wait in line at the front desk to pick up the coded key that would take her up to the penthouse. The elevator seemed to take forever, but the sweep hand of her watch had just ticked off the final seconds of the fifteen-minute deadline when she knocked on the right side of the arched double door.

"You're very prompt," Cody Wunder greeted her.

"I try." A bit winded, she tried not to pant.

Wunder's luxuriant hair swept back from his forehead, revealing a deep widow's peak before falling to his shoulders like a jet curtain. His eyes, deeply set in the bronzed face that gave credence to his story about Native American roots, were the same chilly Arctic blue and as disturbingly free of emotion as the first time she'd seen him. He was dressed entirely in black—black turtleneck shirt, black jeans, glossy black eelskin boots.

"I appreciate you coming." His faint smile, as he welcomed her into a luxurious harbor-view suite, was as cold and dormant as a winter garden, making Laurel wonder how many of the stories of his numerous affairs were true. A woman would be risking frostbite going to bed with this man.

That thought led directly back to the fiery kiss she'd shared with Joe after he'd dragged her from the Wingate.

"Ms. Stewart?" Realizing that he was looking at her strangely, she shook off the memory.

"Thank you for seeing me," she said, hoping he wouldn't notice the heat that had flooded into her cheeks.

"Are you warm? I can turn down the air-conditioning."

Another degree cooler and there'd be frost on the window. He might as well have been staying in an igloo. Adding to the chill was the fact that the suite was decorated solely in shades of white. There was music playing softly in the background, something classical Laurel vaguely recognized but couldn't name, with weeping violins.

"No, I'm fine." She resisted rubbing her bare arms and vowed never to complain about the heat again. She glanced around. "This is quite a contrast to the lobby." Which had been decorated in typically tropical decor.

"I bought the penthouse to use when I'm in Somersett. Since that faux beach look reminded me of a bad Jamaican restaurant, I hired a decorator for this space."

"It's very nice," she lied politely. "Did you buy the apartment? Or did CHAOS?" the reporter in her couldn't resist asking.

"CHAOS is me; I am CHAOS. We've never claimed to be a nonprofit organization," he reminded her. "I didn't know which you'd prefer, so I ordered both tea and coffee. As well as a bottled water and soda."

"Coffee, thanks. Black, no sugar."

He nodded his dark head. "Coffee it is." He moved with a fluid grace across the acre of marble floor to a chrome coffee table set between two love seats covered in alabaster damask, and picked up a sterling pot.

He had beautiful hands, fine boned and long fingered. As he handed her a silver-rimmed china cup, she noticed the CHAOS butterfly tattoo on the inside of a slender, blue-veined wrist.

"Thank you." She sat down on one of the alabaster love seats, cradled the cup between her palms, and breathed in the fragrant, cinnamon-spiced steam.

"It's my pleasure."

The words were correct, but there was no geniality in his tone. She was thinking that Mr. Spock had shown more emotion on *Star Trek*, when she realized his appeal. How many women, she wondered, would fantasize about being the one to break through that reserve, to melt that ice?

He unscrewed a small bottle of water and poured it into a crystal tumbler. "You mentioned something about a friend?"

"Chloe Hollister." Laurel watched his eyes for even a flicker of recognition. Nothing. "She's protocol advisor for the vice president." Still nothing. "Blond, early thirties, very southern."

His brow furrowed. He sipped his water as he gazed out the rain-lashed window toward the fog-draped harbor. "Chloe Hollister." The murmur reverberated in his throat like a cat's purr. "No. I don't believe the name rings a bell." He quirked a brow. "Should it?"

"She attended the Save the Loggerhead Turtle fund-raiser party Happy Aiken cohosted in Georgetown. I thought you might have met." Laurel was beginning to think she'd wasted her time. "Or perhaps gotten her confused with another blond woman who looks a great deal like her." She furrowed her brow, as if attempting to remember. "Sissy something."

"No." His response came quicker this time. His eyes remained flat and cool. "I don't believe I've heard that name, either."

"Sissy's a member of your organization," Laurel prompted, purposefully using the present tense. Since Joe wasn't going to be at all happy she'd come here without him, the least she could do would be to try to help identify his Jane Doe for him.

"A great many people are members of CHAOS. Thousands all over the world. Thanks to the efforts of people like Mrs. Aiken, and that woman you mentioned . . . Sister?"

"Sissy."

"Sissy," he corrected with a thoughtful, agreeable nod. His little frown suggested the name still didn't mean anything to him. "Because of the assistance from our network of volunteers, our message is getting out. Hopefully people will wake up and realize how fragile our environment is before we completely destroy the planet."

He leaned forward, put his water tumbler onto the glass-topped coffee table, and rose with a smooth, feline grace. "Which is why I've brought you here today." When he took a CD from a black briefcase, Laurel thought it odd an environmentalist would have chosen alligator. "I've something I believe you may be interested in."

Laurel angled her head. Studied him. Something was wrong. *Damn.* Why the hell couldn't she get a little burst of Zelda's second sight when she needed it?

She took another sip of coffee, which was a little bitter and not nearly as good as what Brendan O'Neill served at

The Black Swan. Wishing she'd paid more attention to her aunt's instructions on how to center her chakras, she tried to open her mind to Wunder's.

Nothing. Nada. Zilch.

"I don't understand why you'd give any important information to an out of work reporter." The white lilies in the Baccarat vases were beginning to give her a headache.

"There are powerful interests who might be willing to kill to keep this story from coming out. Your having been fired puts you beneath their radar. I have a story I want to get out. You need an exclusive story—a scoop, I believe it's called in the news business."

From the way he'd kept CHAOS in the headlines, Laurel figured Wunder knew as much, if not more, about the manipulation of the news than a lot of reporters.

"So, you're suggesting a quid pro quo arrangement." It was the sort of deal she'd made with Joe. But going into any kind of partnership with this man made her much more uneasy.

"Exactly." When he smiled at her, a cool, patient, benevolent smile, Laurel could have sworn she heard the warning rattle of a diamondback's tail. "Or, to put it in more basic terms, you'll wash my hand. And I'll wash yours."

"I have to tell you, Mr. Wunder, I'm no fan of CHAOS's extremist methods."

"All the better," he said mildly. "You won't be accused of being a flack for my organization."

"How exactly do you expect me to get your story out while I'm unemployed?"

"I'm offering you a tale of crime, corruption, and environmental treachery at the highest levels of government. Believe me, Ms. Stewart, with this in your possession, there'll be a bidding war for your services."

The fantasy of the *New York Times* and *Wall Street Journal* vying to hire her played out in Laurel's mind. Wouldn't that just get Cruella's de Merryman's goat?

She reached out to take the plastic jewel case. When her hand accidentally brushed Wunder's, Laurel felt a jolt shoot from his fingers to hers. The sensation had nothing to do with physical attraction, nothing to do with any alleged second sight inherited from her aunt, but everything to do with journalistic instinct.

This, she thought with a thrill of anticipation, could be the story that got her back in the game.

The fire that destroyed the offices of Dixie Petroleum began slowly, as little more than a glow, like a cigarette burning in the dark. No one noticed. Nor did anyone see the thin wisp of pale smoke curling upward from that small orange light.

Seconds later, the first tendrils of flame unfurled across the carpeting; one wrapped around the leg of a table, holding on, before crawling upward, seeking fuel. A spark leaped free, catching on the edge of the navy-blue draperies.

More flames spread across the floor, hissing and slithering like glowing snakes; the smoke was darker now. More acrid.

The oily smoke suddenly erupted into a roaring fireball, sending voracious flames racing up the walls, along the ceiling. The windows exploded outward, the force so sudden, so violent, that sooty-faced witnesses would later report that, from the way the ground had rocked and rolled beneath their feet, they'd thought for sure an earthquake had struck the city.

As the fire howled, filling the air with thick, black smoke, and chips of safety glass rained down on spectators like falling stars, others, thinking of terrorist bombs, ran for their lives.

Joe had just left the Mustang in The Black Swan's parking lot when he noticed a cab pull up across the street. A spurt of irritation shot through him as he viewed Laurel getting out of the back seat. Dammit, he'd told her to stay put! Where the hell had she gone this time?

A gust sweeping in from the sea turned her bright, rainbow-hued umbrella inside out. She was struggling with it when Joe saw a dark sedan nose around the corner, its headlights dark. With every cop instinct he possessed screaming inside him, he shouted out her name—"Laurel!"—but his words of warning were whipped away by the wind.

She was struggling with the collapsed umbrella, trying to juggle it with an oversize purse as rain poured down like a thick, gray curtain, decreasing visibility. She appeared unaware of the black sedan that was headed straight for her.

Joe took off running.

The engine roared as the car picked up speed.

The wind whipped at Laurel's sunshine-yellow parka as she stepped off the curb.

Shit. If only he'd had the shotgun he kept in the back of the Crown Vic, he might have been able to blow out a tire. Shooting out tires of a speeding car in the dark with a handgun was something that only happened in movies.

Joe sprinted faster as the black car hurtled directly at her.

"Laurel!"

She finally heard Joe calling her name.

"Move, dammit! Now!"

He was running toward her, long legs eating up the cobblestones, arms pumping.

It was then that she saw the huge black car headed straight toward her.

She'd reached the middle of the street. Momentarily frozen in her tracks, Laurel spun a look back at the curb she'd just stepped off, looked forward again toward the walkway on the other side.

Which one? Both seemed a mile away.

Too late.

34

"So you're awake." His voice, coming from somewhere beyond the light, held none of the warmth Chloe was used to hearing in it.

She nodded. *Please.* She turned widened eyes toward the direction of that cold, unfeeling voice. *Please let me go.*

As if hearing her silent words, he came out of his hiding place in the shadows and stripped the tape from her mouth. When she cried out at the pain, he covered her lips with the hand that had intimately explored every inch of her body.

"You have to promise to be quiet. Or I'll put that back on."

Even Chloe's confused, drug-hazed mind could tell it was not an idle threat. She nodded, then wished she hadn't, when lightning bolts flashed behind her eyes.

"Why?" It was part whisper, part croak.

"I don't want to hurt you, darling girl," he said. He bent over her and stroked her tangled hair, as one might soothe a precious favorite child. "And I know this isn't the most comfortable of places, but there's no way I can keep you with me. I told you from the beginning that we needed to be discreet."

"I've never told anyone about us!"

"And how long do you think you can keep that secret once you start to show?"

"I didn't plan to get pregnant." All right, so that wasn't entirely true. But it had seemed like such a good idea at the time, the only way to force what she knew, deep down inside, he really wanted. Unfortunately, he was such an honorable man, he hadn't wanted to claim his own happiness at the risk of hurting so many others. So, she'd taken matters into her own hands and claimed it for him. For them.

"Do you know what happens to naughty girls who don't tell the truth?"

It was the same thing he'd say when they'd play their game. The game where he'd put her over his lap, toss up the little pleated skirt, and spank her bare bottom until it was red. Chloe realized this was no game.

"I'm not lying," she lied. "It was an accident. A mistake." The mistake, she was beginning to fear, was giving her heart to someone who, like so many other men in her past, could never appreciate the gift.

Dark comprehension rumbled, like the thunder before a very deadly storm. She was not going to receive the marriage proposal she'd dreamed of.

"I can't marry you, Chloe," he said, confirming her dread. "Not at this point in time."

"We don't have to get married right away," she said quickly. Too quickly, she realized when his eyes narrowed suspiciously. "We can continue just as we've been. No one would ever have to know whose baby it is." Surely, in time, he'd come to love their child as deeply as she already did.

"You know I'd never risk a scandal that could cost me everything I've ever worked for."

She'd always had wretched judgment in men. From her first affair with her chemistry teacher her sophomore year of high school, she'd been fatally attracted to older men unable and unwilling to commit. She'd once gone to a therapist who'd suggested that these emotionally unavailable men were surrogates for the father she'd lost at such a young age.

At the time she'd protested the idea. Now the truth hit like a knife to her heart.

The pain was sharp. But not deadly.

A strange calm settled over her. Chloe wasn't going to allow herself to get hysterical. It would be bad for her baby.

"I won't be the first woman to raise a child alone." Her voice trembled even as her resolve strengthened. *I'll protect you*, she assured her unborn infant. "I'm intelligent, well-educated, and I can afford to quit work for a time when the baby's born, if I have to."

Hearing the words out loud, amazingly, she, someone who'd never been able to stand being alone, found herself believing them.

"I'd rather not be a single mother," she continued. "But if that's the only choice, well, then." She tried to shrug her shoulders, but was restricted by the bonds he still hadn't untied.

His Arctic-blue eyes narrowed, glittering dangerously

in the yellow candlelight. His face had never been more compelling. Nor as frightening. "That's quite a turn-around coming from such a neurotic, needy girl."

Although she'd just acknowledged the truth of that description to herself, the accusation, stated in a cool, uncaring voice, still stung. It also strengthened her resolve. *I'll protect you.*

"Perhaps it's the hormones."

He studied her and rubbed his chin in that thinking way that she'd once found wonderfully sexy.

"Perhaps." His gaze softened, just a bit. "Are you hungry? I brought you some soup."

She looked at the thermos with suspicion. "I'd rather starve than let you drug me again."

"Don't be foolish." He tenderly skimmed his knuckles up her cheek. "I don't want you to starve, darling. As for drugging you, I'll admit that was a bit extreme. But it was only a little Seconal mixed into the tea. I needed to get you alone, somewhere we could talk uninterrupted about how to handle this problem."

"You can't be asking me to abort my baby."

She'd always voted pro-choice, but about this, about her own life, her child, she'd made her own personal choice the moment she'd learned that she was pregnant.

"You're a young, healthy woman. You can have more children." He reached into his pocket and took out a small plastic vial. "We can have more together," he said with a mild reasonableness she found more threatening than the most deadly shout. "Just not now." He shook out three cylindrical yellow pills into his palm and held them out to her. "Just take them, Chloe."

His lips curved in a gentle, almost kind smile. But when he leaned toward her, Chloe viewed the pistol in the pocket of his black rain slicker; a frisson of icy fear skimmed up her spine as she realized that this man she'd foolishly believed herself to be in love with, the man she'd made a child with, was willing to kill her to keep their secret.

"Goddammit! What the hell did you think you were doing?" Joe roared.

He'd rammed into Laurel, sending her flying across the street. Tires squealed as the car sped around the corner.

And now she was lying on the sidewalk in front of the pub, with him on top of her.

"You don't have to cuss at me. I was working."

"Working?"

"Yes. I believe you might be acquainted with the concept. People do a task which, in turn, earns them money to live on." She bucked beneath him. "And do you think you can get off me any time soon? I'm having difficulty breathing. You probably broke a rib."

"Shit." He rolled off her, onto his feet. "You don't have a job."

"If Wunder's right about this CD, I will." Since she wasn't entirely certain her still-shaking legs could stand on their own, she accepted the hand he was holding down to her.

"You went to see Wunder? On your own?"

"Yes." God, he was sexy when he was pissed. She suspected he didn't get angry often, but when he did—wow, talk about your testosterone overload! "And you don't have to yell."

"I'm not yelling, dammit," Joe roared.

He scooped her up, carrying her through the pub to the interest of the patrons, several who'd cheered him on, and into the elevator. Laurel might have found the entire episode rather romantic—like Richard Gere carrying Debra Winger out of that dreary paper factory in *An Officer and a Gentleman*—if he hadn't been so furious at her.

"You did too yell," Laurel countered. "And curse at me. Which isn't real considerate since I could be bleeding to death."

"You're hurt?" His brows dove down to that strong, straight nose. She thought he paled a bit. "Where?"

"My knees." She lifted her pretty, now-ruined skirt to show him. "You dragged me across about a mile of cobblestones. They're all scraped up."

"It could be worse." His eyes had changed from blazing to relieved as they entered the loft. "That car could have hit you. And you'd be lying beside Sissy Sotheby-Beale in the morgue with a tag on your big toe."

"Sissy Sotheby-Beale? So your brother knew her?"

"Yeah." The storm outside was pounding against the glass wall; the storm inside him had waned as quickly as it had begun. He carried her across the floor, into the bathroom. "Let's clean you up."

"I can do it myself."

"Christ, you can be stubborn. I realize you can do it yourself. But you're bleeding all over your skirt because of me. So it's only right I make amends."

"The blood doesn't matter. Since my skirt's already ruined." It was a bright tangerine silk she'd worn with a tangerine-, lime-, and lemon-striped blouse that should have clashed with her hair, but fortunately didn't since she'd chosen the citrus colors to brighten the gray day.

"Sorry about that," he said as he closed the commode. "I'll buy you a new one." He opened the medicine cabinet and impressed her by retrieving an actual first aid kit. Nothing like being prepared; she doubted either she or Chloe could locate a Band-Aid in their house. "Sit."

"You don't have to replace my skirt." She sat. "You did, after all, save my life."

"So you noticed that." He dampened a washcloth beneath the tap, then squirted some liquid soap on it.

"Of course I did. If you hadn't come along, I'd probably be toast right now." She shook her head. "Some people are just too clueless to live. Even I slow down when it rains. It's too easy to have an accident, and I'm already paying a ridiculous amount for car insurance."

"That wouldn't have been any damn accident." He crouched down beside her. "Jesus, you did take one helluva hit. These look like ground hamburger."

"They look worse than they feel." That was a lie. Now that the shock was wearing off, the nerve endings were coming back to life and screeching bloody murder. His words belatedly sunk in. "What do you mean it wasn't an accident?"

"The driver intended to run you down."

"That's ridiculous." She flinched as he began scrubbing the gravel and sand out of her right knee. "Why would anyone want to run me down?"

"That seems to be the million dollar question. Since we don't seem to be getting any closer to your friend, I suspect it has something to do with you traipsing over to Wunder's hotel after I specifically told you to stay put."

"He called me," she said a little defensively.

"Well, hell, we could have put that on your tombstone."

Beneath the sarcasm, Laurel detected a very real concern. A shiver lanced through her. "You're not kidding."

"I seldom kid about murder." He took a bottle of antiseptic from the white plastic kit. "Well, okay, sometimes I do. I mean, I'm a cop—"

"Yeah, yeah, I know all about it. Dark humor helps you get through the tough stuff without going insane. Shit!" She jerked her leg away at the sting. "You did that on purpose. To get back at me for going to Wunder's hotel room without you."

"I did it so you won't die of sepsis. Or have to have your leg cut off. Which, I suppose, if you ended up with a peg, would make you fit right in during Buccaneer Days."

"You're a riot, Gannon. If you ever decide to turn in your badge you might want to consider going on the comedy circuit."

He ignored that crack and spread a large Band-Aid over the wound. "So what did Wunder have to say?"

"That he has a story that can bring Aiken down, that he doesn't know Chloe, or Sissy, and how could anyone know I was at his hotel in the first place?"

"Maybe because someone followed you?"

"Why?"

"Hell if I know. Perhaps because you've been going

around suggesting that the vice president of the United States is not only having an affair, but may have used nefarious means to get rid of his mistress. Then there's the little matter of a possible break-in into the West Wing."

"I didn't do that!"

"I know that, and you know that, but we don't know if you've convinced the FBI, and finally, slugging a Secret Service agent probably garners a person government attention."

"Good point." She sucked in a sharp breath as he began to clean the other knee. "But the FBI arrests people and I can't believe the Secret Service would try to eliminate anyone who wasn't trying to kill their protectee."

"Maybe Aiken hired himself some private thugs to keep an eye on you."

Her eyes widened. "You finally believe me? About Aiken?"

"He's a logical suspect, if Wunder's information turns out to be important. What's this story that was worth risking your life for, anyway?"

"I don't know. He refused to tell me, but he did give me a CD. Obviously I haven't looked at it yet." She glanced around in a momentary panic. "My purse—"

"Is on the table."

"We need to get it, and see what's on that CD."

"Whatever it is will hold. Are you sure you didn't bang your head on those stones, too?" He ran his fingers through her hair, probing for wounds.

"Just my knees. Why?"

"Because you're being awful cool about this. It seems being matter of fact about a murder attempt is carrying that never-let-them-see-you-sweat motto to the extreme."

"How do you know I'm not trembling like a leaf on the inside?"

"Maybe you are." He studied her thoughtfully, looking hard, looking deep. "You know," he said, "you don't always need to be in charge of everything."

"Yes, I do." It was little more than a whisper, but easily heard in the small room. "I do," she repeated more firmly.

Joe was stunned when her eyes suddenly swam. Depths. The lady had them. Beneath that brassy, independent, take-no-prisoners-attitude, she had fears and uncertainties just like everyone else. Just like him.

"Aw, sugar." He felt his heart tumble and realized that if he was ever going to be able to pull back, it'd be right now. "You're only human." He slid his fingers through the damp silk of her hair. Touched his lips to her cheek and tasted the salt of the single tear she'd allowed to escape. "Maybe it's time to give yourself a break."

She hitched in a breath, then buried her face against his neck. "Maybe I don't know how."

He knew the feeling. All too well. Christ, weren't the two of them a pair?

"You're an intelligent woman, Laurel Stewart." He tipped a finger beneath her chin, lifting her face. "Smart as a whip. I'll bet you've always been a quick learner." He traced her lips, tugging the corners up a little, encouraging a faint smile. "Now see, look at that." He touched his mouth to hers, keeping the kiss light, which was no easy task when he wanted to plunder. "You're already softening, sugarplum."

"I'm not soft." She'd never let herself be. Joe decided to delve into the reasons for that later.

"Wanna bet?" He ran his hand up her leg, deftly bypassing her wounded knee. Slid his fingers beneath that bright, wet, torn skirt and trailed little figure eights on the inside of her thigh. "You feel pretty soft to me."

"That's not what I meant."

"I know," he said against her mouth.

Her sweet, sweet mouth.

Tenderness warred with lust as he kissed her again, a little longer this time. A little deeper, and tasted her soft, shimmering sigh. When her lips opened beneath his, inviting more, the muscles in his stomach tightened.

When he felt the kiss slipping from pleasure to passion, Joe's craving for her soared. He could have eaten her alive, devoured her with one bite, but since there was only one first time with a woman you'd just realized you might be falling in love with, he forced himself to take the time to taste.

When he scooped her back up into his arms and carried her toward the bed, she made one last stab at control. "I'm capable of walking, Gannon. I have, after all, been doing it for nearly thirty-five years."

"I'm aware of that. May I make one suggestion?"

"What?"

"Shut the fuck up," he said pleasantly. She bounced when he dropped her onto the mattress.

"Be still my heart," she sighed dramatically. He could

see the glint of a smile in her eyes as she patted her breast. "You're such a romantic, Detective."

"You told me you didn't want romance," he reminded her.

"I said I didn't *need* it. But I've been wanting to rip your clothes off since you strolled across that squad room."

He cocked a brow. "You wanted to rip my clothes off?"

"Absolutely. And not just because that shirt you were wearing was as ugly as homemade sin."

"Isn't that a handy coincidence. Since I wanted to do the same thing to you."

"Why didn't you?"

"Maybe because I didn't want to get arrested for jumping a reporter in my own police station?"

"We're not in your police station now." The dare flashed in her magnificent eyes like lightning. Hot and dangerous.

"Good point." He tore her citrus colored silk blouse open. Wondering when they'd started making lime-colored bras, he broke the front plastic clasp with a quick, deft twist.

35

Laurel drew in a sharp breath as he possessively cupped her milky white breasts in his hands, then moaned as his fingers tore down her torso and yanked the side zipper of her skirt apart.

"God, Gannon." She bucked as his hand snaked into the open gap to cup her.

"Could you do me a big favor?" he groaned.

"What?" she asked as his fingers thrust into her. She was wet and slick and tight.

He didn't know whether to curse or laugh when, even as her body was clutching at him, she couldn't just give in without questioning.

"When we're in bed . . ." He began to move his fingers. In. "Or on the rug . . ."

Out. "Or maybe the kitchen table."

Her fragrant skin was damp. And hot.

In again. "Or anywhere else I'm making love to you, could you call me something else? Like maybe *darling*."

Out. "*Sweetheart* . . ."

She whimpered and arched her hips toward him.

"Or maybe even *your huge, hot, hunka burning love?*" In.

Her burst of laughter was heard first. Then came a ragged sound—half cry, half scream. It was torn from her throat as the orgasm ripped through her.

"That's the first one," he said against her hair, holding her tight as the energy poured off her limp body in waves. He pulled her skirt away, leaving her wearing only a skimpy pair of lacy panties that matched the bra. "Just to get the edge off." He wanted her limp and naked beneath him, but when he went to yank that minuscule bit of lace away, she drew back. Just far enough to press her hands against his chest.

"Uh, uh," she said. Her eyes, which had gone blind when she'd come, blazed with the same hunger that was burning inside Joe. "It's my turn."

Buttons went flying across the floor. She dragged the shirt down his arms, her teeth nipping, not gently, at his shoulder.

He yanked her down onto the mattress and as they rolled over the bed, he helped her dispense with the clothes between them, exposing more flesh.

There was a clash of teeth as his mouth ate into hers. Joe took what he wanted, Laurel what she needed. Their appetites seemingly insatiable, he feasted on her body as she devoured his. He skimmed kisses up her long smooth legs, bit lightly at the tender skin between her thighs, then stroked her with his tongue until she was twisting beneath him, her hands fisting in the hot and tangled sheets. The low, keening sound she made when she came again was the sexiest thing he'd ever heard.

"That's two," he murmured against her stomach.

"Arrogant bastard."

"That'll do." It wasn't quite as good as a *hunka burning love*, but Joe decided to take it as a compliment.

Oh, God, she was drunk. Drunk on his musky, male scent, drunk on the hot, pungent taste of him, drunk on the feel of smooth muscles beneath that dark, golden skin.

And oh, so very drunk on the power she'd discovered she could wield over a man who, she knew, was not accustomed to giving up control.

She reveled in the way his erection jerked when she nuzzled her cheek against the crisp brown hair between his legs; thrilled at the way he sucked in his stomach when she explored his erection from root to tip. She should have known, she thought, as she circled the hot circumference with her fingers, that Joe Gannon was not a man to exaggerate. About anything.

He was huge. Magnificent. And for tonight he was all hers.

Craving closer contact, she caressed the jutting flesh with her tongue. When she licked the clear moisture from the cleft tip, he moaned her name and reached for her.

"Not yet."

Amazingly, when she took him between her lips, swallowing him more deeply than she'd ever swallowed any man, she came again, in a quick, shuddering climax.

"Three," he said in a half laugh, half groan. "But if you don't stop that, sugar, we're not going to make it to four."

He rolled over, flipping her onto her back. "I knew you'd be amazing." He traced slow, lazy circles in her moist, red curls. "That we'd be amazing together."

He opened the drawer of the bedside table and retrieved a condom. Proving that driving was not the only thing he did fast, he sheathed himself in record time.

His hands looked so large, so dark against the white of her hot, damp skin as he pressed against the inside of her thighs, parting her legs wider, exposing her in a way that would have made her uncomfortable if he'd been any other man.

"Beautiful," he murmured, then lifted his gaze, watching her eyes as he slowly entered her, inch by devastating inch.

They began moving together, in perfect rhythm, as if they'd made love a hundred times before. Her body lifted to meet his as his hips pistoned—deeper, harder, faster. This time they climaxed together, in a pleasure so sharp, so bright, Laurel was amazed she didn't shatter into a thousand crystalline pieces.

"*That's* four," he panted with obvious male satisfaction, as he collapsed onto her.

As a warm, almost unknown peace settled over her, Laurel did something she'd never—ever—done before with a man in bed: she laughed. Then, wrapping her arms around him, she hugged him tight, taking him into her wary, guarded heart.

Laurel slowly, gradually, drifted back, becoming aware of the outside world. It was Blues Night in the pub; the sultry sound of a tenor sax drifted up from downstairs, a musical counterpoint to the percussion of the rain on the roof, the moaning of the wind, the creaking of ships' moorings from the docks.

Somehow, when she hadn't been paying attention, the sun had set; the night lights were coming on all over town, gleaming jewel-like on the other side of the crescent-shaped harbor.

She'd just realized that their hearts were beating in synchronization when he said, "Pizza."

"Pizza?" She lifted her head and looked down at him.

"I promised you a pizza when I got back from Mike's. After all"—the look he skimmed over her had Laurel tingling in places she hadn't even known she could tingle—"we need to keep our strength up."

"For detecting," she reminded him.

He let out a short laugh. "That, too."

36

Laurel was sitting at the kitchen table, studying the screen on her laptop when Joe returned with the pizza. He was disappointed, but not particularly surprised, that she'd gotten dressed in a body-skimming pink blouse and a pair of white shorts creased sharply enough to cut glass. Her feet were still bare, her toes polished in a glossy strawberry pink that had him wanting to suck them.

"You look like something that should be topped with whipped cream and served in a sugar cone." Now that he thought about it, whipped cream wouldn't have been such a bad idea; he should've snagged some from the pub while he'd been downstairs.

"Later," she said distractedly.

He sighed, put the pizza box down on the counter, and went to stand behind her. "So, what's this CD that's going to bring down a sitting vice president?"

"I'm not sure it's that much of a bombshell. But it sure as hell wouldn't be helpful to his campaign if it gets out. Apparently he arranged for one of his cronies' companies to receive a no-bid contract to dismantle an old fleet of ships here in the Somersett shipyards."

"How old?"

"They were built about fifty, sixty years ago, which means the entire fleet of more than a hundred ships are contaminated with PCBs, lead paint, asbestos, and oil, among other nasty stuff."

"Sounds as if it'd be good to get them out of use."

"Well, of course it would. Especially since a lot of them have been rusting away in harbors for decades, and were just an environmental disaster waiting to happen." She tapped on the keys and brought up another window. "But according to this EPA report, while there are a few places here in the States equipped to handle the work safely—or as safely as such a thing can be—Somersett isn't one of them."

"Which means the harbor, not to mention thousands of acres of wetlands, will be at risk."

"Big time," she agreed. "Several groups filed suit to prevent the contract, but it was added to a terrorism bill at the last minute, then classified to keep people from finding out."

"It won't be able to stay secret once the work starts."

"Probably not. But by then the ships will already be here, won't they? And moving them again, to somewhere else, could be more dangerous because they'll be more likely to fall apart."

"You're right about it not exactly blowing the campaign out of the water," Joe agreed. "Since this certainly isn't the first administration to grant no-bid contracts. But what if there's more? What if Aiken took money from the company that's going to do the work?"

"Well, of course he did. That's the way the game is played. That's how campaigns get most of their funds. Contributions from regular people are chickenfeed compared to the millions brought in by PACs and special interests."

"There's a lot of money floating around," he agreed. "Which makes you wonder if it all ends up in the right place."

She thought about that for a long moment. "If he's been comingling campaign funds with personal ones and funneled some into his own coffers . . ."

"There's been a lot of work being done on the old Aiken place out on the river," Joe revealed.

"If he used any campaign contributions for the remodeling, he'd be in trouble."

"And wasn't there talk of a new vacation home down in the islands?"

"Paradise Island." Laurel remembered Chloe mentioning it. It was back when she'd been more strongly involved in the environmental movement and had been worried about what would happen to the undeveloped beaches now that the casino and hotel crowd had found the place. What if Chloe hadn't really been a fan of Aiken after all? What if she'd gone to work for him as some sort of mole to pass information on to Wunder?

"I'll bet public money went into that house. He's also pals with that guy who built one of the casinos." She'd seen a picture in *Newsweek* of the two deep sea fishing together in the Bahamas. Possibilities kept clicking away like one of those old ticker-tape machines they used to use on Wall Street. "What if he's involved in some secret off-shore partnerships?"

"You're definitely talking impeachment," Joe said. "Not to mention jail time."

"I guess we follow the money," Laurel quoted Deep Throat.

"Sounds like it's worth a try," Joe said. He ran a hand over her shoulder. "People have been killed for a lot less."

Shivering at the idea that anyone might have tried to kill her, and beginning to have new worries that Aiken might have arranged for Chloe's disappearance because she'd found something out about illegal dealings, Laurel realized that she couldn't keep her friend's secret from Joe any longer.

"There's something else I haven't told you," she said.

"Oh?"

"I think Chloe's pregnant."

He didn't hesitate. "All the more reason," he said, "to find her as soon as possible."

He finally believed her!

Feeling more encouraged than she had since all this had begun, she began scrolling down the screen, looking for more evidence against Aiken.

"Interestingly enough, the company that got the contract is a subsidiary of an oil company. What a good deal for Dixie Petroleum," she murmured. "They make money dirtying up things, then make more bucks to clean up the mess they made."

"Dixie Petroleum?"

"That's what it says." More scrolling. "Apparently the company's home offices are here."

"Not for long. They're on fire."

"What?" She looked up at him.

"Someone had switched the pub TV to the news. I saw the report." He picked up the remote and clicked on his own large-screen TV, which showed the office tower engulfed in flames.

"I'm amazed it's burning that hot with all the rain," Laurel said.

"It was probably helped along," he guessed. "Maybe Tess will know something."

"Tess?"

"My sister. She's an arson investigator."

"Really?" Yet more proof they didn't know anything about one another, Laurel thought. She hadn't even known he had a sister.

"She used to be a firefighter. Danny—her fiancé—was a firefighter, too. He died shortly before their wedding.

"Jesus." It wasn't often Laurel was speechless. This was one of those times.

"Yeah," he said grimly. "She doesn't talk much about it. Tess is a lot like you. She's not about to let anyone see her sweat."

"Even her brother?"

Another shrug. "She might open up a bit more with Mike, him being in the confession business, and all. But other than having me help with some funeral details while she was still in the hospital with burns from that same fire, she hasn't mentioned it."

"That's sad . . . My mother died," she said as they watched the streams of water from the firefighter's hoses turn black smoke to gray. "When I was five. She'd gone into labor, but there was a blizzard and they couldn't get her to the hospital, so she gave birth to Lily at home." Remembered pain shadowed her eyes. "Something went terribly wrong. And she died."

"That must have been hard."

"I got to talk to her before we lost her, though." Unable to share something so personal face to face, she kept her gaze directed to the screen.

"That's something," he said.

"Yeah. It was." She sighed. "She knew how things were going to end. She told me that she was going to go live with the angels and that since I was the big sister, it'd be my responsibility to take care of Lark and Lily. And my father, since everyone knew he couldn't take care of himself."

"Jesus, Laurel." He ran a hand down her hair. "That's a terrible burden to lay on a five-year-old kid."

"I was the oldest," she said simply. "Besides, it was a long time ago." Nearly thirty years. "I don't remember that much about it."

Liar. Every moment of that time had been emblazoned on her mind—the sleet falling like needles from the darkened December sky on the day of the funeral, Lark looking like a princess, her pale face, framed by white faux fur, giving a hint of the beauty she'd grow up to be, newborn Lily wrapped up in the Stewart plaid bunting.

She remembered how her father, John Angus, who'd always seemed larger than life, had collapsed on the short walk from the chapel to the family cemetery and had to be supported by her uncles as the procession made its way past snow-dusted tombstones.

They all carried their emotional scars from that day. Lily, she suspected, had grown up feeling guilty their mother had died bringing her into the world. The experience had definitely changed Lark. Having originally been the most outgoing, she'd turned quiet, shy, and, Laurel had often felt, too accommodating.

While she herself had become cynical, angry, and determined to never risk depending on anyone for anything.

She was jerked out of the painful thoughts by the familiar face that suddenly filled the screen.

"If people are serious about stopping injustice perpetrated by our government," Cody Wunder was saying into reporters' microphones, "they need to be realistic about what it's going to take to stop that injustice." He was seated on the alabaster love seat in his hotel suite. "Obviously, civil protest involves a variety of tactics, but the life of the planet is so endangered, and so crucial, one form of that protest must include political violence."

"Are you claiming responsibility for the Dixie Petroleum fire?" the blond local television reporter asked.

"Of course not." His smile was as cold as the snake's whose tail Laurel had imagined rattling when she'd been talking with him earlier. "I have a witness who can state I was here at my apartment at the time that fire is reported to have started."

"The bastard set me up," Laurel flared. "He used me as his damn alibi!"

"It appears so," Joe murmured.

"And that witness's name?"

"Laurel Stewart," Wunder announced.

The cutaway shot revealed the reporter's surprise. "Laurel Stewart, the former *Washington Post* journalist?"

"None other." He flashed another of those cold smiles that did not meet his frosty blue eyes. "Whom, I believe, was terminated from her job by powerful interests, to keep her silent."

Back on her game, the reporter obligingly picked up her cue. "Keep her silent about what?"

"The fact that she's working with CHAOS to rid our government of greedy politicians who put money before morals. Politicians who line their pockets at the expense of our planet."

"Dammit," Laurel said. She felt Joe's hand settle on her shoulder as she braced for what was coming next.

"Politicians like Noble Aiken."

37

"How could he do that?" Laurel demanded yet again.

She'd been pacing the floor for ten minutes, the energy sparking around her like heat lightning. He was surprised the earth wasn't rumbling beneath the building.

"He used me, dammit!"

"I believe that's a fair assumption."

She spun toward him, her eyes twin green flames, temper flying in her cheeks. "Don't you dare stay calm while I'm not!"

"Sorry." He held up his hands, deciding that bringing up that old cliché that she was drop-dead gorgeous when she was angry would only get him slugged. And having seen what that clenched fist had done to that Secret Service guy's eye, he decided he'd just as soon pass. "Want me to go over to the Harbor Villa and play Dirty Harry and blow him away for you?"

"Of course I don't want you to kill him. Why should you have all the fun?" She kicked out at the leg of the couch. "Ow! Damn, damn, damn!" He also decided even risking a smile at her hopping around on one foot would not be the wisest move. She threw herself on the couch and began gingerly rubbing her foot. "I think I broke my toes."

"Let me see." He sat down beside her, lifted her foot to his lap, and wiggled the pink toes in question. "Nah. They're just jammed." Still holding her foot, he began massaging it with his thumbs, long smooth strokes from the tips of her toes to her ankles.

She stiffened. "What are you doing?"

"Calming you down?" He refused to let go when she tugged at her foot.

"I don't want to calm down. I want to drag that son of a bitch out of that snow cave he's built for himself and strangle him."

"I don't blame you." His thumbs moved on to pressing circles on the bottom of her foot, lingering on her arch, which was bowed as tight as the rest of her.

"No." She shook her head. "Strangling's too easy. Too fast. I want to draw and quarter him. Slow and horribly. Like King Edward did to Mel Gibson in *Braveheart.*"

"Messy, but effective." He rotated her toes, then cupping his hand beneath her heel, began rotating her ankle. "Give me your other foot."

"That one's not hurt."

"Trust me." He picked it up, twisting her around so she was lying with her head on the arm of the sofa, both feet now in his lap. "I'll still make it feel better."

He felt her rippling sigh all the way to her toes. "I do," she admitted. The flashfire temper was subsiding. "Trust you."

"Thank you." Trust, he knew, was as difficult for her as it was for him.

"He's a hateful, evil man. Even worse than Aiken."

"I think that was determined when he started encouraging his followers to take actions that cost lives."

"I know. If he wasn't so charismatic, he'd probably be behind bars right now." Another sigh. "Although I have to admit that I'm glad he discovered that ghost ship contract."

"What are you going to do with the information?"

"I don't know." She stretched out as he continued to massage her other foot. "My credibility wasn't all that hot before Wunder made it sound as if I were in cahoots with him. And it's not as if I've got editors all around the country waiting with bated breath for me to submit articles." She sighed again, but this time with pleasure. "God, you're good at that."

"Cops are supposed to protect and serve." He skimmed his fingers up her ankle. "This is an aspect of the *serve* part . . . I think I'll go have a little talk with Aiken tomorrow. Want to come along?"

Her eyes had drifted shut. But at his casual mention of the vice president, they opened. "There's nothing I'd love better. But in case you've forgotten, I've got a restraining order that doesn't allow me within a hundred feet of the guy."

"Actually, there isn't any restraining order."

Her eyes flew open. "What? But J. T. Malloy said there was."

"There isn't. I checked." He admittedly hadn't shared that little bit of information because he'd been afraid she'd go getting into more hot water.

"But J. T. and I used to be friends." Her brow furrowed. "Why would he lie?"

"Perhaps because he's still your friend and was trying to keep you out of trouble." Not an easy task, Joe thought. Fortunately, he'd always enjoyed a challenge. "So, want to come?"

Her eyes burned with the intensity of a zealot. "I'd like to see you stop me. Thank you!" She flung herself into his arms and kissed him. Hard. "Now you know what I want?"

"Another round of hot, steamy sex?" he asked hopefully.

"Pizza first. Then the sex," she decided.

"Works for me," he said agreeably.

"But first I have something to do. I just realized who I'm going to give my story to." She retrieved her phone from her tote and scanned through the call numbers until she found the one she was looking for.

"Hello, Ms. Squires," she said as the voice on the other end of the line answered. "This is Laurel Stewart. I had no idea you had such an illustrious background."

Laurel had investigated Sandra Squires while Joe had been downstairs getting the pizza. Surprisingly, the editor had worked as a reporter on political beats for the *Chicago Tribune*, the *Sacramento Bee*, and the *Richmond Times-Dispatch*. Then she'd dropped out of sight.

"I did all right for myself, before choosing to stay home when my children were young," Sandra Squires revealed. "Political journalism on the national scale isn't exactly a family-friendly business."

"Tell me about it," Laurel agreed. One more reason she'd decided against marriage and children.

"Now that my kids are in high school, I thought I'd try putting my toe back into the waters, but as you know,

Washington's a very competitive arena, and people seem to fear I've gotten rusty. I interviewed at the *Post*," she related, "but while she never would have risked saying it out loud, for fear of risking an age discrimination suit, I sensed that Lois Merryman thought I was too old for the job.

"Fortunately, the *Bee*—the Falls Church one, not Sacramento—has a new publisher with deep pockets who was willing to take a chance to hire me as the new editor. Our goal is to shift our focus from a cheery little grocery shopper to a major player in the DC political market. Which was why," she said, "we were so excited about the possibility of you coming to work with us."

"I've been giving a great deal of thought to your offer, Sandra, and I'd love to write for the *Bee*, but for the moment, anyway, I'd prefer to keep things on a freelance basis."

"We can do that," Sandra Squires said without hesitation.

"For my first article, I'll be sending you a report on the vice president's business dealings with a certain southern petroleum company. Oh, and you might want to consider hiring someone to help answer the phones. Since I believe you'll be receiving a lot of calls once the paper hits the stands."

After finishing up the call, she turned back to Joe with a satisfied grin. "The ghost ship report will be running in this week's *Falls Church Bee*. Hopefully, I'll be able to dig up the vacation-home money trail by next week."

Score one, Laurel thought, as she bit into the gooey, thick-crust pizza, for the good guys.

38

The sun rose bloodred, like a match scratched across the sky. *Red sky at night, sailors delight; red sky in the morning, sailors take warning.*

Having awakened unable to remember when she'd felt any better, Laurel didn't dwell on the warning humming in the back of her mind. Good sex was definitely better than a handful of Valium. And great sex . . . well, it didn't get any better than what she'd experienced last night. She stretched, as loose, relaxed, and boneless as a kitten lying in a sunbeam.

The only problem was that she was alone in bed. She smiled when she heard the shower running in the next room.

He had his back to her when she opened the glass door, and just looking at the strong muscles leading down to that firm male butt created a renewed stir of desire.

She paused, second-guessing her plan to join him in the shower. She wasn't accustomed to morning-afters because she usually didn't actually sleep with the men she went to bed with. Somehow, it was too personal, too intimate.

While sex was admittedly as close as two bodies could get, she preferred to think of it as merely recreational. As sweaty as working out in the gym, but a lot more fun. But something was different this morning. Something that was suddenly making her uneasy.

Before she could sort her feelings out, he glanced back over a wide, dark shoulder. "I was just thinking about you." His warmly drawled statement and dazzling smile wiped her mind as clear as glass.

"Were you?"

"Ah yes, the lady reporter needs evidence." He turned around and faced her. "Exhibit A." His body was fully, rampantly aroused.

"Well." She swallowed, then dragged her eyes back to his face. "That is certainly rather compelling evidence. Fortunately, I came prepared."

His wicked-as-sin grin, when he viewed the unwrapped condom she was holding in her palm, gilded his eyes.

As he looped a wet arm around her neck, pulling her into the shower with him, Laurel decided she could figure out the problem of her uncharacteristic nervousness later.

He nuzzled the nape of her neck and cupped her breasts in hands that last night had been every bit as slow and clever as he'd promised.

Warm water was streaming over them; her blood had begun to run even warmer.

She drew in a sharp breath when he nipped at an earlobe she'd never known until last night could be an erogenous zone, then linked her fingers together around his neck.

They were torso to torso, heat to heat when he lifted her up, turning her so her back was up against the cobalt blue tile.

There was a clash of teeth as his mouth crushed hers. Laurel tasted passion and reveled in it. She wrapped her legs around his hips as he thrust into her; her fingers dug deep into his back as they rode into the mists together.

"God, I'm crazy about you," he said later as he tucked in his silk Aloha shirt. Today's print featured blindingly bright tropical fish swimming on a midnight-blue sea.

Laurel couldn't help it. She stiffened. Only for a moment, but as he kept reminding her, he was after all a detective; not much got by him.

"I'm crazy about you, too." Her tone was bright and breezy, and, she suspected, wasn't fooling him for a minute. "And, wow, I've gotta give you credit, you weren't exaggerating. Thanks to you, I beat a personal best."

"We aim to please."

"Oh, you do. I swear, if I'd known about you southern boys—"

"Laurel." He caught hold of the hand she was waving around like a beauty queen on speed. "Relax."

"I am," she lied. "Why, I've never been so relaxed in my life. I was thinking when I woke up, that a night of hot casual sex was even better than Valium."

"I don't think I could ever feel all that casual about sex with you."

She colored prettily, but held firm. "You know what I mean. As long as I'm in Somersett, we'll keep the sex completely apart from the investigation. No strings. No complications." She tugged her hand free and stepped into a short, grass-green pleated skirt that had him wanting to bite one of those smooth silky thighs. "Then, after I've found Chloe, brought down Aiken, and you've arrested Sissy's murderer, we'll go back to our own lives."

"Want to know what I think?"

"Not really."

Since it had kept him awake most of the night, he was going to tell her anyway. "It's not really marriage you're afraid of. It's intimacy."

Her eyes narrowed. "I'm not afraid of anything. I also hadn't realized you had a psych degree."

"Cops have to play shrink from time to time. But you're an easy read, sugar. You like to observe. From a distance." He tilted his head and studied her a bit more. "That's probably why you became a reporter."

"I became a reporter for the same reason you became a cop." Her voice was muffled as she pulled a sleeveless silk top a few shades lighter than the skirt over her head. "To make a difference."

"I'll buy that. But the difference is that my job forces me to get involved in people's lives. I've delivered babies in the backseat of a patrol car on the freeway; I've broken the news to parents that their teenager's been killed in a car wreck; and I've busted mothers for cooking meth while their malnourished toddlers are wandering around the room in filthy diapers.

"While you, on the other hand, built a wall between you and the people you write about."

She tossed up her chin. "That wall just happens to be constructed of journalistic integrity."

"It also allows you to stand back and judge folks from a distance."

"Do you always insult women after you have sex with them?"

"Not as a rule. And we both know that whatever it is that's happening here is more than just sex. Or a one-night stand."

She didn't insult either one of them by lying.

Deciding that there was no point in wading any deeper into conversational waters he wasn't all that eager to discuss, either, Joe took a small box from the top drawer of his bureau and stuck it into the front pocket of his jeans.

"Why don't you get back to tracking down the campaign contributions?" he suggested. "I'll be back in a while."

"You said I could go to Aiken's with you." She shoved her feet into a pair of beaded green sandals.

"You can. This afternoon."

"This afternoon?" She splayed her hands on her hips. "Where are you off to now?"

"Out." He scooped up his keys from the kitchen counter.

"I can see that." She caught up with him at the door and curled her fingers around his upper arm. "Out where?"

"No offense, sugar," he said, "but that's not really any of your business."

"If it's about Chloe, I have a right—"

"Dammit!" He shook his arm free. "When are you going to get it through that gorgeous redhead that not everything revolves around you? You want to keep our lives separate from sex? Fine. I had a life before you showed up in Somersett. I'll have a life after you go back to DC. Where I'm going this morning is on a need to know basis. And you, sweetheart, don't need to know."

That said, he left the loft.

"Well." Laurel blew out a breath and stared at the door he'd almost, but not quite, slammed in her face. Then she snatched her bag from the table and took off after him.

He'd taken the stairs, seemingly several at a time, and was already driving out of the lot when she ran out the door of the pub. Fortunately, what she'd begun to think of as her personal cab was waiting at the curb.

"Follow that car," she gasped, out of breath, as she threw herself into the backseat. "And please, lay off the pirate jargon this morning. I'm not really in the mood."

His dark eyes flashed at hers in the rearview mirror. "Would ye be questioning the speech of Eight-fingers Jake?"

Eight fingers? Laurel absolutely refused to look. "Just follow the damn Mustang. And try not to let him see you."

He was still parked at the curb with the engine running. "Would ye be payin' the usual twenty pieces of eight over the fare, lass?"

Her patience hanging by a thread, she leaned forward and put her hand on the back of the driver's seat. "Look, you biscuit-eating son of a bilge rat," she growled. "I've already crushed ten men between my thighs this morning before I had me breakfast. Now if ye don't want to walk the plank, let's weigh anchor and follow that scallywag."

Flashing a gold-toothed grin, he shifted the yellow cab into gear. "Aye, aye, me buxom beauty," he said happily.

39

The morning sky had faded to a pearly pink when Joe drove down a narrow, winding drive lined with moss-draped oaks at the far western edge of the city. The lush green grounds were draped in fog as he pulled up outside a high, wrought-iron fence rusted by age and weather.

Joe sat in the car for a long, thoughtful time, his hands draped over the leather-covered steering wheel, gazing out at the fog-draped tombs, which looked like muted white ghosts.

It had been three long years since he'd last been here; one thousand and ninety-three days since that rainy afternoon he'd watched the small, pale blue coffin with his tow-headed, dinosaur-loving five-year-old son inside being lowered into the ground.

Unlike many children, Austin had never been afraid of the dark. As an infant, he'd lie in his crib, happily babbling to the moon as it rode the sky outside his window. By the time he was old enough to toddle around the backyard, he'd chase fireflies, a small jar with holes punched in its lid clutched in his pudgy little hand. He'd never catch any, of course. But it was the chase that he loved. Joe'd wondered, more than a few times, if his son might have grown up to be a cop like his old man.

Of course, it had never occurred to him that his son might not grow up.

The night of Austin's fifth birthday, a month before he had been attacked by that killer virus that had taken his life, a month before the shooting that had almost cost Joe *his* life, father and son had camped out together in the backyard after the party in the new tent Joe had bought for the occasion. The warm, sultry air had been perfumed with honeysuckle and Confederate jasmine, and as Austin had gazed up at the clear night sky through the telescope his grandfather had bought him, searching for astronaut footprints on the face of the full moon, he'd suddenly looked over at Joe, his freckled face wreathed in a melon-slice smile.

"This is the bestest birthday of my life, Dad!" he'd proclaimed. "Ever!"

"Glad to hear that, Sport," Joe had said, tousling Austin's blond hair. Not in his worst nightmares could Joe have imagined it would be his son's last birthday.

"Fuck."

He leaned his head against the back of the seat and pressed his fingers hard against his eyes as the visions fast-forwarded to the hospital, the Mass for the Dead that Michael had celebrated for his nephew—never mind that Joe thought *celebrated* was the damn wrong word for such a painfully horrific occasion. Then there'd been the service at the cemetery, where Joe had hammered the last nail into the coffin of his already dead marriage by arriving drunk from the hospital, thanks to a fellow narc who'd smuggled a flask of Jack Black into St. Camillus before the funeral.

It had taken Joe's father, brother, and two hefty fire-fighters from his dad's station house, to haul him back into the wheelchair after he'd sprawled onto the rain-soaked earth. Gwen, unsurprisingly, had refused to look at him.

"Just do it," he told himself now. "It can't be any worse than that goddamn day."

The gate squeaked as it swung open. Although he'd not been back since his son's burial, Joe could have made his way to the grave blindfolded.

"You want me to stay?" the cabbie asked as he pulled into the gravel parking lot of the Queen of Angels ceme-tery next to the red Mustang.

Of all the places Laurel might have expected Joe to be headed, this wouldn't have made the list. "No," she decided, giving the pirate the fare, the usual twenty dollar tip, and an extra ten as an apology for having been snap-pish with him. "Thanks."

"No problem," he said, appearing to understand the gravity of her mission when he finally dropped the pirate jargon. "Good luck."

A statue of the Virgin Mary, holding her infant son, stood guard over the silent graves just inside the gate. Fog curled in clinging tendrils around Laurel's ankles as she stealthily followed Joe past the rows of moss-covered stones; her narrow heels sank into the marshy Low Land ground, making her wish she'd worn flats.

She hid behind a winged angel, watching as he took the small box out of his pocket; retrieving something, he placed it at the feet of a small, white marble lamb. He stood there, looking down at the marker for a long, silent time. Then dragged a hand down his face and sank onto a concrete bench.

He'd been right about one thing. Laurel didn't do intimacy well. She was tempted to leave when—damn—she remembered she'd sent the cab away. So, feeling uneasy about spying on such a private moment, she took a deep breath, came out from her hiding place, walked the few steps to the bench, and sat down beside him.

He didn't so much as glance over at her. Laurel figured he'd known all along that she was following him. She wondered if he was angry about that.

Then she looked at the words carved below the lamb, and her heart hitched. *Austin Michael Gannon. Beloved son.*

"He was five," Joe said flatly. He turned toward her, his eyes dark with strain. "He loved NASCAR Hot Wheels cars, fire trucks, T-ball, and dinosaurs."

That explained the green plastic T-Rex Joe had put at the lamb's base.

"Then he died. And because I'd been so busy playing cops and robbers I didn't make it to his hospital room until it was time to shut off the life support.

"Actually, they could have—probably should have—pulled the plug earlier, but Mike and Tess talked Gwen into waiting for me to show up."

He blew out a breath. "And that's why Gwen and I got a divorce."

"What happened? Was it an accident, or—"

"He came down with this rare type of pneumonia that didn't respond to antibiotics. It just looked like a summer cold when it started, so I didn't give it much mind. When everything went south, Gwen tried to get hold of me, but I'd been in deep cover, workin' up to a narcotics bust for months, and was out on this damn yacht, drinkin' and partying with drug dealers." He pressed his thumb against his teeth and exhaled a deep breath. "Then I got shot—"

"You were shot?"

"Yeah." He shrugged it off. "It was no big deal, things went wrong, bullets started flying, and I sorta got in the way of two of them. One only grazed my arm, but I had to have surgery to get the slug out of my heart."

"That's where you got your scar." She'd wondered about the raised line on his chest.

"Yeah."

He wasn't surprised when she hadn't asked. The lady might be as nosy as all get out when it came to digging around for a story, or figuring out what buttons a person responded to, but she wouldn't have asked about the old wound because, although they'd been about as intimate as two people could be, he understood how that was the kind of personal question she was reluctant to ask; the kind that might risk emotional involvement. Emotional involvement led to complications. To strings.

Joe belatedly realized he'd been wrong when he'd accused her of being the only one of the two of them who kept their distance. He supposed both their careers required emotional walls. He also suspected reporters built those walls the same way he had—brick by brick over the years. The one thing he'd never planned on was for Laurel Stewart to show up with a sledgehammer.

"I'd have traded my life for Austin's in a heartbeat." He snapped his fingers. "I even tried praying, when I got out of surgery and they told me what had happened, but God turned me down. I figure since I'd been giving Him the silent treatment for so long, He just wasn't in the mood for listening. Or maybe Austin's death was a payback for me having killed that drug dealer during the shoot-out on the yacht."

"I don't believe God works that way."

"Yeah. That's what Mike says."

"I'd guess he should know. Being a priest."

"Last I heard, God doesn't hand out his secret detailed instruction plans for the world at ordination."

"Still—"

"A part of me is always going to mourn my son's death," he said quietly, firmly, cutting her off. "Another part of me will probably always have at least some guilt for not having been as good a dad as I should have been while he was alive. Especially on days like this . . .

"Today's the third anniversary."

"Anniversary?" she asked. Joe could tell the exact moment she understood. "Oh." She closed her eyes and exhaled a soft, shimmering breath, then put a hand on his forearm. "Oh, Joe."

"I've developed sort of a routine to get past it. The past two years, I start drinking the night before, about the time when Gwen first took Austin to the hospital." When he'd been playing 007, drinking martinis with a sexy brunette on his arm. "When she first tried to get hold of me. And I keep drinking for the next twenty-four hours."

"You didn't drink last night."

"No. Because although getting wasted had become this sick, depressing ritual, I didn't want to this year. Because I was with you."

He recognized the shields going up. Hell, Joe didn't blame her. She hadn't moved a muscle, but he could see her retreating inside herself. The same way he had for the past three years.

"I don't want that responsibility," she said quietly.

"Of course you don't. Hell, I wouldn't either, if I were you. But I'm not asking you to be responsible for me. I'm just saying that although you can be a real pain—"

"Thank you."

"You're welcome." He liked that she wasn't going to get all maudlin on him. He wasn't sure he could have handled her weeping for him. "But you already know that because you work real hard at it."

"Maybe being a pain in the ass comes naturally."

"Maybe it does. But you're not nearly as hard-boiled as you want people to think you are. A few days ago, I was bored, burned out, and sick to death of my job. All I had to look forward to was more bodies, my upcoming annual, drunk pity party, and getting in my twenty years so I could punch my ticket and get out of the murder business. Then this sassy redheaded reporter walked into the cop shop."

"And got you messed up with a crooked vice president, slimy political staffers, spooky environmentalists, and the Secret Service."

"No one could ever call you boring, sugar."

"Dammit, I'm not any good at this sort of thing."

"What sort of thing?"

"You know. Personal discussions. Relationships." She dragged her hands through the hair that had, last night, felt like flame silk against his thighs. "I'm not a giving type of person, Joe."

"Yeah, that's why you put your plan to clear your name on hold to look for a missing friend."

"That's different. Anyone would do the same thing. I'm not giving," she repeated. "And I'm not soft."

"Now that's a matter of opinion." The desire was back, dark, and dangerous in his eyes. "You definitely felt real soft to me last night. When I was inside you, and making you scream."

"Don't talk like that!" She glanced around, uneasy. "Not in a cemetery. Besides, you don't know the real me."

He laced their fingers together. "Come back home with me and we'll work on that."

40

This was better, Laurel thought twenty minutes later, as they rolled around on his huge lake of a bed. She could handle sex. Especially when it was hot enough to keep her from thinking.

"We're good in bed," she said against his mouth. His gorgeous, sexy, wicked mouth. She felt him go still. Then he drew his head back and stared down at her, really looking at her, hard and deep.

"What?" she asked when the silence stretched.

"We're damn good in bed," he allowed. "Any better and Brendan'd have to be lookin' for a new place to set up his pub because we'd have burned the place down. But it's more than sex, Laurel. More than what fits where—tab A into slot B. We fit in other ways, too."

"If we do, it's only because we're working together. We're partners thrown together to solve a mystery."

"You know, Caitlin Cavanaugh and I've been partners quite a few years now, and not once, even when we've gotten a little loaded to celebrate a righteous bust, have I ever wanted to get naked with her. Ever wanted to touch her here." He skimmed his fingers down Laurel's throat.

"Or here." Over her breast. "Or here." Lower still, over her quivering stomach.

She moaned his name as she felt the desire rise. "This isn't serious."

"Whatever you say, sugar."

"You have your life here." Her hands fisted in his hair as her body poised on a razor sharp edge, helpless as a butterfly pinned to a board. "I have mine in DC . . . Oh, God."

She never could have imagined the desperation that had her digging her nails into his back, her body bowed, aching, desperate.

"Don't fight it." His growl was rough, feral, as he ruthlessly demanded more. "Just let it come, Laurel." His fingers parted her slick, tender lips. "Now." When he scraped his thumb over the hard epicenter of pent-up need, a blinding pleasure close to pain lanced through her, bursting like a supernova in her mind, bones, and blood.

She was still reeling when he plunged into her with a force that had them both gasping. One stroke. Two. "Dammit, I can't hold back," he groaned against her mouth.

"Then don't." Muscles that were still quaking from her orgasm closed vice-tight around him. She gripped his hips. "I want all of you. Now."

On the third stroke, his magnificent male body went rigid. He threw back his head like a wild animal howling at the moon. A savage shudder went through him, and when he cried out her name, although it wasn't the least bit comforting, Laurel knew that the rest of her life would be divided into Before and After Joe.

* * *

"Not that I'm keeping score," he murmured as they lay face to face together afterward, Joe's arms around her, her leg thrown over his hip, "but I believe, counting this morning's shower, that makes six."

"Not that I'm an expert on such things, but shouldn't the counter start over again each episode?" She ran her hands over his slick back, reveling in the play of muscle.

"Well, I suppose that's one way to do it." He brushed some damp hair off her forehead. "Or we could just keep a running tally going. Think how high we could get to by the time we're eighty."

She didn't respond, but he could feel the mood shifting.

It was damn ironic, Joe thought. Ever since the divorce, he'd made a point of only going to bed with women who didn't want pretty words and promises of happily ever after. And now that he wanted to say them, he was lying buck naked with an independent female who definitely didn't want to hear them.

"What if I decide I want more than just a sexual fling?" he asked. She wouldn't stand a chance, but he wanted to hear her answer.

"You'll live." She ran a finger down his chest. "We've already determined that you're a pretty man. You're intelligent, mildly amusing at times, and well off enough to own an entire block."

"Technically it belongs to the bank."

"It's still yours as long as you make the payments, which, from what I see of the business O'Neill's pub's doing, isn't going to prove much of a problem. So, obviously, the only reason you're living here alone is because you want to."

She had him there. At least she would have nailed it just days ago. But things had changed.

"However," she said, obviously trying to keep things from getting sticky, "if you're going to keep that running tally, for the sake of accuracy, you should change the total to seven."

"Seven?" Joe allowed himself to be distracted. For now.

"I believe you might have been a bit, uh, preoccupied, that last time."

"Seven." He rolled over onto his back, taking her with him, and looked up at the ceiling as he considered that little newsflash. "Hot damn."

The tropical storm that had been bringing rain to the city each afternoon had been declared a hurricane and begun prowling the South Atlantic. Forecasters weren't counting on the storm hitting anywhere along the Eastern Seaboard, but the rain shield spreading from Cuba across Florida, into the Carolinas and coastal Georgia, was definitely dampening the final weekend of Buccaneer Days.

The city of Somersett had been founded three hundred years earlier on a land grant from Queen Anne to Admiral James Somersett, a swashbuckling privateer who'd sailed the southern seas, capturing a great deal of pirate bounty for the Crown. Two years later, now a respectable South Carolina colonist, the admiral would help defeat an attack of nearby Charles Town by Spanish and French ships.

"Residents liked to claim that General James Ogle-thorpe 'borrowed' the city plan for nearby Savannah from Somersett's tidy green squares," Joe told Laurel over the clatter of the heavy rain on the metal roof of the Crown Vic he was reluctantly driving because he didn't want to risk hail or wind tearing up the Mustang's rag top. "Unsurprisingly, Savannahians strongly dispute that claim."

"Whatever, they are definitely lovely," Laurel said. Unfortunately, Somersett and Oglethorpe hadn't been around to plan the sprawling development just outside of town, where gas stations, strip malls, and fast-food restaurants had sprouted like mushrooms.

Just past the strip malls were subdivisions with names like Heron's Landing and Plantation Springs. Although there was a Stepford similarity to the developments, the bottle-green lawns were tidy, and the front porches where flowers bloomed in clay pots were more architec-tural detail than a place to sit and watch your neighbors.

They passed through a decidedly working-class area of small, single-story homes—some little more than shanties, barely standing on crumbling block founda-tions. Single wide trailers, streaked with rust, were sink-ing into the ground, seeming to be reclaimed by the red clay.

Then around another bend in the rising river, the lots grew wider and greener again—home from Tara looka-likes to sprawling MacMansions with tennis courts and sparkling pools.

"Welcome to the New South," Joe said, with a touch of irony in his tone.

Approximately ten miles out of the city, they reached serious mansions built by slave labor as summer homes for planters whose rice and cotton plantations were located on the nearby islands. Constructed of brick from nearby Swann Island, the azalea-white house, covered with tabby and stucco scored to look like stone, boasted the quintessentially sweeping double veranda and arched masonry foundation.

The Oaks was set on several splendidly landscaped acres facing the river, which had once served as a highway for visiting guests; dozens of windows flanked by hunter-green shutters, which had protected residents from the stifling heat before the days of air-conditioning and could still be closed against storms, embraced the water view.

"It looks like something from a movie set."

"Like I said, they've been doing a lot of work on it." He pulled into the circular brick driveway, parking next to a money-green Mercedes. The huge, spreading branches of the centuries-old oak trees gracing the grounds, which had given the house its name, were draped in moss that was dripping rain like so many faucets. Water spilled out of an ivy-covered stone cherub fountain in the center of the circle. The front steps were flanked by hydrangea bushes; the way the gorgeous pink, blue, and white blossoms as large as a man's fist were being pounded by the rain, Laurel doubted they'd survive the night.

When the doorbell chimed the opening bars of "Dixie," Laurel wondered how that little bit of musical trivia would play in Boston or New York. A maid, looking like something from a 1930s movie in her black dress and

starched white apron, answered the door, her dark forehead drawing into a worried frown when she viewed the
business card Joe handed her. Laurel was vaguely relieved
when she didn't recognize either of the two Secret Service agents flanking the maid.

"The vice president and Mrs. Aiken are entertaining
guests," she said.

"That's okay." Joe flashed her his best smile. "We
won't be takin' up much of their time."

She drew her lips into a thin line and glanced back
toward a set of double doors upon which a mural of
the eighteenth-century Somersett waterfront had been
painted.

Having grown up in a castle, Laurel wasn't overly
impressed by the antique furnishings, expensive oil paint-
ings, and crystal chandeliers of the entry hall. That Joe
didn't seem to be either overwhelmed or intimidated
didn't surprise her; she may not have known him long,
but she knew that it would take a great deal more than a
show of wealth to impress him.

"Rose?" The double doors opened and Happy Aiken
came out. She was wearing a pink St. John suit with very
good pearls. "Is there a problem?"

"These people want to see the vice president," the
maid said. Her dismissive tone made it sound as if Joe and
Laurel had come to the Oaks to sell Fuller brushes or
hand out religious tracts.

Happy Aiken swept a dismissive glance over Joe. After
making love, he'd changed into a shirt featuring palm
trees and grass-skirted hula dancers, his most obnoxious
yet. Laurel had the feeling he'd worn it on purpose,

either to annoy the Aikens, or to throw them off guard. A descendant of Robert E. Lee, the vice president's wife had always echoed the civility of the South. Not only had she perfected the Nancy Reagan gaze, her dignified demeanor had often been compared to Jackie Kennedy. A bit of that famed dignity slipped when the gaze zeroed in on Laurel. Happy's nostrils pinched together, like a woman who'd just smelled something nasty.

"What are you doing here?"

"Ms. Stewart's with me," Joe said.

"And you are?"

"Joe Gannon. Lieutenant, Somersett PD." He flashed his badge. Unlike Tiffany, the Wingate's day manager, Happy took it from him and studied it carefully. "You're a police detective?"

"You know, everyone reacts that way," Joe said with the winning, aluminum-siding salesman's smile Laurel had come to realize he could turn on and off like a light switch. "I'm thinkin' about growing a mustache, so I'll look more like a cop."

"I doubt that will help," Happy said dryly as she handed the leather case back to him. "This says Homicide."

"It sure enough does, but at the moment I'm working a missing-person case." He smiled encouragingly. "Buccaneer Days use up a lot of resources. Everyone just sort of pitches in."

"Isn't that efficient," she said. "However, I'm afraid the vice president's tied up with important government business," she said. "But if you'll leave your card—"

"I'm afraid, unless the country's going to war in the

next five minutes, I'm going to have to interrupt that business," Joe cut her off. "We'll just take a moment of his time, Ma'am." His voice held just the proper amount of deference. "If you'd like, I can refer the matter to the state attorney general."

Everyone in the entry hall, with the possible exception of Rose, the maid, knew that South Carolina's attorney general had squeaked out a victory in a viciously fought election in which Aiken had backed the loser. It was doubtful that he'd be all that helpful.

"Well, if it won't take long," she backtracked. "My husband is in the library." She turned to the maid. "Thank you, Rose."

"Yes, Ma'am." The maid's quick dip bordered on being a curtsy, making Laurel wonder if anyone had informed Happy Aiken that the War of Northern Aggression was over and sorry, sweetheart, but the North had won.

41

The library was as grand as would be expected in such a magnificent house. The bird's-eye maple paneled walls gleamed from years of being rubbed with oil, the furniture, mostly created from cypress and mahogany, was reminiscent of West Indies colonial days, and shelves of leather-bound books reached two stories high. Laurel wondered if anyone had ever read them, or if they'd been bought by the yard at auction by the Aikens' decorator.

The vice president was with Bishop Cary and Laurel's other nemesis, Warren Wyatt. He broke off in midsentence when Happy returned with Joe and Laurel.

She introduced Joe, who did the badge thing again; unlike his wife, Aiken didn't bother to inspect it. Both the bishop and Wyatt acknowledged Joe; but while the bishop greeted Laurel as well, Wyatt treated her as if she were invisible.

Although Laurel suspected she was the last person the wannabe–First Lady would want in her home, Happy held with tradition, offering both newcomers a glass of sweet tea. Which they turned down. As they did the whiskey—Highlander's Best, Laurel noted with a bit of pride—offered by the vice president.

"We're sorry to interrupt, Mr. Vice President," Joe said. "But I've got this case I thought you might be able to help me with."

Good move, Laurel thought. Make Aiken feel as if he's a part of the investigation rather than a suspect.

"Oh?" The vice president lifted a patrician brow.

"It's about a staffer of yours. A Ms."—he glanced down at the notebook he'd taken from the pocket of the hula girl shirt, as if needing to refresh his memory—"Chloe Hollister."

"Chloe? Has she been in an accident?"

"Not that I know of, Sir," Joe said. "But her friend, Ms. Stewart, seems to believe something has happened to her since she arrived in Somersett."

"Chloe took some time off," Aiken said. "It was a highly inappropriate time, but she claimed it was a personal matter." Laurel wondered if the sheen of perspiration she viewed on the vice president's forehead was real or merely a trick of the light. He dabbed at his forehead with a white linen handkerchief. "A family emergency, I believe she said."

"Then you spoke with her?" Joe asked.

"No. While Chloe is an important member of the staff, she wasn't at a high enough level to come to me with a request for a day off. Warren handles that sort of thing."

Joe turned to Wyatt. "Then it was you who spoke with her?" Wyatt had told Laurel he hadn't. She wondered if he'd stick to his story when questioned by a cop.

He did.

"No," the political advisor admitted. "She left a message on my voice mail. She said something about needing to work out a problem. I didn't save the message, since I had no idea I'd need it, but I seem to recall something about her taking a few days off. Perhaps going to the Caribbean."

"Well then," Bishop Cary said, "it seems that's the answer to your missing person, Detective."

"There's no proof Chloe went to any island," Laurel insisted. "No indication that she's even left Somersett. Her name hasn't shown up on any airline passenger manifest and she's not booked on any cruise line that's sailed from here in the past three days."

"Oh, dear." The bishop's face furrowed into worried lines. "That does sound a little ominous."

"It's Buccaneer Days." Wyatt waved a dismissive hand. "She's probably in one of the beach hotels right here in town. My guess is that she lied about leaving the city, to make it sound as if she'd be too far away for us to call her back to do her job."

"That's a possibility, I suppose," Joe allowed. Laurel, concerned he was just going to dismiss her case, could have kicked him. "Has she made a habit of ditching her duties?"

"Never has before," Aiken replied, confirming what Laurel had already told Joe. "She's been a damn hard worker. Sharp as a tack, too. Even though she does occasionally show poor judgment in friends." He shot a significant look Laurel's way. "Which brings me to ask, Ms. Stewart, what you're doing here?"

"She arrived with Detective Gannon," his wife, who'd taken a seat in a wingback leather chair, informed him, sounding none too pleased at the prospect of any reporter in her home.

"I don't suppose you know anything about Ms. Hollister's uncharacteristic disappearance?" Joe asked Happy.

She toyed with a pearl earring and looked irritated. "Only that she was supposed to be here yesterday to help me with the seating plan for tonight's dinner," she complained.

Joe glanced over toward the windows where the rain-streaked glass had blurred the view of the gardens, turning them into an Impressionist painting. "If this rain keeps up, you may not have to worry about any seating plan."

Happy lifted a chin that looked to Laurel as if it'd had a little work. "My ancestor, for whom I was named, held a dinner party on a night when that pyromaniacal Sherman was camped a mere ten miles upriver. If she didn't turn tail and run, a little tropical storm isn't going to chase me from my home."

"There's another woman I'd like to ask you about." Joe paused and glanced down at his notes again. "Are you acquainted with a Mrs. Sissy Sotheby-Beale?"

"The name doesn't ring a bell," Aiken said, his impatience beginning to show. Or more likely, Laurel decided grimly, his guilt. Yes, that was *definitely* perspiration on his brow. "Is this going to take much longer, Detective? I have a great deal of work to do."

"I understand, Sir. Having work of my own," Joe said significantly.

"You've met Mrs. Sotheby-Beale, Noble," Happy recalled suddenly. "Remember, at the function I cohosted in Georgetown. The one to raise money for the logger-head turtles."

"The one that damn criminal Wunder showed up at?" Aiken glared at his wife. "I still don't understand how his name got on the invitation list."

"I told you at the time." Happy's snappish tone had lost its whispery Jackie quality. "Mr. Wunder crashed the event and I decided that having him thrown out would only gar-ner him the attention he was obviously trying to achieve." She looked at Laurel thoughtfully. Or as thoughtfully as she could manage without creasing her forehead or brows. The woman had definitely been into the Botox. "I seem to recall you being there, as well, that night."

"I'd come with Chloe. In fact, I'd never actually met Cody Wunder until yesterday."

"Ah, yes," Warren said. If he'd had a mustache, he would have twirled it, Snidley Whiplash style. "When you provided him an alibi that allowed his minion to burn a legitimate business's offices."

Laurel glared at him. "I had nothing to do with that."

"Like you didn't make up that negative story?"

"If we could get back to Mrs. Sotheby-Beale," Joe interjected mildly.

"Sissy and her husband are parishioners at St. Bren-dan's," the bishop volunteered. "They're a delightful couple. I can't imagine why the police would be inter-ested in them."

"Because Mrs. Sotheby-Beale is dead."

"Oh, dear God," the bishop murmured. He raised his

eyes toward the coffered ceiling and made the sign of the cross in what Laurel took as a blessing for the dearly departed.

Happy paled a bit beneath her expertly applied makeup. "That's dreadful. Surely you remember her, dear," she said to the vice president. "She was the lovely young blond woman wearing an Albert Nippon suit."

"It was pink," Laurel remembered at the mention of the designer jacket. "She was wearing a pink bustier with black trim beneath the jacket."

The vice president's wife continued to refuse to acknowledge Laurel. "Sissy's husband is—was—a former naval captain," she continued, attempting to refresh her husband's memory.

"He's a doctor at the Academy," the bishop added helpfully. "What a terrible loss. He must be beside himself."

"I remember Beale," Aiken said suddenly, as the name clicked in. "He thanked me for my vote for that new aircraft carrier and wrote a substantial check for the campaign." Having discovered his little habit of transferring campaign funds into his private accounts, Laurel wondered if Beale's check had helped pay for what appeared to be a genuine Ming vase on the desk. Apparently shaken by events, the vice president's hand trembled as he took a long swallow of his drink. "My God, it's *his* wife? She was so young. And beautiful. How did she die?" he asked Joe.

"The coroner hasn't made his final ruling," Joe responded. "But she fell from a balcony at the Wingate Palace."

Happy gasped.

The bishop closed his eyes.

Even Aiken paled beneath his golfer's tan. He sank down into an open-weave cane planter's chair and put his glass next to a Waterford crystal bowl of hard candies on an end table with a pineapple-carved base.

"The doctor must be horribly distraught," the bishop murmured, his voice sounding as shaky as the vice president looked. "Perhaps that's why he hasn't yet called to arrange a funeral."

"He probably hasn't called because I haven't been able to officially notify him of his wife's death," Joe said. "He's not answering the phone at his house, the Academy, or the hotel where he's supposed to be staying. We only learned her identity yesterday, after Father Gannon identified her from a newspaper sketch."

"Yes, she works with him on the literacy program," the bishop remembered. "Gannon," he said, looking at Joe with renewed interest. "Would you be—"

"Father Mike's brother."

Despite the gravity of the topic, the bishop managed a half smile. "Well, isn't this a small world."

"It's definitely a small city," Joe agreed.

"Robert's due back tomorrow morning," Bishop Cary said. "I'm sure he'll help you clear the case then."

Joe made a note. "May I ask how you know when he'll be returning to town?"

"I was scheduled to be part of a foursome with him at Henderson golf club in Savannah tomorrow afternoon, but I had to cancel." His smile was friendly, but rueful. "I never realized being a bishop would take up so much more time than being a monsignor."

"Imagine if you become spiritual counselor to the president," Laurel suggested.

"If God and the electorate will it, I'm sure He'll also find a way for me to fit those duties in," he responded with the smooth flair of a natural born politician.

Which, she supposed, one had to be to work one's way up the Church hierarchy. She was thinking that the rice farm Bishop Cary had inherited probably hadn't hurt his career opportunities, when the end table beside Noble Aiken's chair tipped over.

Tea spilled and the candy bowl shattered, sending candy and crystal shards flying as the vice president crashed, face first, onto the heavy plank floor.

42

"Oh, my God! Call an ambulance!" Happy Aiken leaped off the couch like a rocket. Heedless of the glass, she knelt beside her husband, scooped up a Brach's butterscotch disk, unwrapped it, and stuck it in his cheek.

Laurel dialed 911 while Joe got down on the floor beside Happy and helped turn the vice president onto his side to prevent obstruction to his breathing.

"The paramedics are on their way," Laurel reported.

"Good," Joe said. "Is it diabetes?" he asked Happy.

"Yes . . . Dammit, go get Rose," she snapped at Warren. "Tell her to bring my husband's glucose meter and gel to the library right away."

"Vice President Aiken has diabetes?" Warren's obviously faked surprise was definitely going to keep him out of the running for an Academy Award for best performance by a political advisor.

"You've known that for years. Quit trying to cover your ass." Happy didn't sound like any southern belle Laurel had ever heard. She screamed the maid's name, then glared down at her unconscious husband. "I hope to hell that you're happy, Noble," she ground out, "because you've just blown our shot at the White House."

Laurel and Joe exchanged a look. There was nothing either one of them could say to that.

The maid showed up with the glucose meter and a glass of orange juice, which, being unconscious, Aiken couldn't drink. Laurel wasn't familiar with the protocol for treating a diabetic attack, but thought Happy jabbed the lancet into the side of his finger with a bit more relish than was necessary.

"Dammit, look at this." Happy stuck the meter in front of her husband's face, though with his eyes rolled back in his head, he obviously couldn't read it. "Didn't I tell you to eat regular meals? Didn't I tell you not to drink. God damn you!"

Joe caught her wrist as she went to slap Aiken's slack, ashen cheek. "Perhaps you might want to hold off on that," he suggested, "until your husband's conscious."

"Prick," she flared. Laurel wasn't sure whether she was referring to Aiken or Joe.

As Happy rubbed the glucose gel on the vice president's lips and gums, the two Secret Service agents, who'd come running when Happy had first screamed, guarded the doorway. Against what? Laurel wondered. Terrorists who might want to spike the candy with anthrax?

The ambulance arrived within five minutes, which wasn't bad, Laurel thought, for how far out in the country the house was located.

"He's hypoglycemic," Happy advised the paramedics as they rolled the gurney into the library.

"You sure?" the woman paramedic asked.

"Absolutely." Aiken began to convulse.

"Is your husband allergic to beef or pork, or has he ever had an allergic reaction to any other foods, dyes, or glucagon?"

"No. And you're wasting time."

"It's important to avoid any allergies," the other paramedic said soothingly.

"Okay," his partner said, "let's shoot him up and get him out of here."

She removed Aiken's American flag cuff links, tore the sleeve off the dress shirt, ripped open an alcohol patch, and swabbed his limp arm while her partner took a syringe, injected a substance into a small rubber-topped bottle, and swirled the bottle to mix the substances.

The convulsions stopped almost immediately after the injection.

"Sweet," the male paramedic said as he, his partner, and Joe lifted Aiken's limp body onto the gurney and strapped him in.

The woman glanced back over her shoulder as they got to the door. "Are you coming?" she asked Happy.

"I suppose so." With a heavy sigh, the vice president's wife retrieved her quilted Chanel bag from the desk and followed the little group out to the ambulance.

"I don't think she's real happy with him," Joe said as they left the house behind the Secret Service.

"I think you're right. I wonder how bad he is."

"I'm no expert, but you pick up some stuff when you

work the street." They went through the usual routine as he opened the passenger door for her. "The glucagon seemed to kick in pretty fast and they'll have him on glucose IVs by now, so his chances are good. People rarely die of a hypoglycemic coma."

"That's good to hear." Laurel might intensely dislike the man, but she wouldn't wish death on anyone. "But even without Wunder's evidence, since it sounds as if they've been keeping this a secret for a while, I'll bet his career's just flatlined."

"I'd say you're right." Joe fastened his seat belt and plugged the dashboard flash into the cigarette lighter.

Water hissed beneath the tires as they drove back to the city; even in the heavy boatmobile of a car that was being buffeted by gale-force winds, Joe had no trouble keeping up with the ambulance.

"I want to go to the hospital," Laurel said as the little shanty town flashed by the passenger window. "Stick with the story, so I can get a jump on the rest of the press."

"I figured you would. Sandra Squires's *Falls Church Bee* is really hitting the news jackpot this week, aren't they?"

"Sometimes you get lucky in the reporting business."

Cruella de Merryman, eat your cold, black heart out.

The emergency department was bustling, packed to the rafters with patients and family members. A homeless man had come to get out of the rain, bringing a big piece of sodden cardboard with him, which he was refusing to give up; the weather hadn't appeared to put a dent into

Bucanneer Day celebrations, if the number of alcohol related incidents were any indication, and ambulances kept arriving, sirens wailing and lights flashing, with victims of car accidents due to rain-slick streets and flooded intersections.

Noble Aiken was rushed behind the double doors while a hospital administrator, who'd been waiting for them, ushered Happy to a private waiting room. After a moment to discuss protocol, the Secret Service men split the command, one staying with the vice president, the other with his wife. Laurel was secretly surprised when Happy didn't object to her trailing along; her suspicion was that the woman was grateful enough to Joe to reluctantly put up with her.

"I can't believe this," Happy complained as she glared out the waiting-room window at the rain-draped harbor. "We were so close." She held up her hand, thumb and index finger pressed together. "This close." She closed her eyes and shook her head. "And now it's all over."

"The odds are that he'll live," Joe said, offering comfort.

"Probably. But not to be president."

Laurel shot Joe a *See why I don't believe in marriage?* look. He merely shook his head.

"It was the damn campaign." Happy reached into her bag for a cigarette and, ignoring the No Smoking sign, lit up. "Campaigns are like wars—they're incredibly stressful. People don't sleep, don't eat properly, most days you grab a bite whenever you can because you don't know when you'll eat again, then other days people will expect the candidate to eat whatever nasty little local foods they prepare. Hot dogs, hamburgers, tacos, grilled shrimp, and, down here in the South, of course, cooks have never met an animal or vegetable they didn't believe was better deep fried in lard."

She inhaled deeply, then exhaled a long stream of smoke out of her nose. "I tried to get him to watch his diet more closely, tried to tell him not to drink all the alcohol that was constantly being pushed on him, but would he listen? Hell, no." She cursed. Stabbed out the cigarette on the windowsill, then pulled a gold compact out of her bag and powdered her nose. "If he'd just used a modicum of common sense, he wouldn't have become brittle."

"Brittle?" Laurel was unfamiliar with the term.

"Unstable," Bishop Cary, who had just entered the room, said. Laurel thought it interesting that Warren wasn't with him. The hotshot political advisor was probably burning up the phone lines trying to find a new campaign staff to join, she thought derisively. "Brittle diabetics can experience unpredictable, out-of-proportion rises and swoops in blood glucose, within short periods of time, as a result of very small deviations from schedule."

Of course it was impossible for a candidate to stay on schedule. Laurel also found it intriguing that the bishop obviously knew about the vice president's illness. What else did he know? Could he have any information about Chloe? Might he even know where she was?

"His friends have tried to encourage him to be more diligent regarding his health," the bishop continued, "but of course that same strength of purpose which makes him such a powerful leader occasionally proves a problem when trying to talk the man into slowing down. He's convinced he's on a mission."

A mission to get him and Lady Happy Macbeth into the White House, Laurel thought.

"Will he stay on the ticket?" she asked.

"That's for my husband to decide," Happy snapped, glaring at Laurel as if suddenly realizing she was in the room. "The primary voters put Noble on the ballot. It's their decision."

Not if the national party stepped in. Laurel envisioned winged dollar bills flying out of the campaign to pollsters. Personally, she figured the campaign had taken a fatal wound, but one thing she'd definitely learned during her years in Washington was never to bet against money. The Aiken campaign had already raked in millions; would donations keep flowing in once the ghost ship story and his diversion of funds, not to mention this medical condition he'd kept secret, got picked up by the wire services?

A little silence settled over the room.

"I suppose," Bishop Cary said, after a time, "no news is good news."

"Thank you, Your Excellency," Happy replied with stinging sarcasm. "You must be quite a comfort to your flock."

The bishop flushed, but did not respond.

Another silence was shattered by Joe's phone ringing. He went out into the hall to take the call, Laurel right on his heels.

"Gannon," he answered. "Really? It's about time." He glanced over at the waiting room door. "Okay, yeah, I'll be right in." He closed the phone. "Dr. Beale finally made it back to town, just like His Excellency predicted," he told Laurel. "He's at the station, wanting to claim his wife's body."

43

It was the cold water, washing over her bare feet, that woke Chloe. The air was cold and damp and she could hear the wind wailing outside over a slow, deep Gregorian chanting coming from somewhere beyond the darkness. She'd come to realize, early in her imprisonment, that she was being held in a side cave off of one of the many tunnels that ran beneath the city from the sea. The sea that must have begun to rise, for the water to have reached this far back. If she listened carefully, she could hear the mournful sound of a foghorn drifting on the air. She couldn't tell if it was day or night, but it was getting darker as the tall candle burned down. Soon the wick would drown in the melting wax, causing the cave to go pitch black. And if rain continued, and the tide rose too high, the cavern could fill with water and she'd drown.

No! She wasn't going to let that happen. Even if *she* was prepared to die, which she definitely was not, she had her baby to think of. Fortunately, her captor hadn't thought to check beneath her tongue after forcing her to take those pills. The moment he'd left her alone again, Chloe had spit them out. She'd worried that he'd return and find them on the ground; but the one good thing about the rising water was that it had dissolved the pills, so she might be able to keep her secret a little longer.

The important thing was not to give up hope. The chanting indicated she was somewhere near the Cathedral. Surely someone would realize that the message she'd been forced to leave on Warren's voice mail was coerced. Surely someone would realize that she'd never just drop her responsibilities to go on vacation.

She wasn't stupid or lazy. She'd graduated magna cum laude, after all. She spoke five languages, could speak knowledgeably on art and music, and could name the national anthems of over eighty-five countries without having to call the State Department information office.

She knew it took a staff of 120 to prepare and serve a White House State Dinner. She had memorized every rule of etiquette both Amy Vanderbilt and Letitia Baldrige had ever dreamed up, and while it might sound old-fashioned, she'd built a solid career on such knowledge in government, where social protocol was a necessity.

But more important than knowing the differences between Monet and Manet, or the intricacies of setting a formal table, Chloe knew she wasn't going to die.

Laurel would find her. She'd sensed Laurel hadn't believed her when she'd insisted she couldn't be pregnant. Laurel also knew that there was no way she would have ditched her duty, or missed an opportunity to see the inside of the Aikens' Somersett mansion. There was also the fact that she'd called her to tell her what she'd discovered about Wunder and Aiken, then never called back as promised. By now her best friend had probably shown up in Somersett and reported her missing, and Laurel was like a pit bull when she got her teeth into something. She just wouldn't let go.

As she continued to struggle with the chain attaching her arms to the stone wall, Chloe prayed that Laurel and her search party would reach her before the surging tide.

Doctor Richard Beale was as handsome as his wife had been lovely. Tall, lean, with an outdoor's man's tan, his naval discipline wasn't evident when Joe arrived at the station. In fact, he seemed on the verge of a breakdown.

"I gave him a cup of coffee," Cait informed Joe as they stood on the other side of the window looking in at the man seated at the wooden table in the small cinderblock-walled interrogation room. "I saved the photos for you, since you're the primary. The guy's pretty much a mess. Keeps talking about if he only knew, yada, yada, yada, he never would have left her, it's all his fault. You know the drill."

"Yeah."

It was pretty much what spouses of suicides always said. Of course it was also what spouses who murdered their mates and tried to pass it off as suicide always said. Mike had insisted that Sissy Sotheby-Beale was not a woman to take her own life. But the fact that his brother worked for a Church that considered suicide a mortal sin might color his judgment.

"What's your take on the guy?"

Cait shrugged. "You know I've never bought it as a suicide. Which pretty much leaves the husband as suspect one, with some mystery lover coming in a close second.

Since we don't have a damn thing on a boyfriend, right now Dr. Beale is pretty much the bird in our hands *and* in the bush. How's the VP, by the way?"

"Holding his own. I take it the news has already gotten out."

"Are you kidding? It probably hit the airwaves before the ambulance made it to the hospital. If the Aikens had wanted to keep his collapse quiet, they probably should've paid their maid more. She's been jabbering away on all the talk radio stations, and I hear there's already a book deal in the works."

"Gotta love America," Joe murmured.

Richard Beale looked up when Joe entered the room. His eyes were red-rimmed from crying. Damp tissues were scattered over the table and onto the floor.

"Dr. Beale," Joe greeted him mildly. "I'm Detective Joseph Gannon." He showed his badge. "I'm sorry we have to meet like this."

"I knew I shouldn't have left her." He snuffled loudly, wiped his red, dripping nose with the back of his hand. "I knew she'd been depressed lately, but I'd prescribed some Prozac and it seemed to have been working."

Better living through pharmaceuticals, Joe thought, thinking of the prescription for Wellbutrin he'd never filled. Strangely, since hurricane Laurel Stewart had hit town, he'd forgotten he was depressed.

"We can't always know what's in someone else's mind," he said mildly. "Even the mind of someone we love."

"I'm a physician, dammit. My *job* is to heal. *Do no harm.* That medical principle, first stated by Hippocrates, is the keystone of my profession."

"I've heard it." From a serial killer/surgeon who'd liked to dismember his victims and keep their eyes in mayonnaise jars in his basement. Thinking back on it, the guy hadn't lived that far from Aiken, which might have a prospective buyer wondering about the neighborhood.

"These hands were made to heal." The hands in question trembled as he held them out in front of him. His nails were trim and square, his cuticles neatly clipped. It looked as if he'd had a manicure. Not that there was anything wrong with that. Joe had never, not once, considered getting his nails done, but perhaps patients preferred their physician's fingernails as neat and tidy as their white medical coats.

"To heal," he repeated. "Now they're responsible for the death of a vibrant, beautiful young woman."

Joe leaned forward, just a bit. "Are you saying you took your wife's life, Dr. Beale?"

"Of course not!" Red-veined eyes widened. "I told you, my creed is to do no harm."

"Murder's definitely doing harm," Joe allowed.

"Sissy wasn't murdered."

"Why would you say that?"

"Because of this." He reached inside a linen sport coat, which, since it looked just like something Drew Sloan would wear, Joe figured must be expensive. He took a folded piece of paper from the inside pocket.

It was a letter, mailed to her home address the day of Sissy Sotheby-Beale's death, listing all the reasons why life was no longer worth living. Why, although she was sorry to hurt the one person she loved—"And I do so love you, Richard!"—the words, printed from a computer in bold Times Roman type, stressed her pain was just too great to keep on living.

It was signed, *For eternity, Your Sissy.*

Nice touch, Joe thought. There were just two problems. One was that he could see the indentations in the paper, an indication that someone had traced the signature before going over it with a pen. Then there was the fact, which wouldn't hold up in court, that Laurel had already warned him not to believe any letter Sissy might have been alleged to have written.

Not that Joe totally believed in that psychic stuff.

But he didn't believe Beale, either.

"Had you known your wife was seeing another man?" Joe asked. Adultery had been at the top of Sissy's confessed list of sins.

A shadow moved across the doctor's eyes. He looked down at his hands, sighed, and toyed with a gold Annapolis ring that reminded Joe of what Laurel had said about Sissy's attacker's signet ring slicing into her cheek.

"I know I'll sound like a fool," he said, looking up at Joe again. "But I never had an inkling." Tears welled up. "I probably didn't spend as much time with her as I should have. But we'd moved so much while I was in the Navy, and I was working so hard to establish myself at the Academy." He dragged a hand over his short, black hair. "And she seemed busy with her church work, with Father Mike."

His wet eyes widened. "My God. What if the other man was that priest at St. Brendan's she spent so much time with?"

"Do you think that's a possibility?" Joe asked with studied casualness.

Drew had combed two black hairs out of the victim's pale blond pubic curls. Mike and Beale both had black hair. But there was no way Joe was going to believe his brother was involved. It wasn't that he considered Mike a saint—far from it—but he also knew that if his brother had somehow gotten involved with a married woman, he'd damn well never walk out of a hotel room and leave her with an angry man who'd already demonstrated a propensity for violence.

"I don't know." Beale bit his lip. "I suppose it's possible. Especially given the reputation priests have these days."

Joe curled his hand into a fist beneath the table, all too aware of Cait watching them.

"Naturally, we're not going to leave any stone unturned during our investigation," he reassured the son of a bitch. "I realize this is an extremely difficult time for you, but I was wondering if you'd be willing to look at some photographs for us."

Beale glanced at the manila evidence envelope Joe had brought into the interrogation room.

"Photographs of my wife?"

"I'm afraid so. As you can understand, we need an official identification. And while I might be hesitant to show such graphic photographs to a civilian, I figure you, bein' a doc and all, well, you've seen a lot worse, right?"

The grief lifted from Beale's eyes, replaced by a touch of caution. "That's hard to say without seeing the photographs."

"Good point." Joe drew them out and put them face-down on the table. "Tell you what. I understand that you'd be wanting some privacy, so I'm gonna go outside for a couple minutes. I've been drinking soda all day because of the damn heat, and it's startin' to back up on me."

He knew Cait was rolling her eyes as he slid into his Good Old Boy southern drawl—the one that usually worked fairly well with women and suspects. "Would you like me to heat up that coffee?" he asked, motioning toward the half-empty cup.

"No, thank you," Beale said, his gaze on the stack of eight-by-ten glossies.

"The stuff we've got here is a step down from toxic waste," Joe said easily. "I can have someone run across the street to Starbucks—"

"No." Beale's voice sharpened. Joe could imagine the guy using that tone on a nurse that didn't move quite fast enough for his liking. The doctor quickly caught himself. "No thank you," he said more softly. "I'm fine." A tear escaped and he did another of those lip-gnawing things, which might have been a nice touch, if Joe hadn't seen it at least a dozen times before.

"Okay, well, then, I'll be back in a flash." He stood up. "Feel free to look at those pictures," he said. "Soon as we get a positive ID, we can release your wife's body so you can give her a proper burial."

Beale murmured something that might have been agreement.

"Where's the piece of straw?" Cait asked as he joined her outside the window.

"Straw?" he asked. "Come on, Beale," he encouraged the perp. "Pick those up. Turn them over. See your goddamn handiwork."

"The one that should be stickin' out of your cracker, southern country boy mouth about now," she said in the same slow drawl Joe had pulled out.

"It's like the shirt," he said. That's it, he thought as the physician took the first photograph from the stack. It was a long shot of Sissy Sotheby-Beale sprawled on the hood of the SUV.

"Obnoxious?" Cait gave the hula girls a derogatory look. "No offense, Gannon, but that shirt could make someone with a lot weaker stomach than mine throw up."

"It's an interrogation tool." Joe thought Beale went a little gray. As a doctor the guy would've seen dead people before, but it often made a difference when it was someone you knew. Someone you'd once cared about. "Puts people off guard." Definitely grayish, Joe decided as Beale turned over the second photograph, the one where Cait had moved the camera in for a close-up look at the broken body.

Beale turned over the photo of the blown eye. "Bingo," Joe murmured as the golfer's tan turned the color of Spanish moss.

"I warned you about the vomit factor," Cait said, as the doctor hurled all over the table and tile floor.

"Good thing those photos were copies," Joe said. He was also glad he hadn't worn his new sneaks today. "Guess it's time to get some of the doc's DNA."

"He's going to crack," Cait predicted. "Then you know what you can do next."

"Arrest him?"

"Book him, Danno."

Joe shook his head at the old TV line.

Cait grinned a broad, Cheshire cat smile. "I've been waiting to say that since you first started wearing those dumb shirts."

"You know I live to make your day."

"I know. Which is why I'm going to miss you."

"What makes you think I'm going anywhere?"

She gave him a knowing look. "Sure you are. We've got a pool going. Manning's got Maine; I'll win twenty bucks if you're a murder cop in DC by this time next month."

That idea was even less appealing than staying a cop right here in Somersett. Until you factored in Laurel Stewart. Which was, Joe had to admit, one hell of an incentive.

"Don't go spending your money yet," Joe advised, deciding to think about it later. After he'd gotten the doc to confess and moved Sissy Sotheby-Beale's name to the black side of the murder board.

44

The room was hushed, the only sounds the swish of the respirator and the faint beep from the heart monitor. Lying in the hospital bed, appearing every one of his fifty-six years, Noble Aiken didn't look like a man who was a heartbeat away from the presidency. A man who only a few hours ago had been on the verge of becoming the most powerful individual in the world.

He looked as weak in body as she knew him to have been in morals. And Happy hated him, as she had every day for the past thirty years of their marriage, ever since that memorable afternoon when she'd returned to their honeymoon suite after having her hair done in the Arizona resort's beauty shop and caught him in bed with a cocktail waitress.

She'd wanted to kill him; at the very least she'd wanted to rip that little slut's bottle-peroxide hair out by its black roots, but she'd been brought up to be a lady, and ladies didn't cause scenes. When she'd called home in tears—while Noble had been down in the bar getting drunk—her mama had claimed that tomcatting around was in a man's nature, and if Happy was smart, she'd make her new husband buy her something sparkly to make up for his transgression.

Happy's parents were Old Somersett. Her mother had followed the roles defined by both southern society and her generation, moving through the ranks from Debutante of the Year to the Junior League, then on to head the Somersett chapter of the Daughters of the Confederacy. Happy's father was the quintessential southern wastrel who possessed an unfortunate fondness for whiskey, women, and cards. He began each day with a double Highlander's Pride, often after crawling out of the bed of some society woman whose husband was conveniently out of town. Evenings were spent at the riverboat casino, where his lack of luck kept him in debt to the kind of men who would never have been allowed in his wife's house.

Apparently finally deciding that self-esteem and a good credit rating were more important than jewelry, Happy's mother had thrown him out of the big old Victorian on Queen Anne Square a week before Happy's fourth birthday. But the harm had been done; his daughter had already fallen under his playboy spell.

By her first anniversary, Happy, who'd never considered herself terribly introspective, came to realize that one of the reasons she'd married the dashing, small-town lawyer from Sea Island, Georgia, was because she'd sensed in him many of the same flaws she found so appealing in her father. Noble had married her for her pedigree. Her family roots, which went back to the original land grant from England's Queen Anne, had given him the political clout to make a run for governor, which he'd won easily. Then he moved on to the US Senate.

South Carolina voters, charmed by his smooth ways, and pleased with the political pork he'd bring home from Washington, kept reelecting him. But Happy, who'd become a pragmatist since that day of revelation in Arizona, had always known all that voter admiration could change on a dime if they knew about even half the skeletons she'd helped him hide away in the closet. The bribes, the kickbacks, the women. So damn many women.

At first he'd denied he'd gotten that little college intern pregnant. Then, his story had shifted and he'd insisted that he'd only had sex with her that one time. Why, it hadn't even been a fling; only a late night slip when he'd found himself working alone with her in his West Wing office.

Happy had known he was lying through his bleached white teeth, but since honesty had become a casualty of their marital wars a very long time ago, she'd stood by her man, and prayed the girl's father, who'd once been a political ally, would continue to protect his daughter's reputation, thus protecting Happy's husband's career.

"It wasn't supposed to be this way," she murmured now.

From that sunny spring day when she'd walked down the white satin runner at St. Brendan's on her uncle's arm (her father, who'd gotten drunk at the rehearsal dinner the night before had, unsurprisingly, not shown up), she'd imagined herself as First Lady of the United States. Even after Noble had proven unworthy of her love, she'd contented herself with fantasies of jet-setting around the globe, looking fabulous in one-of-a-kind designer gowns, the envy of women all over the world.

As a young congressional wife who'd been dragged along to charm the press on too many congressional junkets to filthy, war-torn places no civilized person would ever want to visit, her earlier world-traveler fantasy had given way to one where she'd be a First Lady known for her salons, where fascinating, famous people would vie for invitations to the Aiken White House to discuss topics ranging from great books to saving the planet.

Even that idea had, over the past years, lost its glossy sheen. Lately, she'd continued to envision herself as First Lady, but in this new and revised version the designer dress would be a simple black sheath, much like the one Jacqueline Kennedy had worn to her husband's funeral. The famous and powerful would still come, not to discuss Balzac or baby turtles, but to extend their condolences on her loss.

She'd be a model of decorum, befitting her southern roots. And no one in the grieving nation would ever know that behind her black veil, the president's widow would be smiling.

Now, even that dream had been shattered. Bad enough this latest affair with that trashy blonde looked as if it could well blow up in their faces. Other presidents had proven voters might forget infidelity. But keeping his diabetes secret for over a decade would be perceived as a hoax. People'd feel foolish to have bought into the image of the bold politician who demonstrated the same zest for life whether he was shooshing down an Aspen ski slope, deep-sea diving off the coast of Belize, skydiving over New Mexico, or destroying his political opponents.

And even worse than feeling foolish, they'd see the candidate as weak and sickly. Would they risk electing a president who could fall into a coma in the war room if he didn't get three square meals a day, at exactly the same time of day?

And then there were the delusions he'd begun to suffer during blood-sugar swings. Those would undoubtedly come out.

It might not be fair, but Happy had learned that summer of her fourth year that life wasn't always fair. The truth was, whatever the pollsters reported, the Aiken for President campaign was over. Fortunately, that obnoxious reporter had witnessed the event; the bishop had even unwittingly helped out by explaining the seriousness of his friend's condition. By the time Laurel Stewart filed her report, everyone in the country would believe that the vice president had died of natural causes.

She reached into her bag and took out a syringe and the vial of insulin she'd carried with her for years, in the event of an emergency. Noble had a phobia of needles, so as a rule, she'd administered his injections.

As she would for this final time today.

She filled the syringe.

Pricked his arm.

Pressed in the orange plunger.

Then repeated, ensuring an overdose.

As she imagined all that insulin racing to his blood-stream, Happy decided that the one good thing to come out of all this was that mourner's black had always flattered her complexion.

45

It was all over. In the time it had taken Laurel to go around the corner to the vending machine, the vice president had died.

Now that the Secret Service agents no longer had a protectee to protect, Laurel was able to walk right past them into the hospital room where Happy Aiken was seated beside the railed bed, weeping silently into a lace-trimmed handkerchief.

Laurel hated to disturb her, but Chloe had already been missing too many days. Laurel couldn't believe she was dead. She'd know it, dammit, the same way she knew, all the way to the marrow of her bones, that her friend was in trouble.

She'd been so convinced that Noble Aiken had done something to Chloe. Kidnapped her, had her hidden away somewhere until he could come up with a way to rid himself of the problem. Or, she thought horribly, until Chloe agreed to an abortion at some quiet offshore clinic. Something Laurel also knew she would never do.

Laurel had never wanted to be wrong so badly in her life. Because if she was right about the vice president having orchestrated Chloe's disappearance, the only person who knew where she was had just died—possibly, she thought with a sinking feeling, taking the secret with him.

She wanted to scream. Instead, she struggled to focus. "I hate to bring this up right now, Mrs. Aiken—"

"Then don't." Happy's teary eyes narrowed, hardened to chips of blue ice.

Laurel so did not want to fight with a woman who'd just lost her husband. Even if he'd been a son of a bitch, surely Happy couldn't have married him solely for ambition. There must have been a time, when she'd first walked down that aisle, that she'd loved Noble Aiken.

"It's important that I know anything you might know about Chloe's whereabouts."

Laurel could tell it was not the question the widow had been expecting. She looked almost relieved. "I don't know anything more than Warren told you. Chloe was supposed to work this week. She selfishly decided to play hookey instead. End of story."

Happy waved her hand dismissively, then stood up. "And if you have any idea of involving my husband in your friend's so-called disappearance, might I remind you that the last time you published a story without sufficient sources, your editor was forced to fire you. I'm not certain how much credibility you have, dear."

That stated, she walked out of the hospital room. When the medical staff, who'd been waiting outside, came in to prepare the body to be moved to the morgue, Laurel left the room as well.

Happy was striding down the hall, looking pretty

composed for a woman who'd just been widowed. She was accompanied by one of the agents; the other had stayed in the room with the vice president's body. Laurel idly wondered if Happy would have the remains returned to Washington for a public viewing in the Rotunda.

"Where's the bishop?" she asked one of the nurses, who just looked blankly back at her.

"He left a while ago for St. Brendan's," Gwen Gannon, who, luck would have it, was on duty, revealed. "To get the holy oil so he could give the vice president last rites."

"Guess he's going to be a little late," Laurel murmured.

She and Gwen looked at each other, well aware that they were each sizing the other up.

"Well, it was good seeing you again." Christ, she made her living with words. Couldn't she have come up with any better ones than that? "I mean, it's not the best of circumstances, but—"

"I know." A faint smile warmed tired brown eyes. "Not that you'd ask," she said, "but Joe's a good man."

"I've figured that out for myself."

"Good." She angled her head, studying Laurel, as if trying to decide how much to say. "He hasn't always believed that he deserves to be happy, but he does. And although he'd probably rather be gut shot than admit it, he's also ready for marriage."

"It's not that way," Laurel said quickly. "Between us. We're just working together." No way was she going to admit to hot and heavy sex. Not to the woman he'd been married to. Had a child with.

It was obvious from her expression that Joe's ex-wife didn't believe her for a moment. Laurel didn't blame her; she'd always been a lousy liar.

"Too bad," Gwen said. Then turned and walked away.

Laurel blew out a breath, then decided to try to catch the bishop at St. Brendan's. After all, who'd know more about a man than his spiritual advisor? Now that Aiken was dead, there wasn't any reason for Bishop Cary to keep whatever he might know about Chloe secret.

Not wanting to get into another argument about her taking off on her own in case Joe arrived at the hospital to find her gone, she called the station to let him know she was headed to St. Brendan's.

"He's still questioning Richard Beale," Cait Cavanaugh, who'd taken the call, told Laurel. "But I'll pass the message on to him as soon as he's finished. Or when he takes a break, whichever comes first."

"Is it going well?" Laurel asked.

"I'll give him your message," the detective repeated. Then abruptly hung up, as Laurel had done countless times to others over the years.

Reminding herself that detectives viewed reporters as enemies and the police had better things to do than to talk with her, Laurel hoped the fact that Joe had been in with Sissy Sotheby-Beale's husband so long meant that he was gaining ground in finding her killer. After those strange episodes, she felt a connection with the victim.

It would be good to solve her murder.

Even better, she thought, as she climbed into a cab— this one driven by a normal, nonpirate—to find Chloe while she was still alive.

* * *

The water was rising higher. Chloe's head was pounding, a blinding migraine brought on by fear and the stress of her three days of captivity. He hadn't returned since he'd made her take the pills and she was beginning to fear that his plan was to let her die of starvation, or drown, then return later and retrieve her body. If there was anything left to retrieve.

What if she got washed out to sea on the retreating tide? No one would ever know what had happened to her. And her captor wouldn't just get away with murder; he'd be rewarded with even more power.

Her wrists were bloody from twisting them in her restraints, trying to yank the chains from the stone walls. The water was nearly covering her legs. It wouldn't be much longer until it was up to her waist. Then what?

No. Don't think about that!

She would survive. Her baby would survive!

Gritting her teeth, she jerked forward again, putting her entire body into the effort. Success! Finally, this time the mortar crumbled around stones, freeing her right hand. Chloe forced herself onto her knees and began pounding the iron spike against the three-hundred-year-old stones.

I'll protect you.

The man who opened the rectory door was wearing black jeans, boots, and a green Notre Dame sweatshirt.

"Hi," he greeted her. "I'm Father Gannon. May I help you?"

"Father Gannon? Joe's brother?" She never would

have taken Joe and Michael Gannon for brothers. In contrast to Joe's golden athleticism, the priest named for an archangel could have been a fallen angel, washed off the nave ceiling of a Renaissance cathedral. Lush black hair framed a narrow, aesthetic face; his eyes, set above high, slashing cheekbones, were a riveting, intense blue, and his beautifully sculptured lips had been designed to tempt both sinner and saint.

"You're the reporter," he said with a bold, dazzling smile that resembled Joe's. "Laurel Stewart."

"That's me." As much as she'd love to sit down and grill him for intimate secrets about his brother, Laurel got straight to business. "I'm looking for Bishop Cary."

"I believe he's next door at the Cathedral. I saw his car return a few minutes ago, but he didn't come into the house."

"Thanks." She started across the courtyard only to find him walking with her. "If you've got something else to do—"

"Nothing else at the moment," he said easily, matching his long-legged stride to hers.

The sky had gone as dark as the black velvet of an Elvis painting; the courtyard was covered, but the rain was being blown sideways, hitting her face like needles and they both had to bend over to walk against the wind.

"You would have come with me even if you were busy, wouldn't you have?"

"Now you've caught me." He flashed another of those unconsciously sexy grins. If she Googled Father-What-a-Waste, Michael Gannon's picture would undoubtedly have the most hits. "You look concerned. I hope you don't mind, but Joe told me about your friend."

"Did he tell you who I think kidnapped her?"

"He mentioned something about Noble Aiken."

"Who's now dead."

"I heard that on a news bulletin earlier. So I suppose now you're hoping the bishop will tell you something that will help you find Chloe Hollister. Something he might have been holding back. To protect the vice president."

"That's a very good supposition."

"I'm a long-time fan of *Law and Order*. Plus, it wasn't exactly a huge mental leap, since Joe had already asked me whether I'd ever heard the vice president's confession."

Laurel stopped. "He asked you to break the seal of the confessional?"

"I wouldn't put it that way. More like he wouldn't have minded if I'd volunteered. Not that I would have been any help if I'd been willing to break that sacred trust, which I wouldn't, because, as I told Joe, if the vice president *had* received the sacrament of reconciliation, it'd be from the bishop. Who's bound to silence by Church law."

"What if the penitent dies?"

"It's the priest who's under the seal," Father Mike pointed out. "Not the penitent. The rule stands."

Laurel shook her head and began walking again. "That doesn't seem fair."

"We've been entrusted to bring Christ to the people," the priest said mildly. "We've been doing it for two thousand years, and if people don't blow the planet up, or pollute it out of existence, we'll be doing it for another two thousand. Societies and their laws change; grace doesn't. There can't be a loophole."

"What if the penitent isn't sincere in his confession?"

"True repentance requires true contrition and a willingness of the penitent to make a radical change in his or her life and perform penance to make amends for sins. If the contrition isn't true, if the person plans to continue to sin, then it becomes a moral, not a sacramental issue," he allowed.

"I thought so." Laurel nodded decisively. "So, if Aiken didn't mean his confession, he didn't receive absolution, so there's no reason for his confessor to stay silent."

Father Mike slanted her a look. "Do you argue with my brother this way?"

"All the time."

Despite the seriousness of the subject, laughter rose in his intense blue eyes like sunshine on a mountain lake. "Good for you."

St. Brendan's Cathedral had been built in the Gothic style of pinkish-gray bricks made from local clay. Inside, the ceiling was vaulted with heavy timbers, benevolent angels and cherubs smiled down from the fresco in the nave, and the floor was made of the same stones found all over the city. The pews were a softly varnished yellow pine, milled from trees harvested a century earlier, the kneelers worn to a buttery softness by generations of the faithful.

A sanctuary lamp glowed dimly in front of the tabernacle; votive candles flickered in red glass holders, sending prayers and the scent of burning wax upward, as deep, eerily collective voices filled the air.

"Is a choir practicing somewhere?" she whispered.

"It's the stereo in the sacristy," Father Mike responded. "The bishop likes Gregorian chants when he meditates."

"Laurel knew many people found the droning of the Latin chants relaxing. In a dark, nearly abandoned Cathedral, they were proving spooky. She had no trouble picturing fifteenth-century robed monks walking solemnly in line through the gray brick corridors of some millennium-old European church.

Lightning flashed outside the rose window at the front of the Cathedral; dust motes danced in the stuttering burst of light. Bishop Cary was on his knees in front of an altar draped in white linen. His head was bowed; he appeared deep in prayer.

The building had been built in a time when acoustics had been important for organ music, allowing his voice to float over the wooden pews to the back of the Cathedral.

"Forgive me for my weaknesses, Oh, Lord." He directed his words toward the sad-looking Christ hanging in front of the round, stained-glass window. "I've struggled to stay true to your teachings. To do your work here on earth. I may have failed in the end, but I realize now that it was Satan who tempted me."

"Sancte Dei" was booming from the speakers.

Gooseflesh rose on Laurel's arms. She felt a strong, calming hand close over hers.

"Not with treasure or power," the bishop droned on,

"but with the oldest devil's trick in the book—lust."

Laurel looked up into Father Mike's frowning face and knew they were sharing the same dread.

"Satan came to me in the form of a woman. A woman more dangerously seductive than Salome, Jezebel, or even Eve."

An icy fist of fear squeezed her heart. It hadn't been Aiken at all. But another man, just as powerful. Damn! How could she have not seen this coming? Because, Laurel thought, she'd been so fixated on Aiken she couldn't see the truth when it was staring her in the face. The bishop was, after all, the most impossibly unavailable man Chloe could have ever found.

"Lucifer's wickedness has tainted this Cathedral," his voice shook with emotion, "darkened hearts and already cost one innocent life."

Cost a life? No! She couldn't be too late! Laurel would never forgive herself if Chloe had died because she hadn't been able to find her in time.

Her involuntary gasp of fear caught the cleric's attention.

He leaped up and spun around. His eyes bored through them like lasers.

"Oh, damn," Father Mike muttered.

46

"Where is she?" Laurel demanded.

"Take it easy," Mike warned beneath his breath.

"You don't understand." A sob rose painfully in her throat. "It's my fault if anything has happened to her." Shaking off the priest's restraining touch, Laurel marched down the aisle, prepared to do battle. Determined to get answers. "What the hell have you done with Chloe?"

"You dare use such language in God's house?" he thundered over the chanting monks.

"Don't look now, Your Excellency, but I believe God's got other things to be more pissed off about. Like one of his shepherds breaking his vow of celibacy."

"Begone!" The bishop pointed a finger at her, as if banishing a succubus from his Cathedral. The bells of "Paradisum Angeli" began to ring from the surround-sound speakers. "Get thee behind me, Satan."

"You're not helping matters, Laurel." Father Mike caught hold of her again and shoved her behind his back. "Let me give it a shot.

"Damian," he said patiently, "this can be worked out. If we all stay calm."

"Begone!" he repeated, the maniacal look in his eyes a long, long way from holy.

"Is the woman alive?" Mike asked in a steady, calm voice that reminded Laurel of Joe.

"Of course," the bishop responded loftily, regaining the composure that had always played so well on television. "At least she was. Her life, like all of ours, is ultimately in God's hands."

"Is she pregnant?"

"Not anymore." The bishop's face hardened. "She couldn't be allowed to have the child. It was born of Satan's lust. It would have been an abomination."

Rage burned white-hot in Laurel. "You're the abomination!"

Needing to get her fists on the bastard, she dodged to the right, trying to get around Father Mike, who moved right with her. Left. He was there, as well. Blocking her.

"Don't do this," Mike warned grittily. Then his voice lowered. "What you should concentrate on is getting out of here. And calling 911."

Laurel was torn. Dammit, they were wasting time. What if Chloe was alone somewhere bleeding from a botched abortion? Every minute could count.

Go. Stay. Go.

Her mind was swinging back and forth as Father Mike took another step forward up the aisle, his hand outstretched. "We can solve this problem, Damian. Please, don't make things worse."

The unmistakable crack of a gunshot reverberated around the Cathedral. Too late, Laurel realized that the bishop had pulled a pistol from his suit jacket.

Just in front of her, the handsome priest lurched sideways, then crumbled to the stone floor. His body landed behind a pew, but his long, jean-clad legs were still out in the aisle.

"Father Mike!" Laurel dropped to her knees beside him. The chanting, which had grown deafening, was creeping her out as much as the sight of the blood seeping through the shoulder of his green sweatshirt.

"Don't worry. I'll be fine." He didn't sound it. His face was as pale as the altar cloth, his words slurred. "You have to get out of here," he repeated. His eyes were becoming glazed with pain. "Call 911."

"I'm not going to leave you."

"Go." His voice was faint, little more than a whisper. "Now."

No. She had to get Joe's brother to safety. She was struggling to get her hands beneath his armpits, when she felt, rather than saw, the bishop standing over her, a pistol in his hand.

"Get up," he said.

"You shot him!"

"That was the idea."

"How could you do that? He's a priest!"

"He's a troublemaker. One of those rebels who bucks the rules and gives the Church a bad name."

"Sort of like John the Baptist?" Laurel shot back.

"Get on your feet now, Ms. Stewart. Or I'll shoot Michael again. This time in the head."

Oh, God. He'd do it. Laurel could see the murder in his eyes. She'd gotten Father Mike into this mess; now she was going to have to try to keep him alive. Which was not going to be at all easy since he seemed to be unconscious.

"All right." She reluctantly stood with her hands up, palms out. "Please. Don't hurt him." She was not accustomed to begging anyone for anything. She would beg for Joe's brother. "Father Michael doesn't have anything to do with this."

"Neither did you," he said, gesturing her forward with the ugly steel-blue gun. "But that didn't stop you, did it?"

"Chloe's my friend."

"The woman's evil. Sent by the devil to tempt me."

"You're the evil one. And there's no way you're going to get away with what you've done."

The monster actually smiled! "Don't be so sure of that, Ms. Stewart."

He snatched a heavy gold candlestick from the altar and swung it at her head.

47

Joe was feeling pretty damn good as he drove to the Cathedral. Beale had crumbled, as he'd hoped he would. The doctor might have attended the Naval Academy, but it was a good thing the guy had never ended up in a war zone, because he had Jell-O for a spine.

Of course, they'd triggered his temper by having Cait take the DNA swab. Being treated like a common suspect by a woman had been the one thing a guy who considered women beneath him couldn't handle. He'd started taunting her, just as Joe imagined he must have talked to his wife. She came back with the fact that the ME had found ketamine in Sissy's blood. More and more used as a club drug under the names Special K, Vitamin K, and Cat Valium, the drug was a rapid-acting anesthetic used on animals and humans, mostly children. Interestingly, Cait had informed the doctor, cops, even as they were speaking, were searching the Beale house and the doctor's office at the Academy for the drug.

At first he tried to explain away why the police might find drugs in his home. Then, once he started talking, like so many other amateur criminals, he couldn't stop.

Sissy Sotheby-Beale had gotten into the environment big time, which hadn't bothered her husband since it kept her from complaining that he spent too much time either at the Academy or on the golf course. What he had never expected, when she'd attended that fund-raiser for loggerhead turtles in Georgetown, was that she'd meet two men who'd change her life. And eventually cause it to come to a tragic end.

She'd been drawn to Wunder—not sexually, but to the charisma of the man and his message. It had also not escaped the environmentalist's notice that the vice president, a legendary skirt chaser, was interested in Sissy.

Sissy had entered into the affair at Wunder's suggestion, as a way for him to keep tabs on Aiken's actions. That was how he'd gotten the information on the ghost ship deal he'd given to Laurel; Sissy had used the tiny camera he'd bought her at a spy shop to photograph the papers.

The one thing no one had expected was for Sissy to fall in love with the vice president. She'd sworn, with her last breath, that Aiken had been in love with her, as well—something no one would ever know for sure, since both of them were dead.

Joe was still uncomfortable with Aiken's death, but trusted Drew to determine if the politician had died of natural causes or if a crime had been committed. Joe was leaning toward the guy somehow being killed by a wife who'd reached the end of her tolerance for his bad behavior, but then again, he was probably prejudiced, since he didn't run across all that many natural deaths in the murder business.

Joe hadn't been able to save Sissy Sotheby-Beale's life. But at least he'd stood up for her in death.

Now he had to concentrate on finding Chloe Hollister, which might be difficult with the vice president lying on a slab in the hospital morgue.

"Guy definitely had a wandering dick," he murmured as he pulled into the parking lot of the Cathedral.

No one answered the bell at the rectory, which Joe found a little odd, since a check in the garage-door window revealed both the bishop's green Mercedes and Mike's Jeep Cherokee.

The short hairs on the back of his neck rose as he crossed the courtyard to the Cathedral.

Joe's heart lurched, then stopped, when he walked into the Cathedral and found Mike lying on the stone floor. Laurel was sitting beside him, her forehead on her bent knees. Both were bloody and pale as death.

He pulled out his Glock and held it in both hands as he moved down the aisle, his gaze skimming back and forth over the rows of empty pews. "What the hell happened?"

"It appears the bishop's the kidnapper you've been looking for," Mike responded.

Laurel lifted her head. "He's got Chloe! And he shot your brother!"

"And slugged Laurel with that candlestick," Mike added. "He didn't seem all that happy being found out."

"Christ." Joe had reached the altar. Laurel had an egg-sized lump beneath hair that was matted with blood; a dark red stain had spread over Mike's sweatshirt.

"Take care of Laurel first," Mike said.

"Take care of Father Mike before me," Laurel said at the same time.

"Christ," Joe repeated. He ran his fingers over Laurel's head. It was a nasty blow, she undoubtedly had a concussion, and her head was going to hurt like hell once the shock wore off, but she'd live. As for his brother . . .

"We need to get that sweatshirt off you."

"I'll be fine. You've got to find the bishop," he said. "Before he kills Laurel's friend."

"She's still alive," Laurel said. Determination steamrollered over the pain in her eyes. "I'd know if he'd killed her."

After her connection to Sissy, whom she hadn't even known, Joe believed her.

"His Mercedes is still in the garage."

He and Mike looked at each other. Joe knew they were thinking the exact same thing.

"The tunnel," they said together.

"There's one that runs beneath the Cathedral," Joe told Laurel. "From the old days—"

"Of pirates and smugglers," she remembered. "Brendan O'Neill told me about them."

"The storm's going to have the water rising," Mike warned.

"Oh, God," Laurel moaned. She rubbed her temple, then flinched when her fingers connected with the candlestick gash. "We've got to find her."

"You're staying here. With Mike," Joe said.

"I'd like to see you keep me away." She swayed as she stood up. Joe watched with admiration as she clenched her jaw and steadied herself. The resolve in her gaze softened slightly as she looked down at his brother. "I'm worried about leaving you."

"It's only a flesh wound," he insisted. I'll be fine. Though I'd appreciate you calling 911 for me," he suggested to Joe.

"Three minutes ETA," Joe reported back after the call.

"Okay." Laurel turned to Joe. "Let's go find Chloe."

He didn't want her with him. Didn't want to have to worry about her fainting on her face, didn't want to have to worry about the bishop shooting her, as he'd done Mike, didn't want to worry about her drowning if a storm surge filled the tunnel.

From the sound of the rain hammering on the slate roof high overhead, Joe knew that they were running out of time if they wanted to find Chloe Hollister alive. He also knew that arguing with this woman was a lesson in futility.

"There's a trapdoor in the sacristy," he said, giving in as they'd both known he would.

Chloe heard him coming toward her. This time she wasn't afraid; this time she was ready for him.

She leaned against the side wall, making herself as inconspicuous as possible. It helped that it'd gotten so dark in the cave; hopefully, he wouldn't notice, until it was too late, that she'd broken free of her chains.

She felt the long skirt of the cassock brush against her bare legs as he raced past her, then came to a sudden stop when he realized his captive was no longer where he'd left her.

Roaring like an Amazon warrior, she threw the glass candle holder at his face; he screamed, more in shock than pain, as the hot wax hit his skin.

Then she swung the chain around her head, the same way she'd swung that rope lasso when she'd been a little girl pretending to be a cowgirl. There was a loud thunk and the sound of bone breaking when the chain slammed into his nose.

Water splashed her as the man who'd turned out to be a wolf in shepherd's clothing crumbled to his knees.

She paused just long enough to kick him. Hard.

As the bishop fell, landing flat on his broken nose, Chloe took off running for her life.

48

Laurel hated the tunnel. It was dark and damp and claustrophobic, triggering a phobia she'd never known she possessed about being buried alive. A thought that, in turn, reminded her of "The Cask of Amontillado" by Poe. She could only pray that the bishop had not walled up Chloe as Montresor had Fortunato.

Joe had grabbed two flashlights from a cupboard in the sacristy, kept there for times the power went out during storms. The beams of light barely penetrated the surrounding blackness.

They were wading through knee deep water, which slowed their progress. Water was streaming down the stone walls, and their shouts, as they called out for Chloe, echoed around them.

Since it was impossible to run on moss-slick stones, Laurel had taken off her high heeled sandals, but even in bare feet she nearly lost her footing. She reached out to steady herself, touched something wet and slimy that moved beneath her hand, and only halfway stifled her scream.

"What's wrong?" Joe asked.

What wasn't? Laurel thought.

"Nothing. I was just spooked. This place is creepy."

"It was fun when we were kids," Joe said.

"Which just goes to show that you and your brother had a sick idea of fun."

"I guess it's a boy thing."

Laurel guessed he was right. She was also extremely grateful she'd been born a girl.

"I'm still worried about leaving Mike."

"If he says he's going to be okay, he will be."

"That's a lot of faith."

"More a lot of medical experience. He used to be a doctor."

"Your brother went from being a doctor to being a priest?"

"Yeah. He served in the first Gulf War. After he came home, he went into the seminary."

"There must be one helluva story there."

"Must be." Whatever had happened over there in the Gulf appeared to be solely between Father Mike and his God.

"Maybe he'll tell me after this is all over."

"If anyone could get him to spill the beans, it'd probably be you."

Laurel decided to take that as a compliment.

"Chloe!" she called out again. They hadn't gotten any answer so far, but since they also hadn't come across the bishop, Laurel remained hopeful. "Where are you?"

"Laurel?" a voice came out of the darkness.

"Chloe?" Laurel shouted louder as she and Joe swept their lights over the wet stones, searching for some sign of the kidnap victim.

"Laurel! Where are you?"

"I'm here in the tunnel." Duh. How on earth, though, could you describe an exact location without a GPS, which none of them happened to have handy? "You keep shouting, and we'll keep shouting and just keep walking toward the sound."

"The bishop kidnapped me!"

"I know!"

"He tried to make me lose my baby. But I didn't."

Three days ago, Laurel could think of few things worse than Chloe being pregnant. How much could change in three short days. "I'm glad, sweetie!" she shouted out.

"I think he was going to kill me, too. But I knocked him down." Amazingly, a sound like a giggle echoed around them. "I think I broke his nose."

"Good for you!" Laurel would have liked to break his neck. After breaking every other bone in his body. Slowly. One at a time. "We've come for you, Chloe. We'll get you out of here."

She moved faster, pushing through the water, which was now up to her thighs, on a near run. She turned a corner and nearly ran smack into Chloe, who was running the other way.

They both screamed in surprise. Then relief.

They hugged each other, hard, then jumped up and down like two schoolgirls on the playground. Laurel might not let people see her sweat, but there was no way she was going to worry about Joe seeing her cry. Tears were flowing down her cheeks. "We're going to take you home, Chloe. It's okay. You're safe. It's all over."

"Not yet," an all too familiar, deadly voice said from the well of black behind Chloe.

Oh, shit! Laurel's heart sank to her bare feet as the bishop came into view, his gun glinting evilly in the flashlight beams.

"She's right," Joe said. "It's all over. Drop the gun."

"Having been your parish priest, I know you were taught better than that, Joseph Gannon," the bishop chided him, as if there was nothing unusual about him and a former altar boy standing in a tunnel pointing weapons at each other. "It's 'Please drop the gun, Your Excellency.'"

"Sorry," Joe said. "You lost the right for a fancy religious title when you shot my brother."

"That was"—the bishop shrugged—"unfortunate."

"That's one word for it. Not exactly the one I'd use, though," Joe said.

"I've always liked Michael," Bishop Cary said. "Despite his having become a bit of a rabble-rouser these past years. He was one of my best altar boys. He had far more patience than you, Joseph. And he never spilled the wine."

"Guess that's why he ended up the priest."

"He's a good priest. A bit headstrong, and far too familiar with his flock. But learning to distance himself from the laity is something that will come with time."

"I doubt that. And now that we've had this little chat about Father Mike, how about you hand over that gun."

"I'm afraid it's too late for that, Joseph."

The crack of the shot was earsplitting in the close confines of the tunnel. A bullet sang past Laurel's head, chipping off stone.

Joe fired back an instant later.

Chloe screamed.

Blood bloomed on the purple cassock. "Thank you," the bishop said.

"Suicide by cop," Laurel murmured.

"It seems so," Joe agreed as the bishop slid down the wall.

"Joe?" Laurel said as Cary disappeared beneath the water.

"It's okay," he assured her, just as she'd told Chloe.

"I'm feeling a little funny."

"It's probably shock." He took her into his arms. "You've had a helluva day."

"That's probably it." Fighting off the darkness, she attempted a smile. "Thank you. For finding Chloe."

"Goddammit!"

"Could you please not shout so loud?" Laurel asked. "Because I've got a terrible headache." It must be delayed pain from the candlestick, she thought.

"That's not a surprise. Since you've been shot." His voice sounded as if it were coming from the bottom of the sea. He lifted his fingers and glared at the wet blood glistening on them.

"Shot?" Chloe gasped.

"Shot?" Laurel echoed. He was lifting her up, into his arms. Laurel felt as if she were floating. "Really?"

"Yeah. In your shoulder. The bishop's damn bullet must've ricocheted."

"That explains it," Laurel said, as she surrendered to the darkness.

49

Not wanting to wait for an ambulance, Joe drove her to the hospital himself, lights flashing, siren wailing. Strapped into the passenger seat, Laurel was vaguely aware of him cursing a blue streak as he powered the Crown Vic through traffic.

"If only I had the goddamn Mustang," he muttered. Even with her eyes closed, she could feel the car sway as he passed something moving too slowly for him.

"We'd probably all get killed," she murmured, sure he couldn't hear her over the scream of the siren and the blare of horns protesting his driving.

"You're not going to die," he said forcefully. "And shut up. You're wasting energy."

"Yessir, Captain Bligh." She tried to lift her hand to salute, but her arm wouldn't follow the instructions from her foggy brain.

"You're going to be just fine," Chloe's voice offered from the backseat.

Showing a decided lack of cheer, Joe cursed again. Then punched the gas.

* * *

The next thing Laurel knew she was waking up surrounded by white. White walls, white sheets, and an uncharacteristically white-faced man sitting beside the narrow bed.

"Joe?"

"Got it on the first try," he said.

"I'm in the hospital."

"That's two for two."

"Oh, knock it off," she muttered. "That enthusiastic game-show host voice is just too weird coming from you. Why don't I remember getting here?"

He linked his fingers with hers. "Because they shot you up with enough Demerol to knock out a thoroughbred."

"That explains the merry-go-round."

"That's probably it. The bullet was a clean hit through your arm," he assured her. "It didn't nick an artery or anything."

"That's good news." She nodded. Things were starting to come back to her. "How's your brother?"

"He's fine. Gonna be a bit sore for a time, but fortunately, the bishop had lousy aim."

"I'm so relieved." That was a huge understatement. She never would have forgiven herself if Father Mike had been gravely injured. "How about Chloe?"

"She checked out fine. She's in a room down the hall. They're going to keep her for a couple days, make sure her baby's okay."

"That's also wonderful to hear. Did I thank you for that?"

"Yeah."

"Oh."

An awkward little silence settled over them. Which was odd, because of all the emotions this man had stirred in her, he'd never made her feel awkward.

"We made a good team," she murmured.

"Damn good," he agreed.

Another silence, as thick as morning fog.

"I've been thinking," he said.

"I had this idea," she said at the same time.

They both stopped. Looked at each other.

"You first," he said.

"No, really—"

"We're in the South," he reminded her. "Chivalry requires ladies first."

She blew out a sigh. "You're just afraid to bring it up."

"Hell, yes. Besides, you're the mouthy one."

"I'm going to take that as a compliment."

"That's exactly how it was meant."

"Okay. Well." She drew in a breath. Let it out. "Before all this happened, I woke up this morning thinking about what I wanted to do. After we found Chloe."

"That reminds me," he said. "You've gotten a lot of calls. Several from some guy named Barry, who wants you to call him ASAP. Said something about you writing a several-part series about all this."

"Barry's my editor. Was my editor," she corrected. "At the *Post*."

"Yeah, I figured that out. He also sent those." He pointed out an elaborate arrangement of flowers that would've been perfect for a Mafia don's funeral. "The pink roses are from the *Bee* and the daisies are mine. Well, they're yours. From me. They didn't have much selection in the gift shop."

"I've always loved daisies."

"Good, good."

He was acting strange. Could it be that she wasn't the only one who was nervous?

"The switchboard's taken lots of messages from various publishers," he revealed. "Seems a great many people seem to feel there's a book in all this."

"Hmm. I suppose there is. But I think I'll let someone else write it. I've been promised some freelance gigs for the *Falls Church Bee*. Plus, I've been thinking about what you said about back when you couldn't separate work from life. I've never done that, but it might be a good idea to try. I've got this novel I've been working on for what seems like forever. Maybe this is a good time to see if I can finish it."

"I can't imagine you not being able to do anything you put your mind to."

"That's not what you were saying a few days ago."

"A few days ago you were a pain in the ass."

"Everyone needs a talent." This wasn't getting them anywhere. Laurel could not remember a time, not even in Cruella's office, when she'd felt so unsure of herself. And, dammit, Joe wasn't helping a whole lot.

"I was thinking maybe I'd stick around Somersett a while," she said with a casualness that cost her. "I could use a change of pace, and it's a pretty city."

"We like to think so. Or, you might consider one of the shelter islands."

"Oh?" Oh, God, had she misunderstood? Did he want to get rid of her?

"I'll have my twenty years in another ten days. With accumulated overtime and vacation days, I could get my ticket punched now. I received an offer to be police chief over on Swann Island a while back. Told them I'd think about it. It's just a couple miles offshore. Close enough to have all the benefits of the city, small enough that the biggest crimes I'd probably be dealing with would be jay-walking and barking dogs."

"Sounds a little boring."

"Yeah, I came to the same conclusion. Which is why I signed on with this private place."

"A security company?"

"In a way. It's a group of experts—former homicide dicks like me, FBI agents, Secret Service, some Seals and Special Forces. We take on, shall we say, the more diffi-cult cases."

"For a fee."

"You get what you pay for." He shrugged. "And appar-ently we're the best. If what they're offering to pay me is any indication, they're definitely willing to write the checks that'll allow for some in-depth investigation on various cold cases, things like that."

"That sounds more interesting." And since they'd made such a good team, perhaps she could help him with his detecting, when she wasn't working on her novel. "Where is it located?"

"Coincidentally, same place as the other job. Swann Island."

"What would you do with your loft?"

"Stay here and commute. Maybe rent it out. Or perhaps I'll sell the building to O'Neill. Use the money to buy a house."

"Even with that jazzy new job, you could get bored without murders falling into your lap every day."

"I figured maybe I'd take up a hobby."

"Hobbies are nice. Or, so I hear." She'd never taken the time to find out.

"Mike was telling me about these meetings they have at the Cathedral. For sex addicts."

Of all the things he could have said, this was one thing Laurel had not expected.

"You're thinking of becoming a sex addict?"

"Sorta. But I've decided I'd prefer to become a specialist."

"A specialist?"

"Yeah. You know. Focus my addiction on just one woman."

"Well." She blew out another breath. "That sounds interesting."

"I was hoping it would."

Damn him, he was going to make her say it. "Is this a proposal?"

He lifted a brow. "Do you see me getting down on my knees?"

"No."

"Then I guess it's not a proposal."

"Good," she lied.

"I promised you I'd never bring up the *P* word in your presence," he reminded her. "You hate marriage, right? Shackles, and all that."

"That's right. I do." Or did. Before coming to Somersett and having her life turned upside down.

"And I know that we had this deal about not getting involved, and I've always been a man of my word, but the thing is, when Cary shot you, I realized that you could die on me."

"But I didn't."

"You could have. With me never telling you that I love you."

"Oh." She drew in a sharp breath. "I thought the same thing."

"That I loved you?"

"That I could die without ever telling you that I loved YOU." There. She'd said it and it wasn't nearly as difficult to admit it as she'd always thought it would be.

"They've got you pretty doped up. You sure it's not the happy drugs talking?"

"I'm sure."

"Okay, then." He exhaled deeply. But still did not get down on his knees. "I had this idea, but I wanted you to be clearheaded when I brought it up."

When he lifted their joined hands and nipped at her knuckles, which were bruised from the stone walls of the tunnel, Laurel thought how amazing, even through the clouds of Demerol, that he could still make every atom in her body tingle.

"I was thinking that since I love you, and you love me, and we seem to make one helluva team, perhaps we ought to consider extending this partnership."

"For how long a term were you thinking?"

"Oh, I haven't given it a great deal of thought." The

wicked gleam in his lion-gold eyes told her he was lying through his teeth. "The city's celebrating its tricentennial this summer. Knowing how skittish you are about long-term commitments, I was thinking maybe we'd give it to, say, the quadricentennial. Then, if things are still working, we might want to consider renegotiating."

"Well." Her head was spinning in a way that had nothing to do with the drugs the doctors had pumped through her system. "That sounds doable."

Joe had figured her out well enough not to buy that cool act. Not when a sparkle of pleasure had just lit up her gorgeous eyes like Buccaneer Days fireworks.

He'd get Laurel Stewart to marry him, Joe vowed as he claimed her mouth and sealed the deal with a long, sweet kiss.

Eventually.

Because if there was one thing being in the murder business had taught him, it was patience.

Catch up with love...
Catch up with passion...
Catch up with danger....

Catch a bestseller from Pocket Books!

Delve into the past with *New York Times* bestselling author
Julia London
The Dangers of Deceiving a Viscount
Beware! A lady's secrets will always be revealed...

Barbara Delinksy
Lake News
Sometimes you have to get away to find everything.

Fern Michaels
The Marriage Game
It's all fun and games—until someone falls in love.

Hester Browne
The Little Lady Agency
Why trade up if you can fix him up?

Laura Griffin
One Last Breath
Don't move. Don't breathe. Don't say a word...

Love a good story?
So do we!

Don't miss any of these bestselling romance titles from Pocket Books.

One Last Look • Linda Lael Miller
Someone wants her next breath to be her last…

Alone in the Dark • Elaine Coffman
A woman discovers she has a long-lost twin…and is plagued by recurring nightmares of her own death.
Is she…**Alone in the Dark**?

Priceless • Mariah Stewart
A man and woman discover that love is the most precious treasure of all.

Paradise • Judith McNaught
Escape to passion. Escape to desire. Escape to…Paradise.